W9-CPO-788

The Translation of Love

The Translation *of* Love

A NOVEL

Lynne Kutsukake

Alfred A. Knopf Canada

PUBLISHED BY ALFRED A. KNOPF CANADA

www.penguinrandomhouse.ca

Alfred A. Knopf Canada and colophon are registered trademarks.

Library and Archives Canada Cataloguing in Publication

Kutsukake, Lynne, author
The translation of love / Lynne Kutsukake.

Issued in print and electronic formats.

ISBN 978-0-345-80937-7
eBook ISBN 978-0-345-80939-1

1. Japan—History—Allied occupation, 1945–1952—Fiction.
I. Title.

PS8621.U88T73 2016   C813'.6   C2015-905819-8

Book design: Maria Carella
Jacket Images: (girl) Jira Saki/Stocksy.com; (man on bicycle) Wayne Miller/The National Archives Catalog; (Tokaido Road) Lennox Tierney/Special Collections Department, J. Willard Marriott Library, University of Utah; (spine) Svetap/Dreamstime.com
Jacket design: Five Seventeen

Printed and bound in the United States of America

2 4 6 8 9 7 5 3 1

Penguin
Random House
KNOPF CANADA

For Michael

The Translation of Love

Tokyo, 1947

The car is in a parade all by itself. Traffic must stop whenever the boy's father travels, so the road is completely empty. Crowds line the street to watch them. Normally the boy is not allowed to ride in the big Cadillac, the special car reserved for work, but today is special. Today the boy is in the parade, too.

It is a short ride to GHQ, General Headquarters, the office from which his father rules Japan.

"Look at all the people!" The boy raises his finger to the car window. He sees a tiny old woman in a gray kimono, a sunburned man in a white shirt and black pants, a mother with a baby strapped to her back.

"Arthur, don't point."

The voice is firm but not harsh. Even when it reprimands him, it is the voice he loves. "Yes, Father," he murmurs and steals a glance at the figure seated beside him in the backseat. His father has not turned his head once since they got into the car, not toward the boy or toward the crowds.

"Your mother explained about the photographers, didn't she?"

"Yes, sir." He will have his picture taken with his father, and it will appear in all the newspapers and magazines in America.

"You're not nervous are you, Sergeant?"

"No, Father."

"That's right. Nothing to be nervous about. Just a few photos. You should be yourself. Act natural."

"Yes, Father."

"When we're finished, your mother will meet you and take you to the PX. The photographers may want to take more pictures of you. Maybe your mother will get you one of those special hamburgers. Would you like that?"

His father's mouth takes the shape of a smile, but the boy cannot see his eyes. The dark lenses of the sunglasses reveal nothing.

Up ahead, the boy spots two girls lining the route. He can't help noticing other children, especially if they look at all close to his own age. Suddenly one of the girls breaks from the crowd and dashes onto the road. She is heading straight for them, as if she means to run directly in front of the car's path. There is shouting, loud cries in an unintelligible language.

The girl is close to the car now, close enough for the boy to see her eyes. She is staring right at him, locking her wild gaze on him, and he finds he cannot turn away. Then as abruptly as it started, it is all over. A Japanese policeman grabs her and her body snaps backward as if she has reached the end of an elastic band. The boy cranes his neck to see what is happening. He wants to turn around and look out the back window, but he doesn't dare. He wants to tell his father what he has seen, to share this extraordinary thing that has happened on this extraordinary day, but General MacArthur is chewing on the end of his pipe, deep in important and private thought.

1

Ever since her sister had gone away, Fumi looked forward to the democracy lunches with a special, ravenous hunger. The American soldiers came to her school once a week with deliveries, and though she never knew what they would bring, it didn't matter. She wanted it all, whatever it was. Sometimes it was powdered milk and soft white bread as fluffy as cake. Sometimes it was a delicious oily meat called Spam. Occasionally it was peanut butter, a sticky brown paste whose unusual flavor—somehow sweet and salty at the same time—was surprisingly addictive. The lunch supplements supplied by the Occupation forces reminded her of the kind of presents her older sister, Sumiko, used to bring in the days when she still came home. Fumi's hunger was insatiable, and although she couldn't have put it in so many words, some part of her sensed that her craving was inseparable from her longing for her sister's return.

All the pupils knew that the lunches were to help them think clearer, think freer. To become creative and independent. On very rare occasions, hard-boiled eggs were distributed. Eggs were a special treat, high in protein, and while not strictly speaking an American food, they were said to make you democratic faster. They were Fumi's favorite. Throughout the war and ever since the surrender, fresh eggs had been in extremely short supply in Tokyo, almost impossible to obtain except at great expense in the black market.

She knew today was an egg day because Akiko's younger brother

Masatomi had spotted the army jeep at the end of recess and a GI had given him one. From that moment on it was all Fumi could think of. Under her desk, out of Kondo Sensei's sight, she cupped her hand in her lap and pretended she could already feel the weight of the egg in her palm. It was nature's most perfect food, she'd decided, for what else came in its own self-contained package, a smooth thin shell that peeled off in sheets to uncover the slippery skin inside.

The eggs were especially coveted because the Americans never seemed to bring enough to go around. The other items—the milk, the bread, the peanut butter—could easily be stretched so that everyone got something, but an egg was an egg. The elementary grades were served first and inevitably there was a shortfall by the time the older pupils like Fumi, who was twelve and in the first year of middle school, had their turn. On the last egg day, despite jumping up as soon as class was dismissed, she had been pushed out of the way by two larger girls who were determined to beat her to the line. She vowed she wouldn't make the same mistake again. Strategy was key. This time she planned to use her smaller size to her advantage, to slip between everyone's legs, crawl on the floor until she was through the door, and then run down the hall to where the makeshift distribution table was set up.

So Fumi simply couldn't understand why, today of all days, she had gotten stuck with looking after the repat girl.

The new girl had arrived shortly before noon. There was a sharp rap at the door and the principal, who was rarely seen outside the teachers' office, stepped into the classroom. Everyone automatically stood up, bowed in his direction, and remained standing while he and Kondo Sensei conferred in low whispers. The principal was a short, stout man, not much taller than most of the girls in their all-girls class, and Fumi couldn't help noticing that he stood on tiptoe when he was speaking into Kondo Sensei's ear. After this brief consultation, the principal returned to the doorway and reentered, this time followed by a girl who hunched her shoulders like an old woman and hung her head so low no one could see her face. She looked miserable.

"This is your new student," the principal said aloud. He was speaking to Kondo Sensei but now everyone could hear.

"I see."

"Shimamura. Aya Shimamura." He jerked his chin in the girl's direction. "She'll start today."

"Yes, sir. But as the term has already started—"

"Please. Do your best." The principal turned and walked away. It wasn't clear to whom this last remark was addressed.

There was a moment of confusion, with some of the girls continuing to bow toward the empty doorway through which the principal had retreated. Kondo Sensei rapped his pointer on the side of his desk.

"Class, rise!" he said, even though everyone was still standing. "Let's welcome our new classmate, Miss Aya Shimamura."

They bowed formally, but not quite as low as had been required for the principal. After all, this was only another student.

"As of today, Miss Shimamura will be joining our class. We are very lucky." He paused as if uncertain how to continue. "She is from America."

This remark caused an almost electric charge to flow through the classroom.

"From America," he repeated, his voice stronger. "As you are all aware, the mastery of English is one of the goals of our new middle-school curriculum, and I am sure that Miss Shimamura will be able to make many helpful contributions toward this end."

He paused and looked from left to right until his eyes fell on the desk Fumi shared with Akiko in the center of the front row. Briskly he tapped his pointer on the side where Akiko sat.

"Right here. Miss Shimamura, you can sit at this desk. Fumi, it will be your responsibility to look after your new seatmate. Take care of her. Make sure she knows what to do."

Fumi immediately sat up straight. What about Akiko, she wanted to protest. But Akiko had already gathered her books and Kondo Sensei was directing her to a desk at the back.

No sooner had everyone gotten settled than a bell began ringing and Kondo Sensei looked at his watch. He sighed and set his pointer lengthwise across his desk.

"Very good. Class dismissed for lunch."

Fumi was halfway to the door when she heard her name.

"Miss Tanaka!"

The other girls rushed past her and stampeded out of the room.

"Sensei?"

"What are you doing? Come here. Did I not give you a special responsibility?" He tipped his head in Aya's direction.

"But, Sensei, it's an egg day."

"Well, take her with you and help her get something." He picked up a book from his desk and left.

The new girl was frozen in the same hunched posture she had assumed as soon as she sat down, her forehead within inches of resting on the desk. They were alone in the classroom.

"You heard the teacher. Come on!"

The girl did not move or give any indication that she heard or understood.

"Get up, let's go! We have to hurry or we'll miss out." Fumi leaned over and put her mouth next to Aya's ear. "What's wrong with you? Are you deaf? Get up!"

Still the girl didn't budge. Instead, she seemed to be trying to retract her head into her neck like a turtle. Something about that ridiculous action infuriated Fumi and she grabbed the sleeve of Aya's blouse. "Get up!" Fumi tugged once, twice, and on the third tug the thin material tore right off at the shoulder. For the first time the girl came to life. She burst into tears and ran out of the room.

"How's your new friend?" Akiko's laugh sounded a bit malicious.

"Yeah, the repat." Tomoko snickered.

"How should I know?" Fumi muttered.

"My mother says the *imin* shouldn't have come back. The immigrants eat all our food. There's not enough to go around." Tomoko spoke with authority.

"Stupid *imin*," Fumi said. "She can't even talk."

"Do you think she knows Japanese?"

"She can't even move, never mind talk."

"Stupid. *Baka*."

"*Imin no baka*."

Fumi was beginning to feel a bit better. She'd debated running after Aya, but hunger led her to the distribution table, just in case something was left. As she expected, everything was gone. By the time she joined her classmates, they had finished eating and were gathered under the shade of the big oak tree in the far corner of the schoolyard. Her own lunch, minus the hard-boiled egg she had so looked forward to, had been a millet "rice ball," which she'd had to eat very fast because she was late. She could still feel it stuck like a hard stone in the middle of her chest just below her breastbone. It hurt a bit when she laughed. Akiko and Tomoko were laughing, too, and didn't seem to hold it against her that she had to sit next to the *imin*. The three girls joined hands to form a circle and swung their arms back and forth, higher and higher, acting as childishly as the elementary pupils with whom they shared the yard.

Just as Fumi was starting to get a bit light-headed, she felt Akiko and Tomoko let go of her hands and in the spot where they had been standing Kondo Sensei appeared. He stepped directly in front of Fumi and slapped her hard on the cheek with his open palm. Fumi felt the entire schoolyard go quiet and still. Her cheek burned. Although she'd been disciplined many times at school before, this was the first time by Kondo Sensei, the new teacher.

"What did you do to Aya Shimamura!" he shouted. His face was mottled purple right up to his receding hairline, and his thick glasses had slid to the end of his nose.

"She wouldn't move." Fumi began to cry.

"Is that any reason to tear her clothes! How am I going to explain this to the principal? I had to send her home. On her first day!"

There was an audible gasp from Akiko, Tomoko, and the other pupils who were nearby.

"I didn't mean to." She could hardly get the words out between sobs. "She wouldn't get up. I missed my egg."

"Nobody cares about that." Kondo Sensei turned to the other students. "What are you staring at? Go back to the classroom. Immediately! Go!"

The girls began running away before he had even finished talking.

"As for you, Fumi Tanaka, you stay here. Stand facing this tree and don't move until I come back to get you. Do you understand?"

At that, he turned and marched back to the main entranceway, little puffs of dust rising behind his heels.

Fumi kept her head hung low for the rest of the afternoon just in case Kondo Sensei was looking out the window to check up on her. The sun was warm, flies buzzed around her head, and the sand in the schoolyard blew up into her eyes. Her cheek stung for a long time, a prickly tingle like millions of tiny pins. To distract herself, she tried pretending that each tingle was a grain of white rice, that she was being showered mercilessly with buckets of rice. But it didn't really help. So instead she thought about how the shiny oval bald spot on the back of Kondo Sensei's head looked just like an egg. *This* made her feel much better.

It was all the fault of the stupid new girl. Why had Fumi gotten stuck with her? Why hadn't Aya been paired with Sanae? Skinny, ugly Sanae who might be the smartest in the class but who had bowed legs and unsightly blotches on her face. Or Tomoko who was the prettiest, no one could argue with that, but who had a stuck-up nature. For that matter, why not Akiko? At least her father had a proper job. In her mind, Fumi went through the list of all the things she was not. Not the prettiest, not the most popular, not the best at sports, certainly not the one with money. She knew that to most people she was just an average ordinary girl. But her sister had always told her she was special, and whether it was true or not, Fumi missed hearing it. She missed Sumiko and wished she knew how to find her and make her come home.

2

*A*ya was too ashamed to tell her father about the horrible thing that had happened at school. She hid her torn blouse under a pile of dirty clothes and then crawled into the cramped dark closet where they had to store their bedding during the daytime. Pushing her face onto the futon, she cried openmouthed into its worn musty folds. Although she hated the miserable lodgings that her father had found for them, for the first time she was glad to be here, glad only because she could be alone. Everything in Japan was worse than she could possibly have imagined.

Her father had accompanied her to school that morning as if she were starting kindergarten. The school had a long name—Minami Nishiki Elementary and Middle School—so she had expected a much grander structure than the run-down building that stood in the middle of a dirt yard. The roof looked like it was sagging at one end and many of the windows were broken. The concrete walls were full of cracks. Aya's father bowed several times to the principal before producing an envelope from inside his jacket, which he offered with yet another deep bow. Then he told her to remember her manners and left.

Aya was given slippers that were torn at the toe and much too wide, forcing her to half shuffle, half slide in order to keep up with the principal as he led her from the main entrance and down the long corridor. She kept her head low and concentrated on the slap-flap slap-flap of his slippers. His feet hung over the backs, revealing a ragged hole in the heel of his left sock that seemed to get bigger with each step he took. Even though the wooden floors were not very clean, it seemed that no one was allowed to wear shoes inside. Later she would notice that none of the other students wore slippers. They were all barefoot.

The principal stopped at the last classroom.

"Class, rise!"

Aya heard the teacher announce her name and say she was joining the class. He said she was from America. America, America, he kept repeating, and she didn't know how to correct him. Not America—*Canada*. She hung her head even lower until her chin touched her collarbone. Her name was repeated over and over. If she weren't feeling so nervous, she could have understood more of what he was saying, but as it was, the only thing she caught for sure was her own name and "America" and the word "English." *Ingurishu* was what it sounded like.

"You must bow properly. *Zettai wasureruna!* Don't forget!" She recalled her father's instructions delivered in his gruff Japanese. Keep your arms pressed tightly against your sides and bend your upper body at a ninety-degree angle. Hold for as long as you can. It was important to know how to bow, how to behave. Every phrase had a correct counter-phrase, every gesture a precise and appropriate response.

"You have to learn how to behave like a real Japanese or you'll never survive," he'd said. "We're here now. We're here forever."

She realized with horror that she had missed her chance to bow earlier when she was standing in front of the class. Now the opportunity was gone and she was being urged to hurry and sit down. The narrow bench wobbled when she slid onto it. Aya shot a sidelong glance at the girl beside her, who had quickly turned her head away and moved to the far side of the bench. All Aya could see of her was her thick black hair cut straight across just below her chin. The surface of the desk felt rough, the wood unfinished. Aya put her hands in her lap, reluctant to take up any space on top of the shared desk, and squeezed her fists tighter and tighter until the knuckles turned white and shiny. Then, with her head bent low, she stared at the two fists in her lap. They didn't look like her own hands.

Nothing was recognizable anymore, not even her hands.

Aya was in Japan because her father had signed the papers to repatriate. *Go east of the Rockies and disperse, or go to Japan*—that was the choice Canada had given them. No Japanese Canadians would ever be allowed to return to the west coast. In the spring of 1945, even before the war was over, officials arrived in the internment camps with forms to sign and gave everyone three weeks to choose between going "back" to Japan or scattering to unknown parts across Canada.

Aya heard the panicked discussions among her father and other adults. Strange terms like "deportation" and "forced exile" confused her, but other things they said were perfectly clear: "Everything we have is gone," "They want to get rid of us," "How can I start over again at my age?" Clearest of all, though, was this: "They hate us. No matter where we go in this country, they will always hate us." It was her father's voice.

He signed, and with his signature gave the government what it wanted—the ability to deport him. Once the war ended, he was not allowed to revoke what had been done. Aya knew she would have to go with her father. It was just the two of them now that her mother was dead.

They did not leave until the fall of 1946, boarding their train in Slocan City to make the same journey in reverse as when they had been interned. From the interior of British Columbia, they traveled over jagged mountain passes, across endless tracts of forest, along the length of the mighty Fraser River with its thunderous roar pounding in their ears. At the port in Vancouver they waited under guard in the immigration shed for the American military transport ship that would take them to Occupied Japan.

They were told they could take as much luggage as they liked, but they had next to nothing. Aya's mother's ashes were in her father's suitcase, inside a small square box that had been sealed tight and wrapped in a white cloth. Sometimes she wanted to make sure her mother was still there, but she didn't dare open his suitcase to look. Inside her own suitcase she had all her clothes, including the winter coat that had once been too big but that now barely fit her. And in a corner of the suitcase she'd also tucked the handkerchief in which she'd wrapped six little stones from Slocan Lake. They were ugly and gray, not like the sparkly stones she and her friend Midori had collected when they were pretending to be prospectors searching for precious gems. The stones weren't heavy at all. For Aya, they could never be heavy enough.

As soon as their ship came within sight of Japan, a cry had gone out that spread from family to family. "We're approaching the coast. We should be able to see Nippon any minute now!"

It was drizzling, but everyone, including Aya and her father, climbed up to the deck and crowded around the railing. They peered into the thick mist. No land was visible yet, although they could see a few small fishing boats close by dipping in and out of the ocean waves.

"*Mieru*? Can you see?" Her father pointed into the murky distance.

She couldn't see anything, not even the horizon. The sea, the sky, and the rain were all of a piece, a flat wash of gray.

"We're here at last. Our journey is over. Our long, hard journey." His voice cracked with emotion. She sensed that he meant something more than their two-week sea voyage.

"If it weren't for this damn rain, we could see Mount Fuji. That's a beautiful sight, Mount Fuji is. There are lots of beautiful sights in Japan, Aya. You'll see them soon enough. You'll be glad I brought you here."

She looked at his profile. The stubble of his beard was flecked with more gray than ever before, making the shadow of his sunken cheek more pronounced. His jawbone moved just below his ear, in the spot where he was continually grinding his teeth. All the tension and resentment always found its way to that spot.

"If only your . . ." He was staring out at the sea. Rain glistened on his hair and forehead.

Aya knew better than to respond. It had become taboo to talk about her mother, for it made them both too uncomfortable. Her death had pushed Aya and her father farther apart, not closer, as if her mother's absence was a solid mass that sat between them. Absence was not emptiness or nothingness, she had discovered. It was the opposite. Insistent and ever present.

When the rain stopped and the mist thinned, the shoreline came into sight and they could see the sunburned faces of fishermen on boats that bobbed in the harbor. Soon they could even make out tiny figures on land. They were slightly southwest of Tokyo, bound for disembarkation at Uraga.

"Look!" Her father suddenly cupped his hand against the back of her head as if he needed to make sure she was facing the right direction. She could feel his rough calluses. "This is Japan. These are *Nihonjin*! Japanese people. Everyone looks like us. We're home."

They were close to landing. Aya stared at the group of unkempt men in ragged clothing who were running barefoot along the dock where their ship was coming in. These were the *Nihonjin* who had come to greet them. They were shouting something in Japanese.

What are they saying, she was about to ask when she made out the words on her own. Not hello or welcome back, but *"Amerikajin! Cigaretto!"*

Initially they moved in with her father's relatives, an older couple who lived on the outskirts of Tokyo. But it soon became clear that the house was too small, resources too limited, the circumstances too strained. "There's nothing here," the husband said repeatedly, in a weary monotone. "This is what happens when you lose." He was a remote man but not unkind. His wife, whom Aya was told to address as Aunt Ritsuko, terrified her.

"Why didn't you teach her to speak Japanese better? She's thirteen, but she sounds like a six-year-old!"

Aunt Ritsuko's shrill voice echoed throughout the tiny wooden house, and Aya feared her sharp staccato words as if they were capable of drawing real blood. She quickly learned it was better to be quiet, to listen but not speak, and this habit became her way of coping. If she spoke at all, she whispered, and gradually she felt her throat drying up, her voice pulled thinner and thinner like a strand of toffee. She would have liked to stop talking entirely, but it was still necessary to reply if someone spoke to her. Neighbors and shopkeepers peppered her with questions: "Where are you from?" "How long are you staying?" "Where's your mother?"

"Don't tell anyone anything," her father had said right after they arrived. "People here are nosy. This is a country of busybodies." Inside the house, he and Aunt Ritsuko clashed constantly. Whenever he complained about how bad things were in Japan, she would snap, "Well, what did you expect? Why did you come back?" Outside the house, Aya's father had many different voices, depending on whom he was talking to, sometimes formal, sometimes obsequious, sometimes carrying on about topics he knew nothing about. But Aya noticed that the times when he was the most polite to a person to their face was usually when he would turn around and curse them behind their back.

"Not good enough, never good enough," he muttered under his breath whenever yet another odd job abruptly ended.

Everyone here was busy, always rushing. Aunt Ritsuko did everything fast. Despite the way her feet turned inward, pigeon-like, so it looked as if she might bump into herself with every step, she could actually walk faster than anyone Aya had ever known. Dawdlers, it seemed, were viewed with suspicion. Outsiders even more so.

"Don't expect me to translate for you," Aunt Ritsuko said, pushing the loose strands of her wiry gray hair back into her tight bun. "I don't have time. Don't expect me to guess what's on your mind, either."

Sometimes Aya understood, often she didn't. It seemed to depend less on what people said than on how. If they spoke to her slowly and gently, the way her mother always had, then the words were like drops of warm rain that dissolved magically into her brain, and she understood every single word. Aya's mother had come to Canada as a young picture bride to marry Aya's father. She had never learned much English and spoke to Aya only in Japanese. Aya could still hear her mother's soft cadence. "*Aya-chan, ii ko desu, ne.* Aya-chan, you're a good child. You help me with everything. Aya-chan, what would I do without you."

But none of that mattered now. Hardly anyone here spoke like her mother. Everyone was in too much of a hurry. Even after she and her father moved to their own place, Aya found that most people she met sounded just like her aunt, so cross and impatient that it was impossible to understand them. Their words swirled around and around, circling her head like angry black crows.

After the incident with Fumi, Aya was afraid to return to school, but she was more afraid of not going. The other option—explaining to her father what had happened and exposing her shame—struck her as much worse. Her shame would become his shame. She decided she had no choice. She would go back to school, hang her head, and pray. Pray that Fumi would ignore her, pray that the teacher would disregard her, pray that no one would ask her anything, pray that the time would pass and that each day would eventually come to a close. Anything could be endured, she had discovered, if she could only package the time into discrete little packets. She imagined taking the minutes, each one like a pellet, and wrapping them up—one minute, five minutes, fifteen, thirty. Once she had managed to survive a full hour, she could put the packets of time into a box, tie it with string, and push it down a conveyor belt. Just one more minute, one more hour, one more day.

Fumi ignored her. Although this was exactly what she wanted, Aya found herself so confused by the activities at school, she became desperate for someone to ask. Except for the bell and the loud yelling that announced lunch or the end of the school day, she didn't know how to anticipate what was going to happen next. The rhythm of the classroom was erratic. One minute the students were called to the blackboard to write complicated kanji in large exaggerated strokes, the next minute everyone was doing calisthenics in the aisles beside their desks, stretching their arms wildly or jumping up and down. Sometimes they recited aloud. Sometimes they sat in silence reading quietly to themselves. The textbooks were old and the pages inside were covered with thick bars of black ink, long passages the students had been ordered to censor themselves.

By the end of the first week, word had gotten out about Aya, the repat girl, and after class the boys in the lower grades followed her. They called her names and threw handfuls of sand. She was always relieved to reach home until she looked around at her surroundings. The tatami mats were so old and moldy they sank with each step she took, and the wooden walls so full of holes, the dust blew right in. To cook they had to use the charcoal *shichirin* in the outdoor hallway. The communal sink was downstairs; the shared toilet was a hole over which she had to squat, holding her nose and hoping she wouldn't fall in. The other residents of the *nagaya*—tenement house, she learned it meant—were strangers. Through the walls Aya could hear an old lady cackling loudly to herself. A middle-aged man who sat at home all day kept telling her father he should put Aya to work. "Why bother sending her to school? That's a waste of time." Aunt Ritsuko had said more or less the same thing. It was yet another reason why Aya and her father had moved out and found the place where they now lived in the center of Tokyo.

Three weeks passed, then four. Kondo Sensei announced one morning that they would have a short test. Aya sat with her hands in her lap, aware that she had forgotten to bring anything to write with. It didn't really matter, as she would never be able to understand the test. Beside her she saw Fumi reach for her threadbare cloth pencil case and take out a short pencil stub. Then she watched as Fumi pulled out a second stub, just as short as the first, and without turning her head, slid it over to Aya's side of the desk. The stub was less than two inches long, but the tip had been whittled carefully with a knife into a clean sharp point.

Aya didn't know if this was meant to be an apology, but it didn't matter. She took the pencil. She would take anything.

3

Saturday classes were half days, and Kondo usually liked to conduct review lessons to wind up the week. But today the girls seemed more tired than usual. He'd given them an arithmetic test two days ago, and they'd all done poorly. He wondered if it was as demoralizing to them as it was to him. This was his first year at Minami Nishiki, and sometimes he felt as if he were starting all over again as a freshman instructor instead of the experienced teacher that he was. Few of the girls looked up; most kept their heads down, staring either at their fingers or at some blank spot on the top of their desks. The new girl, Aya, was the worst. She never raised her head in class, and so far she hadn't spoken a word.

The school had recently received a donation of maps for the new geography program, and he decided this was a good time to open the kit he had been given.

"I have a surprise for all of you." He could tell by the way they shifted their weight that he had caught their attention. "It's for your social studies lesson. Would you like to see it?"

"Yes, Sensei!"

It was hard to tell if they were genuinely interested or simply humoring him.

"In the past when we studied history and geography, we mistakenly studied bad history and bad geography. We don't want to study bad things anymore, so that's why we have a new program called social studies. As we know, American children are more democratic because they are taught social studies." He cast his eyes around the room. Most of the students were looking down at their desks again. "Do you understand?"

"Yes, Sensei!"

"Very well. This will only take me a moment." He went to the cupboard in the corner of the classroom, pulled out a long thin box, and carried it back to his desk. From the box he took out several long metal tubes. After a few minutes of fiddling, he managed to snap them together into the shape of a stand. He reached into the box again and pulled out a large roll of canvas that he attached to a hook at the top of the stand. Carefully he unfurled the map.

Kondo took a step back and examined his handiwork. The metal roller running across the top was bent so the map hung slightly lower on one side, and the edges of the map were frayed. In the bottom left corner, he could make out "Property of Iowa District School Board" stamped in light blue letters. Everything was in English, but the girls couldn't read English yet except for a few rudimentary words and phrases. Of course the map also looked different in more significant ways. Japan was no longer in the center and the vast stretch of red that had once represented the empire across Asia was entirely gone.

"Class, this is a map of the world," he said.

There was a long silence until a small voice at the back of the room asked, "Sensei, where is Japan?"

After squinting at the map for a moment, he picked up his pointer and touched a spot so close to the edge of the map it looked like it could fall off. "Here. This is Japan."

It resembled a shriveled bean.

"This is what the world looks like. This is what we will study." He moved his pointer to the opposite side of the map and placed it in the center of the United States. "Class, what country is this?"

He looked meaningfully at Aya, but she dropped her gaze immediately.

"Sanae?" he said, picking the one student he could always count on. "I think you know what country this is. Can you please tell the class?"

Sanae looked down at her desk. "America?" she whispered timidly.

"That's it. Speak up so everyone can hear."

"America."

"Very good. And what is America most famous for?"

Again silence.

It was almost time to end class. Kondo wondered if they were tired or bored or simply hungry. He slapped his pointer against the map a second time, hitting it a little harder than he intended. The metal stand wobbled unsteadily. "Come now, it's not a hard question. You know the answer. What is America most famous for?"

Chocoretto. He heard the whisper at the back of the room but he wasn't sure who had spoken. Some of the girls started to giggle.

The bell rang and he set down his pointer. Kondo tried to muster his most authoritative tone of voice—it should be confident, full of energy, in control. He wanted them to look forward to the new social studies program. He wanted them to understand everything that this map represented.

"We'll continue next week. That's all for today. Class dismissed!"

After the last student had left, Kondo sat down at his desk. He listened to the girls' high-pitched chatter grow fainter and fainter as they walked down the school corridor. Once they had exited the building, he was conscious of them again, this time from outside, as their voices floated up to his ears through the open windows and mingled with the cries of the boys and girls in the younger grades who had been let out earlier and were playing in the school yard. From the distance, all their voices sounded so earnest. Every so often he heard shouts of "Stupid!" or "That's mine!"—the little boys seemed particularly prone to fighting—and he felt his heart twist at their innocence and their youth. Even though the students in his class were older, they were still such young girls.

The children struck him as so much more adaptable than adults. The younger they were, the quicker they seemed to make the transition to whatever was new. They switched from miso soup to milk, from rice to bread, and back again with barely any need to stop sipping or chewing. Maybe they were hungry, but it was more than that. Change was in the air, and the children handled it with an insouciance that he envied.

It didn't surprise anyone that the Americans demanded major reforms in the education system. Naturally the old teaching, especially the morals, history, and geography classes, had to go—too feudalistic, too militaristic—to be replaced by a new curriculum that emphasized principles of democracy and individualism. The secondary-school system was also radically revamped by being split into two levels: a middle school of three grades and a high school of three grades. All levels of education were ordered to become coeducational as quickly as possible. Fortunately many elementary schools already had boys and girls attending the same school, so the change was not difficult, but for the higher grades making the shift was more challenging. Many parents found it unthinkable not to have separate education for boys and girls from the age of puberty, so this delicate transition was being phased in more gradually.

The Americans even thought the new middle-school grades should have their own separate buildings (they liked to call them junior high), but everyone recognized the absurdity of such a demand. The economy was precarious and large sections of the city were still in ruins. Many schools, like the one where Kondo used to teach, had burned to the ground during the bombings, and at Minami Nishiki, although they were lucky the foundation had been made of concrete and the building itself survived, there wasn't enough money to repair the classroom walls or windows, never mind erecting a separate structure. So they came up with an eminently practical solution: to create the new "middle school" by simply putting a handwritten sign over the doors of the classrooms used by the girls who were twelve and up. The older boys had been sent to a neighboring school.

If they could, Kondo was sure the Americans would have changed the school year, too, so it started in September the way their schools did. They seemed to have opinions on everything. Just thinking of the enormous disruption such a change would cause made him cringe. Anyone could see that at least in this regard the Japanese way was better. April, when the cherry trees were in full bloom, was clearly the best time to begin a new course of study.

But what difference did the views of one individual like himself make? Whatever was going to happen would happen—a new social studies curriculum, different classroom arrangements, American food for the school lunches. He had to admit that the students seemed to display no resistance at all. Maybe the Americans were right, and even if they weren't, it didn't matter because no one here could stop what was happening. Change was moving fast, like a giant tsunami, and Kondo did what everyone else around him did. He ran as fast as he could to keep from being crushed by the wave.

He was lucky; he knew that, too. Many former teachers had been purged at the end of the war. They were the ones who had been too patriotic, the kind who were a bit too eager to report on others who they felt were not contributing as fully to the war effort as they should. These teachers hadn't thought much of Kondo, whose special subject area was English, the language of the enemy, and whose ineligibility for the draft seemed very suspicious. He explained that he had tried to sign up many times, but no matter how desperate the army recruiters were, even when they were taking older men, they said they had no use for someone so nearsighted. One of them had laughed in his face. "With your eyes, you'd shoot one of us, not the enemy!" In the last three years of the war, he had spent most of his time in a munitions factory, supervising students who had been deployed from school to the war effort. He sometimes wondered what had become of them. How many had been sent to the front and died there?

His relatives and neighbors had felt sorry for him. What a shame he couldn't serve, what a shame he couldn't sacrifice himself for the empire, as their own sons were doing. After the war was over, although no one said it, he sensed that people didn't pity him so much as they resented him. He was alive, their sons were not. He was whole and able-limbed, while their boys had returned damaged and broken.

"Give it back!"

"*Bakayaro!*"

Kondo got up and stood at the window. Two boys in the school yard were fighting. One boy was holding something up over his head, trying to keep the other from getting it.

"Say you're sorry, you *baka*."

"No way! You stink! *Kusotare*."

"You stink more."

"Your father stinks!"

Kondo thought he recognized one of the boys. He looked like the younger brother of one of his students, Akiko Hayashi. What was his name? Masayoshi? Masatomi? Something like that. Both boys wore tattered clothes that were no better than rags and even from a distance Kondo could see the outline of their ribs through their thin undershirts. What could they possibly be fighting over? Probably some useless scrap. Well, let them enjoy their scuffle. He wondered if they knew that they were also the lucky ones. He'd seen plenty of boys their age at Ueno train station, orphaned and forced to fend for themselves. You grew up quickly in a circumstance like that. Those little boys had no compunction about following the GIs and their *panpan* women, cadging cigarettes, chewing gum, and who knew what else. A school-yard scuffle belonged to another era for them.

He turned away from the window and looked at the front row of empty desks, his eyes resting on the spot where the new girl sat. She didn't seem able to talk at all, and he wasn't sure how much she understood of what went on. What on earth was she doing here? Who ever heard about Japanese coming back from America? Why would anyone in their right mind do that? Leave a land of plenty for this. Only the desperate came here, and there were lots of those. They were from places like Manchuria and Korea, boatload after boatload of *hikiagesha*, repatriates driven out of Japan's former colonies. They flooded back to the homeland with nothing except the clothes on their backs and the few possessions that they managed to strap around their shoulders. "Go home." He mouthed the words in English. Was he talking about the repats? Or was he really thinking of the Americans? "Go home, GI Joe." He tested the sound of this phrase, speaking the words aloud this time and listening self-consciously to the echo his voice made in the empty room. It wasn't that he hated the Americans—he didn't even really dislike them—but it seemed as if they had already been here long enough. A year and a half, soon it would be two years, and no sign of anyone leaving.

As for Aya Shimamura, well, he'd done what he thought best, but look at what had happened. How could he have predicted that Fumi would behave the way she had? The principal had some ludicrous idea that Aya's presence would somehow stimulate English-language learning. "Kondo-kun," he'd said, "I want our school to get a head start with all this English study. You figure out how to do it. It's going to be English all the way from this point on, you mark my words." Kondo couldn't quite put his finger on it, but he had the sense that something beyond sheer love of pedagogy was behind the principal's method of running his school. He was a hustler in his own way, yet Kondo had to admit that the principal was able to get things done. Hadn't he managed to make their school one of the first to receive the new maps from America? Of course, all schools were going to get them sooner or later, but the fact that the principal had gotten his hands on one of the first was an accomplishment you had to admire.

Kondo stood up and walked over to the map where it still hung on its spindly metal frame. He was about to roll it up and put it away when something held him transfixed. Slowly, softly, he began pronouncing the English names he saw stamped in thick black letters across the different countries. The world was so vast, it struck him, so much vaster than any of them could ever imagine, living as they did in their one tiny corner of the globe.

He should write the names of the most important countries and capital cities in Japanese underneath the English lettering, he thought. That would help his students. They were good girls but not all of them were as sharp as he wished they were. Yes, he could do that much. He had a fine calligraphic hand, and he would bring his good brush and ink from home. But it would have to wait until next week. Right now he had to set off for his spot in the Alley, a place near Shibuya station that he felt confident none of his fellow teachers knew about. As the weather was so nice, he decided to walk. It would take well over an hour but he wanted to save on streetcar fare.

4

Corporal Yoshitaka "Matt" Matsumoto had the office to himself. Everyone else in the section had left: the officers, the other Nisei, the typists. The room was silent except for the electric hum of the clock that hung high in the center of the wall to the left of Lieutenant Baker's desk. There was something very satisfying about the clock's perfect roundness, the fullness of the sweep of its hands, the large plain numerals stamped in a circle that were easy to see from anywhere in the room. There was no second hand, just the minute needle that quivered ever so slightly before it stuttered into the next position with a faint but decisive *plip*.

Before leaving, Lieutenant Baker had paused at his desk. "Still working on that letter, Matsumoto?"

Matt jumped to his feet. "Almost finished, sir, just a few more lines."

Baker smiled. "Good work. But there's no need to overdo it. Make good use of your pass."

"Yes, sir."

They both knew there was no need for him to work so late on a Friday, yet Matt sensed that Baker was grateful for his dedication. All of today's translations had already been typed up and sent by military courier the short three-hundred-yard trip down the street to General Headquarters. By now the letters were sitting on MacArthur's desk where the general himself, everyone had repeatedly been told, would personally read every single one. A full day's work was something to be proud of, especially given the pressure the translators and typists were under, but there was little time to rest or engage in self-congratulation. Bags of incoming mail arrived twice daily and were emptied on the large oak table in the middle of the room, where the pile was quickly building into a little Mount Fuji.

So many letters!

When a brief announcement had been posted in the Japanese press at the beginning of the Occupation—*The government is interested in hearing from the people*—no one could have possibly anticipated the reaction. This was supposed to be a nation of robots, people who blindly followed their emperor, people who would never challenge authority. Who would have thought they would write so many letters, all of them directly addressed to MacArthur? Who would have thought they had so much to say? The Occupation was already well into its twentieth month, yet the flood of letters to MacArthur showed no sign of abatement. If anything, it seemed to be increasing. Hundreds of letters arrived every day, and while a few were written in English, the vast majority were in Japanese and required translation. Matt was part of the Allied Translator and Interpreter Service, ATIS, a division primarily staffed with Japanese Americans, most of them second generation—Nisei. Some were enlisted servicemen like himself, while others were locally hired foreign nationals, Japanese Americans who had been trapped in Japan during the war and unable to return home. Everyone worked under a handful of American officers, most of whom had received intensive Japanese-language training in the States and had served in wartime intelligence.

The main assignment for Matt's section, currently its *only* assignment, was to translate personal mail addressed to General MacArthur.

Dear General MacArthur, the letters would begin. After that, there was no telling what the writer might have on his mind. Topics ranged far and wide: sugar shortages, land reform, the difficulty in obtaining train tickets, the evils of prostitution, the lack of adequate housing, the high cost of soy sauce, women's rights, corruption among city officials, gambling, smoking in elevators, the need to liberalize taxes. Furthermore, the letters came in all sizes and shapes and materials. Matt was impressed with how inventive people were despite the continuing paper shortage. Anything that could be written on was fair game: paper as thin and translucent as the skin of onions, yellowed sheets from old student notebooks, toilet paper, posters torn off poles, pieces of cardboard neatly cut into the shape of postcards, strips of clean white cloth. He once translated a letter comprised of heavy black brushstrokes written directly onto the front page of an old newspaper. He had felt like an archaeologist holding an ancient palimpsest, his eye constantly distracted by the headlines and advertisements on the faded newsprint.

Most letters came in envelopes sealed shut with sticky rice glue but some were rolled up like scrolls and tied with string. Others were folded so many times they looked like strange forms of origami. Some letters were long—page after page of tiny Japanese characters like rows of dark seeds—and some were short, no more than a line: *We wish you good health*, or *Welcome to Japan*. Some were not kind: *Get out, Americans.* Some letters were written in blood.

There were gifts for MacArthur, too. Ink paintings mounted on silk, calligraphy brushes, white clay Hakata dolls, a Noh mask, serving trays made of polished lacquer. A set of rice bowls, a frying pan (accompanied by a letter offering to provide cooking lessons to Mrs. MacArthur), a tea caddy, a collection of white *tabi*, countless neckties, a dozen silk handkerchiefs, a hand-carved pipe. And many—too many!—folding fans with pictures of goldfish, cherry blossoms, maple leaves, string balls, plump children at play, dancing maidens. One fan came with tiny arrows marked on its spine— *Push this way to open.* The gifts of food included packages of green tea, dried seaweed, white radish pickles, jars filled with homemade *umeboshi*, small pots packed with dark miso paste. A freshly plucked chicken, chunks of salted salmon. A basket of roasted sweet potatoes.

Any notes that accompanied the gifts had to be translated.

Matt smiled to himself, thinking of the things Sab Kawakami liked to say. "Who are they trying to kid? Does anyone really think the Old Man reads all this stuff?" Sab's desk was next to Matt's, and he kept up a constant patter. "I mean, I hope not. Let's hope he has more important things to do with his time. And I bet he throws out most of the presents, except maybe the expensive pictures and pottery. Wish he'd send some stuff our way."

Sab had lots of quips to share. "Hey, Matsumoto, know what GHQ stands for?"

"General Headquarters," Matt had answered solemnly. GHQ stood for General Headquarters, the headquarters of General Douglas MacArthur, the Supreme Commander for the Allied Powers—SCAP. Matt had been so proud to be assigned to work here.

"Nope." Sab tapped two pencils on his desktop like he was doing a drumroll. "Think hard now. GHQ. Wanna guess again?"

Matt shook his head.

"Give up?"

He sighed. With Sab it was always a game. "Yeah, I give up."

Sab beamed. "GHQ. That's short for Go-Home-Quickly. G-H-Q. Get it?"

When Matt shook his head in disapproval, Sab pulled a face and protested. "Hey, I didn't make it up. That's what some Japanese think, you know, deep inside. Not everybody is crazy about being occupied."

Matt returned his attention to what he had translated so far. He was working on a letter urging rapid reform of the ration system and better distribution of goods. The letter was written in a particularly convoluted style of formal Japanese and he'd had to look up almost every word two or three times in different dictionaries to be sure of the meaning. He crossed out the last sentence and rephrased it. There, that was it. He was finished. But the scrawl on his pad was an indecipherable mess, and he would have to write everything out again in a neater hand. It would be faster if he typed it himself, but he was not allowed to type—it didn't matter that he could—because that was the job of the secretaries. Instead, like all the other translators, he had to handwrite his work on lined sheets of foolscap and place them in the big wire basket that was next to where the three secretaries in the typing pool worked. One was Nancy Nogami, a Nisei woman, who hardly spoke a word unless it was absolutely necessary. She spent her days bent over her typewriter so close her nose was only inches from the keys. Every time she made a mistake, she muttered "Darn" under her breath. Sab was betting that she'd say "damn" before the summer was over and he wanted Matt to help keep track of her building frustration.

The other two secretaries were Japanese: an older woman named Yoshiko, whose short graying hair and angular face gave her an air of efficiency and competence that belied her meager output; and Mariko, a young woman who could type like the wind without making mistakes, without jamming her keys, without getting her paper twisted, without fear. Not only was she fast and accurate, she had no problem reading everyone's distinctive handwriting. Nobody in the office knew where she had learned how to type like this, a feat all the more remarkable given that her spoken English was often impossible to understand.

Matt wrote out a more legible copy of his translation on foolscap and deposited it in the wire basket. It would be the first thing the typists saw on Monday morning, when the cycle started up again. He thought about whether to get supper in the mess hall, but he wasn't really hungry. Should he start working on another letter, he wondered, or could he kill time some other way? The guys would be getting ready to go out, the showers full of steam and locker-room banter. If he stayed here a little longer, he could avoid them entirely. Last week they'd teased him mercilessly.

"Matsumoto, how come you never want to come with us? How come you never want to have any fun?"

"You've danced with a girl before, haven't you?"

"Hey, leave him alone, maybe he's never—"

"What do you do by yourself all the time?"

"Hey, he reads. Books and stuff. Isn't that right, Matt?"

"Ah, give me a dame over a book any night."

Eddie Takagi was the worst, he simply wouldn't let up.

"Come on. You want all those girls to go to the white guys? Have some pride." Eddie was the same age as Matt, but he liked to act as if he were a lot older and more worldly.

Then Jimmy Shikaze and Alan Horiya had joined Eddie, and

the three of them had cornered Matt in the shower, white towels wrapped around their smooth hairless torsos. The cloying scent of too much army-issue aftershave made him dizzy.

"Just do what we do. It's easy to pick up a girl here. Cheap, too. And they like us. When was the last time you found a Nipponjin girl who'd go all the way? Where I come from none of them did."

"Ah, c'mon guys. We'd better leave him alone."

Matt sat down at Mariko's typewriter and removed the snug-fitting gray cover. Feeding his plain blue aerogram into the Underwood's roller, he adjusted the carriage until the sheet was even and centered. The keys were perfect round circles, tiny white saucers of black letters, and he set his fingers into position and began to type.

Dear Diane,

How are Mom and Dad? You're taking good care of them, I don't doubt that. And how about you? Is the job okay? You won't have to be a housekeeper forever, you know. Just be patient and you can go back to school, get a degree.

He typed quickly and easily without looking at the keys because Diane had taught him how to touch-type. Instead of hunting for each letter, he could watch the words form before his very eyes. He loved to see the keys bite into the paper—*thwack, thwack, thwack*—metal shapes that pressed their weight with such urgency onto the page. Those were *his* words being forged in front of him. Wordsmith. Oh, he liked that image. That's what he wanted to be.

I'm getting the hang of my new work assignment. I like it better than the Press section I was in before. There's a lot of demand for translators and interpreters here. The Occupation really needs us. But if you're not in the military, it's pretty hard to get decent chow, so I wouldn't recommend it without Uncle Sam's meal ticket.

I've got lots of buddies here. The guys are friendly.

He realized he didn't have much more to say to his sister. Diane claimed that she looked forward to his letters, but he wondered if she really meant it. When she wrote, her letters were always chatty and full of light gossip about relatives and friends. She avoided saying too much about their parents, but Matt knew that his father was severely depressed. Funny, all those years when they'd had the farm, his father had cursed it day in and day out. Stupid strawberry patch. No good. No good fruit. No good soil. But when it was taken away, it was like a limb had been cut off. He wanted it back, all the weeds, all the rocks, all the backbreaking labor. After the war was over and their family was finally allowed to return home, though, it was clear that the people who now farmed their land had no intention of relinquishing it.

Say hi to everyone. I'll write again soon.

He loosened the spring on the roller and pulled out the aerogram. No, there was no easy way to squeeze all of a man's thoughts onto a thin blue rectangle of paper. It was just as well there was no more space left. He'd run out of words.

When Diane had insisted on bringing her typewriter to the internment camp, their mother had been furious. They were allowed only what they could carry. She should have filled her suitcase with dishes and blankets and more clothes, not a useless machine. But Diane had been in secretarial school when the war broke out. When they were shipped to the desert, she'd only been two months away from graduation. She said she needed to practice so she would be ready to work as soon as they got out. How long can they keep us locked up, she said. They've got to realize it's a mistake—we're Americans! But she got tired of practicing and tired of waiting, tired of futile dreaming. When she abandoned her typewriter, Matt decided to take it. He didn't really have anything to say but he liked to punch the keys with his index fingers the way he imagined a hard-bitten journalist or an alcohol-fueled novelist might.

"For Pete's sake," Diane said when she caught him, "if you're going to do it, do it right." And she showed him what she'd learned, how to type with his head erect and eyes looking forward, fingers lightly poised above the middle row of letters, baby fingers crooked.

He put the gray cover back on Mariko's typewriter. After he turned off the lights, he was drawn to the big plate-glass windows that overlooked the main avenue. The sun had just set and thin wisps of cloud were turning pink, then fiery red, then dark maroon right before his eyes. From his office's fourth-floor vantage point, the view was almost panoramic. His building and MacArthur's headquarters—the Dai-Ichi Building—were both six stories high, which made them among the tallest buildings still standing in Tokyo.

To his right, Matt could see the broad marching plaza that was directly across the street from General Headquarters. Beyond the plaza stretched the vast Imperial Palace grounds. The forest that covered the grounds was now shrouded in a dense, impenetrable darkness. Only the broad skirt of massive white stones that formed the palace moat was visible, reflecting the last rays of the remaining early-evening light. Somewhere inside the palace was the emperor. And somewhere just beyond the palace grounds was a flattened city, piles of rubble and jerry-built shacks, a landscape still filled with ruins. It was crawling with a desperate humanity. But for the time being all evidence of the wartime destruction was obscured by the encroaching night.

In the growing darkness, the city looked beautiful.

5

Fumi was not naturally a loner, but lately all she wanted was to be by herself. Home no longer felt right without her sister living with them, and she didn't like the way her mother and father tried to pretend that Sumiko no longer existed. She didn't like being with Akiko or her other friends from school, either, in part because she feared being asked about her family. It wasn't easy to find a private hideout in the crowded backstreets where she lived, but she had discovered two good spots: one was on the grounds of Shotoku Temple, at the back near the tiny cemetery, and the other was the bombed-out ruins of the former local library. Only one wall of the library was still standing—the rest was rubble—but there was a nice sunny spot among these ruins that was hidden from view. This was where Fumi liked to sit. It was a good place to think, to empty her mind of its troubles and let it slowly fill up with ideas and solutions. It didn't always work, but at least for a short period, she felt better.

Fumi unbuttoned her blouse collar and spread it wide so that as much sun as possible could reach her neck and nape. She hoped the sun and its heat would help her think, to puzzle out something that she'd seen a week ago, something that had been bothering her ever since. She was convinced she had been given a sign. The question was how to interpret it. The sign was in the newspaper her father had left open one day after breakfast. The breeze had scattered the pages across the tatami, and as Fumi bent over to pick up the loose sheets of newsprint one of the headlines had caught her eye: GHQ SWAMPED BY LETTER-WRITING FRENZY.

"Everyone is writing to General MacArthur, so I did too," war veteran Hiroyuki Nishio was quoted as saying while he proudly showed off his new American eyeglasses. Fed up with trying to get help from the Japanese health authorities, he had written directly to MacArthur. "I never expected anything to come of it, but this is what democracy means! If you have a problem, write a letter," Nishio advised. "You never know what might happen."

Fumi puzzled over what she had read. The war veteran's problem didn't seem all that serious to her. What was a pair of spectacles compared to bringing her sister home? If a letter could help someone get something as trivial as a pair of glasses, how much more helpful it would surely be in a really important situation. Maybe this was the solution she'd been seeking. But she realized that she didn't know how to even begin writing such a letter, never mind where she should send it or how she could obtain good paper and a decent envelope. She would not, could not, ask her parents. They would disapprove. It was something she would have to do on her own. And yet how?

Before her sister left home, Fumi liked to open the bottom drawer of the dark wooden *tansu* they shared and finger the things Sumiko had hidden under her thick cotton leggings and baggy pantaloon-style *monpe*. She would let her fingers grope through the piles of clothes until they found what she was seeking: something so soft and light it was like stroking moths' wings. Fumi didn't dare pull the stockings out, afraid she might tear them, or worse, that they would evaporate if she exposed them to the sunlight. Not many things were soft anymore.

Fumi remembered her mother's many beautiful silk kimono. They were gone, all of them, sold long ago, one by one, in exchange for shoyu and rice, dried mushrooms and miso. The beautiful stiff wide obi with its intricate design of peonies had been one of the first things to go. They had hoped it would fetch a good price, but when their father took it to market, he didn't get much. The farmers said they already had lots of brocade, and they pointed to the piles of clothing in their carts. In exchange for the obi they gave him a sack of mountain potatoes and some salted fish that later proved to be rotten.

Sumiko, not their mother, was the one who cried each time they sold a kimono. "They're so pretty," she'd said. "Do you have to?"

"They're useless to me, better they bring in something to eat."

Fumi had watched as Sumiko traced her finger over the embossed shape of a heron's wing stitched in glossy braided thread. It was the last kimono they sold. The heron seemed poised to take flight, to tear itself away from the very material of which it was made. Sumiko had followed the wing back to the bird's body and up to the shiny knot of black material that formed its eye. She pressed the tip of her finger into it.

"I wanted a chance to wear this. I always thought you would pass it down to me."

"Sumi-chan, this is no time to be sentimental. What choice do we have? Everyone is selling off their things. Farmers never had it so good." Their mother reached for the kimono. She and Sumiko stood in the entranceway, mother and daughter looking almost identical in their baggy cotton pants and coarsely woven jackets. It was the first time Fumi had noticed that Sumiko was taller than their mother.

What Fumi remembered most about her sister was the scent of her back and her hair. It was a sometimes sour, mostly sweet odor that was uniquely hers, a combination of perspiration and soap and the natural oils in her scalp. When their mother was busy working in the family bookstore, it fell to Sumiko, who was ten years older, to take care of Fumi. From early in the morning, Fumi was strapped to Sumiko's back, her tiny nose buried in her sister's clothing and hair, and there she stayed for most of the day while Sumiko aired the futon, went to school, shopped in the market, helped with the cooking. Fumi was bound with thick bands of cotton that crisscrossed her torso so tightly that, except for her legs which dangled in the air, she could hardly move. It was the most secure place in the world, and she hated to give it up at night when they had to go to bed. Even now, she longed for that sense of protection and warmth. Yet she'd never stopped to wonder if Sumiko had minded the heavy weight she'd had to carry around, whether her back hurt or her legs got sore.

What had once seemed so constant had changed dramatically during and after the war. Their father had lost everything when the bookstore was destroyed in the firebombings and their mother's health was so poor she was unable to leave the house. Fumi herself had suffered a serious case of beriberi and required expensive injections of vitamin B. When Sumiko said she had found a good job that would take care of the bills and bring them food, it seemed like a miracle. Sumiko moved out of the house and into a dormitory in the entertainment district of the Ginza. Gradually she came home less and less frequently, and sometimes Fumi's only clue that her sister had been back was the special American food that suddenly appeared. Lately, though, Sumiko hadn't come home at all. Fumi hadn't seen her in months.

Fumi knew her parents were trying to protect her, trying to hide their fear for her sister. She heard them late at night when they thought she was asleep. Words like *Amerikajin* and *butterfly* and *onrii*—a GI's *only one*. Her mother would make a funny choking noise that Fumi recognized as the muffled sound of her weeping.

Fumi fingered her chest pocket and felt for Sumiko's photograph. She preferred to keep it with her rather than risk having it discovered while she was out, and she also liked the idea of having Sumiko so close by, in her pocket, right over her heart. "*Nechan*," she whispered. "Why did you go away? When are you coming back home?"

In the midst of her daydreaming, Akiko's younger brother suddenly leaped out from behind a pile of broken bricks.

"Want to see what I've got?"

Fumi sat up with a start and clutched the collar of her blouse. "I didn't see you," she snapped. "What are you doing here?"

"Hiding." Masatomi grinned. There were dark brown streaks on either side of his mouth. He stuck out his tongue. It looked dark brown, too.

"Well, you shouldn't hide here," she said crossly.

"Why not? You do. You come here all the time."

"How do you know?"

Masatomi shrugged. He was wearing only an undershirt and when he moved his thin bony shoulders she noticed just how dirty and full of holes it was. He looked every bit the street urchin he could so easily have become.

"Want to see something?" he persisted. He brought a closed fist up to Fumi's face, close enough to make her go cross-eyed. She swung her head back.

"What is it?"

Masatomi opened his fist and in the middle of his small grubby palm lay a twisted clump of dark pink. It was covered with bits of gray fluff.

"What's that?" She wrinkled her nose.

"Chewing gum," Masatomi said triumphantly. "I saved it. I'll give you half, okay?"

"I don't want it."

"It's good. It's from the GI-san."

"When did you get that?"

"Yesterday. No, day before yesterday. I let Akiko chew it yesterday." Masatomi grinned again. "You can borrow it, but you have to give it back."

"Go away."

"I have *chocoretto*, too," he continued undaunted. "But I ate it up. If I get more, I'll give you some, okay?"

"I can get my own."

"No, you can't. You're stupid. You don't know how." Masatomi rolled his eyes skyward. "Hey, I have a surprise. Close your eyes."

"What?"

"You have to close your eyes."

"What if I don't want to."

"Close your eyes!"

Fumi decided to play along. If she wanted him to go away, this would be the fastest way to get rid of him. She felt his hot breath on her face as he inspected her to make sure her eyes were closed.

"No peeking," he said sternly. "Okay, now bend forward."

She leaned forward slightly.

"More!" Masatomi commanded.

She obliged by letting her head fall forward even more and felt her hair brush against her cheeks. She opened her right eye just a crack. She could see her dark blue pants and her toes sticking out between the thongs of her wooden geta. At her feet she saw the gravel and broken pieces of brick. The sun felt hot on her nape and the back of her head. It was a nice kind of cleansing heat.

She felt Masatomi's fingers awkwardly brushing her hair off her neck, parting it in the middle, pushing one half of her hair to one side, the other half to the other side.

"What are you doing?"

"You have nice hair, *o-nesan*. Pretty hair."

It was the first time Masatomi had spoken to her so kindly, even addressing her as if she were an older sister. Maybe he wasn't such a brat after all. She let him continue playing with her hair, pushing it this way and that way to either side of her neck. She tried not to think about how sticky his hands probably were.

"Don't move, *o-nesan*," he said. "Don't move."

She felt his fingers tickling the back of her neck. Then something soft and furry, like cotton balls, brushed against her nape and tumbled down her spine. At that moment she might even have been smiling, the sensation was so pleasant.

A second later she felt a sharp sting in the middle of her back. "Ouch!" She jumped up and felt another sting, then another. Something was inside her blouse and she couldn't reach it. She whirled around like a dog chasing its tail. In desperation, she tore off her top and shook it out. A giant caterpillar fell to the sandy ground and curled up into a round ball.

She stomped on it with her wooden sandal and then in her fury kept on stomping until she had flattened it completely and its gooey insides were smeared across the ground.

Masatomi doubled over with laughter. Two of his friends emerged from their hiding spot behind the broken wall and joined him, giggling and pointing at Fumi's bare chest with their grubby fingers.

"We saw your tits!"

She lunged toward them, snapping her blouse in the air like a whip. "I'll kill you!" she screamed.

"*Panpan* tits! You're a *panpan*!"

"Your sister's a *panpan*!"

"Shut up!"

"Your sister's a *panpan*. *Panpan! Panpan!*" Their high squeaky voices echoed as they ran away.

Fumi could feel herself shaking as she put her arms through the sleeves of her blouse. Horrible boys! She would get back at them, especially that Masatomi. He was a wicked little brat. As she buttoned up her top, she looked down at her chest. Her nipples were darker than usual and a bit hard, but otherwise everything was as flat as ever. Good. Although some of the other girls had started to grow breasts, Fumi was determined that she never would. Her wish was that nothing would change, or better yet that she could set the clock back to an earlier time. She thrust her fingers inside her upper left pocket. The picture wasn't there! A wave of nausea washed over her. It must have fallen out when she was shaking her blouse. She scoured the ground, walking in a spiral from the center of the lot to the outer edges and then back again. Eventually she found it lying in the dirt not far from where she had been sitting, and nearby she spotted the yellowish tissue paper in which it had been wrapped.

She blew off the dirt and stared at the picture. Sumiko stared back at her.

To think that she had nearly lost this! The thought made her heart beat faster. This was a sign, just like the newspaper. And it was also a warning—there was no time to waste.

6

ach time he came to the Alley, Kondo marveled at the density of human traffic in the city. The Alley—its full name was Love Letter Alley (or Koibumi Yokocho)—was really an alley within an alley, a dark offshoot from the narrow crooked line of shops that wound past Shibuya train station and up a long slope. Past the rice ration depot, past the tofu stand, past the storefronts that sold old chipped porcelain cups and battered kettles and pots. A handwritten sign proudly proclaimed DEMOCRACY POTS AND PANS, as if the word "democracy" added a patina of desire to even the most mundane item. Kondo sometimes wondered if he should use it on his sign, too. DEMOCRACY LETTERS—that would be sure to attract lots of customers.

He came here every Saturday after he finished teaching. Usually he arrived by late afternoon and took his time enjoying a bowl of noodles at one of the roadside stalls before opening for business in the early evening. Once he was here, he found it easier to stay overnight. Not only did a lot of customers come late at night but Kondo didn't want to risk being robbed on the way home in the dark; it was safer to wait until daylight.

He had long ago given up hurrying and he was never the first to arrive. Invariably, Nakamura, Yamaguchi, and Tabata beat him to it, their stools already set up in the best spots. Kondo contented himself with a cramped space at the end of the alley within an alley, a place far back from the crowds, tucked away in a nearly invisible nook.

"Letters! Letters read, letters written. Top quality!" Yamaguchi, at the head of the line, began touting his services. He shouted out his slogan in a loud singsong voice. "Best price. Best value. Letters read, letters written."

Despite his appalling English skills, Yamaguchi got a lot of customers because of his location. But Kondo knew that his own English was much better than that of the other translators. His reputation was slowly growing and he hoped that eventually word-of-mouth praise would mean that his customers, all of them women, would actively seek him out, pushing past the other more conveniently located stalls until they found him. For the time being, however, advertising was essential. Kondo added his voice to the chorus of letter writers trying to solicit business. He was at the end of the line, at the top of the slope, sitting in the semidarkness. "Teacher of English writes your letters!" he shouted with all the enthusiasm he could muster. "Superior letters for your American Joe!"

The first woman to approach him was wearing far too much lipstick. Her round face was dominated by her shiny red mouth, making her other features—her small eyes and short, flat nose—fade into insignificance. As if self-conscious of her lips, she pressed them tightly together once she had finished speaking. "I need a letter" was all she said.

"English or Japanese?" Kondo asked.

The woman gave him a funny look. "English," she said. After a pause she added, "Of course."

"To . . . ?"

She pursed her lips again and bent her head down. Kondo could see that her hair was arranged in large symmetrical curls. The woman shook her head ever so slightly, as if afraid to disturb her hairdo.

"You don't know his name?"

When she looked up, Kondo noticed that the rims of her eyes were red.

"GI, huh?"

The woman nodded, this time aggressively. She wrung the handkerchief she was holding in her hands.

"You know a letter in English is not cheap, don't you." It was a statement, not a question. He hated to fish like this, but he couldn't work for free. It had happened all too often before. "And if you don't even know his name . . ."

"I have money." The woman scrunched her handkerchief into a ball and with her right hand patted her handbag. It dangled from a short strap around her left forearm. "I can pay, don't worry. But I want a good letter."

"My letters are good," he said politely.

I only write good ones, the best you can get, was what he meant. He wished he could tell her that she'd come to the best stall in the Alley, that his English was better than any of the other guys here. That he was a teacher and that in university he had studied harder than anyone else, always staying up through the night to memorize one more word of vocabulary, one more tricky idiom. That was before the war, when he had hoped to become a professor or a government bureaucrat, dreaming big despite his poor background. At one point, encouraged by a supportive professor, he had even thought of going into the diplomatic service, to use his language skills for his country. But now, well, there was no knowing which way the winds would blow. Wasn't that the phrase? Which way would they blow? They blew whichever way they wanted, that was the truth, and to hell with effort and study and hard work. To hell with a man's dreams. A few winds, a few bombs. Look at him now. All those years struggling to read Hawthorne, Poe, and Melville; all that studying came down to this: *I miss you and I hope you remember your promise to me,* or some variation. *When will you come back? I am waiting for you. I love you.*

He knew he was lucky. He had a special skill that helped him make enough money to afford food on the black market. One needed a mouth not for talking but for eating. One needed to fill that mouth not with words but with rice.

"I can write you a very good letter, but I don't want you to waste your money. How can you mail the letter if you don't know his name?"

"He told me where he lives. He's in the barracks downtown. If you write the letter for me, I can stand outside the barracks until I see him. I can hand it to him personally."

"Do you have any idea how many GIs there are? It would be almost impossible to find your fellow."

The woman narrowed her eyes.

"Save your money," he said brusquely.

He worried constantly that one of the women who came to him might start crying. What he feared most was a scene, the kind of desperate sobbing that would force him to comfort the woman, tell her everything would be all right. Her Joe would come back. Her Johnny or Harry or simply Honey was a decent man who would do the decent thing. But so far, no one had broken down. They were strong, the women who came to his booth. They came for a transaction: a letter for a fee. They were tougher than he was, he had to admit, but they were stubborn, too. He'd almost given up trying to convince them that "Joe" or "Private Pete" might not be real names. Some even thought they could address a letter to "Charlie, USA" or "Roger, California" and that it would get to their intended. Even when he explained, even when they believed him, they still refused to be discouraged. They opened their purses and pulled out more cash. "What do you need?" they asked. "If it's not enough, I can get more. I can make more."

The woman hadn't moved. "How much?" she asked, fishing in her handbag and pulling out a wad of neatly folded yen with a string around it.

Kondo looked up. "Do you know what you want me to write?"

"Yes."

"Okay," he said, gesturing to the wooden tangerine crate beside his stool. He reached between his knees and pulled out the box where he kept his paper and pens. "Sit down. Now, tell me what you want to say."

7

Just when Aya thought she was starting to understand the strange routines at school, something would happen that would throw her off. The spraying took her completely by surprise.

It began with the principal's unexpected appearance at the classroom door.

"Kondo-kun, the Hygiene Patrol is here," he said, sounding a little short of breath as if he had run down the corridor.

"I thought they were coming tomorrow." Kondo stood at attention in front of the principal. "Didn't the notice say tomorrow?"

"Well, they come when they want to, don't they? Anyway, they're setting up in the yard, so get your students out there now. We'll have them do the older grades first."

"And what about us?"

"The teachers will go last."

"I don't mind getting it with my class."

"Kondo-kun, at our school the teachers go last. That's the way we've always done it."

As soon as the principal left, the students turned their attention expectantly to Kondo, who still stood facing the doorway although his posture was no longer erect. He swiveled toward the class and took a deep breath. "We'll continue the dictation later. The Hygiene Patrol is here. I think you all know the procedure."

Aya quickly shot a glance at Fumi but she seemed to be completely unperturbed by the announcement. After tucking her precious pencil stub in her pencil case, Fumi got up and stood at attention beside her desk. Aya copied her. By now all the other girls were standing, too.

The class lined up and followed Kondo Sensei outside. Three GIs were waiting for them in the middle of the school yard where they had set up a small table on which they had placed their equipment. Two of the men stood listlessly scuffing the tips of their boots in the sand while the third sat perched on the edge of the table, one foot planted on the ground, the other swinging back and forth in the air.

Beyond the mesh fence that enclosed the school, Aya could see the military jeep, a gigantic green metal bug. A group of small children, those who were too young to go to school yet, had formed a circle around the jeep, curious but afraid to get too close.

Led by Kondo Sensei, the class marched across the yard toward the table. As they got closer, Aya noticed that the soldiers' jaws were moving although they were not talking. They seemed to be chewing gum. The soldier who was half sitting on the edge of the table held something that looked like a large spray gun.

As soon as the girls had lined up in a single row in front of the table, the GI with the spray gun walked over to Kondo. "Excuse me. So, we can start the spraying, okay?" He made a pumping motion. "Okay?"

Kondo nodded and moved away.

The soldier approached the first girl in line. It was Akiko. "Okay, sweetheart, close those peepers tight," he said, motioning with his hand for her to shut her eyes and lean forward. He held the applicator up to his shoulder and began spraying a thick cloud of white powder over her hair and shoulders. Suddenly the air was pungent with a sharp chemical odor. The GI went down the first line of girls, and as he moved, each girl bowed her head forward in anticipation of being sprayed. He had almost reached Aya.

He was so close she could see a small piece of pink chewing gum between his front teeth and a few bubbles of clear spittle in the corners of his lips. When he opened his mouth to speak, the chewing gum disappeared. "Your turn, girlie. Now shut your eyes tight.

Bend your head down." He raised the spray gun and pointed it at her. "Close your eyes!"

Aya didn't know what came over her, only that she didn't want to be sprayed by the soldier. She felt a hot rush of blood in her ears, and then she turned on her heels and started to run. She had barely taken a few steps when she tripped and went flying face-first onto the hard-packed dirt. Her chin hit the ground and she felt her teeth bite down on her tongue. Her skirt blew up over the back of her head.

She heard loud laughter, and then Kondo Sensei was kneeling beside her. "*Daijobu desu ka?* Are you all right? What are you doing? You have to get sprayed. It doesn't hurt, I promise."

He grabbed one of her arms and tried to help her upright, at the same time tugging her skirt back down and slapping the dirt off.

Now the principal was here, panting and out of breath. "What's going on, Kondo-kun? We can't have any fuss, not in front of the Americans."

Aya hung her head and felt her face flush. She should have known there was no easy escape. She was aware of a buzz of voices, everyone in the school yard talking about her. She's not clean. She's afraid. She's stupid.

"Holy cow. Now what'd you want to do that for, honey?" the man holding the spray gun said when Kondo led her back to him. He had a look of genuine bewilderment on his face. "Don't be scared. This is for your own good," he said as he raised the spray gun up to his chest.

Aya squeezed her eyes shut and held her breath. A cloud of chemical powder settled over her head and shoulders.

"Okay, you're done! See, that wasn't so hard, was it," the man said. "It's just a bit of DDT. Orders are orders. Every pupil has to be sprayed. It's for hygiene, don't you know."

"Kills all the lice, every last one!" one of the other men chimed in and guffawed loudly.

Aya opened her eyes. The soldier was motioning for her to get out of the way so the next girl could be sprayed. The lower grades were already lining up for their turn, and when Aya walked by, some of the boys jeered.

"We saw your underwear!"

"*Panpan* stinky pants."

Aya tried to keep walking in a straight line past them, but she felt her legs weakening, the world in front of her starting to blur. Suddenly someone clasped her hand in a tight grip and led her forward past the other pupils. It was Fumi.

Without saying a word, Fumi took her back inside the school.

It wasn't the first time Aya had been sprayed with DDT. That had taken place as soon as they got off the ship at Uraga and a team of American soldiers had herded them toward the side of a large wooden building.

"Pick up your bags. Let's go! Okay, set them down over there. Please form a line. That's it."

Aya remembered the look of panic on her father's face.

"Shut your eyes!" one of the soldiers barked. "Shut them tight."

There was no time to talk, no time to ask what was going on. The soldier was upon them in an instant. She closed her eyes and felt a powdery mist fall over her hair, her neck, her shoulders, her chest. It didn't hurt but she didn't dare open her eyes for fear of being blinded. She stood on the spot trembling like a mouse.

"Turn around! You're done. Get a move on. Pick up your suitcase."

Later they would learn that they had been sprayed by mistake. As passengers from an American ship, they hadn't needed to be deloused, but it was too late and no one ever apologized.

The repatriates were housed in barracks that had formerly belonged to the Japanese navy. Here they waited to be processed. Everyone seemed to be heading in a different direction, and it took weeks for arrangements to be made for them to leave for their final destinations. The barracks were run-down and filthy, and the food was worse than anything Aya had ever eaten in her whole life. The rice was gray and filled with so many tiny bits of stone, it was like eating a bowl of gravel. The miso soup smelled fetid. The thin hard pieces of dried fish gave off an odor like unwashed socks, as did the thin hard slices of pickles. One day they received dessert, and she brightened at the sight of a plate of cookies sprinkled with white powdered sugar. She took a bite and gagged—the white powder was mold. The food turned her stomach so much that she refused to eat anything, but after two weeks she was starving. In desperation, she wolfed down whatever she was given, even when the bowl was full of bugs.

One day Aya's father caught her looking at her stones. She'd brought them out when she thought he wasn't around.

"What are those? Where are they from?" he said sharply.

"The lake," she whispered. She was too afraid not to answer him truthfully even though she knew he would get mad.

"Slocan Lake? That place stupid." He kicked the stones and they went flying across the floor and into the thin wall.

A voice from the other side immediately protested. *"Urusai!* What's going on over there!"

"Nothing, everything okay," her father shouted back. He turned to her and hissed, "See, don't make trouble. Get rid of those."

She gathered up the scattered stones and went outside, pretending to throw them away. But she knew she would not, could not. She wrapped them in her handkerchief to hide again later.

8

The sight of Aya cowering on the ground during the hygiene spraying brought out a feeling of pity in Fumi that caught her off guard. It reminded her of what she had seen during wartime bombings when she'd watched the people around her run for cover. They dove into bomb shelters and fell to the floor, flung themselves down and flattened every part of their bodies so that even the tips of their ears and the ridges on their spines seemed to bend inward, making them small and smaller still. She'd seen people trip and fall because they were running too fast or because they were pushed over by others in a bigger hurry to get away.

When the bombing escalated, Fumi and all the children in her school were evacuated to the countryside. But by then she'd seen enough. She'd seen grown-ups crying. She'd seen how fear made big sturdy adults shrink to the size of mice.

Aya's reaction also reminded Fumi of how as a small child she used to run after her older sister whenever she felt abandoned. As soon as she sensed that Sumiko had left her side, she would run down the lane as fast as her tiny legs could take her. Usually she was crying, and she would trip and fall flat on her face. Always Sumiko turned around, picked her up off the ground, and wiped away her tears. Then she would let Fumi climb on her back and she would take her to school or to the market or wherever she happened to be going. Even when Fumi knew she was getting too big to be indulged this way, she never questioned that Sumiko would take care of her.

Fumi started feeling sorry for herself. Then she thought about how Aya had fallen and didn't have anyone to pick her up except the teacher. She felt sorry for Aya, and then she felt very guilty.

Aya wasn't as bad as she'd thought. Because they were seatmates, Aya had begun asking Fumi questions during class. Although her Japanese did not sound quite like theirs—she had a funny accent and used old-fashioned words—you could understand her if you listened carefully. And she was getting better. Actually Fumi was surprised at how much Aya understood and how well she spoke, even if she didn't always know the right word for something. Aya was too shy to speak in front of others, though, so the only one who really knew what she sounded like was Fumi. So Fumi had good reason to feel guilty, for she was the one responsible for starting the worst rumors. She told herself that the other girls were at fault, too. After all, they had encouraged Fumi and egged her on, plying her with question after question, laughing harder and harder the meaner the remark. Hadn't they almost forced her to make things up? Fumi said that Aya gave off a funny smell, a sour foreign stink, and that her hair was not thick and black like theirs but thin and, in the strong sunlight, looked as brown as cold barley tea. Aya didn't know how to do a single thing—just imagine having to babysit someone like that all day long, she'd said. The others nodded sympathetically and giggled.

She knew it was wrong, but she'd been desperate to make the other girls laugh. If she kept them entertained, not only would they like her more but they wouldn't have time to ask about her family. More than once Tomoko had inquired if it was true that her sister had left home. Someone else had used the word *panpan*, not directly about Sumiko, not exactly, but Fumi could tell the girl was sniffing for clues. It was nobody's business, but when someone asked you a question you didn't want to answer, it was very awkward.

What was it that Kondo Sensei had said when he made Aya her seatmate? *It will be your responsibility to look after your new seatmate. Take care of her. Make sure she knows what to do.* At the time, Fumi had considered it a form of punishment but now she wondered if she was missing an important sign. There was a reason for everything even if she didn't always know what it was.

When she'd led Aya from the school yard, it was something she had done out of instinct and pity, and the feel of Aya's hand had been unexpectedly warm. Aya had clutched Fumi's hand like a child.

Take care of her. Fumi thought about Kondo Sensei's words. Well, maybe it wasn't so hard.

Maybe they could even help each other.

Maybe, Fumi thought, she might even be able to show Aya what she dared not show anyone else.

9

Tokyo was hot, dusty, and dirty, but Matt had discovered an oasis only a few blocks from his building: a large public park called Hibiya Park. It was so popular that, especially on Sundays, it felt as if half the city turned out to stroll, sit on the benches, or have picnics on the grass. There were mothers with babies, toddlers learning how to walk, grandparents who shuffled along inch by inch. Young women in colorful dresses stood in the middle of the open lawn, twirling their white parasols around and around. GIs, many in uniform, were also out in large numbers, sauntering alone or in groups, cameras slung around their necks. And then there were the couples. The Japanese couples walked shyly side by side, never touching, but the GIs always held hands with their Japanese girl-friends. In Hibiya Park the sight was so commonplace nobody gave them a second glance anymore. They strolled across the wide lawn with the nonchalance and happiness of couples anywhere. Here, it was possible and right to fall in love. Here, everything felt normal. Somewhere else in the city, the Tokyo War Crimes Trials continued and people held protest rallies against the rising cost of rice, but in this tranquil sanctuary, the promise of romance and happiness held sway.

Matt even had his favorite bench. It was next to an old pine tree whose main bough was supported by a thick post, like a crutch under an old man's arm. A small sign posted at the base of the tree explained that it was three hundred years old. Matt loved to look at the dark gnarled trunk covered with knobs and bumps. It had seen a lot, this tree. It had survived earthquakes and fires, it had survived more than one war. And yet miraculously it still stood, not as tall as before, not as strong perhaps, but upright—proud and determined and undefeated. The tree reminded him of a lot of older Japanese he'd seen, some so bent over they looked frozen into the action of planting rice. They were survivors, just as this pine tree was a survivor.

Matt sat down on his bench, leaned back, and closed his eyes.

A second later a little boy ran up, tapped him on the pant leg, and yelled, "Mr. Soldier!" Just as quickly, he scurried away. It happened a lot. Children who called out "Haro, haro" or "Gimme chocoretto" when they saw him in uniform. It embarrassed Matt to be so conspicuous. If Henry, his big brother, were here, he would have known just how to behave, how to play the role of a true American soldier. He would have laughed and played with the kids. He would have tossed gum in the air and made the children run for it. He would have reveled in his role as a GI in Japan. Henry was that kind of guy.

In the mirror, Matt would sometimes find himself unconsciously looking for Henry in his own facial features, seeking a brotherly resemblance. But he hadn't grown up to resemble Henry at all, not physically or in other ways. Matt was the bookish one, the boy who studied hard, who didn't mind having to go to Japanese school after his regular classes. Henry by contrast had hated school. He was athletic, full of confidence in his body and his strength. He was outgoing, genial, guileless.

Henry, whose Japanese name was Hiro. When Matt was small, he thought his older brother's name was Hero. Every time he heard his mother call out, "Hiro-chan, doko na no?," Matt would hear "Hero-chan! Where's my hero?" He remembered being so jealous. He would have given anything to be called a hero by his mother.

When Henry got older, though, he told his parents never to call him Hiro. He said he wouldn't respond. "It sounds like Hirohito," he complained to Matt. "I hate it." He was Henry and only Henry.

Henry, who was so full of life. He was one of the first in their camp to sign up as soon as Japanese Americans were allowed to serve. He was one of the first to attend basic training, one of the first to be shipped out to the battlefields of Europe with the 442nd. "It's the only way to show we're on the right side," he told their parents. "How else are we going to prove our loyalty? We have to do something. We have to fight."

They received three letters from him before his death. The first two were while he was still in boot camp. The last one came from somewhere in Europe. He couldn't reveal any details about where he was or what he was doing, so the letter had a tantalizing quality, a feeling of mystery behind his mundane accounts. It was raining a lot, he wrote. He hadn't seen so much rain in his whole life. The bread was hard and chewy. He was fine. He missed all of them.

Matt had often tried to picture his brother's last moments in that dark wet place somewhere in the war fields of Europe. The conditions had been terrible—a densely wooded forest and fog as thick as soup. A rifle hidden behind every tree. Henry would have been crawling on his stomach, inching his way forward on his elbows, unable to see beyond the tip of his nose. What had he been thinking about in those last cold moments just before he lost his life?

When Matt decided to enlist, his mother begged him not to throw away his life as his brother had. As it turned out, however, a childhood knee injury disqualified Matt from active service and the army wanted him for Intelligence instead. His Japanese skills were good, and to make them even better, he was sent to study for eight months at one of the army's language training schools. By the time he finished, the war was over. He was privately relieved and then ashamed about just how relieved he felt. When the opportunity to serve in the Occupation arose, he leaped at it.

Matt must have fallen asleep on the bench. When he opened his eyes, there seemed to be more people than ever: families reclining on straw mats, children chasing each other around in circles, couples strolling slowly across the grass. When you took in a scene

like this, he thought, never in a million years could you imagine anyone ever going to war. Directly in front of him, an old man suddenly
pointed his cane in the air, and his gray-haired wife gazed up at the
sky, squinting. Matt looked, too, but saw nothing. Just sky. Beautiful
clear blue sky.

He stood up and walked to the park exit. As he passed through
the wrought-iron gates, a family of five was just coming in. A father,
mother, and three school-age daughters entered in single file, like a
row of ducklings.

The war amputees sat outside the gate, as if by some understanding that it was not appropriate for them to intrude upon the bucolic
atmosphere of the park. They formed long rows flanking either
side of the entrance, some sitting on straw mats or pieces of cardboard, others directly on the ground. They had tin mugs or plates
in front of them, and a few had handwritten signs that they held in
their laps or placed next to their mugs. Many wore their old army
uniforms—"defeat uniforms," Matt had heard them called. Young
people, especially, thought nothing of mocking the now unfashion-
able reminders of the past.

The men sat in silence—nobody begged—letting their scars
and missing limbs speak for them. People passed but hardly anyone
stopped.

The war veterans were everywhere you looked in the city. The
first time he saw them, Matt had felt a confusing mixture of emotions: anger and anguish, disgust and pity, contempt and sorrow.
He didn't know how he felt—how he was *supposed* to feel. As former soldiers, they represented the enemy, and he'd hated the Japanese for bombing Pearl Harbor. If there'd been no Pearl Harbor,
America would never have joined the war. Henry would never have
died. There would never have been camps like Manzanar, Heart
Mountain, Minidoka, Tule Lake. All the people he knew and loved
wouldn't have been forced into bitter factions, some still not talking
to each other. They could have fought over normal things like how
late you could stay out on a school night or what kind of things you
should spend your pocket money on. Not on how to answer a loyalty

oath. Were you a no-no boy or a yes-yes boy? Would you fight to the death? Did you love your country? Oh and by the way, which country was that again?

But the day Matt witnessed a one-legged war veteran being robbed by a gang of young boys, his feelings were suddenly, irrevocably, clarified. The man was standing by himself in front of a bombed-out building on a busy street. He had wooden crutches under each armpit, and his finger was hooked tightly through the handle of his army cup. Every few minutes he shook the cup. On one side his pant leg was pinned up almost to the groin, yet his posture was straight and rigid, as if to say one didn't need two legs to stand at full attention.

The four street urchins who attacked him were so small they couldn't have been more than five or six years old. They knocked the man to the ground, kicked his crutches, and picked up the money that had spilled from his begging cup. As they ran away laughing, they nearly bumped into several passersby, but nobody made any attempt to catch them. The man had groaned and tried to right himself, but without his crutches he was helpless. Matt was about to go over and offer assistance when two young men rushed out of a neighboring building, lifted the man under the arms, and helped him over to a stoop where he could sit.

After that, Matt made it a point to give money whenever he could. It was not a question of pity. These were men. They deserved dignity. Former soldiers, on both sides, had been through something that no one should have been forced to endure. To have mercy was only human; to give was simply the right thing to do. Initially, Matt thought he would select the most disabled man and give him the most money, but he soon discovered how absurd this notion was. For how could he measure one injury against another? Was one leg lost worth more than an arm? Two legs? An arm and a leg? No, if he was going to give, he would give to everyone, spreading his generosity as evenly as he could.

Approaching the long line of men who stood outside the park gate, he reached into his pocket. Along with his army scrip, he always carried some Japanese yen. Inflation was terrible, and it was hard to keep track of how much it was worth. All he knew was that you needed a thick handful of the stuff to buy anything useful. Still, it was better than nothing. He went from one person to the next, stuffing a few pieces of the paper money in each cup. He made it a practice never to look at anyone's face.

By the time he got to the last man in the line, he had run out of all the yen he had. The only thing he could put in the man's cup were two cubes of chocolate that he found in his shirt pocket. They felt soft to the touch, half melted from the heat.

"*Arigato gozaimasu. Goshinsetsu ni.* Thank you for your kindness." The man bowed his head so low his forehead almost touched his tin mug. When he returned to an upright position, Matt noticed his regal bearing. He sat with his legs tucked under him, the way a Zen monk sat for meditation, his back ramrod straight and his head so steady you could balance a book on it.

The man was blind. His face was pointed straight ahead into space, but where his eyes should have been were two sunken holes. Matt wondered why the man did not wear sunglasses. Was it because he did not have the money to buy them? Or was choosing not to hide behind dark glasses a deliberate act of defiance? He had a strong chiseled jaw and high cheekbones, well-defined full lips. They looked almost sensual. He might, at one point in his life, have been very handsome.

"I'm sorry, I don't have any money. What I gave you was some chocolate."

"Oh, thank you kindly, sir. *Chocoretto*, that's a special treat for sure." The man bowed again, holding his head down for several seconds to show his gratitude.

He was wearing his military uniform which, while badly frayed at the cuffs and along the seams, was clean and clearly worn with pride. The original black dye in the material had been bleached out by sunlight and scrubbing so all that was left was a dull blotchy grayness. Matt couldn't take his eyes off him. Anyway, the man couldn't see him.

"You served valiantly in the war." Matt felt he had to say something. Normally he never talked to war veterans; he didn't want to risk getting into an argument about the war or raising bad feelings. He didn't know why he felt drawn to talk to this man. Perhaps it had something to do with the cloak of invisibility the man's blindness had bestowed on him.

"I had the great honor to serve my country." The man bowed again. "But I am afraid I was not worthy."

"I am sure you served very bravely."

"No, sir. I had great fear. It is very shameful."

"We all suffer fear at one time or another. It's nothing to be ashamed of."

"My fear was shameful, very shameful. But there is something even more shameful—I survived."

"Don't say that." Matt spoke more sharply than he meant to.

"Everyone in my unit perished, except me. There is no greater shame."

Matt gazed at the man's face and felt a chill, as if even without eyes, the man was able to stare back at him. He took a deep breath before speaking. "I am a soldier, too."

"It is always nice to meet a fellow veteran, sir."

Matt hoped the man wouldn't ask for details and would simply continue to think Matt was Japanese. Someone from the countryside with a thick dialect, a funny accent. Tokyo was full of demobilized soldiers who either didn't want to go home or had no home to go back to. Even now shiploads of them still arrived from everywhere the Japanese empire had once stretched.

The man bowed again in his stiff formal way. "Thank you for your kindness. I am sorry that this worthless being is such a bother."

"Is there anything special you need?" Matt suddenly asked.

"Sorry?"

"Maybe cigarettes? I can bring some next time. Lucky Strike maybe?"

"*Cigaretto?*"

"Yes, *cigaretto.*"

"Ah, from the black market," the man said, his voice now sly and conspiratorial.

"No, not the black market."

"You are kind. Thank you, sir. You are kind. You are kind." The man's voice had started to take on a rote quality, as if he were already weary of the exchange. Matt got the impression that he was being dismissed.

"I'll come back again. Goodbye."

"Goodbye, sir."

There were many questions Matt wished he could ask but knew he couldn't. Naturally he wished he could ask what had happened to the man. What awful battle had he and his troops been involved in and how had he incurred such a terrible injury. But Matt suspected that not only were such questions meaningless, the answers would be, too. What difference did it make what battle it was, what useless assault, what stupid skirmish. Some of the islands the Japanese had been defending toward the end of the war were nothing more than clumps of volcanic dirt floating in the South Pacific. Had it been worth it to end up like this? Or worse, to have ended up like the other soldiers in the man's unit—all dead.

10

Once a week Kondo was paired with Miss Ikeda, the grade-two teacher, to supervise the lunchtime recess period. Like Kondo, Miss Ikeda was also new to the school, but unlike him, she had never taught anywhere else. She struck him as very young but at the same time extremely confident, with her bobbed hair and sporty way of walking. As they watched the children play, Kondo noticed that she liked to hum to herself and sometimes to sing aloud. She had a lovely voice, sweet and clear, with an impressive range.

Right now she was humming "The Apple Song." After hearing it played so much on the radio, Kondo was beginning to tire of the song's cheerful optimism, but he had to admit it had a catchy melody. The whole country seemed to love it.

He thought he might ask Miss Ikeda if she knew any English-language songs and, if not, whether she would be interested in learning any. When she stopped humming, he ventured, "Miss Ikeda?"

Without turning her head, she put one finger up to her lips. "Shhh." She pointed at the group of small children a few feet away from them. He could only see the side of her face, but she seemed to be smiling. Her head was cocked, in interest and curiosity.

"Are those your pupils?" he asked in a low voice.

"Shhh," she repeated, nodding her head in the affirmative.

One of the little girls was swinging her hips back and forth in front of the group. She put her hand on one hip, jiggled her elbow, and said aloud to no one in particular, "Let's go for a walk, soldier!"

The girl had a vivacious smile and quick darting eyes. She seemed to realize that she was prettier than the other girls and that, even as young as she was, being pretty meant she could get what she wanted.

A boy stepped forward and pretended to give something to the girl. Kondo recognized Masatomi.

"What's that, soldier?" she giggled.

"*Chocoretto.*"

"*Chocoretto* is my favorite!" She made a show of chewing loudly, smacking her lips, and showing her little pink tongue. "Yum, yum. Delicious! I like you, soldier. Here, take my arm." She pumped her elbow up and down.

Masatomi hesitantly put his arm through hers.

"I want more candy!" she cried. "Let's go to American Alley."

"American Alley! Candy Shop Alley!" The children formed a circle and began chanting loudly.

"Hurry, we have to hurry." The girl tugged on Masatomi but he dropped his arm from hers and took a step backward.

"I don't know what you want me to do," he mumbled.

She flung her arms in the air and cried, "Tight! Hold me tight!"

Two of the boys in the crowd shoved Masatomi into the girl. "She wants you to kiss her."

A chorus of giggles erupted, and the circle of children that had formed around Masatomi and the little girl moved in closer.

"Kiss, kiss!"

"Democracy kiss!"

It seemed to Kondo that things had definitely gone too far. He glanced at Miss Ikeda but her mouth was open and she appeared to be laughing. He couldn't believe it. Was she enjoying this?

"Miss Ikeda, shouldn't we do something?"

"What do you mean?"

"This is a school. We shouldn't allow this."

She turned her face toward him; it was a slow movement, graceful like a swan. Imperious, too. For the first time he noticed how long and white her neck was.

"They're children, Mr. Kondo. They're just playing. Aren't we supposed to encourage imaginative play?" He wasn't sure if she was trying to taunt him, but when she turned her head away, he heard a distinct sigh of exasperation.

She clapped her hands. "Children, time to go back to the classroom." Her voice was her regular bright teacher voice, friendly but no-nonsense. He'd heard that she was exceedingly popular with her young charges and very up-to-date in her teaching methods. She'd organized the seating plan in her classroom so that boys and girls sat in alternating seats: boy, girl, boy, girl. She ran toward the door and stood beside it, swinging her arm to encourage the children to run. As soon as the very last child had slipped inside, she pivoted on the balls of her feet like a dancer and turned toward Kondo. Her wooden geta had churned up a small cloud of dust around her bare legs.

"Better hurry, Mr. Kondo. Your pupils are waiting."

With that, she went into the school. He heard the clatter of her putting her geta on one of the open shelves just inside the doorway and then a light pounding sound as she ran down the corridor.

As he made his way toward his own classroom, he couldn't help thinking about the parting look she'd given him. He hadn't imagined it. She'd had a horrible smirk on her face, so unbecoming in a woman, even such a young, pretty woman. You're out of touch, was what the smirk said. It was an expression full of pity and disdain.

11

*I*t was the third week in July, just before the start of summer holidays.

"I have something to show you." Fumi had leaned across their shared desk and whispered this to Aya four times already but refused to elaborate. "You have to wait. I can't show you here."

After class ended, Fumi indicated that they should remain in their seats until everyone had left. Ten minutes passed, then twenty, and finally Fumi abruptly stood up.

"Okay, it should be safe now. Let's go."

"Where?"

"Just follow me."

Trailing half a step behind, Aya let Fumi lead her away from the school and the neighborhood where they lived. They turned down the first street to the left and kept walking and turning, walking and turning, down narrow lanes lined with tiny dark houses. Pots and boxes and plants and hanging laundry spilled into the lane, so there was barely enough room for a person to pass. The houses were made of cheap plywood and the walls had gaps through which Aya could see light shining and sometimes parts of the person who lived inside—a nose, a hand, a bare shoulder.

It wasn't until they reached the end of the last lane that Fumi turned around and said simply, "Here." She pointed at the temple— SHOTOKU TEMPLE the sign said—and gestured that they should enter the grounds.

The temple did not look inviting in the least. The main build-ing, the part that faced the street, was in serious disrepair: The entire structure looked as if it were being pushed into the soil by the heavy clay tiles on its roof. The wood was dark and weatherworn, and the doors to the worship hall were fastened shut. There was no sign of anyone. Except for the fact that the dirt path leading up to the temple had been freshly swept—the thin even lines of a broom were etched into the hard soil—one would think that it had been aban-doned. Had the Buddhist priest or the attendant already left? Did anyone take care of this place?

Something about the dilapidation of the temple made a cold shiver run down Aya's back.

"Come on," Fumi urged when she saw her hesitating. "Let's go."

They walked up the dirt path and skirted around the broad veranda, crouching low to pass under the gnarled branch of an ancient pine tree. They followed the path beside the building, and it eventu-ally opened onto a shady grove of trees and bushes. The grounds were deep, and at the very back Aya could make out some low shapes— monuments or headstones—in a small cemetery. Despite the heat of the day, it was cool here, as if the rays of the sun never touched this part. On the hard-packed earth, moss grew like patches of thick green fur. Mosquitoes began buzzing at her ears.

And it smelled! Aya's nostrils filled with the sharp vinegary stink of urine. She could make out a piece of white cloth tossed in a far corner that looked like someone's underpants. Her father had told her that homeless people will sleep anywhere, even on temple grounds. Stay clear of places like that, he'd told her.

Fumi seemed oblivious. She whirled around and, with her face inches from Aya's, said, "I want to show you something." Aya felt the heat of her breath.

Fumi reached into her blouse pocket and pulled out a piece of yel-lowish tissue paper. She gingerly opened the four corners to reveal the contents and held it out with both hands as if offering a delicate blos-som. It was a small black-and-white photograph. Aya leaned forward to get a closer look but instinctively felt that she should not touch it.

An attractive Japanese woman stood next to a tall American GI.

He had a big toothy grin on his face, but it was hard to tell what he looked like because the camera had caught him with his eyes shut. The woman was not smiling at all. She wore a jacket with wide padded shoulders, and her permed hair was swept off to one side, held up by a pin that caught the light and glittered like a small diamond. She stared straight at the camera and her dark eyes burned with such a strange intensity that Aya couldn't help feeling the woman was actually looking through the camera, directly at her. It was hard to turn away from such a gaze.

"Who is she?" she asked.

"My sister, of course." Fumi sounded impatient. She thrust the photograph into Aya's hands. "Here, have a good look."

Aya dutifully studied the photo. She could hardly see, it was so dark and gloomy behind the temple. If Fumi wanted her to look at her precious sister, why did they have to do it here? Anyway, she didn't think there was much resemblance at all. Were they really sisters? The GI clutched the woman's shoulder tightly, and because he towered over her, he made Aya think of a big bear, even though he was not a heavyset man. His close-cropped hair hugged his head except for one bit that stuck up at the very top like a tiny feather. She decided there was something hard and fake about his too-wide smile. As for the woman, Fumi's sister, well, she had to concede that maybe there was a very slight resemblance in their eyes. Yes, that was it. When Fumi became animated, sometimes she got the same kind of intense look. The photograph had been cut unevenly along the man's right side. In the background, Aya could make out the shape of a gigantic statue of Buddha.

"What's her name?" she asked more out of politeness than real interest.

"Sumiko."

"She looks a lot older than you."

"There's ten years' difference."

"That's a big gap, isn't it."

"No, it's not! Sumiko and I are the closest sisters in the world."

Aya was taken aback by the passion in Fumi's voice. "I'm sorry. I didn't mean—"

Fumi ignored her. "My sister is very pretty, don't you think?"

Aya nodded. Yes, very pretty. More than pretty. She was beautiful. Partly it was the stylish Western clothes she wore, such a contrast to the baggy pants and tops many women were still forced to wear out of necessity, and her fashionable haircut. But there was something else, and Aya wasn't quite sure what it was. An air of dignity, perhaps, but a sadness, too. It was a little like the sadness that her mother had always carried with her.

"My sister gave me this picture to keep. But it's a secret, okay? Don't tell anyone."

Fumi took the picture from Aya and turned it over. A large careless scrawl ran sideways across the back. *To my favorite babydoll.* The next line started with the letter J, but the rest was cut off.

"What does it say?"

How could Aya answer a question like that? Babydoll was not a word she was accustomed to hearing. That was a word used by adults—white men, the kind who wore big suit jackets and greased their hair. She had no idea what an equivalent expression in Japanese would be.

"What does it say?" Fumi repeated. "I thought you knew English. Can't you read it?"

Aya bit her lip. "Let's see. This word, favorite, means—"

"Not that part." Fumi sounded cross. "I know that. What about this?" She stabbed her finger under the word "babydoll."

Aya looked at the ground, at the clumps of moss, at the dirty band across the top of her sandal.

"Babydoll . . . umm."

"What does it mean!"

"Babydoll means . . ." Aya took a deep breath. "It means something like you are cute as a baby and pretty as a doll."

"Oh." Fumi hesitated. "Oh, that's nice. That sounds really nice, doesn't it?"

"Umm, I suppose so."

A slow smile was spreading across Fumi's face. "Thank you. I wasn't sure. It's really nice, isn't it. I thought it might be something nice."

Aya nodded uncomfortably.

Fumi carefully wrapped the photograph in the yellowed tissue paper and tucked it back in her blouse pocket. She looked at Aya. "You know, I, uh . . . I was thinking . . ."

"Yes?"

"Oh, nothing. I was . . . I mean, well, it's really nice, isn't it."

Then she suddenly slapped hard at her neck. "Hey, let's get out of here. There are too many mosquitoes. I'm getting bitten all over, aren't you?"

On the walk home from the temple, Fumi was extremely quiet and subdued, and Aya wondered if she was embarrassed by the picture of her sister with a GI. It was hard to tell, but Aya didn't dwell on it for long because she was soon lost in her own thoughts triggered by the picture. The look of sadness in the eyes of Fumi's sister had unexpectedly set off a series of memories. It had made her think of her own mother, but even more, it made her think of Etsuko, the young woman on the repatriation ship who had helped her. Without Etsuko, Aya didn't know what she would have done.

Even before their ship had docked, something unexpected had happened to Aya. Midway between Canada and Japan, as their vessel plied its relentless way through the vastness of the Pacific, a strange feeling began to occur deep inside her. At first she'd thought it must be seasickness, which everyone including her own father suffered from to varying degrees. Everyone, that is, except Aya. The Ishikawa family, who shared the same set of bunks with Aya and her father, seemed to be plagued by it constantly. Each family member took turns being sick, throwing up into a small bucket they kept in the corner on their side of the hold. They gagged and vomited, but all that came out were thin threads of greenish-yellow spit. With each lurch and sway of the ship, they moaned and clung to each other.

"You have a stomach of iron. What a fortunate girl you are." Mrs. Ishikawa had repeated this comment so often and with such a bitter edge to her voice that Aya had felt ashamed of her inability to share in their misery.

"She's got a strong stomach, Shimamura-san," Mr. Ishikawa joined in, addressing not Aya directly but her father. "She's strong. She can survive anything."

So when she started to feel a funny sensation in the pit of her abdomen, she was almost relieved. She was certain it must be the same seasickness that everyone else was experiencing, but although she waited with patient resignation for the inevitable urge to throw up, it did not come. Instead, she became aware of a mild cramping, as if something was gnawing at her insides in the part deep between her legs. It was pinching her, scraping at her mound. When she stood up, her groin felt sticky. The line for the toilet stalls was long but she waited for her turn. Inside the smelly cubicle, she pulled down her underpants and saw on the crotch a small rust-colored stain, as ugly as the squashed guts of a worm. She touched the spot. It was wet and warm and a bit gummy. She didn't know what else to do, so she pulled her underpants back up and returned to her cabin.

When she went back to the toilet later, the stain was bigger and very wet. It was a brighter, angrier shade of red. She sat on her bunk with her legs pressed tightly together and wondered if she was going to die. If it hadn't been for Etsuko, the oldest daughter in the Ishikawa family, she didn't know what she would have done. Etsuko took one of her own flannel pajama tops, cut it into strips, and showed Aya how to fashion padding to put in her underpants that would absorb the blood.

The day before their ship was due to reach port, Aya came across Etsuko behind a tall pile of wooden cartons in an unlit corner of the ship's hold. She was curled on the floor, her arms hugging her shoulders, blubbering like a baby into her sleeves. As soon as she realized Aya was there, she wiped her tear-streaked face with the palms of her hands and quickly stood up.

"Don't tell my family you saw me like this. I don't want to go to Japan. I'm scared," she said. And then she had looked at Aya with eyes filled with sorrow.

The next time Aya saw Etsuko she was back to her smiling self.

She told Aya not to worry, that it was natural to bleed. "Your body is changing, and that's a good thing." But Aya knew differently. She knew enough to be suspicious of change, of this betrayal of her body.

Blood was never good, nor was change.

Over time, she got used to having her period and knew almost to the day when it would arrive. For some reason it reminded her of her mother's absence in a way that nothing else did. Along with the blood that poured out of her each month, Aya felt a part of her mother was also leaking from her body, a slow ravaged seepage that she was helpless to stop.

12

Matt began putting in extra hours on the weekends to help deal with the backlog of translations. It was strictly voluntary, of course, but as a newcomer to the section, he saw it as an opportunity to improve.

"Are you crazy? Who the heck are you trying to impress?" Sab shook his head in disgust. "Just because Old Man MacArthur works seven days a week, doesn't mean the rest of us have to."

Matt mumbled something about needing to catch up on a few things. In truth, he enjoyed working during the off-hours. He especially liked it when he and Lieutenant Baker were in the office alone, as they were this Sunday. The room was quiet, the silence broken only by the occasional question he posed about some word or phrase and the lieutenant's soft-spoken comments.

The letters addressed to MacArthur were a completely different sort of beast from the bureaucratic memos and documents that Matt had translated in his previous position in the Press and Public Information Section. Everything he dealt with here was unique, each letter suffused with the soul and individual personality of the writer. Many missives continued to haunt him long after they had passed through his hands.

Haikei Makkaasaa Gensui-sama,
Dear General MacArthur,

I am Sachiko Mizumasa, humble citizen in the new postwar Japan. We Japanese people are grateful for your wise rule.

I am a widow, and I write to ask for your kind intercession in the repatriation of my only son, Private First Class, Tadayuki Mizumasa, of the former Japanese Imperial Army, XX Infantry, XX Unit, who to this day remains in Indonesia and unable to return to the homeland. The reasons for the delay in his return are entirely unclear. I have previously made inquiries to various Japanese officials and ministries, but regrettably no one has been able to offer assistance in any form. He was sent directly to the front on his eighteenth birthday, a mere boy barely able to take care of himself.

It is the height of impertinence to interrupt the busy schedule of someone like yourself, preoccupied as you are with many affairs of state and the running of our country, but I beseech you to intercede and hasten the return of my son. Please forgive a mother's unabated concern. He is my only child. I am alone and anxiously awaiting his return.

Yours faithfully,
Sachiko Mizumasa
Tokorozawa, Saitama Prefecture

Matt was told that his job was to translate—to take the Japanese words on the page, turn them into English, and pass the finished product on to the higher authorities. He knew that there was no chance this letter would be answered; at best, it would simply be filed. In fairness, really, what could be done? One soldier among thousands, stranded, alone. It would be impossible to follow up on all requests, even in cases where the information was more precise and useful than in this one. At the same time, though, Matt understood that the writers of these letters depended on *him* to render their pleas into English. A mechanical translation would not do. They needed someone to speak *for* them, and Matt resolved to become their voice—their best, their clearest, their most persuasive voice. That was the job of a real translator.

The letter he was working on now was not even signed, yet it was composed with such poetry and grace that Matt desperately wanted to do it justice. He wondered if he was up to the task.

Dear General Douglas MacArthur,

The spring breezes have given way to hot summer days and much rain. I fervently pray that Your Eminence will enjoy good appetite despite the heat. In summer it is our custom to partake of sweet grilled eel on the hottest day of the season in order to strengthen the body and thicken the blood. Many more hot days lie ahead, I am afraid. If I were not such a poor man, it would give me greatest pleasure to treat you and your esteemed family to a traditional dinner of Japanese grilled eel, but alas it has been many summers since I have been able to enjoy such a feast myself. I live from day to day with memories of meals past. These memories feed my hungry stomach and provide me with the will to continue. My dear children, unfortunately, are too small to have any memories except of hunger.

Sincerely,

A Japanese citizen

"Come here, Matsumoto. You've seen this before, haven't you?"

Matt was just finishing his translation when Lieutenant Baker called him over to the large plate-glass window. From here, they had an excellent view of the crowds who lined the street to watch MacArthur being driven back and forth to General Headquarters. The onlookers came every day, no matter the weather, but Sundays generally drew the biggest crowds.

"Imagine standing in this heat just to catch a glimpse of MacArthur's car. Look how orderly and patient they are. Sometimes I just don't know what to make of it."

"Sir?"

Baker turned to him. "Day after day, month after month. I worry they'd line up in an earthquake."

MacArthur resided at the American embassy with his wife and young son, only a mile or so away from GHQ. He was chauffeured back and forth between his residence and his office four times a day, seven days a week, punctual as clockwork: going in at ten thirty in the morning, returning for lunch at two, back to the office at four, and home for the night at eight. The whole country knew about his legendary work ethic and his unwavering daily routine. "I'll bet the guy even shits on schedule," Sab liked to say. The best spot to wait for his arrival was facing the entrance to the Dai-Ichi Building, where one could catch a glimpse of MacArthur as he emerged from his car, saluted his MP guards, and walked up the broad concrete steps. But the prize location was always packed, so most people had to be content with standing on the roadside and watching as his car drove by.

"It's amazing. What would you call this? Allegiance? Fanaticism? Devotion? Have you ever seen such devotion?" Baker spoke with sudden passion. "I'm curious, what do you make of it, Matsumoto? Would you do something like this? Would you wait for hours to catch a fleeting glimpse of the general who defeated your country?"

Matt was flustered. "I don't know, sir. No, no, of course not."

"Is it a simple transfer of allegiances after the surrender? I know some people think the Japanese worship MacArthur the way they did the emperor. If that's the case, of course that's wrong. We're trying to establish democracy here. But, you know, I think I understand. Something else is going on, something deeper. What do you think?"

"Sir? Um, I'm not sure."

"It's heartbreaking, isn't it. Pitiful. They'll cling to any hope. They're desperate. Why else would they write so many letters?"

"Yes, sir."

"Desperate," Baker repeated, and then he sighed heavily. "Maybe it's more than that, though. I wonder if I would have the fortitude, the courage, to do what they are doing. To pick up and carry on. It was a terrible war."

Nobody else would say things like that, Matt thought. Only Baker. He was the most unlikely officer he'd ever met, the most improbable *man* to be in the military. Matt couldn't imagine him in action, those long delicate fingers pressing a trigger. How on earth had he managed to survive boot camp? It was just as well that he hadn't had to face active combat.

Almost as if Baker had read what was on Matt's mind, he began to speak.

"Do you know how I spent my time during the war?"

"You were in Intelligence, weren't you, sir?"

"Yes. I translated written communication—letters we intercepted or diaries we came across. We were supposed to be looking for military secrets and clues about future maneuvers, but I never found anything of strategic value. Not a single thing."

Baker turned away, fixing his gaze on the window. Matt sensed that he wasn't looking at anything in particular but just staring into space.

"We're all the same, Matsumoto, that's what I learned. But I felt that the Japanese soldiers were more honest. 'Mother, I long to eat your soup. I am cold. Mother, I am scared.' That's the kind of thing they wrote."

"It must have been hard work," Matt ventured timidly, "translating during wartime."

Baker continued to stare out the window. "The diaries were the hardest, you know. Most of them were recovered off corpses. My job was to read the final entries of the dead, their last private moments. I can still remember some of their exact words. 'I have diarrhea again. I dream every night of white rice. The pills no longer work. I cannot sleep anymore.' Every other page had lines blacked out with censors' markers."

Baker suddenly turned toward him, and Matt was conscious of their proximity, their faces only inches apart. For the first time he noticed that Baker's eyes were green, not blue, and that they seemed to be flecked with bits of gold. Running along his left temple was a pale bluish vein, as thin and nearly invisible as a silk thread. It was moving ever so slightly, pulsing like a heartbeat.

"Well, enough of this. Shall we call it a day, corporal?"

"Yes, sir."

Before returning to his desk to pack up, Matt cast a parting glance out the window at the crowds. Baker was right. It was pitiful.

13

Fumi had almost convinced herself that Sumiko really had given her the photograph. *Here, this is for you. Keep this to remember me.* But it wasn't a present or memento. The truth was that Fumi had stolen the picture the last time her sister came home, kept it without really meaning to keep it, took it without knowing that she wouldn't have a chance to give it back. But Fumi was glad she had taken it, so very glad, because if she hadn't, she would have nothing of her sister. Even now, she found it necessary to stare at the photograph over and over to remind herself that someday Sumiko would come home.

It frightened her that there were times when she couldn't remember exactly what Sumiko had looked like the last time she saw her. Instead what she remembered was how she had heard her mother and sister even before she entered the house. She'd slid open the front door and stood in the earthen entranceway, listening to the sound of their weeping coming from the back room. Fumi, who had been let out of school early that day, sensed that she shouldn't interrupt them.

Her sister's shoes were in the entranceway, and Fumi slipped her feet into them. She liked these shoes very much, shiny black pumps with heels so high she had to hold on to the wall to keep her balance. It was a funny happy feeling, being so wobbly. These were the shoes that Sumiko began wearing when she'd started working in the Ginza and moved away from home. Another object of fascination was Sumiko's clutch purse, which sat on the narrow ledge just inside the entranceway. Fumi had seen it many times before; it was made of smooth red leather stamped with a pattern of shells. She had watched her sister flick the shiny oval clasp with her finger to open it, then snap it shut with another quick flick. The shutting sound made a satisfying click, crisp and final. Fumi picked up the purse and opened it. The purse was shallow and the smooth satin lining felt cool to the touch. She poked the contents with her index finger: a tube of lipstick, a cloth change purse, a single key on a chain, three identical hairpins with shiny glass beads on the end.

"You did this for us. You know we're so grateful." It was her mother's voice. "But I don't understand why you can't stop."

"Soon, Mother. Soon. Just a small debt to pay off. It's almost over."

"I wish this had never happened. It's all my fault."

"But it was the only thing to do. You were so sick, and then Father and Fumi."

"I'm better now. I don't need any special food."

Fumi paused what she was doing with Sumiko's purse. Her mother's voice sounded more strident than usual.

"But Mother, you have to keep up your strength."

"I'm better. I don't need anything special. You don't have to do this." She began coughing.

"There, you see. You're still sick."

"Your father takes good care of me."

"Of course Father is doing the best he can. But the Americans have good food, and so much of it. Please don't be stubborn."

For a long time there was silence and then there was more crying. Fumi went back to exploring the items in Sumiko's purse. She picked up a small round mirror and examined her reflection. Then she took the sandalwood comb and ran it through her bangs. But the most interesting thing was what she found inside one of the zippered compartments. It was a photograph of her sister and another Japanese woman standing on either side of a tall American soldier. The soldier had his arms around both women, pressing them possessively against his body.

"Mother, you remember Mrs. Watanabe at the end of the lane?" Sumiko's voice sounded very sad. "How upset we all were when she died. She was so thin, so weak. Remember?"

"Mrs. Watanabe's daughter never went to work for the Americans."

There was another long silence.

"I have a special treat today. I managed to get some sugar. Isn't that great? And I've brought more cans of meat, too."

"It smells funny."

"That's the way it's supposed to smell. It's what they call a processed meat. It's better than eating rancid meat from the black market."

"We don't want it."

"But you ate it before."

"I wish we hadn't. I didn't realize what you have to do . . . to get it."

"Please don't worry. It's not like that. I told you. It's just dancing."

"With Americans!"

"Everyone's doing it."

"Those people killed two of your cousins, don't forget. Look at what happened to the store. Burned to the ground."

"The war is over, Mother. We have to eat. We have to live. You have to live."

"But you look like—"

"Please, Mother. I just dance. I keep telling you. And as for the way I look, everyone looks like this. Everyone wears American clothes now and those who don't, wish they could."

"Not everyone. Not Mrs. Watanabe's daughter."

"But that's my point. Mrs. Watanabe is dead. She could still be alive."

"That's the most disrespectful thing I've ever heard. Take your precious cans. How can I eat something like this? We don't need it."

There was a long silence. Finally Sumiko spoke again.

"How is Fumi?"

Fumi froze when she heard her name.

"She's fine. She's doing well at school."

"She'll be starting middle school in April, won't she. She must be looking forward to it."

"Yes, she is. Your father is so proud."

"Does she . . ." Sumiko paused, and when she resumed speaking her voice sounded hoarse. "Does she ask about me?"

"Of course, Sumiko. All the time."

"Oh."

"You know how bad I feel, but it's better this way."

"Yes, Mother. I understand."

"You know how she is. I can't help but worry about her. I worry about you, too."

"I know."

"Please, Sumiko, you understand, don't you." Her mother's voice dropped low. "Please, we agreed it's better this way, didn't we."

"Yes."

Fumi had been holding her breath, afraid to move, afraid to exhale. She thought her lungs might burst. She wanted to rush into the room and shout. "I'm here! *Nechan*, please stay with us. Don't go away." But her mother had started crying again, that small *chu-chu-chu* sound she made when she was trying really hard not to cry but couldn't help it. She sounded like an injured bird.

"I'm sorry. It's not that we're ungrateful . . ."

"It's all right, Mother. I understand. Please don't cry."

"Why do you have to continue? Why can't you just stop?"

"This will all be over soon, I promise. Just a little longer. I have to make a little more to pay off a small debt."

Fumi heard a series of heavy thumps as if tin cans had rolled off the table onto the tatami mat. The paper-lined doors in the back room banged against their wooden frame and the house shook slightly with the movement of feet. The inner door to the entrance-way was flung open.

Sumiko's cheeks were bright red and there were dark circles under her eyes. "Fumi, what are you doing here?" she whispered. "Why aren't you in school?"

Fumi moved her hand to her waistband and slipped the photo-graph into the back of her pants. She held out the purse.

"Thank you." Sumiko took it from her.

"When are you coming back?"

"Soon."

"When?"

"Shhh. I don't know. Soon."

"Can I come with you? Can I visit?"

Sumiko reached out and ran her fingers through Fumi's hair, across her bangs and over the top of her head. She spoke in such a soft voice Fumi could barely hear her. "No. You have to stay here and go to school and take care of Mother and Father. You have to study hard. You understand?" She opened her purse. "Here's a little money for you. Don't tell Mother. You can keep it in case of an emer-gency. I'll be back again soon."

After her sister left, Fumi crept into the house. In the back room, her mother was sobbing out loud, the disconsolate wails of some-one who thinks that no one is around to hear her. Fumi hoped her mother hadn't heard her come in. She climbed the ladder leading to the room on the second floor that she had once shared with her sister. She pulled out the photograph and examined it. It had been taken in front of the statue of the Great Buddha. Everyone knew the Great Buddha was in Kamakura. Who were those people her sister was with—the American soldier and the other Japanese woman? What kind of people were they that her sister now spent all her time with them and not at home with her family? "*Nechan,*" Fumi whis-pered as she ran her finger over her sister's face. "*Daijobu desu ka? Are you okay?*"

She studied the other woman again and decided she didn't like her at all. She wasn't as pretty as Sumiko but her clothes were more glamorous, brighter and tighter. Her shoes were higher, too. Worse, she was clinging to the GI-san in a funny, unnatural way. Anyone could see that the GI-san must like Sumiko better. He prob-ably wished the other woman would go away. The photograph was small, and Fumi decided that snipping off just a sliver wouldn't matter. With a pair of sewing scissors, she quickly cut the side of the picture. The other woman fell to the floor.

"Fumi? Is that you? Are you home?" her mother suddenly called out, an anxious edge to her voice. She heard her mother's slow, unsteady footsteps approaching the foot of the ladder. "I didn't hear you come in."

"*Tadaima*. I just got back," Fumi replied, shoving the photograph and the money into the bamboo basket where she kept some of her clothes. She picked up the scrap she had cut off and resolved to burn it later with the other garbage.

14

On Friday Nancy Nogami came over to Matt's desk with a type-written translation. It was past suppertime and the others in the office had already gone for the day. The typists usually left promptly at five o'clock, and she wasn't in the habit of staying behind.

"I was just wondering how you feel about translating stuff like this?" She held up a single sheet of paper between the thumbs and forefingers of both hands, and waved it in front of her chest like it was something too dirty to touch. "This one's yours, I believe. I just finished it. Typed it up exactly as written."

Although they worked in the same office, Matt and Nancy hardly spoke. In fact, he couldn't recall ever being alone with her.

"Do you want to look at it again? I've got more, too." She pointed to her desk. "Same topic. I guess I ended up with the whole batch."

"Just put them in the courier box, along with everything else. Same routine as always."

"So you think they should be sent to MacArthur?"

"Well, that's who they're addressed to."

"Yes, but—"

"Miss Nogami, as you know, our assignment is to translate what comes in as it comes in. The content, if that's what you're getting at, is beyond our control."

"Of course, I know that." She rolled her eyes, and something about the way she did it reminded him of his big sister. That look of tolerant exasperation.

"It's just that I really wonder whether these kinds of letters should be forwarded. I mean, do you think it's appropriate?" Nancy brought the sheet of paper in her hands up to within inches of her face and started reading aloud.

Dear General MacArthur,

I am Michiko Hayato, age twenty-four. I am in good physical condition, and full of much energy and enthusiasm. I have heard that Your Excellency is working day and night for the building of our country and for the benefit of all Japanese citizens. I am filled with great hope for our future advancement.

But Your Excellency is in danger of tiring if he works too hard without recreation. Your health is most important. Please retain your vigor and manliness. Please let me know if I may provide any service.

Your most sincere servant,
Miss M. Hayato
Suginami Ward, Tokyo

"Miss Nogami, you really shouldn't—"
"Wait a minute now. Here's a beaut. This one is even better."

Dear Mr. Douglas, General, Supreme Leader,

I have seen your picture in the Asahi Graphic Magazine. You are strong and tall, and I believe you are a good father. You are good-looking and healthy. I am also good-looking and healthy. I am ready to put my womb to your noble service. Our baby would be a handsome boy, a perfect new citizen for the new democratic nation of Japan. Please, let us have a baby who will bring Japan and America together in proud union.

Yours with strong faith and sincere good wishes,
Hiroko Ono
Numazu City, Shizuoka Prefecture

By the time she'd reached the end of the letter, Nancy's voice was quavering. She sounded like she was about to break down in tears.

"Miss Nogami, please."

"You guys think it's funny, don't you." The quaver was gone. Her voice had snapped back to its old sharpness. "Downright hilarious."

He felt relieved that she wasn't going to make a scene.

"I heard MacIntosh and Wilson this afternoon in the hallway," she continued. "They were laughing like a pair of hyenas."

"Well, they're jerks. You never saw Lieutenant Baker laughing, did you." He looked at her. "Or me."

"Lieutenant Baker is a gentleman," she said with finality.

"There are lots of gentlemen here," Matt said. He wanted to add "I'm one, too," but he preferred that she be the one to acknowledge that. She said nothing. Instead, her outrage seemed to be contagious, and now he felt angry, too. Until that moment, he had been fine, glad to see the end of a busy day, the culmination of a full week in which he'd worked hard and accomplished a lot. And now this woman standing in front of him was trying to make him feel lousy. Worse, she was succeeding.

"I'm just doing my job, the way you're doing your job," he said.

Nancy glared at him. "Sometimes I hate this job."

"Well, why don't you quit? I'm sure there are lots of other people who wouldn't mind doing it." As soon as the words were out of his mouth, he knew what a mean-spirited remark it was.

Nancy fell quiet. She walked to her desk and stood with her back to him. He could hear her shuffling papers and opening and closing her desk drawers. When she turned around, she had her purse in one hand and her scarf draped over her forearm.

"You're going?" he asked.

She didn't bother to nod. "See you next week."

Matt regretted his loose tongue. He knew she couldn't quit. She needed the money and no job paid better than one working directly for the Occupation forces. Everyone wanted one of those.

"My sister was studying to be a secretary," he said, "before the war."

A faint smile seemed to cross Nancy's face, although perhaps it was more of a grimace.

"Simpson School of Typing and Shorthand," he continued. "I can still see those green-and-orange textbooks."

"Humph." Nancy crossed her arms. "So she's probably a good typist."

"At one time she was, I guess. Pretty good."

"Well, it's too bad I never went to secretarial school. At least I would have learned how to type."

"You don't seem like the type—to type, I mean."

"Damn right." She paused, as if surprised at the language that had just come out of her mouth. "Oh, I'm sorry. Did I say that? Well excuse my French!"

She and Matt burst out laughing at the same time.

He learned that before the war broke out, Nancy had been sent to Japan to take care of her mother's older sister. Her aunt suffered from rheumatoid arthritis and it was getting worse with each passing year. Her mother wanted to visit, but she and Nancy's father were too busy running a small boardinghouse, so Nancy was sent in her mother's stead. She was loaded down with suitcases full of food and clothing, all gifts for her aunt's family and assorted relatives. When she got here, it seemed to her that her aunt wasn't really all that sick but everyone was welcoming and she made the best of the opportunity she'd been given. Her trip was supposed to be three months, and her return ticket was scheduled for mid-December. Her aunt suggested that she extend her stay longer in order to spend New Year's in Japan, but Nancy wasn't even tempted. She wanted to get home. Of course, no one knew that war was about to break out and that there would be no more ships.

"It must have been awful to be stranded here during the war."

She shrugged. "You learn you can get used to anything. My family back home didn't exactly have a picnic, either, did they. The hardest part was not knowing. You can't imagine what life was like then with no letters. It was torture."

She shifted her purse to her other arm and then turned her head to look at the clock on the wall beside Lieutenant Baker's desk.

Matt was suddenly conscious of how quiet the empty office was once they'd stopped speaking. The hum of the wall clock was all he could hear. "Miss Nogami," he said, "are you usually busy on Sundays? I mean, I thought maybe you might like to go for a stroll."

She looked at him suspiciously. "What do you mean 'a stroll'?"

"Do you think that's a frivolous thing to do? Okay, maybe not that. Perhaps there's somewhere you'd like to go. Some place you'd like to see."

She puffed out her cheeks and thought for a moment. "Sure. As a matter of fact, there is somewhere I wouldn't mind going."

"Where's that?"

"I wouldn't mind going to the zoo."

15

After Fumi showed her the photograph of her sister, Aya felt an even greater shift in their relationship. Fumi was friendly in a new determined way, possessive in her attentions. Now that school was out for summer vacation, she insisted that they meet every day on the temple grounds or in the library ruins. She wanted to tutor Aya, as she had promised. Her enthusiasm for the idea of tutoring, however, far outstripped her ability to teach, and most of the time Fumi simply talked about herself or her family or whatever was on her mind. She described her father's bookstore and how she used to accompany him when he had to deliver or pick up books. "My father says I've got a really good sense of direction," she boasted. "I can find my way around anywhere."

When Fumi got tired of talking about herself, she peppered Aya with questions. "Do you have milk in Canada?" "Do people sleep with their shoes on?" "Does it snow every day?"

Aya was relieved that Fumi never probed in a personal way. If she had asked what had happened to her mother, it would have been impossible to answer. And there wasn't much to say about her father, either. Usually he was out until late at night doing his work. She knew it was hard, although she wasn't sure exactly where he went or what he did. They spoke only about matters of immediate necessity, but it wasn't so different from the way things had always been. For as long as she could remember, her father had been a silent man, and as a child it had seemed natural that she would communicate with him mainly through her mother. After all, she had always been her mother's daughter, and always would be, she thought. Even now.

Sometimes when she and Fumi were sitting among the ruins of the library, boys from school came by to taunt Aya. Whenever it happened, Fumi would shoo them away with a combination of threatening arm movements and invective so rough Aya couldn't understand anything except the fiery tone of her voice.

The summer days passed. The buzz of the cicadas filled the air with an urgent electric throb. Fumi had not covered any of the subjects in their school curriculum, but Aya was aware that her own hearing comprehension had vastly improved. More and more when she thought in Japanese, she didn't hear her mother's slow soft manner of speech. Her brain, her mind, her entire head was filled with Fumi's voice.

Aya was grateful for Fumi's attention, but she knew nothing was for nothing. So when Fumi asked if she could do her a favor, Aya wasn't surprised in the least. What did surprise her was the nature of the request.

"I need a letter in English," Fumi said. "A really important letter for a really important person."

Aya hated being reminded of her English. She hated anything that made her different. English set her apart, when all she longed to do was blend in and be the same as everyone else. Indeed, there were times when she wished she could cut out all the English parts of her tongue and make do with whatever was left. Cut out the parts of her brain that remembered all the other things, too.

"What kind of letter?" she asked. "What's it for?"

"Well, it's . . ." Fumi dug the toe of her sandal into the loose dirt.

They were at the back of the temple grounds again, in the gloomiest section where the trees cast dark shadows. In the distance Aya could hear the sound of the Buddhist priest's broom scraping the ground. *Shaaa, shaaa, shaaa.*

"Remember the picture I showed you of my sister?"

Aya nodded.

"I don't know where she is. All I know is she has a job dancing with *Amerikajin*. I want to find her and make her come home."

Aya thought about the photograph Fumi had shown her with the woman standing next to the GI. "Is the letter for the American soldier? Is that why you want it in English?"

"Oh, no." Fumi looked genuinely puzzled. "I want to write a letter to MacArthur-san."

Aya felt her jaw drop. "To General MacArthur?"

Fumi nodded.

"You can't write to someone like that."

"But everybody is writing to him. Please, Aya, you're the only one who can help me. Please write the letter for me."

"What do your parents think of your idea?"

Fumi shook her head vehemently. "I can't tell them. They wouldn't understand at all. They would try to stop me."

It was quiet. The cicadas had suddenly fallen silent and even the mosquitoes seemed to have stopped buzzing.

"Please. I need a letter in English. You're the only one I can ask."

Fumi bowed her head low in supplication, and Aya immediately felt foolish, and then humiliated, and then angry. Nobody ever bowed to her. It was always the other way around, she was supposed to bow to them. That's what her father said. Bow to everyone, bow as low as you can. It made her feel uncomfortable, the top of Fumi's dark head pointed straight at her. It was as if Fumi had stopped being her friend and had found a new way to make fun of her.

"Okay," she said, mostly because she wanted Fumi to stop bowing. "Okay, I'll do it. Tell me what you want to say."

In the end Aya had to compose the letter on her own because Fumi, for all her natural facility at talking, did not know how to write. She seemed indifferent to the words.

"If you dictate the letter to me, I'll translate it into English," Aya said.

"Just say I want Sumiko to come home."

"But you have to tell me what to write," Aya insisted. "It's your letter."

"I don't know. Something like 'Please find her.'"

"Okay." Aya wrote down the words. "What else?"

Fumi thought for a minute. "You said you are here to help the Japanese people. Please help me."

Aya wrote that down, too. "Isn't there anything else you can think of? Where does your sister live? Where did she go?"

Fumi furrowed her brow. "I don't know. If I knew where she was, I wouldn't have to ask for help, would I."

"But you must have some idea."

"Somewhere . . . in a place where . . . I don't know, some kind of dance hall. In the Ginza."

"Oh . . ." Aya wished she hadn't asked.

"I really miss her," Fumi whispered softly. "I want her to come home."

The expression on Fumi's face in that moment was so forlorn Aya couldn't bear to ask another question. Don't worry, she thought. I can write a good letter for you. I know how.

At the school run by the Nisei teachers in the internment camp, Aya was often praised for her English compositions. She could write a nice sentence, and she understood the importance of good spelling and neat handwriting. She even liked memorizing all the rules for grammar and punctuation. Before the evacuation, in Miss Carmichael's grade-three class, she had learned how to write in a smooth cursive script that looked almost like an adult's, and every day Miss Carmichael had made them practice spelling new words. No child was too young to learn the proper use of the King's English, Miss Carmichael liked to say. It was the most magnificent language in the world.

Of course, Aya had never written to a total stranger before, but she was surprised by the power she felt in using words to command a person's attention. Simple marks on a piece of paper, simple words, which, if arranged in just the right order, could compel even a general to stop and take notice.

It took her many attempts before she finally drafted something that she thought might work. If she wanted to catch her reader's attention, she knew the letter needed to be a little dramatic, perhaps even hint at a bit of danger.

Dear General MacArthur, she began writing.

16

$\mathcal{M}$att had arranged to meet Nancy at the entrance to Ueno Zoo at ten thirty on Sunday morning. He leaned against a wooden pole near the ticket booth and tried to look as casual as any man waiting for a friend. Today he'd decided to wear his civvies, black slacks and a plain white shirt, an outfit that helped him blend into the crowd. But he knew his sturdy leather shoes were a dead giveaway. Most people here had terrible, ill-fitting shoes that fell apart in the first heavy rainfall.

While he was waiting, two uniformed GIs with their Japanese girlfriends approached the entrance to the zoo. The GIs stayed behind, letting the women go up to the ticket booth. Matt shoved his hands in his pockets and pretended to stare up at the trees. It felt good to be incognito, free to dissolve into the background landscape. The men didn't take any notice of him, but one of the girlfriends shot Matt a brittle smile as if to say, See, I don't need Japanese men like you.

"I don't know how I got talked into this," the taller of the two men said. "There can't be much here. Just a bunch of smelly animals."

"Hey, Lily, tell them they should let us in for free," the other man shouted. "We're bringing you freedom, aren't we?"

Matt watched the foursome saunter into the zoo and realized he'd been waiting for Nancy for twenty minutes. He couldn't imagine her ever being late for any appointment. He hoped she wasn't playing a trick on him, but that didn't seem like her, either, and he couldn't remember what had possessed him to suggest that they spend time together outside the office.

And then suddenly there she was, running across the pavement toward him. It was all he could do not to laugh out loud—she looked so comical, her short legs and arms pumping in unison.

"Sorry I'm late. Were you waiting long?" She was panting hard. "The streetcar was so crowded, and then every time it stopped more people tried to get on. I thought it was going to break down." She took a handkerchief out of her purse, wiped her glasses, and then patted her forehead and cheeks. Her short hair stuck out at the sides.

Matt followed her gaze down to her plain straight skirt. The dark navy material was cheap and thin. Wrinkles stretched taut across the front of her thighs, just above her knees.

"Oh, boy, I'm a mess!" she said cheerfully.

"You look fine," he said.

"No, I don't." She puffed out her cheeks.

As soon as Nancy caught her breath, they went up to the booth and Matt asked for two tickets. He was about to pay when she shot her hand in front of him and waved her yen. He tried to push her arm aside, but she insisted.

"I'm paying my own way."

"Okay, okay," he said, accepting Nancy's money. He gave her a ticket and they walked through the entrance turnstile. An arrow pointed to the right and they followed a wide dirt path toward the animals.

Nancy led the way, walking past the cages so briskly that Matt barely had time to read the identifying signs. They passed a pair of dusty-looking zebras, a long-snouted Asian tapir, a crowded pen full of mountain goats. Some cages looked empty, although Matt wasn't sure if the animals were napping and out of sight.

"Are we headed somewhere in particular?" he finally asked.

"What do you mean?" Nancy sounded hostile.

"Well, we're walking past all the cages. I thought you wanted to see the animals. You said you wanted to come to the zoo."

"Oh, that. I thought *you* might like to see the zoo. That's why I suggested it. You're having a good time, aren't you?"

"Oh, sure," he said, flustered.

Nancy finally conceded that the only animals she really found interesting were the monkeys, so they headed to the Primate Pavilion. At one cage, they paused to observe a chimpanzee leisurely peel a banana, at the next they watched a dozen spider monkeys leap from one hanging vine to another. Eventually they came to rest in front of a large cage of Japanese snow monkeys from Hokkaido. The monkeys were sitting quietly in pairs, engaged in intense mutual grooming. Seen from the distance, they almost resembled human lovers. One large snow monkey was grooming a much smaller one, taking special care as it plucked the fleas from the other's back.

"That must be its mother, don't you think?" Nancy said. "Mother and child." She seemed to be taken by this particular pair. The mother monkey, with her thick hood of white fur surrounding her face, resembled a rich old lady in a fuzzy bonnet. She worked her long agile fingers steadily up and down the little one's back with methodical concentration. The baby had not yet developed any fur around its face, giving an impression of nakedness and vulnerability.

"I guess you must miss your family," Matt said.

She nodded but kept her face averted. She continued to watch the monkeys.

"May I ask? How come you're still here?"

"My God, you think I'm here by choice?" She turned to face him. "I can't wait to go home."

"Oh, of course, I'm sorry. I wasn't sure." He felt foolish now but there was no taking back his words.

"I'm waiting to have my U.S. citizenship reinstated."

"But you were born in the States, weren't you?"

"Yes, but everything got all messed up because I was here during the war." She scratched her nose and pushed her glasses up. "I entered my name in the family registry in order to get a ration card. Now I'm told I'm not American anymore, I'm Japanese."

The monkeys had stopped their grooming activity and started

chasing each other up and down the thick branches of a large arti-
ficial tree in the middle of the cage. The mother, too, had abruptly
ceased grooming the young monkey. She lumbered toward the tree
and began slowly climbing. The young monkey ran after her and
tried to climb on her back, but the mother pushed it away with one
broad swipe of her long arm. It was hard to tell if this was an act of
aggression or playful fun. The smaller monkey looked terrified, its
tiny wrinkled face overwhelmed by its large anxious eyes.

Nancy leaned forward, put her fingers through the wire mesh,
and began pushing the fence in and out. The fence moved only
slightly, but it made a loud rattling sound. The monkeys seemed
oblivious.

"Don't do that. You'll scare them."

"Oh, these ones aren't scared of anything. They've lived through
a lot, they're not going to get upset by a little cage rattling. Especially
the ones that lived through the war. They're tough." Her voice rose
sharply. "Hey, you guys, are you scared?"

"Don't shout." Matt looked around to see if anyone else was in
the pavilion. They were by themselves.

"If they lived through all that bombing, they're probably deaf."

The young monkey kept trying to jump on its mother's back, but
each time it was thrown off. How could the mother have turned so
heartless, Matt thought, especially after she had just finished grooming her offspring so lovingly? He wondered if this was what nature
was like in the wild. The youngster needed to learn how to survive
on its own, and survival depended on developing a certain tough-
ness.

"Well, at least they were lucky no one ate them during the war,"
Nancy said. "People were pretty desperate and I wouldn't be surprised if a few ducks and pheasants went missing from this place.
Oh, and the fish. I bet some fish for sure." She laughed at her own
grisly humor. "Let's see, what else? Turtles, they would make good
soup. And eel. I'll bet someone scooped up all the eel. I love *kabayaki*."

Matt didn't think it was funny at all.

"You know why there are no elephants here?" she said.

"There are no elephants?"

"Nope, not a one. They used to have three of them, though." She crossed her arms as if to emphasize her authority in this matter.

"What happened to them?"

"They killed them."

"Who?"

"The government, I guess."

"How do you know?"

"Oh, I heard about it from someone, I can't remember who. It happened during the bombing. Some people got afraid of what would happen if dangerous animals like lions and tigers escaped from the zoo. So they figured it was better to kill them first before they had a chance to kill people."

"But why the elephants? Were they afraid of elephants stampeding?"

"It doesn't make sense, does it. Lions and tigers I can understand. They're a bit scary. But I always think of elephants as being rather gentle. Anyway, as the story goes, the head zookeeper was given orders to kill all the big animals, including the elephants, so he laced their feed with poison. The lions and tigers ate the poison and they died. But the elephants were too smart. They refused to touch their food. Day after day, it was the same thing. Slowly, gradually, they starved to death."

"God, how long does it take an elephant to starve to death?"

"I don't know. They're huge, so it must take quite a while. Months maybe?"

Matt thought about the enormity of an elephant slowly shrinking week by week. He imagined it would have been like watching a giant rubber balloon gradually deflate, growing more and more shriveled as it got smaller, all the gray folds of its hide eventually collapsing inward.

"They didn't eat them, did they?" he asked.

"What a gruesome thought. I don't think so."

"Where do you bury an elephant?"

"And there were three of them!" Nancy started laughing hysterically.

"No, I meant it seriously. I wasn't trying to be funny."

"I know," she said, gasping for air. "Sorry, I couldn't stop think-ing of a colossal elephant coffin." She took a deep breath and com-posed herself. "Cremation. They must have cremated them." She paused. "That must have been an awful sight. Oh, and an awful stench."

They started walking again, leaving the monkey pavilion and returning to the main path through the zoo. Matt glanced at his watch. It was almost one o'clock. He tried to calculate how long it would take him to get back and whether he could go to Hibiya Park later.

"Do you have somewhere you have to go?" She was staring at him.

"No, nowhere."

"Okay, well in that case, do you mind going to American Alley with me? It's only five minutes from here. I have to buy some things, and quite frankly, I'm not comfortable going there on my own. My Japanese isn't good enough to bargain properly. They spot me right away and I always end up paying more than other people."

"Sure, I'd be happy to. But maybe I can get what you need at the PX. It's no trouble for me. Wouldn't that be better? Really, they don't keep track of what we buy, and everything's affordable. I don't mind."

But Nancy was adamant. No, she couldn't impose on him. He couldn't understand why using the black market was better than getting him to buy something for her from the PX. There was no point arguing with her, though. She had already started walking, and she was moving fast. They left the zoo and exited the park, heading down the long slope toward the nearby maze of narrow alleys that formed Ameyoko—American Alley—the biggest black market in the city, perhaps in the entire country. As they got closer, he became aware of an increased din. Shouting, clapping, pounding, the noise of restless movement. His nose also started to detect a mix-ture of smells, some familiar, some strange, some downright putrid. Every so often Nancy turned around to make sure he was behind her but she didn't pause or slow her pace. If he was going to keep up, he didn't dare take his eyes off her for even a second.

Nancy must have been waiting for some time to visit American Alley because she had a long list of things she wanted: soap, cooking oil, shoyu, rice, sesame seeds, toasted seaweed, some charcoal. She led Matt through a maze of narrow passageways lined with tiny open-air stalls squished side by side. Every so often she paused briefly to silently scan the goods arrayed on straw mats spread on the ground, and then she moved on. She did this five or six times until she finally stopped in front of a man sitting cross-legged on a blanket. He was surrounded by piles of soap bars and jars filled with gray, blue, and green liquids.

Nancy leaned close to Matt but even so she had to shout to make herself heard over the noise of the crowd around them. "I need some soap," she said, pushing him in front of her. "Can you find out what he's got and how much."

The man straightened his posture, readying himself for a sale. "Some soap for the lady of the house? American soap? I have shampoo, too. Good shampoo."

Nancy stood behind Matt, so close her chin brushed against his shoulder. "Ask him if he's got any Camay."

When he inquired, the man's response was to nod enthusiastically and reach behind for a bar of soap wrapped in brown paper.

"That's not Camay," Nancy hissed.

Matt repeated his request, and again the man nodded. This time he pulled a small unwrapped bar of soap out of a paper bag. It was ivory-colored and had a flowerly scent. Matt passed it to Nancy who brought it to her nose and sniffed it.

"Well, this isn't Camay, but I guess it will do. Can you try to get a good price?"

Matt wasn't at all sure that he got the best price for the soap or for any of the other goods Nancy bought that day, but each time she seemed satisfied with the amount he negotiated. They went from stall to stall, and as the afternoon wore on, he found he was actually enjoying the challenge of bargaining.

He knew that the black market was the only thing keeping most Japanese people from starving to death, but he'd always held a dim view of illicit activity. It was why he had never been here before. He'd heard that many GIs came regularly in search of booze and drugs like hiropon, while others engaged in their own commerce, stealing army supplies and selling them to the yakuza who controlled the market. What Matt discovered on his visit with Nancy, though, took him completely by surprise. There was a raw, chaotic energy to the place that made him feel caught up in a primitive festival, thrust into a community of wild revelers. All around him he felt the heat and throb of other people pushing, shouting, hustling. He was part of something larger than himself, but it was different from being part of the military or a member of the Occupation forces. That was institutional—he was merely a cog in a bureaucratic machine. No, being in the market felt totally different. It was like being a single wave in a vast ocean, a bird flying in the middle of a huge migrating flock, a molecule in an expanding field of energy.

It was, in a word, intoxicating.

17

*I*t was a while before Sumiko noticed that the photograph she kept in her purse was missing, and when she did, she felt oddly relieved. She should have thrown it out ages ago, she thought. The trip to Kamakura to see the Great Buddha was an event she preferred to forget.

She had only agreed to go because Yoko had begged her. Yoko had just met a GI she was trying to impress. She had some crazy notion that this time was for real and that this man would set her up in her own apartment as his *only* and take care of her. She wouldn't have to work in the dance hall anymore. She wouldn't have to worry about fighting the lines in the black market to get extra food for her parents and younger brothers and sisters. It would be Spam and eggs every day. Besides, Yoko insisted, she was in love for real this time. Everyone she met was a "potential," and Sumiko had grown used to the tales of hope that always ended in disappointment.

According to Yoko, the GI—Sergeant Jake Pickersgill was his name—was really important because he was a driver. That meant he could sign out one of the jeeps on his day off and say he had to check out such-and-such facility in such-and-such region, and then he was free to drive wherever he wanted. As long as he brought the jeep back by the end of the day, no one cared. Jake had told Yoko that he wanted to see the "Big Buddha" in Kamakura. "All the guys talk about it. I want to see what the fuss is about."

Yoko saw this as her chance to make an indelible mark on Jake.

"Please come with me. I can't go alone. That's too risky. But if you come, it will be all right. And I think that Jake has a friend he wants to bring, too."

Sumiko didn't have anything else to do that Sunday and she was fond of Yoko, so she agreed to accompany her. Kamakura was only an hour away, and the trip there, Sumiko had to admit, was quite thrilling. She'd never ridden in a jeep before. Fortunately, she had brought a scarf to cover her hair, otherwise the wind would have blown out all the curls in her new permanent wave. And the noise of the jeep was so loud that she didn't have to worry about making conversation with Jake's friend, Danny, a pale skinny man who looked like he was still a teenager. He called Sumiko "ma'am," and said "yes, sir" to Jake, who constantly ordered him around. Yet while the ride itself—the speed and the rush of wind—was exciting, the landscape they passed through was still a wasteland, much of it barren and flattened. It was a depressing reminder of how much destruction had taken place and how far her country had to go in its efforts at rebuilding.

Yoko was not dressed properly for the outing. Neither her skirt, which was too tight, nor her shoes, which were too high, were any good for walking around the hilly slopes of Kamakura. Jake had to drive everywhere, even down narrow lanes where the jeep barely fit.

"Don't worry, babydoll. I don't want you to injure those pretty feet," he said.

Once they arrived at the Great Buddha, Jake parked the jeep and helped Yoko out by putting his hands around her waist and lifting her to the ground.

"Look at this, Danny. My hands fit right around this gal's waist, she's so tiny."

Danny nodded glumly. Sumiko hastily jumped out of the jeep by herself in case Danny got any ideas that he should try to help. At the Great Buddha, Jake took Yoko's hand and they slowly walked up to the base of the gigantic statue. They circled it, and as they did, Yoko pointed up at various parts and seemed to be explaining things to Jake. By the time they returned to the front of the statue, Jake had his arm around Yoko's shoulder.

"You gotta get up close, Danny. This thing sure is big. Biggest damn Buddha in the world, I bet." Jake threw his head back and laughed. "Biggest damn Buddha."

Yoko laughed, too, but with an uncertain look on her face. Sumiko cringed inwardly on her friend's behalf.

"Hey, Danny, take our picture, would you?" Jake said. "This big Buddha is too much."

"The camera's in the jeep."

"Well, go back and get it!"

"Yes, sir."

"Babydoll," Jake said, "tell your friend to come closer. I want her to be in the picture, too." He gestured for Sumiko to stand on his other side. "Come on, now. I'd like a shot of all three of us together. You know, with the big guy in the background. Gee, his earlobes are huge."

"Big ears, big wisdom," Yoko said solemnly.

"Yours are nice and cute. Good thing you're not wise," Jake said. Yoko giggled loudly.

"Hey, Suzie," Jake shouted again. "Come here and get in the picture."

He grabbed Sumiko's arm and pulled her toward his left side. Yoko peered around from Jake's other side and smiled in a bright, false way as if to say, Please, please, just humor him, okay? Sumiko let him put his arm around her shoulder, but she didn't like the way he gripped her so tightly. He pressed her to his side, squashing her breast.

Danny got down on one knee, looked into the camera, and adjusted the focus.

"Be sure to get all of the Big Buddha in."

"Yes, sir. Okay. Don't move."

The camera clicked.

Jake released his grip on Sumiko and turned his attention to Yoko. "Baby, I want this to be a picture you'll always treasure." He bent over and kissed her on the mouth.

Sumiko turned her head away.

From the Great Buddha, they walked along a narrow path lined with cheap souvenir shops that sold faded postcards of Kamakura, folding fans, ceramic teacups, and miniature replicas of the Great Buddha. Most of the shops were practically empty of wares, but the shop owners sat stoically on their stools by the doorways smiling at the passing soldiers. Yoko and Jake strolled leisurely hand in hand. As soon as they passed one store, Sumiko saw the owner spit onto the ground behind them. Neither Jake nor Yoko seemed aware and Sumiko couldn't tell if Danny had noticed anything.

They walked down the slope and got back into the jeep in the same configuration as before, Jake and Yoko in front, Danny and Sumiko in back. Jake threw his arm around Yoko and pulled her close to him in the driver's seat. He made a big show of handling the steering wheel with one hand, making the car zigzag drunkenly back and forth across the road. There were no other cars, not even a bicycle or cart. Yoko squealed each time the jeep swerved, but it sounded feigned as if she were pretending to be excited.

"Hey, what's that?" Jake suddenly pulled the jeep over to the side of the road where there was a small Jizo statue wearing a red bib. "He looks like a baby Buddha."

"He is Jizo," said Yoko.

"And there's something back there. Down this path. I think I can see more statues. Yeah, looks like a bunch of baby Buddhas back there. Let's go take a look."

"Why?" Yoko asked. Her voice had become petulant. "I want go back Tokyo."

Jake gave her waist a squeeze. "Soon enough, baby. Let's just take a quick look. It might be something interesting." He took her hand and led the way, pushing back the overhanging vegetation with his free arm. "You two come along," he shouted over his shoulder. "And bring the camera, would you?"

They came to a clearing in the middle of which stood a simple wooden structure, a poor cousin of the other temple they had seen. Facing them were dozens of small stone statues arranged in terraced rows, four or five deep and about twenty across. The Jizo statues wore faded red bibs and caps. Toy pinwheels, the kind a child would play with, had been placed in front of some of them. Every so often one of the pinwheels would turn lazily in the hot air.

"Wow, that's pretty weird. Quite a sight." Jake seemed genuinely impressed. "Say, Danny, take a picture of us, would you, standing in front of these statues. They're too much."

Danny raised the camera to his face and began adjusting the focus.

"No." Yoko pulled her hand out of Jake's.

"What's wrong, babydoll? Just another picture of our trip. Besides, everyone has a picture of the Big Buddha, but nobody will have a picture like this."

"Bad luck."

"These are cute. What can be unlucky about taking a picture of them?"

"No good."

"Okay, suit yourself." Jake shrugged his shoulders carelessly. "I'll get my picture taken by myself. Danny, go ahead. Get as many of the statues in as you can fit. This is a great shot. Wait till the other guys see it. They're gonna be green with envy. Maybe we can send this in to *Life* magazine or *Saturday Evening Post*."

Yoko scowled and motioned to Sumiko to walk back to the jeep with her.

"Honey, don't be like that." As soon as Danny had clicked the shutter, Jake ran after Yoko. He caught up to her in three long strides and pulled her into his arms. "Don't be mad. I can't stand it when you get mad at me."

Yoko squirmed briefly but almost immediately gave in to his embrace.

"Okay, that's better. See, you don't have to be mad, do you. Well, I guess we better start driving back."

Once again the four of them climbed into the jeep. During the long ride back to Tokyo, Yoko rested her head on Jake's shoulder as he drove. Sumiko stared at the passing landscape to avoid looking at Danny or at the couple in front. Sumiko wondered if Yoko would explain to Jake the special meaning of the temple they had seen. "You people make the cutest little Buddhas!" Would she explain that this temple was for women to honor the dead babies they had miscarried or aborted? She suspected Yoko would not try. She knew that she herself would not. She didn't think the Americans would want to know.

It was a relief when they arrived at the barracks in downtown Tokyo.

"Danny, I'll be taking care of Yoko here. Maybe you wouldn't mind escorting her lovely friend back home?"

"Yes, sir."

Yoko mouthed "Thank you" over her shoulder to Sumiko as she and Jake walked away.

Danny turned to Sumiko. "Okay, ma'am, looks like I'm supposed to take you home. Where do you live?"

"I'm okay."

"I have to make sure you get home safely. Where do you live?"

Sumiko shrugged. "In Ginza. Near dance hall."

"I will take you there."

"But you get lost."

The streets of downtown Tokyo had always been narrow and mazelike, but since the war, it was much worse and even Tokyoites often got confused. The fire bombings had destroyed so many of the old landmarks.

An anxious look crossed Danny's brow.

"You get lost," she repeated. "I'm okay. By self."

"Well, ma'am, if you're sure."

"Yes."

Sumiko never thought she would see Danny again, but about two months later he showed up at her dance hall. He seemed like a changed man, more confident, even taller and fuller, not as scrawny as she remembered him. At first she assumed he didn't recognize her, but after a few minutes he broke into a grin and began wagging his index finger in the air as he walked toward her.

"I don't believe it. It's you, isn't it. We went to Kamakura together." His finger was only inches from her face. "Where's your friend? Is she here tonight?" He swiveled his head to take in the rest of the dance floor. "I've been carrying around this picture I was supposed to give to her. This is good luck. I didn't know what to do with the damn thing."

Danny pulled a small photograph from his wallet and handed it to her. It was the picture taken in front of the Great Buddha.

"She not here," Sumiko said.

"Well, it doesn't matter. Give it to her, would you? It's a souvenir. Or maybe you want it for yourself. You're in the picture, too."

Sumiko thought about Yoko. All those nights waiting to hear from Jake, sobbing into her pillow.

"Mr. Jake? Is he coming?"

Danny pursed his thin lips, so they formed a crooked red line across the bottom of his long, unattractive face. "Forget it. He's gone.

"Gone?"

"Long gone."

"Where?"

Danny looked down at his shoes. "I'm sorry. I'm really not familiar with any of the details."

When she gave Yoko the picture that evening in the dormitory, Yoko took one look and threw the picture on the tatami mat. She stamped on it with her bare foot. "Stupid man. *Dai kirai*. I hate him. He knew all along he would leave me."

Sumiko wasn't sure why she picked up the photograph and put it in her purse. Perhaps she was drawn to something the camera had seen. The man had his eyes tightly closed and his grin was hard and wolfish. He looked exactly like what he was. But Yoko's expression was complex, fractured. Her bright sunny smile did not match the look of desperation in her eyes, as if the top and bottom halves of her face had been pieced together haphazardly. Sumiko couldn't help wondering if she looked like that, too.

When Yoko left the dance hall a few weeks later, she told no one, not even Sumiko. Sumiko returned to the dorm room one day to find another girl going through the clothes Yoko had left behind, trying to decide what would fit.

18

*A*ya worked on Fumi's letter at home. It took her several days, and each time she sat down to struggle with her composition, she found herself thinking again of Miss Carmichael, the last teacher she'd had in Vancouver. Miss Carmichael, who loved the King's English and who had a broad chest and big hands and thick curly hair the color of a carrot.

It was in Miss Carmichael's class that Aya had begun to yearn for a coat like the other pupils were wearing. Jane Taylor wore a baby blue one, Katie Shirras had a green tartan plaid, and Alice Mead's was bright red.

Aya's mother had frowned. "Red is not a good color. Navy or dark brown are better."

But she must have seen the disappointment on Aya's face because a few days later she announced they would go shopping. "Mrs. Horikawa's daughter told me to go to the big department store downtown. They're having a special sale the last week of November. Everything half price."

They stood in the middle of the girls' section, and her mother held her hand. Aya had never seen so many coats in one spot, racks and racks of different colors and fabrics. She grew dizzy watching the uniformed saleswomen swish past carrying armloads of coats, and her feet sank deeper and deeper into the thick plush carpet, giving her an unsteady sensation, as if she were standing on sponges. But it didn't take long for her to notice how customers who came later were being served ahead of them and how the saleswomen refused to make eye contact. Suddenly she didn't want a new coat. She only wanted to go home, but her mother's grip on her hand had progressively tightened until it was like an iron vise. It hurt so much, Aya began to feel afraid. There was no question of leaving. They'd come too far to retreat. Her mother was staring straight ahead, as if summoning some force deep inside herself.

That was when, through the forest of coats, Miss Carmichael appeared. She was walking straight toward them.

"Hello, Irene," she said in her clear classroom voice. "Fancy meeting you here. Is this your mother?"

Aya's mother bowed her head.

Please don't bow, Aya prayed silently. You're not supposed to do that.

Miss Carmichael smiled. "It's so nice to meet you. Irene is one of our best pupils. You must be proud of her."

Please don't bow. But her mother kept on bowing and smiling, bowing and smiling. She didn't try to speak, nor did Aya, who found herself completely tongue-tied. Miss Carmichael didn't seem to notice at all. She was a teacher, used to filling the silences in her classroom with her own voice.

"Are you shopping for a coat? This store has the best in the city. Any coat you get here will be a very good buy."

"Miss Carmichael?" A tall saleswoman with tight blond curls and a large nose appeared. She smiled broadly, her lips shiny with bright coral lipstick. "I'm sorry to have kept you waiting. Here's the coat for your niece." She handed Miss Carmichael a gift-wrapped box.

"Excellent! And while you are here, I hope you can assist my pupil and her mother." Before leaving, Miss Carmichael gave Aya's arm a tight squeeze. "I am so glad to have met your mother."

"And what exactly are we looking for?" The saleswoman's voice was polite but cold.

Aya hesitated. She knew she was expected to speak for her mother in English as always, but she didn't know what to say. That was when her mother shocked her.

"*Kouto,*" she said in English. She pointed at Aya.

The woman smirked. "Coat-o? Well, yes. That's what we sell."

"For daughter, *kouto.*"

"Well, I really don't know if we would have any coats suitable for someone like—"

"*Puriizu.*" Aya's mother had raised her voice and a few customers had turned their heads. It was mortifying. "For daughter."

The saleswoman was silent for a moment. She shifted her gaze to Aya and said sharply, "What size are you?"

"I—I don't know."

The woman rolled her eyes. "Oh, all right. Give me a minute."

They waited for what seemed like an eternity. Aya didn't really expect the saleswoman to return. When she came back, she had only one coat over her arm, something mustard yellow with large black buttons. Aya tried it on. The sleeves flopped over her hands and the shoulders sagged. The hem fell to the floor. It was clearly several sizes too big. Aya looked helplessly at her mother, feeling her eyes well up with hot tears.

The saleswoman's smile had returned, only bigger and wider, with a thick oily smear of coral lipstick on her teeth. "Oh, isn't that a shame. I'm afraid this is the only coat we have in stock, for people like you. Well, I guess it doesn't fit."

They went to Mrs. Yoshimoto, who took Aya's measurements and promised to make a good sturdy coat. It would be dark brown, so as not to show the dirt, with wide seams and a deep hem that could be let out to accommodate a young girl's growth.

"And I have some nice buttons left over from a previous order," Mrs. Yoshimoto said, reaching into a drawer and pulling out a handful of shiny silver buttons. "These will look nice."

But after Pearl Harbor, Mrs. Yoshimoto was overwhelmed with work because everyone was afraid to go downtown. Aya's mother said not to bother with their order, but Mrs. Yoshimoto insisted. When Aya and her mother were finally told that her coat was ready, they discovered Mrs. Yoshimoto had mixed up the orders and made the coat much too big. It was almost as large as the coat they'd been shown in the department store.

When she realized her mistake, Mrs. Yoshimoto started to cry. "I'm sorry, I'm sorry. Too much happening. Too much worry." The rumors of forced expulsion that had been circulating ever since the start of the war were now turning to fact. Soon all of them would have to leave the west coast.

Aya's mother tried to assure her it was fine. "I can sew. I can fix. A big coat is good."

Mrs. Yoshimoto continued to cry. "Thank you, Mrs. Shima-mura, thank you. No, no. No need to pay. I will make a new coat, a proper coat, sometime when we come back. I promise."

19

*P*lease don't come when Fumi is here," Sumiko's mother had begged her. "It's better this way." And though it had been hurtful, Sumiko did as her mother asked, timing her visits home for the hours when Fumi was in school. But Fumi must have been let out of school early that day when Sumiko found her in the entrance-way playing with her shoes and purse. The chance encounter had surprised Sumiko, but it had also provoked a crushing awareness that her mother was right to be worried. Fumi was much too curious a child, much too interested in new things. And she would soon no longer be a child. It was terrible to realize that one of the people she most wanted to help was someone she needed to push away, but Sumiko saw clearly how she would influence Fumi without meaning to.

As for herself, Sumiko still strove—at least in her heart—to be a dutiful daughter, a good individual, a kind sister. She hoped that her family recognized that. But she wasn't the same person who had left home and moved to the Ginza. The life she'd taken up had meant that certain things about her previously sheltered existence had changed entirely.

What was the real price of a can of peaches or a bag of sugar? Not even a chocolate bar was really free. She told her mother that she just danced but kept the details as vague as she could. She didn't explain, for instance, that the cookies and chocolate she brought home were things she received in exchange for letting a man stroke her hair or nuzzle his face against her neck. She never explained that a peck on the cheek might yield a jar of peanut butter but getting Spam and a small box of salt might require a long embrace. Letting an arm rest around her shoulder might be good enough to get her a bag of soft white bread, while resting *her* head on the man's shoulder would definitely allow her to ask for the special kind of sugar-coated biscuits her sister loved so much. What she did wasn't bad, she reminded herself. What she did was essential to survive.

Initially it was thrilling to feel so powerful and in control. She was making money; she was supporting her family. She came home every weekend loaded down with gifts of food she'd received, some of them things she didn't even know you could eat. Meat in a can, caramel popcorn, fluffy white things called marshmallows, so sweet they made her teeth ache. The presents delighted her sister and put color back into her mother's cheeks. If the neighbors cast disapproving looks in her direction, if the words they whispered—"disgusting" and "brazen"—were just loud enough for her to hear, she did her best to ignore them. She knew she wasn't the only woman doing exactly what she was doing, or worse.

Yet there were times when she wished she could visit in her old clothes and plain hair and sensible shoes, not only for her mother's sake or to avoid the stares of the neighbors. She wished she could just be her former self, but she couldn't. Somewhere along the way, she had become the clothes that she wore. It was as simple as that.

The manager of the dance hall, Mr. Harada, had approached Sumiko when she was standing in one of the ration lines in the fall of 1946. Although the war had ended more than a year earlier, the food shortages were worse, not better, in peacetime. She couldn't imagine how she must have appeared then. Thin, tired. Shapeless in the same faded blue top and baggy *monpe* that she'd worn throughout the war. They were all exhausted then, malnourished not just in body but in spirit. That there would be even less food available than during wartime was something no one had anticipated. During the war, they had been told to sacrifice for country, for emperor, for their brave soldiers on the front lines. But after the war, they didn't have anything left to sacrifice. They just wanted to eat. There was no longer a purpose to hunger, and sheer starvation had reduced them to animals.

Harada stood out among the others in the line. He was better dressed than anyone else and gave off an air of prosperity. They fell into conversation. He was friendly and had a way of making her want to open up. Was she married? Did she have a fiancé? No? How was that possible, a pretty girl like her? Did she live at home? How old was she? Did she know any English? How was her family? She hadn't thought it odd at the time. She was eager to talk. She realized that no one had expressed any interest in who she was or what she was doing in a very long time. Everyone was too preoccupied with trying to survive. She told him about some bills they owed and how when the bill collectors started coming to the house, they had to hide inside and pretend they were out. That was when she couldn't help it and the tears fell.

He touched her shoulder with his hand, very formally, politely, to comfort her. He said that bill collectors were the lowest form of human being. What right had they to take advantage of others in need? He wanted to help. He offered to give her some money.

No, she couldn't accept that, she'd said. But it was no trouble, he was adamant.

"I don't like to see decent folks suffer," he'd said, then gestured to his own fine attire. "I've got a bit of money now. Those who are fortunate owe it to help those who are not."

No, she couldn't possibly accept.

Well, in that case, perhaps she could consider accepting a loan. He would give her a loan to help her family pay off their bills, and she could pay him back by coming to work for him. He was in the entertainment business and was hoping to start a dance club for American guests. Did she know how to dance? No? It didn't matter. Everyone would get dance lessons. It would be a high-class dance hall, he insisted, not at all like those other cheap places she might have heard about in the Ginza. Very "high collar." Everyone would have to learn basic English, though. Was she willing to do that? She would receive a special wardrobe and makeup.

Sumiko didn't accept right away. It wasn't until Fumi developed beriberi and required special injections their parents couldn't afford that she brought out the business card he had given her.

That was when she discovered the other part of herself, the part that had been hidden behind the good girl and dutiful daughter. The part of her that thrilled at the chance to taste this new lifestyle. She never told anyone, of course, but secretly she was just a little bit glad she had an excuse. More than a little bit. To work in a dance hall was not something a proper girl should do—it was too shady and risqué—and she was above all a proper girl. She had been raised to be demure and polite, trained to serve tea and offer a guest a cushion to sit on, told to keep her eyes downcast and not speak unless spoken to. A proper girl did what her parents asked her and did not voice her opinion too loudly. She did not get a permanent wave in her hair; she did not wear skirts with a slit up the side or shoes with heels so high they forced her to swing her hips from side to side. So how was it that such a proper girl could want to wear clothing like that? Why would she covet the hairpins and handbags and lipstick? Perhaps it meant she was shallow. Sumiko was willing to accept that. But she knew it might also mean that this was the type of woman she had always been. Someone who wasn't a proper girl.

In her old life, Sumiko would have been expected to have an arranged marriage and to be happy with her father's choice for her. Her family had not been wealthy but they were not poor, and her father's bookstore was considered a very respectable business. She would have been a good wife and a wise mother, just as she'd been trained to be. But even then she must have harbored some rebellion, because hadn't she hoped there might be a way she could convince her father to choose Takeo Shoyama, the young carpenter who lived a few doors away and who had once repaired the steps in front of the bookstore? Just a laborer, she could hear her father say. Whenever Sumiko bumped into Takeo, they would stop and talk for a few minutes. He made her laugh, and although everything was innocent, she had felt a growing attachment. She didn't know if that was what they meant by love, but it felt nice and she wanted to know him more. But before anything could happen, Takeo was conscripted and never returned from the front, his death neither confirmed nor denied. It was as if he had vanished into thin air. Whether he was alive somewhere in the Philippines or whether he was already dead, nobody knew. And so, although Sumiko had never been embraced by Takeo, had never even held hands with him, she felt in limbo.

After months of being stricken at the thought of his death and buoyed by the possibility that he was still alive, Sumiko's emotions turned increasingly black. So many young men did not return. She knew it was irrational but she began to resent, even hate, Takeo for not coming back alive and then she hated him even more for not dying outright in a clear, unambiguous way.

And because she had never told a soul how she'd felt, and because her father and mother would never have suspected that their dutiful daughter might have thought about marrying someone her father hadn't specifically chosen for her, the fact that Takeo had not come back was not something she felt comfortable openly mourning. It was a secret that had to sit locked inside her heart, a tight knot of sadness and confusion and remembrance that stirred restlessly whenever she found herself in the arms of a GI. In an unexpected way, these feelings protected her. She would not sell her body; she would not sell her heart. No matter what her mother feared, she was not a *panpan*, and she felt no desire to become anyone's *only*. Perhaps another woman would have reacted differently, justifying her actions because of her pain. But Sumiko was different. Whether it was because she was perverse and stubborn, or because her heart was too hard or maybe not hard enough, Sumiko didn't know.

Whatever the reason, it was the reason. It was the reason she just danced.

She accepted the loan Harada offered. She accepted the job. She felt powerful and wanted and superior. She enjoyed the way men—and women—looked at her, took in her sharp clothes and her wavy hair and her high-heeled shoes. She basked in their stares, relished the envious glances.

In the early days, she was a fool.

It was only later that she fully comprehended what she'd gotten herself into. While Harada was very generous at first, she hadn't realized that the loan incurred interest at a steep rate, and eventually it became clear that, after deductions, the job didn't pay nearly as much as she thought it would. She had to pay rent for her part of the crowded dorm room; she was even charged for the blanket and the futon. She was in well over her head, dropping deeper and deeper into a bottomless hole.

20

*F*umi announced they would deliver the letter in person.

"How?" Aya asked dubiously.

"We'll go to MacArthur-san's headquarters," Fumi said. "I know where it is. I've seen pictures in the newspaper. All kinds of people wait in front of his building to say hello."

She didn't elaborate on the details of her plan. She'd been dreaming about it for so long, she didn't want to spoil anything by putting it into words. The very idea of what she was about to do was so bold, so audacious, it gave her chills. She saw exactly what would happen. She and Aya would stand in front of GHQ. General MacArthur's car would pull up and he would get out, rising tall as he unfolded his lean fit figure. He would wave his pipe to the crowd, he would give them all a crisp salute. And then he would see Fumi and beckon her to come forward. This was real democracy! Even a twelve-year-old could greet the general. She would follow him up the broad white steps of General Headquarters, and just before he entered the building, he would turn to her. *Young lady, don't you have something for me?* He would hold out his upturned palm. She would give him the letter.

Please find my sister, she would say.

Don't worry, he would reply. *I am the Supreme Commander. I can do anything!*

Each time she imagined this scene, she couldn't decide whether

MacArthur would be speaking Japanese to her or whether she would be speaking English. It was a small but nettlesome point.

"We should go as soon as we can," Fumi said. "Maybe this Friday afternoon. My mother will be out."

It was the end of August and the summer holidays were coming to a close. There was hardly any time.

It took much longer than Fumi expected to get to General Headquarters. She knew the location and the direction in which they should walk, but many of the streets were crowded and narrow. To make matters worse, it was a very hot day. Aya could not walk as fast as Fumi, and because of the heat she kept wanting to stop and rest in the shade. Fumi tried not to be impatient, but she felt a mounting urgency. It took more than an hour and a half to reach the vicinity of GHQ.

When they arrived, it was impossible to get anywhere near the Dai-Ichi Building. There were far too many people. Fumi and Aya were forced to look for a place along the roadside, but it was crowded here, too. The only spot they could find meant standing behind several other people. They couldn't even see the road.

"The car is in sight. He's coming!"

The animated voice of a bystander caused the people around them to stir, and Fumi thrust her arm through Aya's, pulling her tight against her body. "Push!" she ordered Aya, although Fumi was the one who had to do all the pushing. It was worse than forcing her way through the crowd of schoolgirls at lunchtime or pushing herself onto a packed streetcar. "*Sumimasen*, excuse me, *sumimasen*. Please let us through." And then, miraculously, they broke through to the front row and there was nothing between them and the empty road. Fumi pulled out the letter and unfolded it. The English words swam before her eyes. She couldn't read it, but she was heartened by the sight of Aya's handwriting. Somewhere in here were the words: *Please find my sister. Please help.* That was all she needed to know.

The car was coming closer, driving up the wide dusty boulevard. It had a lonely feel to it—she couldn't have explained why. Perhaps because there were no other cars or bicycles or rickshaws. Only the American car, moving so slowly it was like a shiny black ship, advancing with a prideful, majestic certainty. There was nowhere else for it to go except right past Fumi.

It was close enough that the old woman beside her had started to bow, and next to her a young man in wire-rim glasses began waving the paper flags—one Japanese and one American—that he held in each hand.

"He's coming, he's coming." The murmurs around her swelled into a single voice that roared in her ears. This was Fumi's chance—her only chance. And then everything fell silent, as if she had tumbled into a separate universe with only the car and herself.

She hadn't planned it. Later she would swear over and over to Aya that it had just happened spontaneously. She had lifted one foot and as soon as it came down slightly ahead of the other, as soon as the weight of her body had shifted so that its balance was altered and her hip pitched forward, it was inevitable. Unstoppable. She pushed off from the side of the road and began sprinting, drawn like a moth toward lamplight, like a bird toward the sun. Headlong toward the car that seemed to be waiting only for her. She clutched the letter in her hand. It was unfolded and flapping in the air, and she wished she had folded it before moving, but it was too late. She had to deliver it. She had to reach the car. Although she was aware of the rapid pumping of her heart, she also felt as if everything was happening in slow motion. She was moving toward the car, and the car was moving toward her. They would meet in the middle.

The afternoon sun was bright, casting the interior of the car into darkness. She could make out the silhouette of a driver in the front seat, a featureless shape wearing a cap, but where was MacArthur? The backseat was all blackness and shadow. Until suddenly, she saw a face. An American boy's pale face was pressed against the window in the backseat and he was staring straight at her. He was clearly as startled as she was, and for a moment their eyes were locked in surprise and bewilderment. Then her foot stumbled.

The noise of the world shot back into her ears.

"Got you!"

Someone grabbed the seat of her pants and then the collar of her blouse, and she felt herself yanked back. The letter flew out of her hand.

"Let me go!"

"What do you think you're doing!" The policeman dragged her back to the side of the road. A crowd immediately formed around them.

"What's your name?"

"Please let me go."

"We can't have behavior like this, young lady. Where do you live?"

"I'm sorry. It won't happen again."

"Where are your parents?" He cast an inquiring look at the faces in the crowd. "Are they here?"

"I came by myself."

"Even worse! Your parents are responsible for you. What kind of parents would let a young girl run around by herself?"

"It's not their fault. I didn't tell them."

He shifted his grip to her shoulders and began shaking her back and forth, as if he could shake some sense into her. "Okay, once again. What's your name? Where do you live? Don't waste my time."

"Officer, she's just a kid. Leave her alone," someone in the crowd yelled.

He addressed the circle of onlookers who had gathered around them. "The city is overrun with lawless children like this one. Lawless parents, too. I have to report her. It's my duty."

"What about democracy?" someone else said. "Aren't we supposed to be free to do what we want?"

The policeman blushed and looked stunned as if this line of reasoning had never occurred to him. At this distraction, Fumi felt his grip loosen and she used the opportunity to slide out of his grasp.

"Hey, come back here!" the policeman shouted after her.

But she had already slipped through a gap in the circle of people and was running as far from the street as possible in the direction of nearby Hibiya Park. She ran until her lungs hurt too much and she had to stop. She hid behind the thick trunk of a large oak tree, hoping that the policeman wouldn't catch her. When she looked back, he was nowhere to be seen.

To be on the safe side she waited in hiding for as long as she could. By the time she circled back to look for Aya, the crowds were gone. Aya was sitting by herself on the roadside almost exactly where they had originally been standing.

Aya raised her head as Fumi approached, and jumped up. "Thank goodness you came back. I was scared. I didn't know where you were so I just waited here." She pulled out a crumpled piece of paper. "I got the letter. After everyone left I ran out onto the road and picked it up."

At the sight of the letter's condition, Fumi felt her heart sink. What a stupid fool she'd been, making such a terrible mess of things. Now her letter was not fit to give to anyone, never mind the most important person in Japan. She felt tears burn in her eyes.

"Aren't you happy?" Aya said. "I got the letter for you."

"Give that to me. It's a stupid letter." She made a move to snatch the letter, but Aya pulled it back out of reach.

"It's okay." Aya smoothed the paper with the palm of her hand and brushed off the surface dirt. "Look, it's as good as new. If you want, I can write out another copy for you. But, please, first let's go home."

For some reason, Aya's words made Fumi feel worse and she squatted on the ground and began wailing like an infant. She knew she was making a scene, her face covered with tears and snot, but she didn't care.

She felt Aya's hands on her back, rubbing and patting ineffectually. "Please stop. Get up. Please get up." Then she felt Aya reach under her armpit and tug like she was trying to pull up a tree root. But Fumi was stronger, and she pushed her weight down into her haunches and willed her body to stay on the ground. She yanked her arm out of Aya's grip, twisted around to face her, and instinctively pushed with all her might. Aya teetered briefly, then fell backward onto her rump. She let out a funny "oomph" sound when her body hit the ground.

"*Baka!* Stupid!" Fumi spat out the word. It was not directed at Aya but at herself. She had been so close and yet she'd failed. In her mind she saw the shiny black surface of the car, saw the window, saw the American boy's face, saw those eyes filled with a special kind of loneliness. He'd stared at her as if he understood something deep inside her, as if he knew all the yearning in her heart.

21

*E*veryone in the office except Matt had left shortly after lunch. It was the last Friday in August and hot as hell, but that was not why they had been given time off. All the officers in the section had been called over to GHQ, and as a result the enlisted men were also told to knock off early. The staff was on high alert because MacArthur's son was making a special visit to General Headquarters today.

"The rumor is the Old Man's getting ready to seek the Republican nomination next year," Sab announced.

"How do you know that?" Matt said.

"Come on. Showing off your wife and son and what a perfect family you have? I heard extra photographers from *Life* and *Look* were flown in from the States to be sure the photos come out just right. Everyone knows he wants to run for president."

Matt shrugged.

"I'm going to take my camera and see if I can get any good shots," Sab said.

"What a hypocrite you are. I didn't think you were such a big fan."

"I'm not. But maybe somebody'll want to buy one of my pictures. Come on with me."

"I'm going to finish up here. I'll see you later."

Matt thought it would only take him ten minutes to complete what he was doing, but his efforts had not gone smoothly. He was still struggling with what turned out to be a very difficult translation when he heard loud shouts. All the windows in the office had been left open in an attempt to let in any stray breeze.

When he looked outside he saw that the crowds were impressive, many more people than even a couple of hours ago. There was extra security, too, in the form of Japanese policemen. One of them had just apprehended someone, and a circle of onlookers was forming in the middle of the road.

Matt watched as a young girl was being scolded by the policeman. He heard the phrase "Where are your parents?," but after that, with so many people yelling at the same time, it was hard to catch anything else.

He went back to his desk and finished his work. By the time he was ready to leave, all the sounds outside had subsided, and he assumed the crowds had dispersed. It was very quiet. Looking out the window, he saw that indeed the crowds had gone, but on the roadside by themselves were two girls. One was the girl who had been scolded by the policeman earlier. As Matt watched, she suddenly squatted on the ground and brought her hands up to her face. She was crying. The other girl crouched beside her and began rubbing her back. Then this girl stood up and tugged on the crying girl's arm.

The girl on the ground yanked her arm free, swiveled around, and gave the other girl a hard shove. That girl stumbled backward one or two steps and fell on her rear end. Now both girls were sitting on the ground.

What on earth was going on? Girls of their age shouldn't be out on their own, should they? Hey, you two, hurry up and go home, he wanted to yell. It was getting late. Friday evening was not a good time to be out.

He grabbed his things and ran down the stairs, emerging from the building to find the two girls in the same state.

"Good evening," Matt said in polite Japanese. He was a little out of breath. "Are you girls lost? Do you need some assistance?"

Upon seeing him, they scrambled to their feet.

"Please don't be frightened. I'd just like to help. Are you lost?"

"We're not lost!" The shorter of the two girls spoke in a voice that seemed unusually loud and sharp. He was momentarily taken aback. Weren't Japanese girls supposed to be more reticent?

"Oh, that's good. Well, I'm sorry. But it's getting late, you see. I think that you young ladies might want to head home. Would you like me to get a policeman to escort you?"

"No policeman!" She was practically screaming.

"Okay, okay. No police. I didn't mean to offend you. Would you like a chocolate?" He rummaged in his pockets only to realize that he didn't have any on him.

"I'm sorry," he said. "I guess I don't have anything."

"That's okay." The girl spoke in a more friendly tone.

"I saw you from my window." At this, Matt gestured toward his building across the street.

"You work there?"

"Yes."

"That's where the *Amerikajin* are."

"That's right. Let me introduce myself. I'm Corporal Matsumoto. I'm very pleased to meet you. What are your names?"

"Fumi," the girl with the loud voice replied. The other girl did not speak.

"Do you two girls live nearby?"

"Sort of. Not really."

"What are you doing here? Were you waiting to see General MacArthur's car?"

"Are you an American soldier?" the girl Fumi suddenly asked.

"Yes. I'm with the Occupation forces."

"With General MacArthur?"

"Yes, with General MacArthur."

"General MacArthur is the most important person in Japan."

"Well, I don't know about that."

"He *is*," the girl said emphatically.

"All right, yes, he's very important."

"Do you know him?"

Matt shook his head.

"But he's your leader. You've seen him, haven't you? In person."

Matt thought about how whenever he opened *The Stars and*

Stripes, it was impossible not to see MacArthur's face staring out at him. And yes, he'd seen him in person, too. Shortly after he arrived in Japan, Matt had marched with his unit past MacArthur on the parade plaza in front of GHQ, saluting smartly at the tall figure standing on the podium.

"Yes, I've seen him," he said.

"A lot?"

Matt couldn't help smiling. Now this was unexpected. The little girl was interrogating him!

"Let's just say that he's hard to avoid. He's everywhere. He's the big boss." He chuckled at his own wit.

The girl's eyes brightened. "He's *your* boss, isn't he?"

"I suppose so, in a manner of speaking." Matt smiled again. This was pretty funny. "He's the commander in chief, so in a sense you could say he's my boss."

He watched the girls turn their heads away and whisper to each other. They seemed to be having a disagreement. Then suddenly it was over and the talkative girl, Fumi, approached him. She bowed very low and extended both arms toward him, offering him something. It looked like a piece of paper folded lengthwise.

"Sir, I beg of you, please deliver this to your general, to General MacArthur. It is of the utmost importance."

Matt looked at the other girl, but her eyes gave away nothing.

"Please." Fumi pushed the paper into his hands. "Please deliver this."

"What is it?"

"A very important message for General MacArthur."

"Well, I'm really not sure what I can do." He tried to hand the paper back to her but she refused to accept it.

"Please give it to him. You have to. I think you are the only person I can trust to deliver it to him."

"But I really don't think I should . . ."

She reached into her chest pocket and pulled out a small square of yellowed tissue paper. She seemed to be unsure of what she wanted to do, for she put it back in her pocket, then pulled it out again. She touched her lips to it just before pressing it into his palm.

"What's this?" Matt said. There was something in the tissue paper, he could feel it.

In the second that he glanced down, the girls turned around and ran away like rabbits bounding off into the shadows.

He unwrapped the tissue paper. It was a photograph. A typical shot of a GI with his Japanese girlfriend. The piece of paper he'd been given was a little crumpled. He unfolded it and saw immediately that it was a letter. *Dear General MacArthur*, it began.

To his surprise, it was written in English.

Two weeks passed and Matt still had the girl's letter. He didn't know why he was holding on to it. It was in English, which meant it was supposed to go straight into the basket for English-language mail. All correspondence addressed to MacArthur was supposed to be sent to GHQ without delay. The envelope (if there was one) and the letter itself were to be stamped with the red oval ATIS stamp and the date of receipt inscribed in blue ink. Simple mechanical actions performed by the office secretaries that gave the letters legitimacy and turned them, irrevocably, into government property. But this letter from the girl was different. He couldn't bring himself to submit it. It was written in pencil in a neat cursive script slanted slightly to the right. Every time he read it, he couldn't help but smile. It was rather charming in its quaint language, its earnestness.

Dear General MacArthur,

I am writing to ask for your great and kindly help. I have a serious problem. My sister is missing! Please help me find her.

My sister's name is Sumiko Tanaka and she is twenty-two years old. She works in the Ginza but I don't know where. She used to visit me at home but she doesn't come back anymore. I want to find her. Please find her for me.

I am very, very worried. Maybe she is sick and cannot move or talk? Maybe she had an accident and lost her memory?

She is the kindest sister anyone could have. She made money to take care of me when I was sick. She took care of my mother and my father too. I miss her and want her to come home.

You are the only person in Japan who can help. You said you want to help all the Japanese people. Please help me. Please find my sister. Thank you very much.

Sincerely,

Fumi Tanaka

First-year student at Minami Nishiki Middle School

Chiyoda Ward, Tokyo

P.S. I am already twelve years old and I promise to work hard for our new democracy.

He always chuckled when he got to the postscript. And then he would feel bad. Oh, that poor kid, that poor little twelve-year-old. She was waiting to hear about her sister. She was waiting for help. She was waiting for a goddamn miracle. Honestly, MacArthur was scarcely going to drop everything to send out search parties for a missing bar girl.

Sometimes he looked at the letter and the accompanying photograph when he was by himself in his barracks, taking a short break in the middle of the day. Matt's sleeping quarters were rooms on a different floor of the same building in which he worked, former offices that had been converted into barracks for some of the men in his division. The room was outfitted with six narrow bunk beds; twelve guys, all Nisei, shared the same space. He felt lucky to have drawn the straw that gave him a lower bunk and a measure of privacy.

He took the photograph out of its tissue wrapping and brought it close. The woman was looking directly at the camera with such seriousness of purpose that he couldn't help but feel she was staring straight at him, challenging him in some way. She was an attractive woman, for sure, with delicate, well-proportioned features, and he enjoyed studying her face. But something was missing. He was increasingly aware of how different he was, and how the things that aroused him were not things he could easily share with others.

"Hey, lookey, lookey. This your girl?" Eddie Takagi's head swung down from the upper bunk like a monkey in a tree and his arm sliced through the air. Before Matt even knew what was happening, Eddie's nimble fingers had snatched the photograph.

"What the hell! What are you doing here?"

"Went to sick bay and they told me to go to bed, my own bed. I think they think it's just a hangover, but it's not. It's the flu. I'm sick."

"Give me my document back!"

"Document?" Eddie's guffaw echoed off the ceiling.

"Yes, give it back. Before I—" Matt began climbing up to the upper bunk.

Eddie was sitting up in bed. He held the photograph over his head, and his hand almost touched the ceiling. "So she's the reason you never want to have any fun. How come you never told us you had a girlfriend?" He flapped the photograph in the air and grinned.

"Give it to me, Takagi. I'm warning you."

"Wait a minute. Let me have a good look at your gal. She must be something if you've kept her a secret like this." Eddie squinted at the picture. "What the heck?"

"That's government property. Give it back."

"Matt, you're a pathetic sack of shit. What are you doing with some other slob's photo?"

"Come on, Takagi. I'm not kidding."

Eddie turned the photo over and smirked. "'Babydoll'? You stole this, didn't you."

"I did not."

"Oh, I'm supposed to believe this is your sister?"

"Cut it out. It's none of your business."

"Yeah, well, I can tell you a thing or two about that guy."

"Are you serious? You know the man?"

Eddie brought the photograph up close and made an exaggerated show of scrutinizing the picture. "Okay, let me get a good look here."

"Are you sure? He's got his eyes shut, it's hard to make out his face."

"I can see enough. Yup, I know him." Eddie paused. All trace of his earlier jocularity had vanished. "Maybe not him personally, but I know that type."

Matt exhaled heavily. "Oh, yeah, that type."

"They're everywhere. I know the woman, too."

"Her type's everywhere, too, I guess."

"Well, not exactly." Eddie brought the photograph close again. "No, I'd say she's a little special. A looker like that."

For a moment Matt felt an irrational jealousy at the sight of Eddie staring at Sumiko's picture.

"Actually, she reminds me a bit of someone who used to work at the Midnight Club."

"The big dance hall in the middle of the Ginza?"

"Yeah."

"How long ago was that?"

"What?"

"That you saw her."

"Oh, this was months ago. Could be even a year ago."

"Do you think she might still be there?"

"Wait a minute. I'm not sure it was her. Not at all. Just someone who looked a bit like her."

"But you just said she was special. You'd remember her, wouldn't you?"

Eddie set the photograph down on the bed and slid it in Matt's direction. "Did I? Matt, they're all special. And they're all the same. For God's sake, she's a bar girl."

The weeks passed, and nobody complained when the summer heat and humidity gave way to the crispness of autumn weather. Like everyone, Matt enjoyed strolling up and down the main Ginza boulevard, which during the daytime was packed with people from all walks of life. GIs and Japanese alike were especially fond of congregating in front of the Hattori Watch Building, which had been converted into the Tokyo PX. You could get anything you wanted at the PX—it was hard to imagine a busier intersection in all of

Japan. A private named Barrymore told Matt he saw lots of potential here. "Clean it up and get some lights, we could fix it up like Times Square in New York," Barrymore had said eagerly, somehow conveniently forgetting about the stretch of flattened structures only a few blocks away. "My uncle back home is in real estate. He would know what to do." Barrymore and his buddy had fashioned a handwritten sign out of a piece of broken plywood. BROAD WAY, JAPAN, the sign said in big, slightly crooked letters, accompanied at the bottom by a crude line drawing of a wavy female figure. They had managed to hang their sign over the main entrance to Ginza station but the MPs took it down the next morning. No sense of humor, Barrymore complained.

On the Ginza, everyone was watching everyone else. The Japanese were studying the Americans, and the GIs were eyeing the Japanese women. There was an element of theater to the tango of humanity that, depending on Matt's mood, alternately amused and depressed him. The Japanese clearly didn't know one rank from another, and the way most of the GIs swaggered, you could bet the stories they told were far from true. No doubt, everyone was a general or at least a colonel. The women only saw well-fed, healthy young men who looked like giants compared to their own fathers or brothers. You couldn't blame them for believing the lies they were told, for wanting to believe. Their own stories might not have been entirely truthful, either.

Every so often a young woman would smile at Matt, and he would quickly turn away, embarrassed and flustered. He realized he might have been at fault for staring at her and giving the impression that he was interested. Unconsciously at first, and then with increasing awareness, he found himself scanning the faces in the crowds for the woman in the photograph.

22

It was always too hot in the dance hall where Sumiko worked, it didn't matter what season it was. To prevent anyone from peeking inside, Harada kept the windows tightly shut with all the curtains drawn, and the temperature quickly rose from the heat of so many bodies packed into a single small room.

Why give them a free look? he said. Anyone wants to see, let them pay. But the heat made it hard to breathe, and when she first started to work here an unfamiliar smell assaulted her senses. She asked the other women what it was, but nobody knew what she was talking about. Over time, instead of getting used to it, Sumiko's sensitivity only grew. Finally she identified the odor as a foreign smell, a GI smell. For the longest time she thought the Americans gave off a special odor because of the food they consumed, all the milk and butter and beef and bacon leaking out of their pores as they perspired in the tight confines of the dance hall. Later she came to understand that what her nose detected was more than sweat. It was lust. On a crowded night the dance hall was pungent with this odor. The women smelled different, too, different from ordinary Japanese women. Their bodies oozed a salty perfume of cigarettes and liquor.

Despite his ambitions, Harada's operation was quite modest compared to the really big nightclubs and dance halls. It consisted of one long narrow room about thirty feet by fifteen, with a wooden floor that had been hastily constructed out of scrap lumber and plywood. A coat of watered-down red paint had been slapped on the walls in an attempt to make the room look lively and sensual, but it only highlighted the bumps and fissures in the uneven walls. It reminded Sumiko of the way a woman's lipstick faded and cracked by the end of the night. Every evening she joined the line of women leaning against the red wall and waited to be picked for a dance.

In those early days, she had enjoyed learning how to dance and how to banter in bar-girl English. At first she practiced with other women who were newcomers like her. They held hands and shuffled their feet and pressed their cheeks against each other. One of the women in her dorm, Namie, taught Sumiko how to hide a long sewing needle in the lapel of her blouse which, if necessary, could be used to poke a dance partner who was getting fresh.

"You jab it through their shirt around the midriff like this. They get real startled, don't you know. They can't figure out what's happening. The needle is small so they can't see it."

Sumiko tried it once, but it didn't work.

"That needle's too short," Namie said when Sumiko showed her. "Get a longer one. Loop some thread through the eye so you can pull the needle out fast when you need it. Tuck it under the collar of your top."

Sumiko quickly learned that to dance meant to touch. That was her job—to touch and be touched. Hand clutching hand, hand on her back. Cheek against shoulder, cheek to cheek. Dancing with a GI was different from practicing with one of the dance-hall women. Sumiko would find her face pressed against the buttons of an olive shirt or her nose shoved into a smelly armpit. If the man bent over to shorten his height, her face would end up rubbing against a stubbly beard. Sometimes it scratched like sandpaper.

There was all kinds of touching, she learned.

As they swayed to the music, a hand might start to roam like a curious animal exploring the terrain of her body. If the man held her too tightly and she couldn't reach for her needle, she gave him a kick in the ankle. "Oh, sorry" was the usual mumbled response. And the hand would move up to its proper place, temporarily.

This was the job, and she got used to it.

If a man was decent and polite—and didn't touch too much—

she didn't mind dancing with him. Some GIs were barely older than teenagers, with gangly arms and sweaty palms and feet that were too big. She didn't feel bad letting someone like that press his cheek against hers if it meant she could ask for a package of cookies or a jar of jam. She might even let them run their fingers through her hair for nothing more than a box of Cracker Jack. But she didn't get to choose her partners. Whoever bought a ticket was entitled to a dance. There were plenty of scary men with huge arms and greasy smiles who clenched her in a too-tight embrace.

Once she danced with a GI who had a cluster of red pimples scattered across the bottom of his chin. He seemed nervous and held her at a formal distance, as if he had never danced with a woman before. She'd smiled at him, mistaking his nervousness for innocence and inexperience, until he suddenly pulled her flat against him and shoved her hand along the front of his pants, against the hard lump in his crotch. The buckle of his belt scraped the skin on her forearm when she pulled her hand back.

He'd laughed then. An openmouthed guffaw, as if it was the funniest thing in the world. The pimples on his chin danced in front of her eyes, bouncing red spots.

She didn't scream or even speak. She didn't dare, for fear of how the manager would discipline her afterward. All she could do was stand motionless in the middle of the floor, her head cast down. She wondered if anyone had seen what had happened, but the music played on and the other couples continued dancing, occasionally backing into her.

"Hey, we gotta finish our dance." The man reached forward to put an arm around her waist. "Don't be sore. It was a joke."

She wasn't sure what he had said, but she heard "dance" and she understood they had to finish. He'd paid for a ticket. He'd want his money back, or more.

"Smile for Christ's sake. I said I was sorry."

Yoko had told her the way to survive was to keep smiling. If you didn't understand what a man said, just smile. Americans liked Japanese women who smiled.

It wasn't easy to size up each situation. The cues were all different. No meant yes, yes meant no, or sometimes it didn't matter if you said no or yes, because everything meant yes, yes, yes. Give in and don't make any trouble. Give in and do what you're told. Smile, because no one wants to dance with a grump. Before he opened the doors each evening, the manager ordered them to stand in a line and practice smiling. Put your hand over your mouth to show modesty. Smile, laugh, even when you had no idea what the man was saying. They used words like "honey" and "baby" and "swell" and "shit," and she soon picked up a new vocabulary, which was not at all like the English lessons she had listened to on the radio after the war ended. And what she didn't understand didn't matter. She just smiled and pretended, pretended and smiled.

After the incident with the pimply man, Harada began acting strangely toward Sumiko. When she handed over her ticket stubs at the end of that evening, he didn't count them as he usually did. Instead he reached forward and took her hand.

"Suzie"—he called everyone by their dance-hall names—"how are you doing?"

"Fine." She stared at the dirty ticket stubs she'd placed on the table where he sat. She preferred his businesslike manner, licking his thumb as he counted the money twice before handing it over. She didn't like this sudden friendliness.

"Suzie, Suzie."

He pulled her hand closer and made a show of examining her forearm. The GI's belt buckle had made a long scratch on her skin.

"Does it hurt?" he said with oily concern.

"No, not at all." She tried to pull her hand free, but he had tightened his grip around her wrist.

"You know, everything in life is a lot harder when you resist. I was watching earlier this evening. I think that young man simply wanted you to keep him company."

"Please, it's late."

"You know, when a person has a debt to pay off, she should consider the possibility of making some supplemental income. If you like, I can help you. I can make arrangements."

She tugged on her arm again, but he wouldn't release her.

"Nobody likes a stubborn woman. It's not an attractive feature. Sooner or later, you'll see how important it is to be flexible. That's the kind of girl we like." He fixed his eyes on her meaningfully. "Don't get any bright ideas about going into business for yourself. I always get my cut, don't forget that." He jerked her wrist hard to let her know he could snap it if he wanted to. Then he flung her hand away.

"Please, I'm tired. Could you please pay me for tonight's work." She stared at her pile of ticket stubs.

But Harada made no move to reach into his cash drawer. He pretended to busy himself with writing figures in his ledger.

Keep smiling and pretending. That was what Yoko always said.

Don't resist. That was another rule.

Things happened fast on the dance floor or in the dark alleys. You had to develop a sense for danger, had to smell it coming before anything happened, before it exploded into something ugly, before it turned violent and hard. The safest way to react was not to react. To give in, to be passive. To fall limp, to make yourself small, to curl into yourself and not be a threat.

Don't resist, don't be a fool. Don't resist if your life is in danger.

23

*W*hy the heck would you want to go there?" Eddie said when Matt finally took the plunge and suggested going to the Midnight Club. "If you're looking for that dame, forget it. You're not going to find her."

"Didn't you say you saw her there?"

"I corrected myself, didn't I? I said her *type*. There are a lot of women working in a lot of bars."

"You have to admit someone who looks like that would stick out. That's why you remembered her, surely."

"I told you, I don't remember her. I'm sorry I mentioned it. I was just kidding."

Matt hated to beg but he didn't want to go alone. Everyone knew the Midnight Club was special, more like a high-class nightclub than a regular dance hall. Rumors were that it was very expensive, and that they served potent cocktails that could set your head spinning. More than three of those would knock the average man flat on his back. The place looked intimidating from the outside as well. It was set in a dark alley, and the walls and roof had been painted black. There were no windows. It reminded Matt of a squat black tank, a place you crawled into and hoped you'd come out of in one piece.

"Look, you're always haranguing me about not going out enough. Now I'm saying I want to go to this place. I'll pay for both of us. Are you going to come with me or not?"

Eddie raised his arms in the air to indicate surrender. "Okay, okay. Don't get so worked up."

"This coming Saturday?"

"Yeah, yeah. But she probably won't be there, you know. You're barking up the wrong tree." Eddie was uncharacteristically negative.

"That's fine, but can't we just check it out?"

Eddie shrugged nonchalantly but his brow was furrowed.

On Friday Sab leaned toward Matt and said loudly, "Hey, I heard you and Eddie are gonna paint the town red tomorrow."

Matt looked around nervously to see if anyone had heard. Was there no such thing as privacy around here? Eddie really had a big mouth.

Sab immediately dropped his voice. "Look, it's none of my business, but you don't drink much, do you?"

"Me? No, I'm not a drinker."

"I didn't think so. Well, just a bit of advice to stick to beer and stay away from the hard stuff. You'll get a terrible hangover."

"Like *kasutori*?"

"Oh, that's just ordinary rotgut. I'm talking about the real bootleg." Sab lowered his voice even more. "Did you know they sometimes spike drinks with lubrication fluid?"

"What!"

"Yeah, the alcohol used in airplane engines. Add a bit of sweetener, and you've got something with quite a kick. They call it the *bakudan*—the bomb. After the war ended all the stockpiles went underground. There's a huge surplus of the stuff."

"How do you know all this, Sab?"

"Me? I've just been around. You'd be surprised at what goes on. People will do anything to make a profit."

Although Matt had never been to a place like the Midnight Club, he'd been to any number of cheap dance halls before, the kind frequented by ordinary servicemen. Some were innocent places where you bought a strip of tickets for an evening of dancing, one ticket per dance. You got the chance to briefly rest your hand on a pretty woman's hip and press your cheek close to hers. On those occasions Matt hadn't had a bad time, although initially it had been depressing to see the long line of women standing against the wall waiting to be picked. There were attractive ones, true, but the majority were quite ordinary-looking, some even downright plain, not glamorous in the least despite their standard-issue red lipstick. Once, Matt had danced with a woman who was so tired she nearly fell asleep in his arms. "My baby," she apologized sheepishly. "Cries all the time, I can't get any sleep." He wondered how many of the other women he danced with were war widows.

But other places were out-and-out brothels and made no attempt to hide their real purpose. He'd entered one of those by mistake once and walked straight out, it was so appalling. Cheap plywood booths without doors lined the walls. The only concession to privacy was thin curtains that didn't even reach the floor. The GIs stood in line, each waiting his turn. Matt prayed that Sumiko was not involved in a place like that.

On the evening he went out with Eddie, he showered and put on freshly ironed olive drabs. He combed his wet hair and made a neat part on the right side, and then combed it again and made a new part a little closer to the center. On the walk over, he was so anxious and preoccupied that he didn't notice how quiet Eddie was.

Two Japanese men in ill-fitting suit jackets stood at the entrance to the Midnight Club, and when Matt and Eddie approached, they shifted their weight slightly so their shoulders almost touched. They weren't tall but they gave an impression of heft.

"Good evening." Eddie lowered his head in a short bow and addressed them in polite Japanese. "Is there any chance we might get in tonight?"

Neither of the suits replied, but one smirked faintly.

Eddie tried again. "We understand there's an entrance fee. We can pay in yen, army scrip, or real dollars, whichever you prefer."

The smirker continued smirking. His partner did nothing.

"How much is it?" Eddie said brightly. He turned to Matt and muttered, "We might have to go a little high, okay?"

Matt nodded and reached for his wallet. The two door guards were as impassive as ever. Neither spoke or moved.

Behind them the door swung open, and the man with the smirk quickly turned to grab the handle and hold the door. He now wore a serious expression.

A couple emerged. The woman was Japanese, and her escort was a thin white officer with narrow, rounded shoulders. It was hard to tell in the dim light, but the woman looked like she was at least ten years older than the man on her arm. She swung her hips in a studied side-to-side movement.

She briefly glanced at Matt and Eddie, giving them a cursory assessment. Then she tugged on her escort's arm. It was like signaling a horse to move forward. "Come on, honey," she said in English.

As soon as the couple had left, Eddie tried again. "Well, I guess there's room inside for us now."

The silent guard finally spoke. "*Amerikajin dake.* Americans only."

Eddie swore and began stabbing his chest with his thumb. "We're Americans! Look, GI uniform. *Nikkeijin. Amerikajin.*" He reached into his pocket and Matt thought he was going to show his ID. Instead, he pulled out a ten-dollar bill.

The two doormen did nothing.

"I thought you said you'd been here before," Matt muttered.

Eddie waved the money in the air. "Come on, guys, let us in. Please! *Onegai dakara.*"

"Forget it." Matt began walking away as fast as he could.

"Let us in," Eddie said one last time. He turned and hurried to catch up.

When they reached the end of the lane, Eddie cupped his hands over his mouth and yelled, "Assholes! *Bakayaro!*" That clearly made him feel better, for he looked at Matt and grinned. "That's a shithole anyway. Come on, I'll take you to a much better place."

Pale lanterns were hung here and there along the lane, illuminating a series of tiny bars and outdoor noodle stalls. Some had signs written in English. WELCOME GI JOE. DRINKS, BEERS, HAPPY. AMERI-KAJIN, O-KAY. They'd passed the first sign sometime ago: OFF-LIMITS TO ALL MILITARY PERSONNEL.

"You want a drink?" Eddie asked. "You got yen on you, right? I don't want to waste my greenbacks here."

Matt rarely went to off-limits bars; in fact he didn't even like to drink. But tonight he felt depressed and reckless at the same time. He also wanted to get the evening over with fast, and he sensed that Eddie would be willing to head back to the barracks as soon as he had a drink or two. They ducked their heads under the curtain that hung over the doorway of one of the bars.

"*Irasshaimase!* Welcome!" the bartender shouted out his standard greeting. He stood behind a makeshift counter built of scrap lumber and some boxes. Seating consisted of five rattan stools, all of different heights.

"What are you up for?" Eddie asked Matt when they sat down. "They make some pretty strong stuff out of barley. Want to try?"

Matt declined, and they ordered two glasses of beer.

When the bartender heard their English, he gave them a funny look. Matt had seen it before, that look of confusion that turned into a kind of unreadable blankness. It happened all the time, and he hated it. People didn't know what to make of him, a Nisei in an American uniform. A Nisei in any clothing. How could you be Japanese and American at the same time, was the unspoken question. If you're supposed to be American, how come you look Japanese? If you're supposed to be Japanese, how come you don't talk like us? Or, if your Japanese was good and you did talk like them, the question became, How come you don't *think* like us? There was always one more hurdle placed in front of you, another barrier to acceptance.

Of course it was not as bad as back home in America. No one here had told him "We don't sell to Japs" or thrown a stone through his family's front window. Still, it was complicated. There was envy, and who could blame the Japanese? Anyone who worked for the Occupation forces ate well, dressed well, and generally seemed without a worry in the world. But mingled with that envy was distrust. Who *were* you really? Whose side were you on?

Matt had a cousin in Tokyo, and had once tried to explain to him what it had been like in the camps. The cousin was his own age but a stranger; they had never met until Matt arrived with the Occupation forces. Not surprisingly the cousin didn't know anything about what had happened to his relatives in America during the war. "They shipped us to the middle of the desert," Matt said. "There was nothing around us, nowhere to go, but they built barbed-wire fences and kept armed guards on all the watchtowers." He was surprised at his own passion, for he hardly ever spoke about the experience. None of the other Nisei in his barracks liked to talk about it too much, either. But the only part of his story that made an impression on the cousin was that they'd been forced to eat in a big mess hall, rather than privately with their own families. "What'd you eat?" the cousin kept asking. "What was the food like?"

Eddie chugged his beer and looked at Matt's still-full glass. "Drink up, man. The evening is young."

"I'm okay. I'm nursing this."

"Sure, but you don't mind if I have another, do you?" He lifted his empty glass at the bartender as a signal for a refill. "I need to reward myself. I've had a pretty shitty week, if you must know."

Matt groaned inwardly. He could picture himself stuck for hours with Eddie, a man he really didn't like that much. They were just too different. But it was his own fault for trying to use him, he supposed. He should have guessed that Eddie had never been to that nightclub before, that he had no special connections. The guy was always bragging—bullshitting was more like it. Even the way he looked was unappealing. He had a barrel chest, a thick neck, and a round face with a strong jaw. When he pushed his lower incisors out, he looked just like a bulldog.

"Hey, Matt, ever get those assignments where you want to punch the guy's face into a bloody pulp?"

Matt turned his head to look at Eddie. He was staring at his beer glass.

"I don't know why they picked me but I had to escort some stupid officer—Dexter Johnson, what a stupid name, huh—had to take him shopping. Bigwigs always have stupid names, don't they. Anyway, shopping for souvenirs in Asakusa. He should have gone shopping for his own stinking souvenirs by himself the way everybody else does, but no, I have to take him and translate for him because he thinks he'll get a better price that way. First thing he wants is a Jappie doll. That's what he calls it. 'A Jappie doll, a real cute one for my fiancée back home.' Then he says, 'I'm so glad to be getting out of here, going back Stateside. I suppose for you it's different. You're from here.' I say, 'No, sir, I'm not from here.' He gives me this real queer look, so I explain that I never set foot on Japanese soil till I joined the military. 'Well, I'll be darned,' he says. 'But you came from here, right? Originally.'

"Anyway, that's not the part that drove me crazy. The guy confesses that he initially thought his Japanese girlfriend would help him with his shopping, but when she found out he had a girlfriend back home—a fiancée, no less—all hell broke loose. He stopped in the middle of the street and rolled up his sleeve. 'See this?' he says. 'The bitch bit me. That's a permanent scar. I was lucky I'd already had my tetanus shot. You know, I don't know what the hell got into her to act like such an animal. We had a good time, and then she had to spoil it all. They're not civilized here. They're not. Some of these women are crazy. She thought I was going to marry her and take her back with me to the States. I never promised anything of the kind.'

"The guy was such a prick, I really wanted to sock him right then and there. I wish I had. It would have been worth it. I would have felt better." Eddie seemed unaware that he had clenched his fists so tightly the knuckles had turned shiny white. "Can't you just see me at my court-martial?"

"Hey," Matt said softly. "I'm glad you didn't do that. I don't want to have to train another bunkmate, you know. You're bad enough."

Eddie swallowed a mouthful of beer. The glass was still two-thirds full.

"Let's go," he said, abruptly sliding off his stool. "This stuff tastes like piss, and it's not having any effect. I have a feeling that no matter how much I drink tonight, I won't be able to get good and blasted."

24

*A*ya's father, Toshio Shimamura, had succeeded in becoming invisible. Knowing this was what gave him the strength to do his job. Whether he was pushing his mop down the corridor or wiping windows or hauling out barrels of muck, no one gave him a second glance. The soldiers were used to him by now, the wiry gray-haired Japanese man with a mop whose wooden handle was almost as thick as his skinny forearms. He pushed his mop on the mess-hall floor, sometimes deliberately running it under the tables when the men were still eating, so that occasionally someone got mad and said, "Hey, watch what you're doing. You just got my shoes wet." And he would bow and bob his head up and down and pretend that he couldn't speak English but it wasn't really pretending because his English wasn't that good and anyway it didn't matter because nobody cared. They went back to eating and talking and gossiping and joshing around. They went back for seconds, and sometimes even third helpings. They filled their big American bellies with red meat and mashed potatoes and boiled peas and fat wedges of apple pie. They forgot about the skinny Japanese man who was cleaning the floor of their mess hall, and who would later clean their latrines.

He was so invisible that once, when he'd had to clean in the office where the Nisei translators worked, not one of them even noticed him. They went right on shuffling their papers or chattering away in English or scratching their heads with the ends of their pencils, and if they happened to glance up, they looked straight through him. Why should anyone look twice at an old man with a broom pushing a pile of dust out the door?

He hated this job, but he needed it. He hated his need and that it had forced him to go to Ozawa, who was the friend of a friend but not a good man. He hated how he'd begged for his help.

The job was only temporary, filling in for someone else, but even so Shimamura found that the only way he could cope was to become invisible. To the people around him and to himself.

Ironically it was one of the best jobs you could get, working for the Occupation forces. Everyone wanted a job like this, but not Shimamura. He had never told his daughter where he worked and he never would. She should go on thinking that he continued to pick up odd jobs on the street, as he had when they first arrived. The shame he felt came from working for *hakujin*—American, Canadian, they were all the same—after he'd sworn that he would never work for a white man again. Not after what the white people had done to him and his family. To all of them. What kind of man had so little pride?

But he had to make money. He didn't want Aya to work; she had to go to school and learn, there was no choice. He'd brought her to Japan and now he had to make sure she learned enough Japanese— good Japanese—to make something of herself here. It was the only thing that mattered. Everything was too late for him, but for her, it had to be a new beginning. And if he had to leave her on her own for much of the time, he was sure that she was all right. She was old enough to go to school by herself; she was old enough to manage. After all, hadn't he gone to Canada when he was barely older than she was now, a mere youth of sixteen when he'd crossed the Pacific by himself to join his uncle, who had helped him find work in the sawmills?

"The Occupation needs lots of English speakers," Ozawa had said, "but your English is lousy. They want Nisei, not Issei like you."

"I know *Ingurishu*." He was indignant.

"Hardly!" Ozawa had snorted. "Your kind of broken English is no use. Well, let me see what I can do. I'm sure I can find something. I'll ask my connections."

Shimamura hated that he'd bowed his head and then pretended to offer Ozawa some thank-you money.

"That's okay. Maybe you can help me some other way."

The first time Shimamura had gone into the dispensary was half by accident, half out of curiosity. The hallway was empty; it was that quiet time in the midafternoon when everyone was away doing their jobs, doing something else. The dispensary was at the other end of the corridor from the mess hall, and he had been looking for a sink in which to empty his dirty water to avoid lugging his bucket all the way back to the janitors' room down two flights of stairs. He hadn't expected the dispensary door to be unlocked, and he certainly hadn't expected to find a room with a wide gleaming counter behind which were rows and rows of white cabinets. He opened one cabinet. The shelves were full of bottles of pills and glass vials and rolls of bandages and safety pins and syringes. Aspirin. Talcum powder. Tooth powder. Diarrhea pills. Suppositories. Everything a patient could need was in these cabinets.

He heard footsteps coming down the hallway and quickly closed the cabinet. Grabbing his still-full bucket of dirty water, he faced the door.

"Who the hell are you? What are you doing in here?" The man was in a medic's uniform but his tie was askew, and although it wasn't even three o'clock yet, his breath smelled of alcohol.

Shimamura lowered his head and muttered "Sorry" in Japanese.

"You're not supposed to clean in here. Didn't anyone explain?" The man's face was florid but his voice was calm. "Here, look." He gestured to Shimamura to follow him out into the hallway. Then he pointed at a sign high at the top of the door. RESTRICTED ACCESS. KEEP OUT. "I guess you can't read that, can you. Anyway, it says don't come in here. Those are the rules. Got it?"

Shimamura put on his best display of obsequiousness. He gritted his teeth and bowed again. He hadn't noticed the sign, but he could read it. Although his English was rudimentary, some words he knew by heart. KEEP OUT. Words he'd come to hate more than any other words in the English language. JAPS KEEP OUT. He'd learned what those words meant pretty quickly.

The man let out a big sigh. "Jesus, I wish they hired people who spoke better English. How hard can that be? Oh well, I guess it's not your fault." He reached forward and made to put his hand on Shimamura's shoulder, but, as if thinking better of it, let his arm fall to his side. "Anyway, I don't know how the heck you got in. The door's supposed to be locked." He spoke under his breath, muttering to himself, and made a big show of locking the door. Again he pointed to the notice, this time even more theatrically.

KEEP OUT.

If it hadn't been for that sign, Shimamura might not have come back.

After that encounter, he slipped into the dispensary at times when he knew the medic was sneaking a rendezvous with his Japanese girlfriend. It was safe then. He quickly discovered where the medic hid the key to the main door, and after a little exploring he found a ring of keys that opened the special cabinets, the ones that contained medicine. For the longest time he took nothing. He just looked: little white boxes labeled in English with the names of complicated drugs he couldn't understand but whose value he immediately sensed. If it was locked up, it was valuable to the Americans. If it was valuable, he would take it. Benzedrine, codeine, laudanum, morphine, and much more.

He didn't care if he got caught. But somehow he knew he wouldn't. Even if the doses were counted and someone got suspicious, he knew the medic would only be worried about being disciplined himself and would do anything to hide the discrepancy.

It was always about the taking, not about the money. That was something Ozawa never understood. Shimamura regretted the day he had bragged to Ozawa about what he had discovered. "Bring me some." Ozawa's eyes had lit up. And later, "Bring me more, bring me whatever you can get your hands on. I'll pay you."

Shimamura accepted the money, but he didn't give everything to Ozawa; some he kept at home just to remind himself why he was doing what he was doing. And if anyone had asked, he would have explained what should have been perfectly obvious: He took because white people took.

First they took all the fishing boats and impounded them. Then they took all the cars and the trucks. They took cameras, shortwave radios, and anything that looked like an antenna. They took the farms. They took the restaurants, the grocery stores, the clothing shops, the houses. Shimamura didn't have a boat or a store or even a car, just a small wooden house that had taken all his savings to buy. They took it.

They called him an enemy alien and sent him to a road camp in the Rocky Mountains near the border between British Columbia and Alberta. The Japanese Canadian men would work on sections of the Trans-Canada Highway, clearing forest and building road. The land was rock-hard and unyielding; that was when Shimamura truly understood that this was a country made of stone. They gave him a pick to dig out the boulders and a shovel to scrape at the earth—only the white foremen could set the dynamite—and they paid him twenty-five cents an hour because, after all, this was Canada where they did not believe in slave labor. He would be paid, if only a pittance. But then they deducted the amount he owed for his food and bunk in the road camp, and because he had a wife and a child, they further docked his pay to help cover the cost of their internment in a ghost-town camp in the interior mountains that no one had ever heard of. By the time they added up all the deductions, there was next to nothing left.

They took his dignity and his honor and his pride and his sense of self-worth and still it wasn't enough. They took whatever they could but they always wanted more—his will, his bitterness, his anger. No, he wouldn't give them his anger. That was his to keep. He wouldn't lie down and be meek.

So wasn't it natural that he should want to take? That he should want to know just how it felt to take something from somebody else?

It didn't feel good, though. It didn't make up for what he had lost. Because what he had lost was everything.

25

*A*re you happy?" the GIs always asked.

The Americans loved that word.

"Happy to see me, honey?" "Let me make you happy, baby." There were dozens of variations, but the key word to listen for was "happy."

Sumiko knew she had to smile. If she smiled, it meant she was happy, and if she was happy, the GIs were happy. It didn't matter if she was depressed and homesick, she had to smile and pretend.

Since Yoko's departure, she no longer cared to go to the trouble of making close friends in the dormitory or dance hall. There were too many newcomers, some so young-looking Sumiko was sure they were lying about their age. One insisted she was sixteen, but she couldn't have been much older than twelve or thirteen. Twelve, Sumiko thought with a shudder. That was Fumi's age.

She took the girl aside one day. "You shouldn't be working in a place like this. Leave while you can."

But the girl had given her such a blank look Sumiko wondered momentarily if she were deaf or slow of mind. When she finally spoke, her voice was like a robot, flat and monotone. "You don't understand. My father is dead. My mother is dead. I have a younger brother and sister, and I'm their sole support. I've tried other things, but we're still too hungry. This is a really good job. You don't understand how happy I am."

It was a good reminder, Sumiko thought. Whenever she started to waver about visiting home, she would think about that girl, and her resolve would be strengthened. No, she would not go home, not yet. Fumi should never be allowed to think this was a glamorous job. This was not a happy place.

From time to time, Sumiko went by herself to Wada's bar, a place she used to frequent with Yoko after work. It was not like the other bars and snack clubs that catered to GIs. It was far enough away from the main Ginza district that the customers were ordinary working-class Japanese. Mr. Wada, the owner, had lost everything during the war—his wife, his son, his home, his business—yet he had somehow never lost his determination to keep on going. To Sumiko, he was an inspiration. When Wada first started out, the "bar" didn't even have four walls. It was an open-air stall that stood all by itself in the middle of an empty field. The counter was made of a broken door laid sideways. Gradually he made significant improvements, cobbling together pieces of scrap wood and bamboo screens and straw mats and anything else he found discarded nearby until he'd created a modest establishment with four sturdy walls and a roof. It was just a tiny square of space, but to Sumiko it felt comfortable and inviting. The progress of Wada's bar had always struck her as a way of measuring how things were improving in the city, and perhaps that was why she liked it. That, and Mr. Wada's delicious noodles. Often he fed her without charge.

He always asked her the same question: "What are you doing here?" Meaning what was she doing working in a dance hall. "Go home," he would say. "You don't belong here." She would try to explain her problem with the debt, but he pooh-poohed this.

"Don't let yourself be bullied," he said. "Your dance-hall owner is a cheap punk, nothing more. His sphere of influence doesn't extend one foot beyond his doorstep. Besides, that type is lazy. When was the last time you saw him go after someone who left the dance hall? Why would he bother when he's got an endless supply of women?"

"Maybe you're right, but . . . It won't be too much longer, I hope."

"All right, but at the very least, you should go see your family. They must be worried."

She told him about her fears that she would influence her impressionable younger sister.

"How old is your sister?"

"Twelve."

"Hmm. That's a tricky age. Half child, half adult, not a child anymore but not an adult, either. But maybe you don't give her enough credit. You seem to believe she can't think for herself."

"It's not that. There are a lot of temptations." Sumiko didn't like to recall how she herself had fallen for some of those very temptations.

Wada kept a picture of his wife and son in a small altar that he'd set up behind the counter. He said he talked to his wife every day and asked her for advice. "The one thing she couldn't help me with was the name," he said. "You and Yoko were the ones who named my bar."

"Your place doesn't have a name," Yoko had said one night.

"What do I need a name for?"

"It's good for business. Something in English would make your place really stand out."

"Okay, so how about My Bar?"

Yoko wrinkled her nose. "That's boring."

"Tell me a better name, then."

"How about Lucky Strike, like the cigarettes?" Sumiko suggested.

Yoko clapped her hands together. "That's it! Let's call it Bar Lucky."

"Lucky, huh," Wada said. "Well, I suppose it can't do any harm."

He found someone to embroider the words BAR LUCKY in large English letters onto the navy blue *noren* that hung over the doorway.

Although the curtain was now soiled from the grease of so many heads that had brushed against it going in and out, Wada said it would be bad luck to take it down for even one day to wash it.

Once Sumiko had asked Wada about those days right after the war ended and how he'd managed. She had been in a self-pitying mood that day—homesick and also missing Yoko's companionship—and maybe unconsciously wanted to hear about someone else's suffering. Wada became pensive.

"The war was terrible. I saw men do awful things, unimaginably horrible things. It was a miracle that I survived. Our commander went insane; those of us who had not been killed in combat were all slowly dying of dysentery or cholera or starvation. But I was determined to make it home. When I finally returned, I discovered that my house had burned to the ground and my wife and young son were dead. At that moment I realized what a stupid mistake I'd made. I shouldn't have tried so hard to stay alive. What was the point? Now I was going to have to figure out a way to do myself in, and this would require some real effort. I went to the Sumida River and marched back and forth along the banks trying to decide the best place to jump in. I can't swim, so I figured this was a foolproof method. But something kept pulling me back, quite literally. Every time I tried to jump, I felt a tugging on my pant leg, but when I turned around there was no one. And then I knew it was my son. He was seven when he died, but I hadn't seen him for three years because I'd gone to war, so he was four when I remembered him last. Such a small boy, he had a habit of pulling on the back of my pant legs when he wanted my attention."

Sumiko could hardly breathe. "So it was a ghost. Your son came back as a ghost."

"I don't know about that, but I do know that I suddenly realized that I owed it to him to continue living. He was so young when he died, he'd hardly had any chance to experience the bounty of life. So then and there I resolved that I would live my own allotment of life but also his share, the part that he didn't get to live. I think we owe it to the dead to do that. We're luckier than they are, so we have a responsibility."

"I'm so sorry," Sumiko cried out, ashamed of what she'd done. "I didn't mean to make you relive such a painful experience."

"It's all right," Wada said quietly. "Anyway, there's nothing I can do about it. I have to accept it."

26

I think you might enjoy this," Baker said when he handed Matt the book.

The exchange had taken place after five o'clock when they were alone in the office. The official announcement of Baker's transfer had been made only the day before.

"Do you know Natsume Soseki?" Baker continued. "*Kokoro* is one of his most famous novels. I really hope you like it."

Matt turned the book over in his hands. The characters for the title and the author's name were stamped in gold leaf on the burgundy cover and down the smooth spine. Heart. The title *Kokoro* meant heart. The leather binding was soft to the touch, as if it had been caressed by many hands over the years. "It's a beautiful book. It looks very expensive."

"Oh, no, it was cheap. I got it in Kanda, the used-book district. I go there all the time. I'll take you there." Baker paused. "I mean, after I get back."

"Do you . . . do you know how long you'll be in Osaka?"

"Oh, you know the army. They won't tell me anything except that I'm to work on some secret project where they need my translation skills. I guess I'll find out later. It's a temporary reassignment but I have no idea for how long. I was told to pack up all my things."

"Oh, I see. And you're leaving tomorrow?"

Baker nodded. "Yes, crack of dawn. You know, I really wish they'd given me more notice."

Matt bowed his head and focused his gaze on the book he held in his hands. "Well, sir, it's a good opportunity to see another part of Japan, isn't it." When he looked up, he met Baker's eyes.

"Yes, it is . . . corporal," Baker said softly.

"You'll be just in time for the autumn leaves. The *momiji* in Kyoto are supposed to be beautiful. I hope you get to see them, sir."

Baker didn't reply.

Suddenly Matt thrust the book forward. "Are you sure you want me to keep this? Maybe you'd rather take it with you."

Baker pushed the book back at him, and for a few electric seconds Matt felt Baker's hands on top of his own. His grip was strong. "No! No, it's for you. I want you to read it."

They stared at each other, and then Baker pulled the book from Matt. He took out a pencil and started laughing as he wrote something on the inside. "Here you go, Matsumoto. It's a loan. That way you have to give it back to me when I return."

"Yes, a loan." Matt laughed and hugged the book to his chest. "I'll give it back to you. That's a promise."

Of course, Matt didn't tell a soul about the book, and he wasn't about to bring it out when the other guys in his barracks were around. He started taking it with him to the park, always carrying a dictionary along too because he had to look up a lot of words. It was the first time he'd ever tried reading a whole novel in Japanese and it was slow going. Sometimes he just liked holding the book in his hands—the feel of the soft leather cover on his fingers, the feel of Baker's fingers on the backs of his hands.

Kokoro. Why had Baker given him a book called "Heart"?

From the time he was a child, Matt had learned to keep the matters of his heart private. In his family, the word "love" was never used. The stomach is the most important organ of the body, his father always said, patting the *haramaki* he wore wrapped snuggly around his belly, winter and summer. Got to keep it warm! His sister was thoroughly American, but even Diane never talked about love. She'd had her share of Nisei boyfriends before the war, and later there were others she met in the camp. She would walk up and down the dust-filled paths with them, from one section of the barbed-wire fence to the other. Observing them, it had always struck Matt as a bit mechanical, as if they were doing it out of duty or to put on a show for the guards in the watchtowers. To prove that romance was still possible, even here.

Matt's habit of reticence and secrecy was so deeply ingrained that sometimes he wondered if he was guarding his heart from himself. What did his heart feel? What did his heart yearn for? Since coming to Japan, Matt felt this question arise with greater frequency. He considered the hearts of all the people he'd met here. There was Nancy, who was clearly unhappy and wanted to go home. She bewildered him. Sometimes she was confident and bossy, other times insecure and dependent. She expected him to take charge, but she wanted to tell him what to do. There was the missing woman, Sumiko, whose picture he carried with him all the time. She was an enigma. She was only a celluloid image, but why did her stare haunt him so? Then there was her little sister, Fumi. She was crazy if she thought that MacArthur would help her—MacArthur wasn't going to help anyone. In that case, who would?

These random thoughts floated through his mind as Matt made his way toward his favorite bench in the park. He couldn't wait to continue reading again. So when he reached the section where the footpath curved and the bench came into view, he was mightily annoyed to see that someone else was on *his* bench. Not just sitting on it, either, but lying down, stretched out along the entire length. Some drunk or derelict, he supposed, sleeping off a bad night. Who else would fall asleep like that in the middle of the afternoon? By the time he was within a few feet, however, Matt could see that the figure was too small to be a man. It was a woman.

She had her back to him and her shoulder blades stuck out through her thin cotton yukata like a pair of wings. Something about the way her body was awkwardly bent reminded him of a grasshopper. Her feet were bare, the soles dirty and calloused. A pair of wooden sandals was tucked underneath the bench. She did not appear properly attired for the cooler weather. As he was staring at her, she casually rolled over. "Hello," she said, gazing up at him sideways. She looked like a teenager, not much older than a girl.

"I'm sorry. I thought you were asleep."

"I wasn't asleep." She pushed herself up into sitting position and her long braid swung forward. "I'm just killing time."

"I see."

"If they ask me to leave the room for a while, I always come to the park. This is a good place to kill time."

"Who asks you to leave your room?"

"The big sisters. It's not my room anyway, it's theirs, so I have to do what they ask, don't I. When they bring a GI friend over."

Matt frowned.

The girl continued. "I really like it here. It's quiet and peaceful, don't you think?" She looked up at the tree overhead as if seeking confirmation from the vegetation. "Say, can I ask you a question?"

He nodded.

"How come you're dressed like a GI?"

"I'm an American."

"But you look Japanese."

"I'm Japanese, too. I'm Japanese American."

The girl pondered this for a moment, then broke into a grin. "I want to go to America."

"Really."

She grinned again and nodded vigorously. The space between her two front teeth gave her an impish appearance, and it was hard not to be infected at least a bit by her enthusiasm.

"Japan is nice, too, you know," he ventured. "This is a very nice country."

"America is better. It's got everything. Someday I'll go."

"Well, I hope you will."

"Oh, you bet I will! Say, what's your name?"

"Matsumoto. What's yours?"

"My name's Hisa—I mean, Betty." She had a slight lisp and pronounced it *beh-chi*.

"Betty?"

She nodded.

"That's a nice name. I'm pleased to meet you, Betty."

She beamed. "Me, too." Suddenly she pointed at his watch. "What time is it?"

"Almost four o'clock."

"Oh, I have to go. I might have killed too much time!" She quickly slipped her feet into her sandals. "Bye bye," she said in English, waving her hand.

It wasn't until after she'd passed out of his range of sight that he noticed a scrap of paper on the bench where she'd been sitting. He picked it up. Heti, Bety, Betti, and other English names had been written in hesitant wobbly letters—the girl had been trying to spell her new name. On the other side of the paper she'd written in Japanese characters: Ginza, Yurakucho, Hibiya, Nihonbashi over and over, as if practicing the kanji or learning a new geography. Matt thought of the girl's silly smile as he put the paper back on the bench and turned to his book. He began reading, but after only a couple of pages he gave up. No, he didn't feel like reading. Something about the girl had made him think of that other girl, Fumi, and now it was hard to concentrate. Matt sighed and glanced at the empty space on the bench beside him. The scrap of paper had already blown away.

27

Ever since they had delivered the letter, it was hard for Fumi to contain her impatience. She was back at school, but who could concentrate on studying when so much was happening in real life? She could barely sit still.

Her mother seemed to have an endless number of chores to keep her occupied after school and on the weekends, but whenever she could, Fumi sought to escape the confines of her home and neighborhood. The wide world was waiting, and she felt an overpowering urge to embrace it.

She was always on the lookout for junk, an activity which was by no means frivolous. Whenever she found something discarded on the street—a scrap of cloth, a cracked plate, a cushion splattered with mud—she investigated and usually picked it up to take home to her father who, ever since their bookstore had burned down, made his living collecting old newspapers and magazines for recycling. He went all over the city begging for unwanted papers, which he hauled in a makeshift wooden cart. Along the way, he often picked up other garbage. Not everything had value, of course, but Fumi had learned from him that sometimes you could be surprised. Scraps of material, for instance, might still have buttons attached or even a fancy clasp, and a cracked plate could be fixed with some glue. A few times she had been lucky to find empty tin cans, which were valuable for the metal they contained. Her father sold what he collected to a variety of dealers, most of whom gave him a pittance for his troubles.

Occasionally her father met people who were desperate enough to sell their books for next to nothing. He would pile what they gave him into his cart, head for a sunny corner, and spread the books neatly on the roadside. Then he waited for customers. A book here, a book there—often he made no money at all—but it was almost like the bookstore days again. He told Fumi that nobody wanted to read the classics anymore. Penny romances and pulp magazines were the current rage. Some of the covers she'd seen were illustrated with men and women embracing, their lips almost touching, and the captions promised exciting stories of romance and love. When she'd asked if she could read them, her father had winced and said they were too contemporary for a young girl like her.

Sometimes people recognized him as the former owner of Tanaka Books. Fumi had been with him a few times when it happened. "Is it Tanaka-san? How nice to see you. You look so healthy." But all the while the person was studying her father's dusty clothes or staring at the wooden cart and its contents. People liked to compare. To measure how far another had fallen was to confirm how fortunate you were.

Akiko and Tomoko still made Fumi laugh with all the naughty things they said about other girls in their class—how Michiko's father wore a toupee or how Sanae tried to straighten her bowed legs by binding them with string—but Fumi now spent most of her time with Aya. She was grateful that Aya was not a talker or a gossip. It had been a big risk confiding in her and asking for help with the English letter. A different type of person might easily have pressed for some kind of advantage. Fumi shuddered to think what that would be like.

That letter! She counted on her fingers—eight weeks had passed. What was taking so long? Why was her sister not home yet? Didn't General MacArthur say he was here to help the Japanese people? Wasn't she one of the people he was supposed to help? Even if he was a busy man, that didn't lessen her sense of frustration. She yearned for his full attention but had to content herself with the pictures of him she saw in the newspaper. He was often seated at his desk, pen in one hand and pipe in the other, gazing straight into the camera.

Whenever Fumi saw one of these pictures, she whispered: "Listen to me! Answer me!" She did not know how long it was reasonable to wait for a reply.

※

One Sunday Fumi persuaded Aya to accompany her to Kanda. It was only a twenty-minute walk.

"I'll show you where my father's bookstore used to be," she said. "I hardly ever show anyone where it was." The truth was that she sought an excuse to see it again for herself and didn't want to go alone. Lately she felt a desperate need to confirm that the store had existed, as if that fact would also prove that her family had once been whole.

While few stores in the book district had escaped damage during the wartime bombings, some were hit much harder than others. Tanaka Books had been located on a narrow side street at the far end of the district, and when it caught fire, it and the bookstores on either side burned completely to the ground in a matter of hours. The winds had been against them, and the books and wooden bookcases had provided the perfect fuel. They were supposed to be thankful that no one was in the store at the time. Fumi's father had never owned the land or the building, just the contents, all of which were lost. Once the store was razed, the plot of land on which it had stood looked ludicrously small, a space hardly bigger than a closet. Without walls, a roof, or a floor to define the space, without the books themselves to suggest function and purpose, there was nothing but a square of gray, dust-filled air.

"Hello, girls. You want to buy a pot?" A thin woman wearing a dirty apron sat on the ground where the bookstore had been. She pointed her chin at Aya. "You there, you need a democracy pot for your family?" At the woman's feet lay a small pile of battered saucepans. Some were burned black on the bottom.

Aya shook her head and backed away.

Fumi spoke up. "My father used to have a bookstore here."

"Where?"

"Right where you're sitting."

"Is that so? I never heard that." The woman shrugged.

"Why are you selling pots and pans here?" Fumi asked.

"Why not?"

"Most people around here sell books, don't they?"

"Pots are better than books. You can't eat with a book." The woman laughed and her tongue stuck out between a gaping hole in her front teeth. "Move along now. If you're not buying, don't block my other customers."

It seemed impossible that the lumpy patch of soil where the woman sat had once supported her family's business. Fumi tried to picture the exact spot where her father used to sit behind the cash box, the place where they kept the ladder for climbing up to the top shelves, the cupboard where Sumiko stored the dustcloths and supplies. But she couldn't remember. The pots had asserted their right to take up residence on the site and they had taken over for good.

As soon as they were out of earshot, Aya asked why the woman had called her wares "democracy pots."

"Because that's what they are. That's what they're called."

"But why?"

"How should I know! Everything's democracy now."

"I'm sorry. I didn't mean to make you angry."

"I'm not angry."

Fumi was walking faster and Aya had to rush to keep up. "Was it a nice store?" she asked. "It doesn't look like it was very big."

"Of course it was a nice store."

"I'm sorry."

"You can't help it. You have no imagination. Just because you can't see anything now doesn't mean it wasn't nice in the past."

"You're right. I'm sorry."

"Oh, stop apologizing." Fumi abruptly turned the corner. "Well, that's enough. Let's go home. We can take a shortcut down this back lane."

The lane was very narrow and lined on either side with shacks made of corrugated sheeting. There were no spaces between the shacks and no windows in any of the walls. Although it was a sunny day, in the lane it was as dark as if a thunderstorm were brewing. It didn't look like many people ever came down here.

"Let's hurry," Aya said, pulling the collar of her blouse close to her neck.

"Oh, look." Fumi pointed her finger straight ahead. "Hey, do you see that?"

In a patch of tall weeds against one of the walls something caught their eye. Aya realized it was the metal strap around a wooden bucket, the kind of bucket that people here used for everything from storing rice to making pickles to hauling water. The bucket was nestled in the weeds, and someone had tried to hide it by laying some long stalks of grass across the mouth. The effort had been done too hastily, though, for the bucket was clearly visible.

"A bucket," Fumi said eagerly. Her bad mood was completely forgotten. "I bet my father can use that."

"We should leave it alone. It's not ours."

"Don't be ridiculous. It doesn't belong to anyone. I'm going to take it." Fumi stomped on the weeds to flatten them and brushed the stalks of grass from the top. "What did I tell you. Look, there's something inside."

Aya leaned forward. Inside the bucket was a rolled-up bundle of cloth, a blue-and-white print covered with a pattern of bamboo shoots. In contrast to the dirty bucket, the cloth looked clean and new.

"It looks like someone's yukata, doesn't it," Fumi said. "A nice yukata, almost brand new."

"Do you think the person is going to come back for it?"

"Not likely. But if they do, well that's too bad, because I'm taking it home."

"You can't."

"I can. You can tell this was thrown out." Fumi reached into the bucket and pulled out the bundle. "Oh, there's something inside, I can feel it. You know, it might be something valuable."

Aya watched as Fumi put the bundle on the ground and began unwinding the material. They shouldn't be doing this, she thought. They were going to find something bad, she just knew it—stolen goods or a piece of rotting fish—but she felt helpless to stop Fumi, who was practically grunting as she struggled to loosen the tightly wrapped cloth. Then, maybe because she was thinking of rotten fish, Aya became aware of a bad smell.

"Ugh!" Fumi jumped back so hard she fell on her rear end.

For a second Aya thought she might faint, but she didn't. She stared straight on, without flinching. She held her breath, but did not avert her eyes. With her last tug on the material, Fumi had exposed the baby's face. The rest of its body remained tightly swaddled.

They stared at their discovery, too shocked to move.

Fumi spoke first. "Do you think it's . . . ?"

Holding her hand over her nose, Aya bent closer and gingerly pulled more of the material away from the baby's head and shoulders. Fumi crouched down beside her.

The baby was tiny with very dark skin, a deep rich hue of brown like the color of the earth after a long rainfall. It had a surprisingly thick head of hair, damp springy little curls that covered its miniature skull. Its thin lips were primly pursed in a wiggly line, and its eyes were closed, as if it were sleeping. They could see two lines of thick curly lashes rimming the bottom of its large round eyelids. What if it opened its eyes, Aya thought. What would they do?

"Is it dead?" Fumi whispered.

"I don't know."

"Why does it look like that? It doesn't look Japanese."

Aya didn't say anything at first. Finally she said, "I think we should put it back, don't you? Maybe its mother will come back soon."

Aya put her finger on the baby's tiny cheek. Its skin was slippery and a little cold. She wrapped the cloth over its face and put the bundle back in the bucket where they had found it. When she finished, she realized she was shaking uncontrollably. Next to her, Fumi was shaking, too.

Without exchanging a word, they both began running.

28

*A*fter working all Saturday night in Love Letter Alley, Kondo usually didn't get home until early morning. He would crawl onto his thin futon in his underwear and, exhausted from the long night, surrender immediately to the dark pull of sleep. But no matter how tired he was he never allowed himself to sleep in too late. Sunday afternoons were the only time he had to himself, and he used it to browse the used-book stores, a practice he had begun as a student long before the war. It was one of the few pleasures he permitted himself. During wartime, the English-language books he loved so much had been taken off the shelves, and he had missed them greatly. He'd had to content himself with perusing the Japanese classics—this was not a bad thing, for there were many works he hadn't read—and even some German books, though he knew hardly a word of German. Having little or no money to buy books had never been a problem, for browsing was free. But Kondo wanted more. He wanted to own his books, to have his own personal library. As much as he could, after buying the food that he needed, he set aside the rest of his extra money for this purpose.

The book district was slowly beginning to recover. At first there were only a fraction of the original number of stores, and even they were mainly empty, their stock having been destroyed during the bombings. A few stores had miraculously been spared; their walls remained intact, their books unscathed if a little dusty. But other stores had been obliterated. Kondo knew that the father of one of his students had lost everything. He remembered the store—Tanaka Books—and even recalled having had conversations with the owner, but that seemed like a lifetime ago. Now if he came across Tanaka hawking cheap pulp magazines on a street corner, he tried to avert his gaze. It was the best way to preserve what remained of the poor man's dignity. He wondered if Tanaka would do the same for him if he spotted Kondo at work in Love Letter Alley.

Today he thought he might go to Kobayashi Shoten. The store specialized in art books and lately had begun carrying works on European art that were hard to find elsewhere. Kondo liked the impressionists. How he enjoyed looking at the works of Renoir—the facial expressions the man created were exquisite. Toulouse-Lautrec was another favorite. Those sad drunken faces brought him an odd solace. Why was that? Was it simply knowing that there were other people in the world like that? Even if you were white and European, he thought, you might be lonely, too.

He had just turned the corner onto the street where Kobayashi Shoten was located, when he almost collided with Fumi and Aya. Or rather, they almost collided with him, for they were the ones who were running recklessly down the narrow sidewalk, unmindful of the book displays outside the stores and of the other people who were strolling in the district.

"Miss Tanaka! Miss Shimamura!" He automatically assumed his teacher's voice.

The girls had been running hard. Their hair was messy, their brows shone with sweat, their faces were tear-streaked and blotchy. Their shoulders heaved up and down.

"What's the matter?" he said. Now he was really concerned. They were his pupils, and it was obvious that something was wrong. For a second it crossed his mind that they had stolen something and were running away from a shopkeeper. If so, he would have to give them a lecture on ethical behavior. He straightened his posture and made himself a little taller. "You can tell me," he said. "What's the matter?"

"Terrible, Sensei. It was awful." Fumi spoke haltingly between loud gulps of air.

"What?"

"We have to show him," Fumi said to Aya. She turned to him. "Kondo Sensei, please come with us."

The girls hurried back in the direction they'd come from, and Kondo had to quicken his pace in order to keep up with them. They threaded their way down the crowded main street and past all the used-book stores until they reached a passageway between two stores that led to a sunless back lane. It was near the site of the former Tanaka Books.

Fumi and Aya walked halfway down and stopped.

"Over there," Fumi said, pointing to a wall where overgrown weeds sprouted thickly.

"Where?"

"In the weeds. There's a bucket. There's something inside."

He went over. Sure enough there was a bucket and inside there was a bundle of cloth. It was probably someone's clothing. He turned around to look at the girls who hung back several steps, and wondered if they were playing a prank on him, but their faces were if anything more strained and anxious than before.

"Please, Sensei, it's not our fault. We found it by accident."

As soon as he picked up the bundle of clothing, he realized there was something inside, something that smelled a bit off. The cloth—a lightweight yukata—was clean, so it couldn't have been exposed to the elements for very long. He lifted the top folds of the material and saw the baby's face. He'd never seen one like this before though he had heard there were lots of them now.

"Sensei, it's not alive, is it?" It was Fumi's voice at his side. He shook his head. There were no signs that the baby was breathing. He wondered if it had even taken its first breath.

"No," he said quietly. "No, it's not."

Maybe someone else would have examined the baby right then and there. Perhaps he should have unwound the cloth completely and taken a good look. Later, when he watched what the police did at the station, he realized that there might have been something tucked inside—an amulet or a note with a name—and he could have been the first to discover it. But he didn't want to touch the baby. Not because of its color or the fact that it was dead. No, he didn't want to sully the baby by putting his dirty life-soiled fingers on its beautiful body. The baby struck him as so pure, a tiny Buddha come to earth. He felt he didn't have the right to touch it.

At the neighborhood police station, they treated the matter with such callous indifference, Kondo regretted letting the girls come with him. They had walked together to the station, and the whole time Kondo had cradled the baby gently in the crook of his arms. It didn't matter that it was dead. The girls flanked him on either side, leaning toward him in an uncharacteristically intimate way, as if he were their father. Maybe they had wanted to protect the baby, too. The officer on duty took the baby like he was handling a clump of unwashed clothes and set it down on the dirty counter. Kondo shuddered. He hated to think what else had touched that counter recently—some punk gangster leaning his greasy shirt against it as he offered a bribe, or a woman of the night sprawled drunkenly across it. The policeman quickly unwound the cloth, and laid the naked infant on its back. He turned his attention to the material.

Kondo saw that it was a boy. The baby's tiny fists were clenched tightly to its chest like a boxer ready to fight.

The policeman shook out the yukata, snapping it in the air several times.

"Got to check for ID or a note, just in case," he said. He made a show of looking on the floor. "See, nothing at all. That's the way it always is."

He rolled the yukata into a ball and put it back on the counter beside the tiny body. Then he opened a drawer, got a small label, and in black ink wrote "Unknown," followed by the date and time. He tied the label to the baby's foot with a piece of thin wire.

Kondo wished he could pull some of the material over the baby's body. Instead he said, "I suppose there is no way to trace the mother?"

"You can see there's no note. No identification."

"Yes, I can see that. But do you think there might be other clues? Perhaps the yukata might be a lead."

"Not possible. This kind of cheap cotton kimono. Besides, it's dead, isn't it. Even when they're alive, we can't do anything. There're too many of them."

"Oh, I see. Yes, I suppose so." Kondo was conscious of the girls standing next to him and hoped they didn't really understand.

"Are you kidding? You wouldn't believe!" The policeman laughed crudely. He was a thin man with leathery skin and deep wrinkles around his mouth. "A lot of them look like that, too."

He picked up the baby and took it into the back room. When he returned to the counter, he looked surprised that they were still there.

"Hey, you don't want that yukata, do you?" he asked, pointing at the material on the counter.

"It's not mine," Kondo said.

The policeman fingered the yukata as if assessing the thickness of the cotton. "It looks pretty new. Well, I guess we better keep it here at the station."

Kondo knew that the policeman was going to take it home and give it to his wife or daughter. There were some bloodstains but those could be washed out. The material was still good. It could certainly be reused. A policeman's salary was as bad as a teacher's.

"What are they going to do with the baby?" Fumi asked as soon as they left the station.

"Don't worry." He tried to sound reassuring. "The police will take care of it properly."

"Will they give it a funeral?"

"Maybe. I'm not sure."

All three of them were silent for a moment. Then, just when he thought Fumi was finished with her questions, she spoke again. "Sensei, why did the baby look like that? Why didn't it look Japanese?"

He wasn't prepared for her directness. Fumi often struck him as naïve and worldly at the same time.

"Actually, he was half Japanese and half—"

"*Amerikajin.*" Aya completed his sentence. "American soldier."

When he swiveled his head in her direction, he was surprised by the heat of her gaze.

Now it was Aya's turn to question him. "Who is going to tell the baby's mother where he is?" she asked. "How is she going to know where to find him?"

Kondo wasn't prepared for this question, either, but an answer came to him immediately. "Aya, a mother always knows where her baby is. Don't worry, she is praying for him in her heart."

Thank goodness for the sweet-potato peddler. His cart was passing at just the right moment, his singsong chant—"*Yaki-imo! Yaki-imo!*"—growing louder as he moved in their direction. The potatoes were roasted whole over a small charcoal fire that he stoked in a metal tin.

"Are you girls hungry? I hear the sweet-potato cart, don't you?"

Kondo watched the girls struggle to peel off the crisp outer skin and devour the sweet orange flesh of the potato without burning their lips or fingertips. They were smiling, and he hoped that, with this distraction, the baby would be forgotten.

29

*A*ya wondered if the baby gave Fumi the same kind of nightmares as he did her. For a long time after they found him, he came to her every night, always naked but each time somehow bigger and more muscular. He lay on his back, his chubby arms and legs churning energetically in the air, his powerful fists clenched over his chest. His head was gigantic, and although he sometimes opened his mouth wide as if waiting to be fed, his eyes remained tightly shut, just as when they had discovered him. The dream refused to release her, and she feared the moment when he would open his eyes. The terror was so real that in the morning her nightgown would be drenched in sweat. She knew that when he opened his eyes, the first person he would see would be her. And she knew he would ask, "Mother, why did you leave me behind?"

It was the question she always asked. It was the question that had no answer.

Aya had seen a dead baby before. In the internment camp, there was a young mother whose baby died at birth. For a full week, the woman refused to give it up, screaming hysterically if anyone tried to take it from her. As soon as she could get out of bed, she went from person to person, even among the children, asking if they wanted to take a look. Aya had caught a glimpse of a tiny skull with a tuft of black hair; it was poking out of a bloodstained towel. "Don't look!" Aya's mother had pulled her away, tried to cover her eyes. But it was too late. She'd already seen it.

Aya was too young at the time to fully understand what was happening, but the hushed voices of the other women lingered in her mind long after the event had passed. The woman's husband had been sent even farther away than Aya's father—to a place somewhere in the wilderness of northern Ontario. A POW camp, someone whispered.

"It was worry that killed her baby." The old grandmothers talked among themselves in the bathhouse. "*Kawaiso.* So pitiful. Worry is a poison. It went straight into her womb."

Aya didn't know what a womb was, but she pictured a soft pink sac that sagged heavier and heavier as it slowly filled with the black fluid of worry. Fearing the young mother might do something to herself, the other women set up a watch and took turns following her around. Aya's mother seemed particularly affected by the woman's grief.

Aya's friend Midori said that dead babies went to *Sai no Kawara*—the Children's Limbo. The banks of the River Sai were rocky, and there was nothing to play with except the stones on the shore. The children built little piles of stones here and there, little piles of memory so no one would forget them. No sooner had they built a pile but it would be knocked down and they had to start all over again. Was it cold there? Aya wondered. Were they lonely?

When winter came to their camp, the temperature plunged and it began to snow. White pellets fell ceaselessly from the huge gray sky. Aya had seen snow only three times before in Vancouver, soft fat flakes that fluttered to the sidewalk like feathery petals and dissolved as soon as they touched the ground. She remembered trying to catch them on her tongue. But in the mountains the snow was different. The flakes were small and hard and persistent. The snow fell for days without stop until the lake was covered and all the pine trees on the mountainsides wore heavy capes of white. The ground, the shore, the peaks, the sky: The whole world looked like it would remain white forever.

Each day was colder than the one before until it became too cold to snow. Too cold to breathe. Too cold for blood to flow. Inside their tarpaper shacks, they put on every piece of clothing they'd brought with them, even their Sunday dresses, layering one on top of the other like clowns.

"The government knew all about this," Mrs. Takahara said to Aya's mother. Aya and her mother shared a cramped, freezing shack with another family, Mrs. Takahara and her three children. "They studied the long-range weather forecast and picked this as the coldest place they could send us. They knew exactly what they were doing."

"Bobby and Tom are going to walk across Slocan Lake." Midori threaded her arm through Aya's as they walked in the snow. "Don't tell anyone. It's a secret, of course."

"But they can't," Aya said. "It's not allowed."

Their ghost-town camp had no barbed-wire fence, but the mountains and lake formed natural barriers. Aya imagined an invisible line in the middle of the lake dividing the Japanese Canadians from the rest of the world.

"Bobby said the lake is frozen solid. They've been testing it, walking out a little bit farther each time. Bobby said I could watch. He said I could bring a friend." Midori clapped her mittens together, perhaps in praise of her brave cousin Bobby or perhaps simply because she was cold. "It might be tomorrow. If not, then the day after. I'll come and get you. You're my best friend."

Aya thought about Bobby and Tom's daring plan and felt sick with fear. All the children had been warned about the lake. It had been formed by a glacier, and was narrow across but at its center so deep it was said to be bottomless. During the summer some children had liked to swim and play water games, but they were warned to stay close to the shore. Never swim across. Never go out too far. The lake had moods that shifted suddenly. It was swiftly roused to anger, and with a swoop of mountain winds or a rush of underwater currents, the placid glass-like surface could turn violent and mean in an instant. When winter came, the warnings were sharper. Never walk on the ice. This lake has no bottom. If you fall in, your body will never be found.

During the silver rush half a century ago, an old white prospector had drowned in the lake and his body was never recovered. The story was that he lurked in the depths, ready to grab your leg and pull you down so he could have company. Some said they heard him cackling with glee in the middle of the night. "All you Japs are in ghost towns. It's lively here again. New Denver, Sandon, Kaslo, Slocan—whichever one you're in, it don't matter. 'Cause you can be a real ghost now and stay with me!"

"Girls are so stupid. That's a bunch of baloney," Bobby used to say. He and Tom had swum in the lake all summer.

Aya pictured her body plunging down, straight as an arrow, toward the bottom she could never reach. Down through an unending shaft of icy blackness. Would she encounter other falling bodies along the way, all of them seeking a place to stop, to rest?

On the day of the crossing, Midori came for her. They went to the lake, to their usual spot on the shore. It was a cold crisp morning, and their breath left their mouths in fat white puffs like smoke from cigarettes. They hurried, pursuing their breath. Bobby and Tom were already there. They wore thick lumber jackets and had scarves wound around their necks.

"Where've you been! Girls are always late. I'm sorry I said you could watch." Bobby's voice was changing, and every so often it crackled like something was broken inside his throat.

Tom laughed. He was a year older, with a deep voice and a thick neck that looked even fatter with his scarf on. "Let's go," he said.

The boys began taking deliberate steps toward the lake, their feet making crunching sounds in the snow. When they reached the ice, they had to steady themselves. The snow had blown off the surface in many places, and it looked slippery. Midori and Aya stood on the shore watching. The boys walked slowly, sliding their feet forward and holding their arms out to the side like tightrope walkers. When they were about thirty feet out, Tom turned around and yelled, "This is fun! Why don't you come with us?"

"*Baka*," they heard Bobby say to Tom. "Midori, you stay where you are."

Don't go any farther, Aya wanted to shout. It's dangerous. *Abunai!* Instead she looked at Midori, whose gaze never left the boys. It seemed to take forever until they reached the middle of the lake. Aya thought for sure they would turn around and come back, but they kept on walking. When they reached the other shore, they waved their arms and jumped up and down, and the sound of their hooting echoed across the still lake. They disappeared into the forest behind them.

"What should we do?" Aya asked.

"Just wait, I guess." Midori had scrunched up her face, out of worry or cold, or maybe both.

In about fifteen minutes the boys reappeared several yards farther down the shore and began walking back across the lake. It seemed to Aya that they were moving faster than when they first crossed, either in a hurry or simply more confident in their balance. Midori and Aya walked down the shore toward the point where they were approaching.

"Nothing to it," Bobby said when he stepped off the ice. "It's frozen solid."

"Yeah, we could go back and forth as many times as we want," Tom said.

"If we wanted to."

"Yeah. Back and forth."

"Were you scared?" Midori asked brightly. "When you were way out in the middle."

"*Baka.* Don't be stupid. There's nothing to be scared of. Only girls would be scared. Anyway, there's nothing on the other side. It's worse than here." Tom pulled his scarf tighter around his thick neck. His hands looked like they were trembling.

Bobby swung his gaze from Midori to Aya then back to Midori. "You two, you better keep your mouths shut about this." He shook his mitten in front of Midori's face, so close that crystals of snow flew onto her cheeks and eyelashes.

※

By late spring, an elementary school had been started in the camp by the Nisei women who were high-school graduates. They would teach the younger children all the same subjects taught in a regular school; they didn't want them to fall behind. Aya was doing composition exercises when Bobby burst into the room, sweaty and breathing heavily.

"There's a body floating on the lake! They're gonna haul it in any minute," he shouted, his voice equal parts excitement and terror.

The teacher ordered him to sit down, but he ran back outside.

"We'll continue with our lesson," she told the class. "Whatever it is, it's adult business. Nothing to do with you."

Two minutes later, though, a group of women rushed in, including Aya's aunt, and the teacher quickly ended the lesson. Everyone except Aya was free to go.

Her mother had been wearing her winter coat. That's what pulled her under, some said. Poor thing couldn't swim in a bulky coat like that. Nobody wanted to point out the obvious, to ask why she had gone into the lake wearing a heavy wool coat. It was almost summer. At least in front of Aya, they pretended it was an accident.

But she heard their secret whisperings everywhere.

She was lonely.

She was afraid.

She was weak.

She was selfish.

She was foolish.

She was worried.

But we're all worried.

What's going to happen to Aya now?

How could a mother do this to her daughter?

Aya didn't ask any questions. Nobody had the answer to the only question she wanted to ask, to the only question that mattered: Why did you leave me behind? Why didn't you take me with you?

Aunt Yae took care of the funeral. She was the widow of Aya's father's uncle, and the closest relative Aya had.

"There's no telling when my letter will reach him," Aya overheard Aunt Yae say of her father. "I can't wait. I'm responsible. I have to take care of her body. I have to take care of things."

After the funeral people came up to Aya and said how sorry they were and what a terrible accident it was and how the lake was a dangerous place and if there was anything they could do. But Aya was numb and hardly heard a word, nodding but not listening.

She didn't find out about the coat pockets until several days after the funeral service. Old Mr. Takeda, who had built the pine coffin, came to the door.

"Is your aunt here?"

She shook her head. She was the only one at home.

He stared at her through his thick old man's glasses, his eyes so magnified he reminded her of a bug. He blinked several times, then very slowly he moved his head from side to side. He did this for a long time until at last he spoke.

"Well, let me return this to you. Your mother's coat."

He held the coat toward her and she raised her arms to receive it. Suddenly he grabbed her hand and pushed it toward one of the pockets. Immediately she felt the resistance. The top of the pocket had been sewn shut.

Mr. Takeda regarded her again with his solemn bug eyes. "*Kawaiso,*" he murmured. So pitiful.

After he left, she spread the coat on the floor and examined the pockets. Although the opening of each pocket had been sewn securely shut, the pockets themselves were made of thin material and the bottom seams had ripped wide open. Presumably the contents of the pockets had been heavy. Through the material Aya could feel a few lumps. When she pulled them out she saw they were small stones, the ones that had not fallen out. The shore of the lake was covered with stones, and when she and Midori had played their game of prospector, they collected only the most colorful ones. Aya knew that her mother had not been so picky.

Without asking anyone, she instinctively understood what had happened. How the strong underwater currents would have easily torn the sheer pocket bottoms which were already straining with the weight of the stones. It was thus that the stones would have been released. Even now a cascade of stones was falling. Falling toward a bottom they could never reach.

She sat for a long time with her mother's coat on her lap. The coat was gray and shabby and still damp in places. It gave off a peculiar musty odor like a sick old dog, and it seemed to Aya that it would never dry out. She pushed her hand against the tops of the pockets, the openings that had been sewn shut, repeatedly testing how much pressure the seams could take. But they had been sewn with tight, close stitches, stitches that were meant to hold. Her mother had always been a good seamstress. Only six stones remained, six small ugly stones barely larger than pebbles. They weighed next to nothing. Aya wondered how many of them her mother had pushed into those pockets, filling them to bursting, before sewing them up. She wondered how long she had spent in contemplation and planning.

She gave the coat to her aunt but kept the stones for herself.

After her mother's death, Aya lived with Aunt Yae.

"She could have talked to me," Aunt Yae said to the adults who dropped by. "She was stubborn. She never wanted any help. But what she did . . . How could she be so selfish?" She lowered her voice to a whisper. "What about Aya? What's going to happen to her? As if things weren't bad enough for all of us."

Three months later they received word that Aya's father and other married men would be released from road camp and allowed to join their families in the internment camps. The single men, however, had to remain. When her father arrived, the first thing he and Aya did was to go to the small cemetery on the hill behind the apple trees where her mother's grave was next to Mrs. Negita, Mr. Okada, and the baby who had died last summer, a row of Japanese Canadian graves that was set apart from the much older graves of the white prospectors. Her father did not cry but he closed his eyes for the longest time and clenched his teeth so tight and so hard, she thought his face might crack. Then she observed the bones in his jaw begin to saw back and forth and she knew he was grinding his teeth. Grinding whatever he was feeling back down into himself.

He didn't want to talk about her mother's death except to berate Aunt Yae.

"Why did you bury her?"

"I didn't know what to do." Aunt Yae always broke down in tears. "You weren't here. I did my best. I had to take care of her body."

Sometimes Aya saw her father return from the cemetery, his hands covered in dirt as if he had been pawing the soil on her mother's grave.

Time passed and shortly before they were to be shipped to Japan, Aya's father approached Mr. Takeda.

"Are you sure, Shimamura-san?"

"I can't leave her in the ground here. Not this ground. Not all alone."

The grave was dug up, the cremation performed. The ashes were placed inside a small wooden box that was sealed tightly and wrapped in a square of white cloth, knotted twice.

The box was very light, almost weightless. It struck Aya that the soul was a compact thing indeed.

30

Even after Baker's departure, Matt continued to work on the weekends. He accomplished a lot when he was by himself. Today, for instance, he quickly finished off a letter requesting assistance with a license to export worms to the United States. *Japanese worms have superior qualities*, the writer stressed. It wasn't clear why exporting these worms halfway around the globe would be of any benefit, except the author of the letter seemed to be under the impression that Americans loved fishing and had a shortage of bait. Another letter was taped to a folding fan with MacArthur's face printed in the center. If the general found it to his liking, the writer of the letter pleaded, would he please consider putting in an order? Maybe for enough fans for each member of the Occupation forces? Please! Yes, work was therapeutic. At times like this, Matt thought he understood his father's attitude—forget about the heart. Forget about nonsense like what made the heart happy, what made it skip a beat or pound hard as a hammer. What made it thrash inside your chest like a wild salmon caught on a hook. Concentrate on work, his father would say.

Baker had been gone a month, but his desk remained vacant and so far no one else had been assigned to sit there. Lieutenant Duncan, who was currently in charge of their section, seemed content to issue his commands from an office down the hall. Whenever Matt could, he would steal a glance at that empty desk, and today, with no one else around to observe him, he had even tried sitting in Baker's chair for a few minutes. He felt very silly. The top of the desk was completely clear and the drawers were empty.

Work! Concentrate on work. He forced himself to go over to the mail table to pick up another letter to translate. No matter how hard he and everyone else worked, the mountain seemed to grow higher each day. It was frightening how many people were writing. Awe-inspiring, but frightening. Such faith in the power of written supplication, such faith in the power of words. There it was, a gigantic mountain of hope. Suddenly he felt overwhelmed and bent forward to bury his face in the letters. Instead of the smell of ink and paper, he felt he was inhaling the scent of human sweat and desperation and desire. He wished he could crawl into the very center of the pile.

"Matt?" It was a female voice.

He snapped to attention.

"What the heck are you doing?"

It was Nancy. He stared at her. She never worked on the weekend. What was she doing here?

"I was looking for a letter." It sounded stupid, but he had to say something.

"Did you find it?"

"No. But that's okay. I don't really need it."

Nancy gave him a quizzical look and then headed over to her typewriter. She took off her jacket, hung it over the back of her chair, and plucked off her typewriter cover.

"What are you doing here?" Matt said.

"I asked Lieutenant Duncan if there was any overtime I could do. He arranged it. I've decided I need to save more money in case I can go back to the States." Nancy made a face. "Sorry, *when. When* I go back. I'm going to think positively. I just heard from a Nisei girl I know who lives in Kyoto. She recently got her citizenship reinstated, and her case was even more complicated than mine. Oh, by the way, you won't mention this overtime business to Yoshiko or Mariko just yet, will you? I don't want to stir up any resentment."

"Of course not. Don't worry."

"Thanks. Say, I didn't know you'd be here. So you have to work on the weekends, too?"

Nancy didn't seem to expect an answer, for she bent her head over her typewriter and began rolling a fresh sheet of paper into the carriage. She and Matt worked for an hour and a half without talking or taking a break. As Matt listened to her type, he realized that she'd improved. While she still hit the keys in an uneven rhythm, there was a steadiness to her pace that he hadn't heard before.

"It's one o'clock. Aren't you going to the canteen for lunch?" Matt asked.

"I brought something from home. Why don't you have some? I made plenty."

He knew it was a lie. "I can't do that. I can't eat your food."

"Please. Think of it as a thank you. Remember how you helped me pick up some things in the black market?"

"That was nothing. Anyway, it was a long time ago."

"Well, never mind that. You helped me, and I'm not the type to forget. Please have some. It would make me feel better."

⁂

They fell into a comfortable routine of working quietly together in the office on weekends. One Saturday Matt walked Nancy partway home at the end of the day.

"I like to walk." Nancy started talking without any prompting. "I used to go for long walks by myself whenever I could. I would think about everything I missed. My sisters, Mom and Dad. My friends. But you know what I kept thinking about more than anything else? A good old-fashioned bologna sandwich! Sounds crazy, huh? I guess that was the height of my homesickness. Anyway I had no privacy, so being outside was the only way I could be by myself. It was the only way I could think.

"I'd head to the Sumida River after work. I was trying to figure things out, I guess, trying to fathom how I had ended up here and wondering if I would ever see my family again. I would go before twilight, and although I wasn't supposed to be out after dark because of the blackouts, sometimes I just couldn't bear to go inside. I would walk along the riverbank until it got so dark I couldn't see in front of me. Even then, I'd keep going. One foot after the other. That's usually when I got asked. *Ikura ka?* How much? The first time a man asked me, I thought he was trying to sell *me* something. For the life of me I couldn't figure out what it was. I kept smiling and saying sorry, I didn't have any extra money to spare. He kept offering different prices, going slightly higher each time. When I finally understood what he was driving at, I got so mad I yelled at him in English. 'Go to hell!' Sometimes it even happened in broad daylight, and it got to the point where I recognized that sick lewd smile men wore when they approached me. I always told them to go straight to hell. It didn't do any good, but it made me feel better for the moment. Of course, as soon as I got home, all the tears would come out. I'd just cry myself to sleep."

She gave Matt a crooked smile. "Sorry, I don't know what made me tell you that! What a maudlin story."

"It's not maudlin. Being here during the war must have been terrible."

"Well, it wasn't easy. I make it sound like I was wandering around like a woman of leisure, but I had to work in a parachute factory, and half the time I was jumping in and out of bomb shelters. At first I thought, Hooray, the Americans are coming and they'll rescue me. Then I realized I better duck for cover because they were dropping bombs all over the city. I can still hear the drone of those B-29s. It's something you can never forget."

She shuddered and looked away.

31

Sumiko was the last to leave the dance hall, and even though her dormitory wasn't far, her feet hurt more than usual so she was walking slowly. Her shoes were tight and blisters had formed on the backs of her heels. Once again Harada had refused to pay her for the tickets she'd collected tonight—he said the till was empty and he would have to reimburse her another time, but she knew it was a lie. She hobbled on. A rickshaw pulled up beside her.

"Need a ride?" The driver, a gaunt wrinkled man of indeterminate age, set the arms of his rickshaw on the ground and put his hands on his hips. She recognized him as one of the regulars who waited outside the dance hall hoping for a fare. He looked her up and down, smiling broadly. Even in the dark she could see the glint of his shiny yellow teeth.

"No, thank you."

"Come on. It's a slow night for me."

She did her best to ignore him.

He picked up the arms of the rickshaw and began walking alongside her. She kept her eyes fixed on the road, well aware that he was leering at her. She thought she could even hear him smack his lips. By now she was supposed to be accustomed to the ogling—it was part of her job after all—but it wasn't something you could ever get used to, and it made her angry and disgusted and most of all afraid. Every so often she passed a streetlamp and caught a glimpse of the man's arms, which were like hard knotted ropes. He was thin and sinewy, but he also looked as strong as a wild boar.

She deliberately walked past the corner where she would normally have turned for her dormitory because she didn't want him to know where she lived.

"Hey, no need to walk on those sore feet. You look like you've had a long night. I'll help you out. Ha, ha. I know how hard you girls have to work."

She walked to the third lamplight, turned at the tobacco shop on the corner and continued down a lane so narrow the man could no longer pull his rickshaw beside her. He was forced to walk behind her, and she thought this would make him give up, turn around and leave, but he was undeterred. She'd reached the limits of the main Ginza district, and was entering an area of empty lots and open fields overgrown with weeds and strewn with garbage. If she kept on going, eventually she would reach Bar Lucky.

The rickshaw driver tried again. "Tell you what, there's no charge for a ride tonight. You don't have to pay me. Well, not in cash anyway." He laughed.

It wasn't until she was right outside Wada's bar, standing in front of the navy blue *noren*, the curtain that hung over the doorway, that she finally had the nerve to face the driver. "Go away. Leave me alone."

The man sneered at her. "*Panpan* like you think you're too good for us Japanese men, don't you. You only want that white meat. Well, I won't forget you. Someday you'll be sorry, and I'll be there watching."

Sumiko didn't wait to see what the driver would do next. She ducked her head under the Bar Lucky *noren* and entered Wada's bar.

"Sumiko! Good to see you. Come in. We're just finishing up here."

Wada was standing in his usual spot behind the counter, and another man stood in front. This man turned around to look at her before returning to his conversation with Wada.

"So what do you say? Is it a deal?"

"Too expensive," Wada said.

"But this is good stuff. Got it from a special source. Once your customers get a taste of this, they'll be willing to pay a little more."

Wada held a bottle up to the single lightbulb that dangled from a cord overhead. It had no label but was clearly recycled from an American whiskey bottle. The liquid glowed a clear pale amber, like spun gold.

"Look, I've sold to all the bars in this area. You don't want to be the only one left out, do you?"

The man took the bottle back and unscrewed the cap. "This one's pure. It's a secret formula. Give me a glass, would you? No, make that two." He poured a small amount into each glass. "Try it, but first take a long sniff. That's the way you can tell this is good stuff. It doesn't stink like that other *kasutori* crap."

The man demonstrated by bringing one of the glasses up to his nose and inhaling deeply. He didn't drink but set his glass down on the counter. Wada picked up the other glass and sniffed.

"Not bad."

"Not bad! This is the best you can get."

Wada reached into his cash box and tossed a few crumpled yen bills onto the counter. "That's all I've got. Take it or leave it."

The man wrinkled his brow and drummed his fingers on the counter. Then he scooped up the money and stuffed it into his pocket. "That'll do. I'll bring more next week."

After the man left, Wada turned to Sumiko and shrugged his shoulders. "Everybody's trying to make money any way they can. Say, are you hungry? You want something to eat?"

"I don't have any money."

"Don't worry."

He carefully wiped the counter and set out two pair of chopsticks, two small bowls of cold rice, and a plate of cabbage pickles. "Here's something else you'll like," he said, putting a large ripe tomato on the counter and resting his knife next to it. "Doesn't this look good? I'll slice it up and we can share it."

He pushed one of the glasses toward Sumiko. "We shouldn't let this go to waste."

She smiled but shook her head.

"Come on now," Wada said, raising his glass. "I can't enjoy it unless you keep me company. *Kanpai!*"

She picked up the shot glass and clinked it against Wada's. "*Kanpai!*" She was just about to take a sip when she saw Wada freeze, his glass halfway to his lips. She quickly turned around.

The American in the doorway was so still he looked like a statue. She wondered how long he had been there and whether he had been watching them since the other man had left. Although he was not as big as some of the GIs she'd met, he was still much taller and bulkier than Wada. The only part of him that moved were his eyes. They were wide and wild, and they darted all around the tiny enclosure, back and forth between Sumiko and Wada.

He was filthy. If she hadn't known better, she would have thought he had walked in off a battlefield in the jungle. His hair was uncombed and his face was covered with a thick black stubble, his uniform dirty and stained with dark blotches. There was a particularly large stain on his left thigh, and something dark and viscous was dripping from it.

The silence was broken by Wada.

"*Sumimasen*, no money." Wada tried valiantly. "So sorry."

As if this were his cue, the man rushed forward, snatched the knife from the counter and clamped his arm around Sumiko's neck, all in what seemed like a single smooth, uninterrupted motion. His chokehold was so tight, she could hardly breathe. Just under her jawbone, she felt the sharp warning prickle of the knife tip, forcing her to keep her head erect. She thought about what they always said in the dance hall—don't resist, don't resist. But she couldn't have resisted if she'd wanted to.

"*Kane ga nai.* No money." Wada was whimpering now. "So sorry."

The man didn't seem to hear or comprehend. Just as suddenly as he had grabbed Sumiko, he released her by slamming her hard against the counter. He held the knife in front of him, slashing at the empty air and jerking it recklessly back and forth between Sumiko and Wada. Then, with his free hand, he picked up one of the bowls of rice from the counter and shoved his face into it, eating from the bowl like a dog. He did the same with the second bowl. He bit into the ripe tomato, heedless of the juice spilling down his chin, and after he had devoured it, he picked up the Japanese pickles with his fingers and pushed them one by one into his mouth. At the first sour bite, he made a face, but he continued to chew with a fierce determination until everything on the plate was gone. Sumiko had never seen a white man eat like that; she'd never seen a white person who was so hungry. After the man had devoured everything before him, he downed the contents of the two shot glasses one after the other, and then picked up the bottle and brought it directly to his lips. He choked on his first large gulp, but after he recovered, he took another swig. And another and another. Each subsequent swallow seemed to be easier. As he drank, he pointed the knife at them, holding it straight out like an extension of his arm as if to demonstrate he meant business.

Sumiko watched the man's every move but she couldn't do anything. She couldn't even scream. It was like a bad dream in which her throat had been stuffed with seaweed. Wada seemed similarly paralyzed.

After finishing almost half the bottle, the man set it down on the counter and turned his head toward Sumiko. He began staring at her in a way that was different from the way he'd looked at her before. She tried averting her eyes but he stared so hard and so fixedly that eventually she felt compelled to return his gaze. He'd lowered the knife, and his eyes had stilled, all their wildness completely gone. Now they were glazed and unfocused, filled with a morose puzzlement and confusion, as if the man were scanning her face, searching for something just out of reach. His eyes were, in fact, large and quite striking, a startling shade of blue fringed with dark lashes as long as a girl's. In another circumstance, she might even have said they looked pretty. What struck her now was how mournful they were, like the eyes of some sad frightened animal.

"Keiko, I'm sorry," he began speaking for the first time. "I'm sorry, I'm so sorry." He seemed to think she was someone else. To Sumiko's astonishment, he started to blubber. Rubbing one big hand over his dirty face, he began sobbing like a small boy. It was so unexpected and even embarrassing that Sumiko's first reaction was pity. Then she came to her senses. He'd let the knife slip out of his grasp, and she dropped to the floor to grab it.

That was what she remembered most clearly, the feel of the knife in her hand. The smooth wooden handle had a comfortable grip and the knife itself was small and light. She had just wrapped her fingers securely around the handle when she turned her head to see a blur of movement. A dark mass hurtled toward her, smashing into her so hard it knocked the wind out of her lungs. When she came to, she was lying on her back and the man's body was on top of her. Wada was standing over them. In his hand he held the neck of a broken bottle.

"I knocked him out. Don't worry, Sumiko, it's over," Wada said. He got down on his knees and rolled the GI off her. Then his face turned ashen.

Even before looking, somehow she already knew. Somehow she was aware that her hand was empty and that the knife was gone. When she saw the man on the floor, her first impression was that he seemed much smaller lying down than he had standing up. The knife sticking out of his side looked bigger now.

She touched her hair and pricked her finger on a splinter of glass.

It's over, Wada had said. The words now had a different meaning. A man was dead. Not just any man, but an American. Sumiko bit her lip hard to make sure she wouldn't scream.

Wada grabbed her by the shoulders and shook her. "We have to get out of here. You understand, don't you? This is my place, so I'm in more trouble than you, but you . . . you, too . . ." He glanced at the body, and she followed his gaze to the knife.

"The police," she finally managed to say. "We have to go to the police."

"Are you crazy?"

"It was self-defense. It was an accident."

"The Japanese police can't help us. We have to run. We have to take care of ourselves."

Wada emptied his cash box, wrapped the framed pictures of his wife and son in a tea towel, and shoved his belongings into a small bag. "When they find this dead guy, there's going to be hell to pay. The Americans won the war. They're in charge, and they can do anything they want to us."

"But what about your bar?" she said. "After you worked so hard for it."

Wada looked her straight in the eye. "Don't you know that everything you have can be taken away from you in an instant?"

32

They spent the night hiding among the crowds of homeless who filled the underground passageway at Ueno train station. They were exhausted but unable to sleep. It wasn't just the sheer terror of what had happened that kept Sumiko awake. She was cold and wet and aching all over. Before they left the bar, she'd hastily tried to wash the blood off the front of her blouse. "Don't bother," Wada said. "We have to hurry." But she'd insisted because the blood had been sticky and warm and it felt like a part of the man was still plastered to her. The most she'd been able to do, though, was wipe her blouse with a dishrag that she had dampened with water. Now as she sat on the concrete floor in the underground passageway, she was convinced that the smell of his blood was all over her. It had seeped into her skin, a raw rank odor that she could never get rid of. The blood mixed with other smells—her sweat and the cloying sweetness of the perfume she'd put on earlier in the evening—but worst of all was the powerful smell of fear. It was the scent thrown off by a wounded animal hiding in its lair, and it came from her and from Wada. She listened to his shallow irregular breathing and sensed his constantly shifting movements by her side.

As soon as the trains started running in the morning, Wada insisted they had to flee. "Let's go to Hokkaido, as far north as we can go. It's big up there. The Americans will never find us."

It sounded so far away, almost like another country.

"I need some time to think," she pleaded.

"We have no time. Don't you understand? It's not safe to stay here. A dead Japanese, who cares? But a dead American! They'll be coming after us."

She covered her face with her hands and the image of the man's body with the knife in his side came back to her.

"You know me by now," Wada said. "I'm a good man. I'll always take care of you. I'll protect you."

By evening, she'd made up her mind. He was a good man, probably better than most, but she knew instinctively that it wouldn't work. The dead GI would always be between them. *We* killed an American would someday turn into *you* killed him. He'd hit the man over the head, but she had been the one holding the knife. No, she would have to take care of herself. She had to, she wanted to. It was better this way.

She told him to go alone.

Wada was shocked. "How can you manage by yourself? You're a woman. There's only one thing you can do to survive. Do you want to end up doing that?" He kept shaking his head as if he couldn't believe her stubbornness. "Okay, if that's the way you want it, but you better be careful. Get away from Tokyo."

He slipped into the fast-moving throng of people headed toward the platforms to board night trains.

Sumiko sank back against the wall in the passageway and, to her surprise, almost immediately fell asleep. She woke after a few hours in the middle of the night. The passageway was pitch-black, and perhaps because she was now alone without Wada, the darkness felt thicker and denser than the night before. Yet though it was dark, it was not quiet. All around her, there was sighing, sniffling, wheezing, snoring. A child whimpered and was hushed. A man coughed and spat. From somewhere in the passageway Sumiko heard a low moan that was repeated every few minutes. She couldn't tell if it was male or female, young or old, or even if it was human.

Later, when it grew quieter, Sumiko pricked up her ears again, and this time she detected scuttling sounds. Instantly she felt her scalp tighten. The scuttling was faint, the telltale tiny taps of small sharp claws running across a hard surface. Sumiko hated rats. From that point on, whenever anyone brushed against her body in the overcrowded passageway, Sumiko couldn't help imagining a swarm of rodents coming to get her.

Wada had given her a little money before they parted company. "Get a train," he urged. "Go anywhere." She'd put the money in her shoe so she could feel the uncomfortable bulge under the ball of her foot, so she would know for sure where it was at all times. But although her shoes were tight and she did not take them off, she woke up one morning to find the money gone. Not only had the thief skillfully removed her shoe without disturbing her, he had somehow also managed to put it back on her foot.

She sat in her spot in the station and spent her days watching people hurry past. The longer she sat, the less need there was for movement. She was convinced she was so still that the people who rushed by didn't see her at all. Then it came to her: Here was a solution. If she remained still enough, for long enough, eventually she could simply dissolve into thin air. It seemed like a fitting resolution. A man was dead and she would will herself to melt away. She didn't think of it as starvation. It was more like evaporating.

With each day that she did not eat, she felt a little lighter. Each hour without water, she grew lighter yet. She stopped needing to go to the bathroom. She stopped needing to move. Even her breathing was transformed into the rapid quivering of a tiny bird.

She lost all sense of time. Then one afternoon a squad of Japanese policemen arrived at the station and as passengers got off the train and passed through the exit turnstile, they began frisking them.

"Up against the wall. Random inspection."

Sumiko felt her chest turn to ice. This was the end, the worst thing that could happen—the police had arrived and they would arrest her for sure. She wasn't invisible to them. With every ounce of her depleted flesh she wanted to run, but she didn't think she had the strength to even stand.

The police seemed especially intent on targeting women. Any woman wearing baggy clothing, regardless of age, was made to lift up her top and show her belly, then turn around and show her bottom.

"Come on, you're not all pregnant. Let's see what's strapped under those *monpe*. There, look at that. A clear violation. That's well in excess of your ration allotment."

"They're checking for rice smuggling," the woman next to Sumiko muttered. "But everyone knows the rations are ridiculous."

As if he'd heard what she just said, one of the policemen pointed at the woman and the other homeless people, including Sumiko. "All of you, stand up! Now!"

Sumiko struggled to get to her feet.

"Stand up!"

She clutched the pant legs of the person next to her, desperately hoping somehow to haul herself up, when a woman in a wide black robe rushed over.

"*Hazukashiku nai!* You should be ashamed of yourself," the woman snapped at the policeman. "Can't you see how weak she is?"

"But everyone has to—"

"Look at her clothes. It's obvious she isn't hiding any rice."

"Well, but everyone—"

"Just look at her! She is clearly a victim of society. You men have done this."

Then the woman tapped the front of her gown with authority, and Sumiko realized the black robe was a nun's habit. "This is a fallen woman and she is my charge. I'll take care of her."

The policeman backed off.

The nun helped Sumiko to another area of the station away from the inspection. She reached into the folds of her robe and produced a baby bottle, unscrewed the top, and held the bottle to Sumiko's lips. "Drink this. It's sugar water." Then she gave her a slightly squashed bean-paste bun that she pulled from another hidden pocket. While Sumiko slowly chewed on the bun, the nun studied her in silence.

"My name is Sister Izumi. You don't have anywhere to go, do you?"

Sumiko looked up. Sister Izumi had a round face and small

crinkly eyes. A few short strands of black hair peeked out from the sides of her head covering.

"Do you?"

Sumiko shook her head.

"I didn't think so. Well then, you should come with me."

"Where?"

"It's not too far. You can lean on me if you're feeling weak. There's nothing to be afraid of."

Sumiko thought about the police who were still in the station. It wasn't a hard decision to make. She extended her arms toward Sister Izumi, who pulled her up to standing position and gripped her tightly against her side.

"Come, I've got you. You won't fall. We have to take the train."

Sumiko fell asleep on the ride. She woke briefly just when the train was pulling into Yokohama station, and then a second time when Sister Izumi shook her. "We're almost here. It's the next stop."

They got off at a small town somewhere close to the sea. Sumiko couldn't see the ocean, but she could smell the salt air.

"Are you rested?" Sister Izumi asked. "We have a short walk but then we'll be home."

"Home?"

"Home is the orphanage." She smiled, and her crinkly eyes disappeared into the crests of her high round cheeks.

The orphanage was located at the top of a steep hill, and when they reached the gate, Sumiko was exhausted. She looked back over her shoulder at the dirt path they had just climbed. It was lined on both sides by rows of tall bamboo trees that curved inward toward each other, swaying gently in the wind. From this perspective the trees appeared to form a long narrow tunnel. At the far end, at the bottom of the slope, she could see a pale circle of light.

As if reading her mind, Sister Izumi spoke. "We call this the Tunnel of Separation."

Sumiko felt a breeze brush her cheeks. The air no longer smelled of the sea but of something else, something fresh and clean like pine trees and flowers. As soon as she stepped through the gate, Sister Izumi locked it behind them.

33

The arrival of colder weather forced Kondo Sensei to alter his moonlighting schedule completely. Instead of staying overnight in Love Letter Alley, as he had in the summer and early fall, he switched to Sundays, working all day and into the early evening. All the letter writers came earlier in the day and left earlier, as did their customers. Kondo missed the rhythm of summer, missed meeting his customers in the middle of the night when both of them had been able to conduct their exchange under the protective cover of darkness. Darkness brought anonymity, and anonymity supported dignity both for the women who came to purchase his letter-writing services and for the letter writer himself. They could all pretend they were someone other than they were. But the weather changed that. No one wanted to sit outside in the cold at night.

Some of the letter writers, like Yamaguchi and Tabata, grouped together, huddling around a charcoal hibachi that one of them had bought. They invited Kondo to join them, but he always politely declined and now they didn't bother anymore. He knew he had a reputation as a bit of a snob. The professor, they called him, sarcastically, not just sensei but *kyoju—Professor* Kondo—as if he put on airs like the faculty member of a big university. But he preferred to be left alone, and he liked his isolated spot in the Alley nowhere near the front, where the others clustered. They liked to joke about the content of the letters they were asked to translate or to write. Not another one of those! Oh, these women are all the same! Kondo wanted to avoid that kind of shoptalk. If he began demeaning the women who asked for his services, where would it end? Wouldn't he only be demeaning himself?

"Just a few weeks before the Americans have their Christmas. This is the best time of the year." Yamaguchi rubbed his thumb against his fingertips to indicate that lots of money could be made. "Be prepared to put in long hours but it's worth it. All the bar girls are getting letters and every letter needs translating."

"Is it mostly good news or bad?" Kondo asked.

"What do you think?" Yamaguchi laughed outright. "The Americans start feeling guilty when Christmas rolls around. They get more letters from home than usual, they even get presents. If they're married or engaged to someone back home, they feel bad about having a Japanese girlfriend, so they decide they better make a clean break. As for the ones who've already gone back to America, they feel guilty about what they did here and if they weren't up front with their girlfriends before they left, they figure they can digest their Christmas dinners better if they've gotten things off their chest. We do our best business at this time of year. Everyone's writing letters back and forth. Even the lousiest translator can make a bundle."

Kondo did not say anything to Yamaguchi, but recently he had begun thinking about quitting the Alley. While his schoolteacher salary was still too low to survive without supplementing it in some fashion, he'd heard about GIs who were interested in studying Japanese in a serious way, not just to pick up bar girls but because they liked Japan and its culture. They would pay well, exceedingly well. Besides, it looked like the Americans would be here forever. Maybe it was time to try to make friends, or if not friends, then to strike a truce.

An incident earlier in the day had added to his sense that maybe he was becoming unsuited to this type of work.

The woman had arrived in the morning, shortly after he had set up his stall. He had been busy retrieving his stool and tangerine crate from his secret hiding place and arranging his brushes, ink, pencils, and paper when he looked up and saw her standing patiently in front of him. She had a freshly scrubbed face and long straight hair. Kondo was used to the heavy makeup and permanent-wave hairdos of the bar girls who usually sought his services, so he was surprised and also a little amused. Then he took in her figure. She was wearing a thin cotton smock that came down to her knees and billowed out as she shifted from one foot to the other. From the way the material fell around her middle, he guessed she was probably several months pregnant.

"You're one of the English letter writers, aren't you?"

"I am. How can I help you?"

"I have a letter from America. I just got it. Can you tell me what it says?" The woman spoke with elation. She reached up the sleeve of her smock and pulled out a thin blue envelope.

"You haven't opened it yet," he said, turning the envelope over in his hands.

"No, I came here right away. Someone told me there were people like you who would translate my letter. It's an important letter, so it has to be read by a real expert." She took the envelope from Kondo and tapped her finger over the address written on the back. "There, see? That's him. It's from him." Kondo looked at the return address. All it said was *Derek Smith, Omaha, Nebraska.*

Kondo gestured to the tangerine crate. "Please have a seat, miss."

"Thank you for helping. Thank you so much. It's a very important letter. Did I mention that?" The woman slowly lowered herself onto the crate. Her legs were bare despite the cold, and on her feet she wore short split-toe socks and an old pair of wooden geta. Her ankles, he noticed, were very swollen.

"Are you comfortable?" he asked. "You don't have to worry. It won't break."

She smiled at him and shifted her weight gingerly. "It's cold today, isn't it? Please excuse my appearance. I'm wearing so many layers." She smiled at him again, even more broadly and excitedly, and wrapped her arms around her middle. Her cheeks were flushed. She almost looked drunk.

Kondo reached into his satchel for his wooden letter opener, carefully slit the top of the airmail envelope, and pulled out the letter. There were two pages of onionskin paper, as sheer as the wings of a butterfly. The man's handwriting slanted backward, but it was neat and thankfully not hard to decipher. Some letters Kondo had worked on in the past were so full of spelling and grammar mistakes, he'd really struggled to figure out what the writer was trying to say. He wondered if in America some soldiers had never gone to school. But this man was educated. His English and his message were very clear. Several times he called himself a sinner. He mentioned his wife and his two small children. He asked for forgiveness.

Kondo rubbed his temple. What on earth was he going to do with this? The woman was gazing at him sweetly, and it was obvious she had no idea what her boyfriend had written. She was expecting some other kind of news, not the bombshell this letter contained.

He cleared his throat. "You were probably waiting a long time to hear from him."

"I've tried to be patient. I know he was very busy with all the preparations. He told me it might take a long time. There are lots of documents to file."

"Documents to file?"

"Yes, for my papers."

"Papers for . . . ?"

"For bringing me to America." She smiled at Kondo as if he were a little slow and she had to be patient with him. As if she had to indulge him, because he was not as lucky as she was.

He quickly dropped his gaze back to the letter in his hand. "Umm, I need to consult my dictionaries, I'm afraid. English is a very complicated language, and I don't want to make a mistake. I'm sorry, but this will take a bit of time."

"Of course. I don't want to rush you." The woman unconsciously rubbed her stomach. She leaned back as if to give Kondo more space to think. "I admire people like you who know English. I've been studying, but I find it so hard."

He flipped open his dictionary, pretending to look up some words. He'd read hundreds of letters like this since he started working in the Alley. They varied in the names and details, but he knew the storyline cold. Upon returning to the States, the man found his hometown girlfriend still waiting for him. Upon returning to the

States, the man went straight back into the embrace of his wife. Upon returning to the States, the man discovered a world of eligible young women more than happy to help a serviceman readjust to life back home. Kondo acknowledged to himself that those who took the trouble to write to their Japanese girlfriends were the decent ones. The others didn't even bother.

The longer he worked here, the more aware he was of the power he wielded as a translator. He could translate word for literal word, each one like the blow of a hammer on tin to the listener. Or he could take it upon himself to soften the message. He could say that the man was sorry, when the letter contained no real apology. He could say the man felt affection, even when there was no explicit declaration of love. And if he came across phrases like *I made a mistake. I never really loved you, it was just that I was in a strange country and feeling lonely,* well, he would change that into something kinder. *I was so glad that I met you. You helped me during my stay in a strange land, and you took away my loneliness. I will never forget you.*

It wasn't lying, not really. He never changed the essential message of a letter, although he knew a lot of the other translators did. They bragged that they made things up all the time because it often meant being rewarded with a nice tip. A happy bar girl was a generous bar girl, they liked to say. But Kondo didn't believe in misleading anyone, not even a bar girl he would never see again. Dishonesty never helped anyone. Besides, a job should be done honorably. He was being paid to translate what someone else couldn't read, and he owed it to them to respect their need for the truth. It was just like teaching his pupils—he never ever wanted to lie to them. Children didn't respect you if you didn't tell them the truth, no matter how hard it was. They were tougher than they looked. They could take it.

Of course, not all the letters brought bad news. Some were filled with hope and cheeriness and ardent messages of love. Kondo saw many examples of tenderness and devotion against all odds.

"Did you know each other a long time?" he asked.

The woman blushed. "A while."

"I'm guessing maybe not all that long, right?"

"Everything happened a little fast. We had just met and then he was ordered back to America."

"That must have been hard."

For a moment she looked like she might start crying, but when she spoke her voice was bright. "He said he would pray for me every night and that we'd be reunited soon. Never lose faith, he said. What we have is true love."

"I don't mean to pry, but does he know . . . ?"

"Pardon me? I don't understand."

Kondo gestured with his hand clumsily toward her body, toward the bulk of her stomach. She looked so vulnerable that he immediately regretted his words. Her face, so young and fresh, did not seem ready for the changes taking place in her body.

"I don't know what you're talking about." The woman abruptly stopped smiling. "I'd like to know what my letter says. What does he say about my papers?"

"There's nothing about any papers, I'm afraid."

"You mean they're not ready yet?"

"No, there's no mention of any papers." Kondo paused and took a deep breath before continuing. "I don't think he intends to bring you to America."

"That's impossible."

"I'm really sorry. I also have to tell you that he's married. It's in the letter."

The woman's face turned red, first a fiery bright red, then dark as old blood. "But *we're* married," she said.

"I'm sorry."

"We're married, I tell you! He made me put my hand on his Bible and his friend was there as a witness. He said we'd have a proper wedding ceremony when I came to America." She put her hands over her face and began sobbing.

Kondo carefully folded the onionskin paper along the existing crease lines and tucked the letter back into the envelope. "I know it's not much comfort, but you're not the only—"

Abruptly she stopped crying and snatched the letter from his hands. "*Uso tsuki*. Liar! I don't believe anything you say. You're making it all up."

"I'm sorry the letter—"

"You don't understand English."

"I can see how upset—"

"Fraud! You can't read English. You made everything up."

"You know that's not true."

"I'm not paying. You only tell lies."

"That's all right. I will waive the fee. I'm sorry the news wasn't good."

"You bet I won't pay. I'm going to find a real translator, not a fraud like you."

"Whoever you find will tell you the same thing."

The woman turned to leave and as she did, her foot slipped out of her geta. The movement had been quick and violent, and she let out a short yelp, like a wounded animal. Kondo worried that she might have twisted her ankle.

"Are you all right?"

She bent over and picked up the wooden sandal. The strap between the toes had pulled right off. She stared at it with a strange glittering look in her eyes.

"Are you all right?" he asked again. "Did you hurt yourself?"

"See what you made me do!" She waved the geta in front of him. "Look at this. The strap broke. Do you know how many years of bad luck this is!"

For a moment he thought she would throw her geta at him but instead she turned around and began walking away. It was a sad comical limp. He knew he had handled things badly, and yet he didn't regret telling her the truth. There was no way to sugarcoat the contents of a letter like that.

That evening it took Kondo a long time to fall asleep. The woman had upset him more than he realized, though at first he didn't understand why. Her situation, while sad, was not unusual.

He'd translated many letters like the one she had received. But as he lay awake on his futon, he thought of another woman, a distant cousin, and he had to admit that something about the woman tonight reminded him a little of her. They had the same long thick hair, the same fresh-scrubbed face. He hadn't thought of her in a long time.

She'd come to Tokyo from the countryside to work in one of the textile factories, first sewing women's pantaloons and later gloves and uniforms for the military. As he was the only relative she had in the city, they would meet from time to time, and on her day off he would take her for walks in Ueno Park, where they strolled by Shinobazu Pond and watched the ducks. She always called him Uncle because he was older. Over time he realized that he had fallen in love with her but he knew he could not tell her. She told him about her fiancé, how he had trained to be a fighter pilot for Japan's mighty imperial navy, how proud she was of him, how much she missed him. When she received news that he had perished in a battle in the Strait of Malacca, Kondo was the one she came to. They met in Ueno Park, and in front of the placidly swimming ducks, she'd cried into his shoulder, sobbing as he'd never heard any woman sob before. It was as if she were wringing out every ounce of water inside her, draining her very body of all its fluid. He didn't know what to say, so he said nothing. He wanted to tell her that *he* was here. He remained. Couldn't she see that? He would take care of her forever, if only she would let him.

After she had finished crying, she sat back and thanked him. For being the only one in the world she could talk to, for being so understanding and kind. He walked her back to her factory dormitory. They did not speak any more about what had happened to her fiancé. Instead, as they walked, they paid attention to the sounds of different birds in the high treetops. She stopped at one point to pet a stray cat, but it ran away. At the doorway to her residence, she bowed and waved goodbye to him. He never saw her again. A week later, her dormitory went up in flames during one of the firebombings. None of the factory girls survived.

34

Sumiko could stay at the orphanage if she worked. That was the arrangement Sister Izumi came up with to convince the other three nuns and Mother Masako that Sumiko would pull her weight. In exchange for doing the heavy chores, she was given food and a place to sleep. That was all she asked for. A place to be, a place to hide, she was grateful for that. Here she was safe. No one would ever think to look for her in a place like this.

And she welcomed the work. She was asked to clean the floors, wash the clothes, cut the vegetables, cook the rice. The more exhausting and menial the work, the better as far as she was concerned, for it was then that she could truly lose herself in the grueling physical labor. The laundry—it mainly consisted of diapers and sheets—was endless. Everything had to be washed by hand in cold water using a wooden washboard and a harsh chemical soap designed to disinfect. When an ugly rash erupted on her hands and traveled up her forearms, she welcomed that, too. It helped, if only temporarily, to block out her memories of the night in the bar.

The story behind the orphanage was this: In the last years of the war, the nuns had taken shelter in an old house on a large estate which, for reasons no one understood, had been abandoned. After the surrender, having nowhere else to go, they simply stayed on until one day, a little over nine months after the arrival of the Occupation forces, someone left a GI baby in front of the gate. Sister Izumi had taken it in. After that, word quickly spread that mixed-blood infants could be abandoned at the Tunnel of Separation, and the old house was turned into an accidental orphanage. Several times a month, there were new arrivals.

It was assumed that children like this would face intense hardship in Japan, so the orphanage started keeping detailed records of each infant in the hope that overseas adoption might be possible. The information was written down on cards: weight, length, color and shape of eyes, color and texture of hair, color of skin. The reverse side of the card bore the final distinguishing mark. The sole of the baby's foot was brushed with ink and pressed onto the card to form a "signature."

If any notes had been left by the mother, these too were carefully recorded.

Please take care of my beautiful daughter.
Look after my baby. He is innocent.

More often, though, there was nothing. Alive for only a few hours, the infants already had such complex silent histories.

To Sumiko, all the record keeping seemed irrelevant. One had only to look at the child, she thought, to see an entire personal narrative written directly on his flesh. Although some infants looked Japanese or almost Japanese, the majority were obviously *konketsu*, of mixed blood. Foreign but not foreign enough. Japanese but decidedly not pure. The story of their parentage—of their very conception— was plainly visible for all to see.

Usually it was Sister Izumi who checked the gate early in the morning, but sometimes she sent Sumiko. The first time she came upon a small wicker basket on the ground, Sumiko was struck by the delicate pink handkerchief draped across the top. She peered down the path, through the mysterious tunnel shaped by the bending bamboo trees, but there was no one in sight. When she lifted the handkerchief, the baby she found wrapped in a clean white napkin was tinier than any baby she had ever seen. She didn't know that any living creature could be so small. Its eyes were shut tight but its miniature mouth moved almost imperceptibly like a small fish kissing the empty air. Sticking the tip of her finger into the baby's squirming mouth, she instantly felt the powerful tug of its sucking.

It surprised her so much, she pulled out her finger. With that, the tiny baby parted its tiny lips and let out an ear-piercing cry.

The furious force of that little mouth. Whenever she thought about the babies, it was that physical sensation she recalled. More than anything else, it seemed to symbolize their fierce determination to thrive. The odds were against them, but they persisted unaware. The instinct to survive was in all of them, Sumiko thought, and it started from the moment of birth. The babies were selfish. Everything they wanted was for themselves.

That was how you stayed alive.

You had to be selfish.

"I'm sure you are aware of our need for more space." Sumiko was called into Mother Masako's office in late December and the conversation had begun in this meandering way. "As you know, the room at the end of the corridor is currently being used for storage purposes. If it were cleared out, it could easily be converted into another nursery."

Sumiko knew about the storage room. When the orphanage was first established, there had been such severe shortages that every sheet of paper, every scrap of tin, every piece of glass was saved for reuse.

"There's no one else I can ask. Some of the Sisters, if I may say, are most reluctant to part with old items." Mother Masako cleared her throat and set her mouth in the mildest suggestion of a grimace.

Sumiko nodded. She understood that this was a reference to Sister Naoko who, everyone knew, had a penchant—a compulsion—for collecting things. Every time she went out, she brought back something she had picked up off the street. "For the children," she would retort whenever anyone challenged her. "It's all for the children."

The string collection was useful, as was the box full of pencil stubs and the mismatched buttons. The scraps of fabric could be used for patches.

"But those old newspapers . . ." Mother Masako shuddered. "We have to consider the danger of fire and other hazards. It would be very helpful if you could tie them up so we can sell them to the junk dealer."

When Sumiko went to the storage room, she could barely open the door wide enough to squeeze through. Indeed, the trouble was the newspapers, piles and piles, some as high as the ceiling. How could so much have accumulated? Sister Naoko had undoubtedly intended to sell them to raise money for the orphanage but had never been organized enough to do so.

Sumiko started with the piles closest to the doorway and worked her way back into the interior of the room. Armed with a giant ball of string and a small pair of scissors, she began tying the newspapers into neat, uniform-size bundles. As soon as she had made a number of bundles, she took them out to a spot just inside the compound gate. The junk collector would be making his rounds of the area next week, his last visit before year-end. She was determined to finish by then. It would be a good way for the orphanage to start the new year.

As she worked, occasionally a front-page headline might capture her attention and she would momentarily be distracted from the task at hand. Most of the news was about Occupation policy, about this or that reform or commission. There was land reform, there was education reform. But interspersed among the official announcements of progress were veiled references to worker rallies and hints of discontent. The Japanese press was censored, and you had to read between the lines.

By the end of the week, she was close to finishing and not bothering to read the headlines anymore. She worked as fast as she could, anxious to get the task over with, already thinking about the upcoming celebrations at the orphanage. Although she'd never attended a Christmas festival before, she could tell by the exuberance of the Sisters that it would be very special. But then she thought about how that would be followed by the traditional New Year's festivities and how she would not be able to spend it with her family. How she would never be able to spend Oshogatsu or any other holiday with her family again.

She pressed her fists against her eyes to staunch any tears before they started. When she took her hands away, she knew she would not cry.

She reached for the next pile of newspapers. To her surprise, they were in English. How had Sister Naoko acquired English-language newspapers? she wondered, and then recalled something Sister Izumi had once said. It wasn't uncommon for babies to be wrapped in newspaper. Often it was the cleanest thing on hand.

The quality of the newsprint was better than the Japanese newspapers, and there were many photographs. She flipped through the pages. There were pictures of GIs posing in front of Mount Fuji and of sailors waving from the decks of ships. Remarkably, the newspapers were in relatively good condition. But when she picked up the next one in the pile and turned the page, her heart stopped.

It was him. The photo was grainy but she knew him instantly. He looked different of course. His hair was close-cropped, he was clean-shaven and smiling. He had been alive then.

She checked the date at the top of the newspaper. Ten days after it had happened.

So it had been in the newspapers. Wada was right, the Americans knew. How could she have thought otherwise? They were Americans. They had power and they knew everything and they could do whatever they wanted. They would find out where she was, if they didn't already know. When they came for her, the last thing she wanted was to put the orphanage in danger.

Her whole being filled with a strange fog, and she could hardly see in front of her. Although she'd thought she was safe, she wasn't. It had been an illusion. She hoped that Wada had made it to Hokkaido, that he'd taken on a new identity and made a whole new life. Because if the picture of the GI was in the newspaper, it could only mean the worst. A newspaper like this would surely only publish the worst.

Sumiko stared at the man's face, trying to will him to talk to her through the newsprint. Who are you? Why did you come to the bar? Next to his picture was a mixed-up jumble of *abc* letters, words that made absolutely no sense to her. The English words seemed to be taunting her, mocking her ignorance.

Mingled with her cold fear, too, was anger and resentment. The Americans were free to write about whatever they wanted, weren't they. She assumed this article was their version of the man's death, of how he had died like a dog in a Japanese bar, of how the Japanese had attacked him, of how he was an innocent victim. Wasn't that the sort of thing they would write? The more she scrutinized the paper, the more frustrated she felt. And then, amid the incomprehensible English letters, two words leaped out at her—Bar Lucky. A roar of blood filled her ears.

Sumiko didn't know how long she sat in the storage room. It could have been hours. It could have been only a few minutes. But when she finally decided what she needed to do, she experienced a sense of deep clarity. She tucked the newspaper into her sleeve. This she would not, could not, put out for the junk collector.

That evening Sumiko did not take supper with the others. She said she was tired and needed to sleep. When everyone else went to bed, she crept into the tiny windowless room that Mother Masako used as her office and opened the wooden box on her desk. There was hardly any money inside, just enough to pay for the deliveries of milk and rice. She didn't want to take it all, but there was so little she had no choice. She needed enough train fare to get back to Tokyo and a bit extra. She felt terrible, but she also knew that it was worse for Mother Masako to be housing a murderer.

There was a large gray shawl in the storage room—one of the few items Sister Naoko had picked up that was actually useful—and Sumiko wrapped it around her head and neck. It was cold, and she was glad to have the shawl as she made her way in the dark through the long bamboo-lined passage—the Tunnel of Separation—and back into the world.

35

On the Sunday before Christmas, Nancy arranged two chairs in front of the big plate-glass window so she and Matt could have a special lunch looking out at the view. Today she was wearing a bright red blouse that Matt had never seen on her before, and her hair looked different, curlier and shorter. He wasn't sure but he thought she might even be wearing some lipstick. She had packed rice balls wrapped in nori, black beans, vinegared carrots, and some tiny dried fish no bigger than the tip of a pencil. Matt's contribution to the feast consisted of two bottles of Coke.

Except for the giant "Merry Xmas" banner that hung on the front of General Headquarters, there were few obvious signs on the street that Christmas was just around the corner. Here the big celebration was New Year's, and for most Japanese, Christmas Day was merely another workday.

"Hard to believe it's Christmas again and I'm still here," Nancy said.

"Maybe it won't be much longer."

"You think so? Oh, who knows." She let out a deep sigh. "Anyway, let's enjoy our lunch. I have to say it's fun working in the office when no one else is around. Look at this view. I bet it's every bit as good as the one MacArthur has from his office."

"It's not bad."

"And below, all those people lining the route. Just for a glimpse of MacArthur. Say, do you suppose they can see us from here?" She stood up and began waving her arms back and forth in large sweeping motions as if she were practicing semaphore. The sleeves of her bright red blouse fluttered like little flags.

"What do you think of him?"

"Who?" Nancy continued waving her arms.

"MacArthur."

"Well, I really don't know. He's got one heck of a job ahead of him, I guess. What about you? What do you think?"

Matt remembered that day on the marching plaza when MacArthur addressed the troops with a megaphone. Tall, vigorous, confident—a man who had total power and knew it.

Matt wondered what it must be like living with a man like MacArthur—a man filled with restless drive and energy, a man perpetually on the alert and ready to go to battle at a moment's notice. His much younger wife and his son, Arthur, upon whom he doted, were always by his side through war and peace—in the Philippines, in Australia, and now in Japan. Although MacArthur was by now in his late sixties, from the distance anyway, he exuded no sign of aging or diminution. What was it that gave him such a commanding presence—his stature, his leanness, his proud eagle-like nose? Maybe it was that leather jacket he favored or his dashing aviator glasses. Matt couldn't put his finger on it. Maybe it was just power, pure and simple. All he knew was that his own father was a decade younger and already he looked like an ancient grandfather. He could no longer stand up straight, either because his bones had crumpled or out of an unwillingness to look the world in the eye. His back and his spirit were both bent in an ever-shortening curve toward the ground.

"Hey, how about that!" Nancy began jumping up and down. "You know, I think someone just waved back. Well, this is fun. There are two girls down there and they're waving at me. Do you see them?" Nancy got up on her chair and waved even more vigorously. "Hello! Hello down there!"

Matt looked where Nancy was pointing. The crowd was larger than ever. It felt as if half the city had turned out. In the front row, almost directly opposite their building, were two girls. Their heads were tilted back and they were clearly looking up in Nancy and Matt's direction. One girl held her arm over her head like she was asking a question in class, while the other waved more conspicuously, carving a wide arc in the air with her arm. It was *those* girls! Fumi and her quiet friend, the ones who had given him the letter and the photograph. He was sure of it. He never imagined he would ever see them again.

He took a deep breath. His rational, cautious mind told him to ignore the scene unfolding before his eyes. Just ignore it. He had nothing to say to those girls. They were part of a mass of desperate people, and it was best to stay away from desperate people. Nancy was still flapping her arms like an excited kid.

"Oh, look at them! I know they line up all the time, but I've never had a view of the whole crowd from up high like this. It's really something. That old goat, MacArthur, he must have quite a swelled head by now." Nancy turned to Matt laughing. "Hey, are you okay?"

To hell with it. It was better to speak now, before he had a chance to think. Before he had time to let his rational, cautious mind get the better of him.

"I know this sounds strange, but I think I know those girls. I have to go out and talk to them. They have a problem. I promised to help." Nancy was looking at him strangely, but he continued nonetheless. "I . . . please . . . can you come with me? Can you help me? Please."

She was still giving him the same funny look, but she nodded slowly. He smiled with relief. It was only then that he realized he had been tugging on the sleeve of her blouse.

Nancy turned out to be a woman of action.

Matt explained that he'd met the girls in the summer and that Fumi had wanted him to deliver a letter to General MacArthur. He showed Nancy the letter.

"Nice handwriting." She pursed her lips thoughtfully. "Did you forward a copy to MacArthur?"

"No, of course not."

"Why not?"

"It's a hopeless request. No one is going to pay any attention to something like that."

"But did you say you would deliver the letter?"

"Well, I suppose I sort of promised. I felt sorry for them. I never thought I'd see them again. What would you have done?"

She waved her hand impatiently in the air. "It doesn't matter what I would have done."

"I shouldn't have accepted the letter," he said. "I gave them too much hope, false hope. So I should set the record straight, shouldn't I? I mean, it's not good to mislead them, to let them believe that MacArthur can fix their problems."

Nancy turned her head away. She seemed to be staring at a spot on the far wall. "Makes you think about all the letters we get here, doesn't it. I'm not enthusiastic about typing up some of them, I think you know that. I don't like to see people beg, even if they lost the war. But hope—I figure that hope is one thing nobody can have too much of, not these days. It's what keeps most of us going." In a soft, barely audible voice she added, "Giving someone hope is a good thing. Maybe you did those girls a favor."

Down below, the crowds were starting to disperse and move onto the road, but the girls were still in the same place. MacArthur's car must have passed by.

"You'll come with me, won't you?" Matt said.

"What do you need me for?"

"I don't know. Moral support maybe."

"Okay, better not waste any time," she said, starting to move toward the door. She didn't even bother to put on her jacket. "Whatever it is you want to say or do, you can figure it out on the way."

By the time they raced down the stairs and out the building, Nancy was several steps ahead of him. She crossed the road and walked straight up to the two girls, Matt hurrying after her.

"*Kon'nichi wa*. We saw you from the window." Nancy smiled broadly at Fumi and Aya. "What're your names? I'm Noriko Nogami. *Hajimemashite*. Pleased to meet you."

"Nancy," Matt said.

"What is it? I thought you wanted to talk to them."

"Maybe we should go somewhere else." A man with round glasses and unruly hair was glaring at him.

"Where can we go? Can we take them back to the office?"

"No, of course not."

"Excuse please." The man with the unruly hair addressed Matt in English. In Japanese, he continued, "You should leave those girls alone. They are too young. You *Amerikajin* . . . And as for *you*." He glared at Nancy.

"No, you don't understand. I'm not . . . I know these girls." Matt turned to them. "Do you remember me? We met before, didn't we?"

Fumi nodded.

The man squinted suspiciously at Matt before turning to Fumi. "You don't have to be afraid of his kind, you know."

Matt was trying to think of a comeback when Fumi spoke up in his defense.

"Don't worry. He's my special friend." She beamed at Matt. "You know where my sister is, don't you! That's why you're here."

"Oh, I see." The man's voice was filled with disdain as he turned away. "Your *sister*."

Fumi was oblivious to the stranger's comment. "I'm so happy to see you. I knew that coming here again was the right thing to do. You've found my sister, haven't you!"

That was when Matt made his big mistake. He hadn't been prepared for such a direct question, nor had he anticipated Fumi's strong reaction to seeing him. She'd clearly had total faith in his ability to help her. He should have made something up, told her what she expected to hear, what she so desperately needed to hear. At the very least, he later thought, he should have understood that he needed to soften the blow.

"You've found my sister, haven't you!" she'd chirped in that bright, hope-filled voice. And how had he responded?

"No." Just one hard bullet of a word. He hadn't even added he was sorry. Then he watched as the color instantly drained from her face.

He tried to compensate, assuming as authoritative a tone as he could muster—"These things take longer than expected, you must have patience"—but he could tell by the look Fumi gave him that he'd failed her.

She turned her head away as if she couldn't bear the sight of his face.

It was Nancy who broke the awkward strain of the moment.

"Why don't we all go for some dessert? Let's find a nice coffee shop and get something sweet." She wrapped one arm around Aya and the other around Fumi, and began walking. Over her shoulder she called out to Matt, "Come on now. There's got to be someplace we can go. How about in the Ginza? We can all use a treat. It's almost Christmas, for heaven's sake."

Fumi's mood improved significantly when they got to the coffee shop. Her eyes widened when Nancy asked her to pick from the wax food models in the shopwindow and she pointed without hesitation at the dish of sweet red beans. Once seated at their table, she appeared content to concentrate on eating, barely looking up from her dish.

Nancy, meanwhile, had discovered that Aya was from Canada. She immediately switched to English.

"My goodness, we were meant to meet! You have to tell me all about yourself." She patted Aya's shoulder. "How's the dessert? My relatives here eat *tokoroten*. Seaweed jelly! That's their idea of a dessert, but I just hate it. I wish I had some Jell-O to give them. Now that's a real dessert. Jell-O with whipped cream. What's your favorite dessert?"

"Ice cream," Aya said a little hesitantly.

"Oh, me too. I wish we could get some real ice cream here." Nancy turned to Matt. "Look at that. She's just like us."

Matt had to admit that Nancy's instinct about taking the girls to a coffee shop had been just right. He and Nancy watched as they went to examine the wax models in the shopwindow again. He heard them giggling as they tried to pick a second dessert.

"You're terrific with them," he said to Nancy.

"I like them. They remind me of my kid sisters." Nancy spoke softly. "You know, it really bothers me that I wasn't there for them when they needed me. Getting thrown in the camps and all that. It must have been horrible. Well, they're big now. They went through the worst experience of their lives without me to help them. Maybe they don't need me anymore."

He detected a tone of sadness he'd never heard in her voice before. "You had an even worse time here," he murmured, but she did not reply.

Afterward they accompanied the girls to the streetcar stop. Aya and Nancy walked side by side still talking, followed by Fumi and then by Matt. Matt gave Fumi money for the fare. While they waited, Nancy grabbed Aya's hand and pulled her close. "Did you and Fumi have enough to eat? It was lots of fun, wasn't it. You know, you remind me so much of my youngest sister. Next time we meet I want to tell you about her. You'd like her."

While they waited for the streetcar, Matt repeated to Fumi what he'd said earlier. "I'm sorry your sister hasn't been found yet, but don't be discouraged. General MacArthur has your letter and he always keeps his promises."

He hoped that by saying it over and over it might fix things. But Fumi glared at him coldly, her dark eyes flashing, and he realized that no amount of syrupy dessert was going to make up for today's disappointment or assuage her feelings. Nancy and Aya were too preoccupied with their own parting to even notice.

As soon as the streetcar arrived, a group of people rushed for the doors and Aya and Fumi were swept up with the crowd and pushed on board.

"Oh, wait! Aya! I wanted to ask you—" Nancy shouted, but her voice was cut off by the clanging of a bell. The doors of the streetcar slammed shut.

"I didn't realize it would be so crowded," Matt said. "It doesn't look like it will be a very comfortable ride."

"Oh, that's nothing. It's always crowded." Nancy sounded irritated for some reason. "You army guys don't know how pampered you are. Special jeeps, special reserve cars on trains. If the Occupation forces had to travel the way ordinary Japanese people do, they probably wouldn't go anywhere."

The late-afternoon sun was low in the sky, forcing Matt to squint into the brightness as he looked at Nancy. Her red blouse seemed to be on fire. She was rubbing her hands briskly up and down her arms and he realized she must be freezing.

"You'll catch cold," he said.

"Oh, don't worry about me. Believe me, I went through a lot worse during the war. I'm made of tough stuff. Even so I'm not half as tough as some people here." Nancy stuck out her jaw provocatively. "In this country, can you guess who is made of the toughest stuff? Japanese women, that's who. Don't ever think otherwise. Don't ever believe that hooey about the delicate Oriental flower. They're tough as nails."

Abruptly she bent down, and Matt watched as she brushed some dirt off her skirt hem. Did he dare ask her, he wondered. He really needed help. He couldn't do it alone.

"Thanks so much for coming today."

"I'm glad I came."

"I think the girls really liked you."

"Well, I liked them."

"Say, can I show you something?" Matt reached into his pocket and pulled out the photograph. "This is Sumiko, Fumi's missing sister."

Nancy took the picture from him and studied it in silence.

"She's very pretty," she finally said. "Is that her boyfriend?"

"I don't know. I guess so."

"Humph."

"You were so helpful earlier, I was wondering if you have any suggestions about how one could search for someone like this. I mean, I was thinking, maybe I should look around. For Fumi's sake.

She was awfully disappointed today. You know, you're really good at . . . What I mean is, if there's any help you can give me . . ." His voice trailed off.

She handed the picture back to him and shook her head. "You know, people have to do what they can in order to survive. But they make their own decisions. I'll bet she's making more money in a week than most people make in a month, and she's sure as hell living a lot better. You can count on that. Maybe she doesn't want to be found. Did you ever consider that? Maybe she's having a grand old time."

36

*A*s soon as the doors of the streetcar closed behind them, Aya tried to turn around so she could see Nancy through the glass, but she couldn't move an inch. In fact, she could hardly breathe. Yet despite her discomfort, she couldn't stop smiling. It had been such a wonderful afternoon, and she wished she could have stayed with Nancy longer. Nancy, who held her hand and liked Jell-O and didn't walk in that funny pigeon-toed way or cover her mouth when she laughed. And she laughed a lot. Aya had even told Nancy she was called Irene back home. What's your name, Nancy had asked her in English, and out it had come, her Canadian name. Of course, she asked her to call her Aya, so that Fumi wouldn't get upset. The best thing, though, the most important thing, was that she and Nancy could speak in English. In English! She could be her old self. For a short time this afternoon, she was Irene Shimamura, and Nancy was like the big sister she'd never had. There was so much she wanted to tell her, but how would she ever see her again? She had waited for Nancy to ask for her address or to suggest when they could next meet, but it never came up and before Aya knew it the streetcar had suddenly arrived and she was pushed from behind onto the steps and inside. She didn't even have time to wave goodbye.

The streetcar traveled in a jerky, uneven movement, sometimes fast, sometimes slow. It stopped several times but the doors remained shut, and it wasn't until the fifth stop that the doors were flung open. Before the people waiting at the stop could board, Fumi jumped out, pulling Aya with her. The drop to the ground gave Aya an unexpected jolt.

"What happened? Was it the wrong streetcar?"

"We're not taking the streetcar." Fumi started walking briskly.

"Where are we going?" Aya could barely keep up.

Fumi headed back in the direction of the coffee shop where they had just had their dessert. The street was still as crowded as before. Maybe Nancy had returned there, too, Aya thought, and her hopes were raised when she spotted Nancy's bright red blouse, but when the woman turned around it was someone else.

"What are we doing?" Aya asked. "Are we looking for Nancy and Matsumoto-san?"

"Forget about them. Good, it's getting dark."

"Yes, you're right, it's late. Shouldn't we go home?"

Fumi stopped so abruptly Aya nearly bumped into her. "Don't you understand? We've come this far. We have to look for my sister."

"But what can we do? You have to leave it up to the adults."

"Adults!" Fumi spit the word out. "You can't rely on adults."

"But Matsumoto-san—"

"He doesn't care about finding my sister. He doesn't care one bit. I should have known that I couldn't rely on him. Nobody cares about my sister. Only I do." She pulled Aya into the doorway of the nearest building. "And *you*. You care. You're the only friend I can count on. Let's look for her ourselves. See this. See what I have." Reaching into her blouse Fumi pulled out a small silk pouch that hung around her neck on a slender cord. "I don't know why I decided to bring this today. I just had a hunch I might need it. Something told me that I should be prepared."

"What is it?"

"My sister gave me some money a long time ago. For an emergency."

"Good, so we can take the streetcar home."

"Not that. I meant a real emergency. We have to find my sister."

They turned down the first street they came to and entered a maze of narrow, crooked lanes. Everywhere looked dark and grimy. The area was deserted.

"Wouldn't it be better to come back another time, in the day-time?" Aya said.

"We can't leave until we find her."

"*O-nesan*, pretty *o-nesan*." A child's voice came out of nowhere. "Over here." Two small boys stepped out of the shadows. They wore dirty sweaters full of holes. One had an unlit cigarette butt dangling from his lips. He moved with an exaggerated swagger as he approached.

"Big sister, you want to meet a nice Joe?" The boy addressed Fumi.

"Beat it!" Fumi said.

The boy moved closer. He pushed his lower jaw forward so his cigarette brushed against Fumi's chin and he tried wiggling the dry butt to tickle her. Fumi jerked her head to the side. The cigarette fell from his mouth, and the boy caught it midair with a practiced motion. He started laughing.

"Come on, I can help you make some good money."

"Leave us alone."

"Okay, sure." The boy raised both hands in the air in a show of goodwill. "But before you leave, can you give us poor boys a little something? Anything you can spare is fine."

Fumi motioned to Aya to run but it was too late. The boys had clearly been observing them, just waiting for the right opportunity to strike. The one with the cigarette butt grabbed Fumi's pouch, broke the flimsy strap with a quick tug, and began running down the lane. "*Dorobo!*" Fumi screamed. She set off in pursuit, yelling "Thief!" at the top of her lungs, but the other boy caught up to her and pushed her to the ground before running off himself. Fumi scrambled to her feet and started running again. By the time Aya reached her, Fumi was on the ground once more, clutching her legs in pain.

"They got it. They got it all," Fumi said between gasps. "I was running as fast as I could but they disappeared."

Her legs were scratched and bloodied, and she'd lost her sandals during the chase. Her white socks were completely black. She looked dazed.

"There, you see? We better go home right away," Aya said.

"No."

"You'll never find your sister like this."

"I'm not giving up."

"But we have to go home."

"You go home if you like. I'm not leaving."

Aya had reached her limit. "Can't you see how dangerous it is? Look what just happened. How can you be so stupid?"

"Stupid?" Fumi's tone had shifted. "Look who's talking. You're the one who's stupid."

"That's right, call me stupid. But you're the stupidest of all." Aya's words came out in a rush. "You're looking for your sister, but she's not looking for you. How do you know she even cares if she sees you again?"

"That's not true. She loves me!" Fumi's face turned purple. "You're jealous. Because I have a sister, and you—you have nobody. You don't even have a mother. Nobody cares about you. You're nothing but a stupid repat."

You have nobody. You don't even have a mother. The words were like hammers chipping off pieces of her heart. Aya felt the truth in those words and then she felt a cold blackness close in all around her. It was as if she had fallen into the bottomless lake.

In that instant she saw Fumi for what she was, a selfish scheming girl who didn't care about anyone except herself and her sister. She didn't care about Aya, she had only wanted to use her. Aya turned and slowly began walking away. She felt a strange numbing calmness.

"Where do you think you're going?" Fumi's voice sounded distant, muffled. Distorted by an ocean of separation and refraction. "You'll never find your way on your own!"

Where was she going? Aya wasn't sure. She was falling fast. She was sinking like a stone.

37

*Y*ou're right, forget it. She's just a bar girl. Not worth bothering about." Matt shoved Sumiko's picture back in his pocket. He and Nancy were still standing on the sidewalk near the streetcar stop where they had seen Fumi and Aya off.

"You think I'm a prig, don't you," Nancy said.

"I never said anything of the kind."

"Sure you do. A moralistic, holier-than-thou old maid."

"Nancy, please."

"Remember what I told you about how people thought I was a streetwalker. How would you feel? Just because of the way I walk, like an American, not shuffling and pigeon-toed like the women here, or because I speak with this heavy accent. Just because I'm different. People make all kinds of assumptions about others, don't they. They take one look at you and they assume they know all about you, when they don't know a damn thing."

"Nancy, I'm sorry you—"

She paid no attention to him. "Everything goes wrong when people make stupid assumptions and don't even try to get to know you as a person. As a human being, for God's sake. It just stinks."

"Nancy . . ."

Her eyes glistened behind her glasses. "Anyway, never mind. Show me that picture again."

"What?"

"The photograph. If I'm going to help you, you better show it to me."

"But I thought you said—"

"Look, am I a prig? Probably. Am I moralistic? Well, maybe that's just the way I was raised. But I'm a human being and so is Sumiko. She's a person, not just some bar girl. I don't know why she's doing what she's doing, but it doesn't matter. I'll help you. You want me to help you find her, don't you? Isn't that what you want?"

"Yes, but are you sure?"

"Matt, I just said I'll help. Don't you believe me?"

"Of course, well, as long as you're sure." He paused, uncertain how to express his gratitude. "When are you free? How about next weekend?"

"For heaven's sake, let's start right now. We're already in the Ginza. We can go to the big dance halls and show them Sumiko's picture. Surely someone will recognize her. Maybe we can find her tonight."

They set off, marching quickly with a sense of grim purpose. Nancy had such a determined set to her jaw that, although she looked very cold—she was almost shivering—Matt was afraid to say anything. When they reached the bar district, Nancy suddenly turned to him and said, "From here on, you better lead the way."

"But there are hundreds of bars and dance halls. Actually I don't know that many."

"Well, you're still one up on me. I've never set foot in a single one. Stop shilly-shallying, Matt. If we're going to find Fumi's sister, we have to start somewhere."

They turned down a side street that Matt knew would bring them close to the infamous Lily Pad Dance and Drink Hall. Two men squatted in front of the door, smoking cigarettes. They did not stand up when Matt approached, so he had to bend over to show them Sumiko's photograph. He returned to where Nancy was standing several yards back.

"They didn't know her."

"This is only the first place we've tried. Did they have any suggestions where else we should look?"

"I didn't ask."

"Oh, Matt." Nancy sounded exasperated. "Okay, shall we just continue down this street?"

The next dance hall was much smaller and more cheerful looking. The walls were painted with colorful palm trees, and a bright orange neon sign flashed on and off. The door was closed.

"Guess they're not open yet." Matt shoved his hands in his pockets.

"Somebody must be there though. The sign's lit." Nancy went up to one of the windows but the bottom sill was a good foot above her head, too high for her to see inside.

She returned to the front of the building and knocked on the door. There was no response.

"It's probably too early," Matt said. "Let's go."

No sooner had he spoken than the door swung open and a middle-aged man with a pencil-thin mustache peered out. He was wearing a wrinkled white shirt, and behind one ear was the stub of an unlit cigarette. He looked at Nancy, then at Matt, and then back at Nancy.

"We're looking for someone." Matt spoke quickly. He showed the man Sumiko's picture. "Have you ever seen this woman? Do you know where she is?"

The man took the photograph from Matt and held it at an angle close to his face. "Sorry, can't help you. Never seen her before." As he handed the picture back to Matt, he tipped his head in Nancy's direction. "If she needs work, though, we might have an opening. Can start right away."

"Thanks for your time." Matt tugged on the back of Nancy's blouse to pull her away.

They walked for a few minutes in silence until Nancy suddenly exploded. "What a creep! He must have thought you were my pimp."

They continued trudging up and down the back alleys of the Ginza. At each bar and dance hall they came to, it was Matt's job to go inside and show the photograph. Everywhere they went, it was the same. Searching for one woman among thousands, he realized, was madness. Inwardly he cursed the stupid idea he'd had, and he cursed Nancy's willingness to help out.

"We're going about this all wrong." Nancy plucked the photograph from his hand. "We're asking the men when we should be asking other women. All these women are in the same position as Sumiko is. Somebody has to know her; somebody will recognize her."

She began running up to women on the street who were alone or in pairs. "Excuse me, *sumimasen*. Do you know this woman by any chance? No? You're certain? I see. Well, thank you for your time."

One after another, women looked at the photograph and shook their heads until the last one Nancy approached. This woman had some advice. Pointing down a squalid-looking unlit lane, she said, "I'm sorry I can't help you, but you might try going this way. There are a lot of dormitories and rooming houses on this dead-end street. Maybe you'll find the person you're looking for there."

The narrow lane looked distinctly unsavory. After they thanked the woman for her tip, Matt turned to Nancy. "It's getting really late. I think we should give up and go home."

"Are you ready to give up so easily?" Nancy started down the lane ahead of him. "Come on."

At the first building they came to, she knocked loudly on the door. "*Sumimasen.* Sorry to bother you. *Tomodachi o sagashite imasu.* We're looking for a friend."

Door after door, no one answered.

"Nancy, let's call it quits."

"Okay. Just one more place."

They had reached the end of the cul-de-sac. A crudely lettered sign, TACHIBANA DORMITORY, stood next to a row of battered mailboxes. A miniature American flag was stuck in one of the slots.

"One last try," Nancy said, pounding on the first door. "*Sumimasen!* We're looking for a friend."

As with the other places they had tried, no one answered. After five doors, Matt put his arm in front of Nancy to stop her from continuing.

"That's enough," he said.

They retraced their steps toward the now extremely crowded streets where they had begun their search. The temperature had fallen, and the dance halls and bars were too busy for them to make further inquiries. They didn't dare approach any more women on the street, either, for most were no longer walking alone; they clung to the arms of their GI clients or boyfriends.

Even Nancy had to admit defeat. "Oh, Matt, I'm really sorry. It's so disappointing. I honestly thought we could find her."

"Let's forget about it."

"It seemed like such a good idea. Maybe we can try again tomorrow."

"We've done enough."

"I'm serious, there must be something else we can do."

"No."

"But it might be different if we have a fresh start."

Her persistence touched a nerve and he snapped at her. "I said forget it, Nancy. It's pointless."

"Don't you want to find her?"

"What? A missing bar girl? You're the one who said she probably doesn't want to be found."

"I shouldn't have said that. It was wrong."

"Well, you've convinced me."

"But don't you want to find her for Fumi's sake? Didn't you say you felt bad about letting Fumi down?"

"I can't help Fumi. She should learn to accept reality."

"But you *can* help her, Matt."

"No, I can't. I can't help her. I can't help anyone."

"But I'm sure you can."

Matt stopped abruptly in the middle of the street. People streamed around them. "Why are you doing this?" he demanded.

"What do you mean? I want to help. I want to help *you*."

"Well, you're wasting your time. It's pointless."

"What is? Trying to help another human being? Trying to do the right thing? Is that pointless?" She had a look of utter confusion and hurt on her face.

"Yes, goddammit. Especially trying to do the right thing. Nobody ever thanks you for doing the right thing."

"Don't get mad at me, Matt, please." She put her hand on his arm and the unexpected gesture made him stiffen involuntarily. She dropped her hand.

"I better go," she said. Without waiting for a reply she turned and was immediately swallowed up in the crowd.

Matt stood where he was, letting his body be buffeted by passing groups of *panpan* and GIs. Everyone seemed to be drunk or pretending to be.

"Move out of the way, would ya," a beefy GI yelled. He gave Matt a stiff shove with his shoulder, slamming him into the side of a building.

Matt put his hands in front of his face just in time to avoid having his nose broken against the wall. Out of the corner of one eye he saw the kaleidoscope of humanity swirling past—white skin, yellow, black, brown. Close by, a woman shrieked with laughter. When the crowd had moved on and he had room to maneuver, he reached into his pocket and pulled out Sumiko's photograph. It was too dark to see anything, not her face, not her eyes, not the sparkling hairpin in her black hair. But it didn't matter because he already knew what was there. He ripped the picture in half, then in quarters, and continued tearing as many times as he could until the pieces were too small to grip with his fingertips, too small to tear. Until there was nothing left of the woman at all.

38

*Y*ou'll never find your way on your own," Fumi shouted after Aya's retreating figure.

She wanted to add "Good riddance! I'm glad I don't have to take care of you anymore." But she didn't say those words out loud—she let them ring inside her chest—harsh, mean words that she suddenly felt ashamed of even thinking. She watched Aya walk away, and although she was tempted to run after her and say she was sorry, she did nothing. Whatever regret she might have felt for what she had said in anger, some core of stubbornness and willful pride that she'd had since she was a small child made it impossible for her to chase after Aya. She could only stay right where she was and wait. Aya would come back, she was sure of that.

"You'll get lost," she muttered under her breath. "You need me."

In the distance Aya turned the corner and disappeared from sight.

"You're jealous," Fumi had said. But wasn't the truth that *she* was the one who'd felt jealous watching Aya and Nancy in the coffee shop? The way Nancy kept grabbing Aya's hand, the way they had chattered in English, completely ignoring Fumi. Nancy looked Japanese but she didn't act like one. She had a loose way of moving her arms and legs, and she laughed with her mouth wide open so you could see her teeth and sometimes even her tongue. She didn't have a loud voice, but somehow it felt loud. It had filled the coffee shop, echoed off the walls. Aya had laughed at everything Nancy said. She had looked at her so eagerly it was pathetic, like a puppy anxious to be petted.

But what bothered Fumi the most was this: What if Aya was right? What if Sumiko really was happier without Fumi in her life? The moon had risen and now shone like a tight drum in the cloudless sky. The air felt cold and dry. Fumi retraced her steps, scanning the ground for her sandals, but they were nowhere in sight. She tried seeking shelter in the entranceway to a small tobacco shop, but there wasn't much protection from the wind, so after a few minutes she went all the way to the end of the lane where a low narrow building blocked any further passage. The rows of doors along the side of the building stretched back into the darkness, and in front was a large sign—TACHIBANA DORMITORY—and a set of mailboxes. Someone had glued a miniature American flag to a chopstick and pushed it into the top of one of the slots. Fumi was about to reach up and touch the flag when she heard someone coming out of the building. She crouched behind the mailboxes.

It was a GI and a Japanese woman. When they were almost in front of Fumi, the man turned around and pulled the woman toward him. All Fumi could see were their legs, so close together the woman's tiny feet were almost standing on top of the man's big shoes. They stood like this for what felt to Fumi like an eternity before walking away.

"Gosh, that's so romantic, don't you think?"

The voice came from behind her. Fumi turned around to find herself face-to-face with a girl who didn't look all that much older than she was. The girl grinned broadly, revealing a big gap between her two front teeth. Fumi felt her face flush. It was mortifying to be caught watching the couple, but the other girl didn't appear to be embarrassed in the least.

"I can't wait to be an *only*. How about you?" The girl had a rough accent. She was wearing a cheap kimono and her hair was tied back in a braid. "Haven't seen you here before. You new?"

Although she wasn't sure what she meant, Fumi nodded.

"Me, too," the girl said. "You come from far?"

"Not too far," Fumi said vaguely. "Do you live here?"

"Of course! Want to see our room? I can't tell you how nice it is. My big sisters are all really nice, too."

"Your sisters live here?"

"They're not my real sisters, silly. They're showing me the ropes, and I have to run errands for them. Most of the time they're out or too busy, though. It's okay. It's not really that hard."

"You don't know Sumiko Tanaka, do you?" Fumi decided she had nothing to lose in asking.

"No. Who's that?" The girl opened her eyes wide and stared at Fumi, scrutinizing her with renewed interest.

"My sister."

"Oh, so you came to work with your sister?"

"No, I can't work. I'm still in school. I'm just looking for her."

"School! How old are you anyway?"

"Twelve."

"Twelve! No wonder you look so young." The girl narrowed her eyes. "I'm fifteen. Well, who knows. Maybe they'll hire you. You can lie about your age." She pulled her braid forward and chewed on the end. "It's fun. You get to dance and listen to music. The GIs have to buy tickets, one ticket for one dance. I'm still learning how to dance, you know. Some of the other sisters at the club are teaching me. They said I have natural talent. It's Western dancing, you know. They call it the cheek-to-cheek style." The girl leaned one cheek toward Fumi coquettishly. "You touch cheeks. The GIs like that."

She pulled out the band around her braid, and ran her fingers through her long hair to untangle it. "As soon as I get a bit better, I'll have my own partners. Then I can start to make money. I'll get some proper clothes, too, and some makeup."

Fumi looked at the girl. Even in the shadows it was clear she was still just a country hick.

"Don't you want to come inside with me?" the girl asked.

Fumi considered her options. She glanced up and down the dark alley. There was no one in sight, certainly no sign of Aya. It was cold, she'd lost all her money, and who knew when Aya would reappear. On the other hand, if Fumi went inside, how would Aya know where to find her? Should she wait where she was or should she follow this girl inside?

"Hey, where are your shoes?" The girl suddenly pointed at Fumi's feet.

Fumi looked down at her filthy socks and scraped shins as if seeing them for the first time.

"Don't worry," the girl said. "Come with me. I can give you a new pair of shoes. Come inside and get warm."

Fumi followed the girl down the side of the building to the last door. The girl reached up to the ledge over the doorway and felt for something. She moved her hand back and forth across the ledge, tapping like a blind person.

"Oh, there's no key," she said, a bit surprised. "It's supposed to be here. I don't know what to do. Sometimes the others don't come home all night."

But when she tried the door, the knob turned easily. It wasn't even locked. Before they went in, she pointed at the women's shoes that were lined up just outside the room.

"You can have your pick," she said. "Whichever ones you like."

Once inside the girl reached up to pull the cord on the ceiling light. The harsh fluorescent light flickered and buzzed. The room was very small and all the bedding had been rolled up and shoved into the corner. Clothes spilled out of the closet and were hung helter-skelter on hooks that had been nailed into the walls. The stale scent of perfume filled the air.

"Isn't it nice," the girl said, picking up some towels and tissues that were strewn across the tatami. She plopped herself down in front of the low tea table in the middle of the room. On top of the table was a small lacquer box. She raised the lid of the box and motioned for Fumi to come sit beside her.

"See here, this is lipstick." The girl picked up a metal tube from the box, pulled off the top, and swiveled the bottom so that a stick of bright red shot up. She adjusted the mirror in the lid of the box and applied the lipstick to her small chapped lips. The color was too stark, and it made her look as if she had cut her mouth. She poked her finger through the box again and this time retrieved a small brown pencil. She licked the tip and made a tiny dark spot on her cheek near her lip.

"This is a beauty mark," she said, examining her face from different angles in the cloudy mirror. "How do I look? Oh, wait. I forgot my rouge." She poked through the contents of the box again, but couldn't seem to find what she was looking for. "Hmmm, someone must have taken it."

"Is all this stuff yours?" Fumi asked.

"Oh no. Say, you want to try some lipstick?"

Fumi shook her head.

"It's okay. Don't worry. I'm not supposed to use the big sisters' makeup, either, but when they're out, who's to know? Anyway, I have to practice, don't I?" The girl went back to looking at herself in the mirror. She puckered her red lips. "What's your name?"

"Fumi."

"What an old-fashioned name!" The girl made a face. "You better change it."

"Why?"

" 'Cause the Americans don't like Japanese names. I'm changing mine."

"Yeah? What's your name?"

"I haven't decided. Maybe I'll be Betty. What do you think? You think Betty is a good name?"

Fumi didn't know what she should say, so instead she asked, "What's your real name?"

"Hisayo." The girl wrinkled her nose. "Nobody can remember that."

Hisayo suddenly stood up and pulled aside a thin curtain that covered a makeshift closet in the corner of the room. She selected a pink blouse with a frilly collar and cuffs and a long wide skirt made of a stiff-looking fabric. She held the outfit against her body and twirled around as if she were dancing.

"What do you think?" she asked.

"It's pretty," Fumi said obligingly.

"Of course." Hisayo set the clothes on the tatami mat and began undoing her kimono. She stripped down to her undershirt, and Fumi could see her nipples poking through the thin material, like little azuki beans. Her breasts were small.

"The first outfit I buy for myself is going to look just like this one," Hisayo said as she slipped her arms through the pink blouse and buttoned it up. It was much too large and the frilly collar sagged in front; the sleeves fell over her wrists and covered half her hands.

"Well?"

"You look very pretty."

Hisayo beamed. "Thanks." She carefully unbuttoned the blouse and hung it back up in the closet. She didn't even attempt to try on the skirt, instead hanging it up, too. She ran her hand back and forth across the clothes hanging on the line. The different fabrics rustled against each other.

"These kinds of clothes must be expensive," Fumi said.

"You bet. You see how many nice clothes the big sisters have." Hisayo sighed. "Say, you better not tell anyone I looked at their clothes, okay? You'll be in trouble, too, you know." Her tone had changed, a harder edge to it now.

"Don't worry, I won't say—"

Before Fumi could finish, Hisayo cut her off. "Shhh. Be quiet."

She pulled the cord attached to the ceiling light and the room turned dark. From outside Fumi could hear the faint sound of knocking and a woman's voice repeating "*Sumimasen, sumimasen.* We're looking for a friend."

"What is it?" she whispered.

"Shhh. Don't make any noise."

The knocking stopped but Fumi didn't dare move until Hisayo finally turned the light back on.

"What was that?"

Hisayo shrugged. "I don't know. Might have been the police or the landlord."

"But it was a woman's voice."

Hisayo shrugged again. "Beats me. All I know is that the big sisters never like to open the door unless they know who it is. They said that anyone who has to knock doesn't belong here."

Hisayo went over to the side of the room and crouched in front of a small pile of soiled-looking clothes. She pulled out a tattered yukata.

"If you don't mind, I'm going to get changed for bed. It's a bit early but let's go to sleep, okay? I'm bushed."

She turned around and undressed, quickly exchanging her cheap kimono for the yukata that served as her nightgown. When she was finished, she looked Fumi up and down again, taking in her baggy pants and threadbare jacket. "You going to sleep like that? In your clothes?"

"I don't have anything else."

"I'd give you a nightgown, but I don't have an extra one. But here, maybe you can use this." Hisayo reached into a cupboard and pulled out a gauzy piece of material. It was the shade of a peach, and so sheer it was practically see-through.

"What's that?" Fumi asked.

"It's an American nightgown. It's what a real woman wears. Why don't you sleep in this."

"But it's someone else's."

"Oh, go on. You don't want to sleep in your clothes, do you?"

"Why don't you wear one of these?"

"I will, soon enough. Anyway, don't worry. Whoever this belongs to probably won't come back tonight. Sometimes they stay out all night. They're having lots of fun. Here, put it on. Let's see what you look like."

Fumi took off her blouse and put the nightgown on over her undershirt. Hisayo giggled. "You don't even have breasts yet, do you."

Hisayo unrolled a futon and motioned for Fumi to do the same. She pulled the blanket up to her shoulders. "I'll be asleep in two seconds. Can you turn off the overhead light?"

She wasn't kidding. Almost instantly, Hisayo's breathing took on the slow, steady rhythm of sleep and she began snoring lightly. Fumi lay in the dark listening to her. She knew she couldn't possibly go to sleep. She was much too worried.

Besides, she had to think. She had to focus. Concentrate, concentrate! Despite her exhaustion, she had to come up with a proper plan to find Sumiko. That was the whole point of her efforts, wasn't it? Everything she'd been doing was to find Sumiko. Lying in the dark, Fumi realized she did not have the slightest idea how to find her sister. Even worse, she no longer felt confident she could recognize her. For even if Sumiko looked the same on the outside, Fumi was afraid that she might not be the Sumiko she knew from before. If she were, why wouldn't she have come back to visit? Why would she have vanished so completely from Fumi's life like this? Again the hateful thought came to her unbidden: What if her sister had simply forgotten about her?

Over the past months Fumi had tried very hard to imagine what her sister's life was like. She'd tried to fill her mind with the same thoughts her sister might have had, tried desperately to dream the same way. But she had come up blank. Certain details were easy: Sumiko's new clothes or hairdo, or the way she might laugh when a handsome GI approached to ask for a dance. But inside, that was hard. What was going on inside? If a man put his arms around your waist and drew you close, how did that feel? Many of the new pulp magazines featured pictures of fallen women on their covers. The pictures were confusing; Fumi liked to look at them but knew they were somehow bad. Her father seemed to think he was shielding her from this world of pulp fantasy, but Fumi already knew what lay between the covers of those magazines, as did all her classmates at school.

Her parents also thought they were protecting her by not talking about Sumiko, as if her sister had never existed. Neither of her parents were the same people who had raised her, who had fed her rice porridge when she was sick, who had brushed the sand off her knees when she fell, who had told her with pride how she would grow up to be a fine wife and mother in the new Japanese empire and how wonderful her life would be. All that had changed as life shrank to the bare essentials of getting by.

Nechan, where are you? Why don't you want to come home?

She should never have given away the photograph. What a fool she had been. It was the only solid evidence that Sumiko still existed. She did still exist, didn't she? Didn't she?

Fumi tried to conjure the image of Sumiko's face, but somehow the only face that came to mind was Aya's. Aya was taking up the space where her sister should be. It made Fumi mad, and then it made her want to cry. "Stupid," she muttered as she clutched the dirty blanket and pulled it tighter. "*Baka.*" She was angry at Aya, and at the same time she was afraid for her. Afraid for both of them.

It was cold tonight, so cold that even inside the room she could see her breath when she exhaled. The futon was thin, the blanket even thinner. It was very quiet. All she could hear was a wintery wind whistling softly through the spaces between the window frame and the wall. The wind played snatches of a sad off-key little tune. It was, Fumi decided, the song of loneliness. She pulled the blanket up to her chin and then over her entire head.

She shouldn't go to sleep. She should go outside and wait for Aya to return. What if the person knocking on the door had been Aya? Fumi should get up and look for her. But the cold made it impossible to move, and Hisayo's steady breathing was hypnotic. Against her will, against her better judgment, Fumi started to feel very drowsy.

39

*K*ondo Sensei felt awful. It was one of the coldest days they'd had so far, and he knew it was foolish to be sitting outside in the Alley in weather like this. But it was the last Sunday before Christmas, and once again Yamaguchi was going on and on about how much money was to be made at this time of year. Most of the other translators, in fact, intended to work every night until New Year's. Over the past few weeks, however, Kondo had developed a bad cough that he couldn't seem to shake, and now his throat was so raw it sometimes hurt to talk or even to swallow. He rubbed his dry, chapped hands together and tucked them under his arms to keep them warm. Even his fingertips were numb, so he periodically blew on them, trying to keep the blood circulating. It didn't seem normal to feel this cold all the time. Deep in his chest he felt a dull heaviness.

Although it wasn't very late, he began packing up his things. Business had been steady throughout the day and he had made decent money. He rolled his brushes and ink sticks in newspaper, wrapped his pencils and pens in an old handkerchief, and placed everything in the top of his worn black satchel. He would stop somewhere and have a bowl of oden and maybe treat himself to a bit of hot sake. He pulled the scarf around his neck tighter. Yes, that was what he really craved, something to warm him from the inside. He felt energized by this small promise to himself. To hell with Christmas, to hell with these *onlys* and butterflies. He would go home and go to bed.

"Excuse me, you're not leaving already, are you?"

He turned around. The woman wore baggy pants, a plain blue top, and a large gray shawl around her shoulders. While her clothes were not those of a *panpan,* she had a direct gaze that suggested she was accustomed to looking at men. He stared back at her. She brought her face closer to the candle and something about her, especially around the eyes, reminded him of someone, but he couldn't place who it might be. He cast the thought aside. He saw so many women that they were all starting to look alike.

Maybe one more job wouldn't hurt, he thought, but then he felt the fire rise in his throat again. It reminded him that he needed to get some rest. "I'm done for the day. There are other letter writers at the entrance. You must have seen them."

"Yes, I saw them."

"Ask one of them."

"They were talking together in a group. I didn't want to disturb them. I want someone who will work in private."

Kondo pulled his scarf tighter around his neck. The winter air was so dry it felt like bits of sand were lodged in the lining of his throat. "Sorry, I'm finished for the evening."

The woman didn't blink. "Couldn't you please take a quick look? I've come a long way."

"All right," he said gruffly. "Let's stop wasting time. Show me your letter."

"No, it's not a letter."

Kondo narrowed his eyes. "If it's something you want me to compose, come back another time. I have to go home."

"I need a really good translator. Someone who is completely accurate."

He gritted his teeth and thought about the incident with the woman with the broken geta. Sometimes accuracy wasn't what people really wanted.

"And someone who's discreet. You look like a serious type. Not a chatterbox. Not like those other men I passed on the way here."

"Why don't you just show me what you have."

She set the *furoshiki* she'd been carrying on the ground and unknotted it. Inside was another cloth, a smaller *furoshiki*, which she also unknotted. Judging by the care with which she had wrapped the contents, Kondo assumed it must be something very valuable. When he saw the newspaper, he waited for her to unwrap it as well. Instead she picked up the paper and held it in front of his face. *The Pacific Stars and Stripes*. For the first time, it crossed his mind that she might not be quite right in the head. Despite her appearance, she might be one of the damaged ones, just a crazy lady trying to sell issues of the U.S. Forces' newspaper that she'd picked up from the garbage outside the barracks. There was no telling what people would try to sell.

"Do you know this newspaper?" she asked.

"Of course. It's for the American military."

She nodded, as if affirming that he had passed the first test. "I need you to translate it."

"The whole paper?"

"Well, I . . ." Her voice was hesitant.

"Miss, this is not even current. Quite frankly, I don't think you want to waste your money on out-of-date news."

The woman closed her eyes and was silent for a moment. Then she pulled a thin envelope from her purse and placed it on the tangerine crate. "Please. I don't know how much your services are and I suppose this is nowhere near enough, but if you are willing to accept this as a down payment, I will return with the full amount."

Kondo was again conscious of the scratchiness in his throat and the ache in his chest. Damn woman. Even without opening the envelope she offered, he could tell it had hardly anything in it. The whole business was too humiliating for both of them.

He pushed the envelope across the crate toward her.

"Please, I need to know what this says. As quickly as possible. Please reconsider." The woman's voice had lost its crisp edge. She slid the envelope back to his side of the tangerine crate.

Kondo sighed. Everyone always wanted him to do something for them. As a teacher, as a translator, as a letter writer. He picked up the envelope and began tapping it against his wrist.

"In a hurry? For old news?"

The woman winced.

"Tell me, are you in some kind of trouble?"

She shook her head. No.

"I see. But there's something important in these newspaper articles, am I correct?"

She nodded.

"Obviously you don't want me to translate the entire newspaper. Don't you think you better give me some guidance?"

She stared at her hands and began pulling on the frayed edges of her shawl. "A friend needs to know."

Her voice was barely audible and Kondo leaned forward to hear better.

"A man was stabbed to death." The woman's voice cracked, then fell even lower. "An American."

The candle flickered, as if in acknowledgment of the gravity of her statement. Kondo held his breath waiting for her to continue, but she simply hung her head as if it had taken all her energy to make that statement. When she recovered, she picked up the newspaper, folded it open to an inside page, and handed it to him. The headline in large typeface said BAR LUCKY NOT LUCKY, OFF-LIMITS MEANS OFF-LIMITS! Next to the article there were pictures of five GIs.

What the hell was this about? Kondo was going to refuse when he was overcome by a fit of coughing. He doubled over, and when his coughing subsided, he became aware of her hand rubbing his back. She tried to wrap her shawl around his shoulders. He shooed her arm away.

"You're not well."

"I'm okay. It's just a cold. I'll take this home and look at it there. Come back next week."

"Next week?" Her voice sounded distraught. "Can't you do it sooner?"

"How soon do you need it?"

"As soon as—"

"All right, all right. Tomorrow evening after six." He stuffed the newspaper in his satchel. Then he returned her envelope. "You can pay me when I've finished the job."

"I can't tell you how—"

"Forget it." He waved his hand in the air to cut her off and started down the slope ahead of her.

"Thank you so much," the woman called out after him. "I will be here at six. I will be here without fail."

When he arrived at his boardinghouse, Kondo took off his shoes, his gloves, and his hat, but kept his overcoat and scarf on. As was often the case in the winter, it actually felt colder inside than it did outside. He wondered if his landlady had opened the window while he was out and forgotten to shut it, but the window was closed. Cold air blew in around the edges where the glass met the ill-fitting wooden frame. Every few minutes, the glass pane rattled ominously.

The bowl of noodles he'd had on his way home had helped to warm him but the effect was only temporary. How he wished he'd come back in time to go to the public bath. A long soak in the hot *sento* would have heated his blood enough so that by the time he crawled into his futon, he would be fast asleep and dreaming of warm places. Once asleep, you didn't feel the cold. A deep sleep killed all pain, masked all discomfort. He thought about asking Mrs. Kanehara if she would prepare a hot water bottle for him, but it was already very late and his landlady was a prickly type.

He decided he might as well tackle the translation. Why on earth had he agreed to do it? The woman must have bewitched him. As for promising to return tomorrow evening—Monday—well, that was even more proof that he was getting soft in the head. He had to teach all day.

He located the article—BAR LUCKY NOT LUCKY, OFF-LIMITS MEANS OFF-LIMITS!—and quickly scanned it. It was puzzling because he didn't see anything about the stabbing the woman had mentioned. He sighed. It happened all too often, didn't it. Women who got their facts mixed up and jumbled. Well, it wasn't his problem.

All U.S. servicemen are sternly reminded once again not to enter any area designated as off-limits. Violations of these regulations will be considered as prejudicial to the goals of the Allied Occupation of Japan. For good reason SCAP has determined that certain districts must be out of bounds. Protect yourselves. Obey all regulations.

There was more but he was tired now. The thought of having to teach tomorrow made him realize that he needed to go to bed right away. He would get up early and finish the article in the morning.

40

Fumi woke to the caress of warm yeasty breath on her face. Her first thought was that Sumiko had come for her.

"Little thief! Look, she wear my nightgown."

Fumi opened her eyes. The woman leaning over her had her face so close it was hard to focus. Fumi made out a set of charcoal-rimmed eyes and scarlet lips.

"Aw, don't get upset, honey. I'll buy you all the nighties you need." The GI stood in the doorway of the apartment, filling the frame.

"But it mine." The woman pouted.

"I'm gonna buy you brand-new ones. What do you need that old thing for? Leave the kid be. Pack up your things and let's go."

"O-nesan, what's going on?" Hisayo sat up and rubbed the sleep out of her eyes.

"I came to get my things."

"You're leaving?" Hisayo sounded panicky.

"Who's the kid wearing my nightgown? Did you bring her here? Did you give her my nightgown to wear?"

"O-nesan, she's new. She wants to work here. I told her what a nice place this is."

The woman snorted. "Good, I'll sell her my stuff." She tugged on the nightgown Fumi was wearing. "You want to wear my clothes so much, huh. How about if you pay me for them."

"What's the matter, honey?" The GI remained standing in the doorway.

"Nothing," the woman replied in English, standing up. "Everything okay."

She was dressed like she was going to a party. Her hair was piled high on her head and she wore round earrings that looked like small white clams. Her dress was cinched in tightly at the waist and flared out wide with a skirt of crinoline. The material was sheer and looked more suitable for summer. Over her shoulders she wore a thin navy cape.

The woman put her hands on her hips. "So, you want to work here."

"Sure she does," Hisayo broke in. "We want to be like you."

The woman shifted her gaze from Fumi to Hisayo. "You're too young. You think this is a game, but it isn't."

Fumi wondered if she had been the woman she'd heard knocking on the door earlier. "Were you looking for someone? I'm looking for my sister, Sumiko Tanaka. Do you know her by any chance?"

"I'm afraid not. There are a lot of us here." The woman shook her head sadly. She gestured with her thumb to the American waiting for her in the doorway. "I have to go. He's setting me up in my own place. Says he wants to have me all to himself. Maybe that's what happened to your sister. Maybe she got lucky and found someone who was sweet on her."

The woman quickly pulled a few clothes off the hangers on the wall and rolled them up into a large purple cloth that she knotted at the top. She handed the cloth bundle to the man.

"That everything?" he said.

At the entranceway the woman stepped into her high heels and slipped her arm into the crook of the man's elbow. She didn't look back. Fumi listened to the sound of their shoes as they walked away, the woman's heels clicking lightly, his shuffling heavily.

Hisayo sighed loudly. "Gosh, that's romantic. I can't wait to be somebody's *only*."

Fumi didn't respond. She lay down, pulled the blanket up to her nose, and squeezed her eyes shut. Was that what had happened to her sister? Was that why she would never come home?

After the woman and her boyfriend left, Hisayo went right back to sleep. Fumi had never known anyone like her. Nothing bothered her. As she listened to Hisayo's faint snoring, she wondered how a person could become like that and she almost felt a little envious. She herself was trapped in a whirling cycle of anxiety—first about Sumiko, then about Aya, and finally about her parents. She had never stayed away overnight and knew they would be worried sick. She would really be in trouble when she got home. By morning, she had worked herself into a state.

"Are you going to sleep forever?" She poked Hisayo's shoulder.

"Umm?" Hisayo rolled over onto her other side.

"I have to leave. I have to go home."

"Home? So early?" Hisayo quickly sat up. "Don't go yet. Have something to eat first. Aren't you hungry?"

"Well, I suppose . . ."

"There's always lots of stuff lying around here. The big sisters get so many presents. Candy and cake and . . ." Hisayo reached into one of the cardboard boxes on the floor next to her and began fishing inside. "Usually I can find something. You know, the first day I came here, I ate some chewing gum by mistake. I didn't know you're not supposed to swallow it. I kept putting pieces in my mouth, chewing and swallowing, chewing and swallowing. I ate a whole pack of Chiclets! I'd never tasted anything so sweet. The big sisters found out and I thought I was really going to get it for taking someone's gum, but instead everyone burst out laughing. Boy, the next day my tummy wasn't feeling too good, let me tell you!"

Hisayo laughed and put her hands on her knees. "Gee, there's nothing here. I guess we'll have to go out and see what we can find. I know where one of the restaurants nearby keeps its garbage cans."

At the doorway, Hisayo again gestured to the pile of shoes.

"You'll need something for your feet. How about these?" She held out a pair of high heels.

Fumi picked a pair of wooden geta similar to the ones she had been wearing.

"I hope we can find something," Hisayo said. "But if we can't, don't worry. I'm sure the big sisters will have something to share with us when they get home."

They passed the mailboxes and began walking but they hadn't gone very far before they noticed a figure in a brown coat squatting by the side of the lane.

Hisayo picked up her pace. "Do you see that woman over there? I bet that's one of the big sisters coming home. Hello! *O-nesan*, hello!"

The figure stood up and as soon as she did, Fumi let out a scream.

"What's the matter?" Hisayo said. "Oh, I get it! Is that your sister?"

But Fumi was already running as fast as she could. When she reached Aya, she didn't say a word. She simply grabbed her hands and squeezed them with all her might.

41

*M*r. Kondo! Mr. Kondo!"

He woke with a start to the sound of his landlady's panicked cries. For a moment he thought the house was on fire. Mrs. Kanehara abruptly slid open the door to his room without knocking. She was in a padded house jacket that she had thrown over her nightgown.

"The principal of your school is here," she announced breathlessly. "He insists on seeing you. Imagine, at this hour. It's still dark outside."

The principal peered around her and pushed his way into Kondo's room.

"Kondo-kun, sorry to bother you so early in the morning but this is an emergency."

"What happened?"

The principal wouldn't talk until Mrs. Kanehara had left the room and her footsteps could be heard going down the stairs. "Trouble, nothing but trouble," he muttered. In a more audible voice he said, "Fumi Tanaka didn't come home last night. Her parents came to see me yesterday evening and they wouldn't leave until I agreed to go back home with them. We've been up all night waiting. I finally persuaded them that the best thing would be if I talked to you."

"Me?"

"I said you might have some idea. The mother was hysterical. She was sobbing so loudly I can't imagine what my neighbors were thinking. Tell me, you're Fumi's homeroom teacher. Do you have any idea where she might be?"

Kondo shook his head. "Why would I know?"

"No idea at all? You're her teacher. Sometimes a teacher observes things in a pupil, changes in behavior, you know, that sort of thing."

"No, I'm sorry. I don't have any idea. Shouldn't this be a matter for the police?"

"No police, please. I told the Tanakas that we—the school—could handle this."

"Why would you say that? What can we do in a situation like this?"

"We don't want any gossip. I have to think about the school's reputation. This is the sort of thing that is best handled privately."

"But this is a serious matter."

"Our reputation! I really hope this can be solved without going to the police. And it's for the girl's protection, too. I think the Tanakas are worried about any damage that could be done to Fumi's reputation. Anyway, I told them you could help. What a mess! The school was doing so well, and now this. It could become a scandal. Mrs. Tanaka raised her voice to me, you know. It was most unpleasant. She said her daughter had never done anything like this before. What kind of things was the school teaching her, she said. Wasn't this the result of too much freedom and democracy."

"But democracy is the pillar of our new curriculum."

"Yes, yes," the principal said impatiently. "Democracy, yes, but not freedom. Little girls are not supposed to be taught they can do whatever they want."

"Sir, with all due respect, they are not that little."

"Precisely! See what I mean? This could turn out very badly. What am I going to do? What am I going to tell Mrs. Tanaka?"

"Well, maybe I can ask some of the other pupils. Someone might know something. Is it all right if I question one of her friends? I'll do it discreetly."

The principal wrung his hands. "Yes, discreetly. Please, we don't want any bad rumors circulating."

※

Kondo hoped that when class started he would find Fumi sitting in her seat just as always, but not only was she not in attendance, Aya's seat was empty, too. Had they run off together? Would Kondo be held responsible for both of their disappearances?

It would be a long day, and to make matters worse his voice was hoarse and his throat on fire. He told the students to read the assigned lessons on their own and called Akiko over. He took her into the hallway and shut the classroom door behind them.

"You were seatmates with Fumi Tanaka for a while," he said in a low voice. "You're close friends, aren't you?"

"Not really, Sensei."

"But you girls like to talk about things, don't you. Did she ever mention any plans? Did she ever talk about going anywhere?"

Akiko stared at the floor.

"Can you think of any reason why she might not be in school, why she might not have come home last night?"

"She didn't come home last night?" Akiko looked shocked.

Kondo winced. No, he shouldn't have said that. That was revealing too much. The principal would be furious. "What I meant was, *if* she hadn't come home, do you have any idea where she might go?"

Akiko shook her head.

"Please, Akiko, please think hard."

Akiko thought for a moment. "Fumi once said that if I ever wanted to go to the black market, she would take me."

"The black market? Which one?"

"The big one in Ueno, Ameyoko. Fumi said you can get anything you want in American Alley. I thought she was just bragging."

Kondo groaned inwardly. The market was huge, and young girls would be easy prey for the yakuza there.

"Akiko, do you think she might have gone to American Alley?"

She shrugged helplessly. "I don't know. I'm scared, Sensei. Is Fumi lost?"

Kondo forced himself to smile. "Everything's absolutely fine,

Akiko. There's no need to worry. You can go back to your desk now, but please don't mention this to anyone."

He hurried to report to the principal. For sure he would now have to agree that the police should be called in. But the principal wasn't in the teachers' room and as Kondo rushed out, he nearly collided with an old man who was standing in the doorway.

"Excuse me," Kondo said.

"Sensei?"

"Yes. Can I help you?"

"You're not Kondo Sensei by any chance, are you?"

"Yes."

The man rolled the brim of a worn cloth hat round and round in his hands. "I'm Shimamura. I'm looking for my daughter."

So this was Aya's father, Kondo thought. Now that he realized who the man was, he could see the resemblance. Most telling was the way he carried himself, slightly stooped with his shoulders hunched forward. That was exactly like Aya. Kondo had often been struck by her habit of rolling the top half of her body forward as if she were trying to make herself shrink or even disappear.

"My daughter," Shimamura repeated. "Do you know where she is?"

"Shouldn't you be the one to tell us? Don't you have any idea?"

The man hung his head. "She . . . she's never done this before. She's a good girl, always obedient. She's a good girl in class, isn't she?"

"Yes, she's a good student."

Shimamura looked relieved. "I told her she has to study hard. Maybe I shouldn't have left her on her own so much. But I thought she was old enough."

"Another classmate, Fumi Tanaka, is also missing."

Shimamura looked startled. "Who's that?"

"Fumi Tanaka."

"I don't know her."

"She and Aya sit together in class."

"Aya never told me what she does at school. I'm away at work and I don't get home until late."

"Times are difficult. Many people work long hours."

"She leaves for school before I get up. Sometimes I don't get back from work until she's asleep."

"Many of us have to work long hours," Kondo repeated dully.

"So she's . . . So you don't know where . . ." Shimamura seemed to be mumbling to himself. "So she's gone . . ."

Kondo wanted to scold the man for not taking better care of his daughter, but he held his tongue. The self-justification he thought he'd seen in Shimamura a second ago had vanished, replaced by something else. Something more commonplace and careworn: an attitude of defeat.

"Are there any clues that Aya planned to run away? Are her clothes missing, for instance?"

Shimamura grunted. "I don't know anything about my daughter's clothes. Ever since her mother died, Aya takes care of those things by herself."

They stood in silence for a moment.

"Obviously we all hope that Aya and Fumi will come ho—" Before Kondo could finish his sentence, Shimamura had dropped to his knees and flattened himself on the floor. His forehead was only inches from Kondo's feet.

"*Tanomu.* Please help me. I shouldn't have left her alone so much. I am to blame."

"Please get up, Mr. Shimamura. That's not necessary. Please, you're getting dirty."

But Shimamura refused to budge. His shoulders began shaking, and Kondo realized that the poor man was crying.

Kondo bent down and patted Shimamura gently on the back. "Please don't be upset. Maybe we could search for your daughter together. And for Fumi, too."

"Yes," Shimamura said, quickly rising to his feet and wiping his face with his hands. "That's a good idea. We should start now. She could be kidnapped or lost or hurt. What if she's hurt?" He looked into Kondo's eyes searchingly. "What if it's already too late?"

"I'm sure we'll find her. Please give me a minute to get ready. I'll meet you outside in the school yard."

Miss Ikeda was walking down the hall and Kondo hastened to catch up with her. He explained the situation, asking her to look after his class for the rest of the day and to let the principal know. Outside, Shimamura was pacing back and forth in front of the school gate.

"Where should we begin?" Shimamura asked as soon as Kondo approached.

Kondo recalled what Akiko had said about the black market in Ueno. "One of my students thinks there's a good chance they might have gone to American Alley."

"Impossible!" Shimamura exploded. "The black market! I strictly forbade Aya to go there. She wouldn't dare disobey me." A thick vein on his forehead began to throb visibly. "That place is full of scum."

Kondo was taken aback by the sudden force of Shimamura's reply, but he pressed his point. "This is the only clue we have. And unless we hurry . . ." He left the thought dangling.

Shimamura closed his eyes. Kondo studied the throbbing vein, the man's clenched fists, the tightness in his jaw. Then, as if a storm had passed, Shimamura opened his eyes and nodded.

"You're right," he said. "We'd better hurry."

42

I was so worried. Where were you all night?" Fumi demanded. She refused to let go of Aya's hands, clutching them as if her life, both their lives, depended on this connection.

Aya squeezed back, surprised at how relieved she was to have found Fumi and how quickly her fury seemed to have vanished. Surprised, too, that this simple act of touching brought such a deep sense of comfort. Of all the people she had come to know in Japan, it was Fumi whose friendship she craved; it was Fumi she needed the most. This bossy, irritating slip of a girl was the only friend she had. Yet last night she had been so angry and hurt, her only thought had been to get as far away from Fumi as she could. Her heart had been pounding with such violence she thought her chest might crack open. *You don't even have a mother.* Walk away, walk away. *You're nothing but a stupid repat.* Don't turn back. One foot after the other. Just keep going. As long as she didn't stop, she would be all right. She would run away from school, from the children who made fun of her, from the terrible apartment where she lived, from Japan. She would run away to the docks and find a ship—an American ship, any kind of ship—and stow away.

"Where were you?" Fumi repeated. "Where did you spend the night?"

Aya pointed to the shed in front of them. "I hid in here."

When Aya had walked away from Fumi, she'd had no idea where she was or which way to go. She got to the end of the lane, turned the corner, and continued walking in what she hoped was the direction of the main boulevard running through the Ginza. If only she could find Nancy, she'd thought. Nancy would help her. They would run away together, take the American ship and sail away home. If only she could spot Nancy's bright red blouse, if only she could hear Nancy's loud American laugh. Then, as if in response to her wishes, she began hearing English. Up ahead she could see clusters of GIs surrounded by groups of Japanese women, and immediately she regretted her decision to leave Fumi. Some formed couples, and with arms linked, staggered together drunkenly. Others were in groups of four or five, the colorful costumes of the women catching the bright moonlight and making them appear like twisting wraiths.

"You skivvy honcho!" A woman's shrill voice rang out in the night air, followed by a man's coarse guffaw. There was more male laughter as the woman's shrieks rose to a hysterical pitch.

Aya turned around and retraced her steps, moving as quickly as she could. She returned to the place where she had turned the corner and then walked down the lane where she had left Fumi. She went up and down the lane but Fumi was nowhere in sight and every single building she passed was dark, not a flicker of light coming from inside. Then to her left she saw a pale gray shimmer like a fluttering of wings. It seemed like a miracle. When she got up close, she realized it was a small shed whose door was slightly ajar. Moonlight shone in through a hole in the roof, and the wind was causing the door to move back and forth ever so slightly, just enough to create the sensation of something shimmering. She slipped inside.

It was dim but she could make out tools of some sort and stacks of ceramic jugs and pots. In the middle was a tall wooden screen, and behind it, a large plump sack. She leaned down to touch it. It was soft, as if it were filled with cloth, and it smelled clean. She took off her dark brown coat to use as a blanket and lay down to go to sleep, resting her head on the soft sack. But after a few minutes she shifted her position. Instead of using the sack as a pillow, she pulled it next to her, hugging it close to her body the way she used to hug her mother when she was small and slept in the same bed. She swore to herself that if she survived the night, she would never again do anything so foolish. If she could only manage not to be attacked or assaulted, she would be grateful to be alive and in one piece.

She heard the distant sound of voices and laughter late into the night, and finally fell into a fitful slumber hours later. When she woke, she didn't know what time it was but sensed it was morning. She put on her coat and crouched outside in front of the shed, waiting.

"So this is where you spent the night," Fumi said, peering at the shed. "Actually we weren't very far away from each other."

"Where were you?"

Fumi pointed at Hisayo. "I spent the night with her."

As if this was the introduction she'd been waiting for, Hisayo stepped forward and grinned. She unhooked Fumi's hand from Aya's and replaced it with her own. "Hi, my name is Betty. What's yours? Want to see our room? Come on."

Tugging Aya by the hand, Hisayo led her to the dormitory. Fumi followed behind. Inside the room, Hisayo used one bare foot to push a rolled-up futon back against the wall and pointed to the space she had created on the tatami mat. "Come in and relax. See, there's plenty of room."

Aya looked uncertainly at Fumi.

"We have to go home," Fumi said.

"Home!" Hisayo snorted. "Why do you want to go home when you can stay in a nice place like this. Come on." She plunked herself down on the tatami and reached up to grab Aya's hand. "Sit here beside me."

Aya tried to resist but Hisayo's grip was strong and she pulled Aya onto the tatami.

"Good. Now I want to show you some makeup," Hisayo said cheerily.

"But I'm not sure . . ." Again Aya looked at Fumi.

"Oh, I guess it's all right, but not for too long," Fumi said somewhat reluctantly. "Maybe just for a little while."

"Of course," Hisayo said. "Just for a while. You'll be glad that you stayed."

They sat on either side of Hisayo at the low tea table and watched as she opened the lacquer box and began applying lipstick just as she had done last night.

"You can try some if you like," she said, offering the tube of lipstick to Aya.

Aya shook her head.

Hisayo shrugged and shut the makeup box. Leaning toward Aya, she began stroking her arm. "Let's be friends, okay?"

"Okay."

Hisayo stood up and gestured for Aya to stand up beside her. "You have a beautiful coat, a real American coat. Can I try it on? Just for a minute?"

Fumi's reaction was swift. "Don't you dare!"

"I'm not doing anything."

"You can't have her coat!"

"I just want to see what I look like in it. What's wrong with that? Anyway, this is a nice room, isn't it? I'm sharing it with you." Hisayo crossed her arms and puffed out her chest.

"It's okay. I don't mind." Aya took off her coat and handed it to Hisayo. She wanted to avoid an argument at all costs. After last night, she didn't want to fight with anyone ever again.

Hisayo put one arm through the right sleeve, then pushed her other arm into the left. She struggled a bit but finally managed to shrug the coat up over her shoulders. It was clearly much too small for her.

"What a beautiful coat. It's so soft and warm. I've always wanted a real American coat." She stroked the worn collar and faded lapels.

"It doesn't fit you at all," Fumi said.

"Yes, it does."

"No, it doesn't. It's too small. You can't even do up the buttons."

"Yes, I can. Wait." Hisayo sucked in her breath and quickly began doing up the buttons starting from the bottom. The material strained across her chest and shoulders but she managed to fasten all the buttons except the top two. Her arms stuck out stiffly at her sides. "How do I look?"

She was such a ridiculous sight, Aya almost laughed out loud.

Fumi was furious. "Take it off!"

"See how good I look," Hisayo taunted. "I'm so pretty. In my American coat!" She twirled around in an effort to make the hem of the coat lift in the air.

Fumi reached for the coat, but Hisayo danced out of her grasp. That was when she tripped on a pile of clothing on the floor and went flying backward. As she flung her arms out to break her fall, they all heard the sound of the coat ripping. As loud as a sail snapping in the wind. Aya gasped.

"You ruined it!" Fumi shouted. "I told you not to try it on. Now look what you've done."

Hisayo rolled over onto her stomach to push herself off the floor. There were more ripping sounds. As soon as she stood up, bits of cloth started falling to the floor, as if the coat itself were unraveling from the inside.

"You ruined it," Fumi repeated.

"I didn't mean to," Hisayo cried out. "I just wanted to see what it felt like. I've never had a coat."

She began struggling to wriggle out of the coat but every movement she made caused more bits of material to tumble out. The coat had ripped wide open in the back and under the arms, and the lining had been torn from the seams in several sections. It appeared as if old rags had been cut into small pieces and stuffed inside the lining for added insulation; these scraps of material had fallen out and now lay scattered across the tatami.

Fumi got down on her knees to take a closer look. "What are these things? Aya, this one has your name on it." She handed Aya a small strip of white cloth.

Aya got down on the tatami, and Hisayo, too, and together they sifted through the bits of fabric.

The strips of white cloth had Aya's name on them in the indelible ink her mother had used to identify all her clothes. The writing, in Japanese, was in her mother's neat hand, her careful calligraphy.

But there was more than just her name. Each strip also had a short message: *Tsuyoku narinasai.* Be strong. *Yoku benkyo shinasai.* Study hard. Many were the same messages written over and over. *Grow tall. Respect your elders. Be resolute. Never forget. Don't give up.*

"What is this all about?" Hisayo said. "Why on earth would anyone put these things inside your coat where you can't even see them. That's the dumbest thing I've ever heard of."

Aya didn't even realize tears were rolling down her cheeks until Fumi brought out a handkerchief and began wiping her face. "Come on, Aya," Fumi said. "It's time for us to go home."

Hisayo did her best to dissuade them. "Why are you in such a hurry? Stay one more night with me, please. We can try on more of the big sisters' clothes."

"We can't," Fumi said. "Our parents are really worried about us. I'm sure my mother hasn't been able to sleep at all."

Aya saw how Hisayo stiffened.

"Parents." Hisayo sniffed derisively. "Who needs parents? You're still such a baby, aren't you."

"I'm not."

"Yes, you are." She turned to Aya. "What about you? You want to stay with me?"

Aya shook her head vigorously.

Hisayo shrugged. "Okay, suit yourself. You don't know what you're missing." Before they left, she tried to make Aya take something to wear in place of the coat.

"How about this," she said, pulling a satiny blouse off a hanger. "No good? What about that one over there? You want it?"

By the time Aya and Fumi walked out the door, it was late in the afternoon.

Hisayo cheerily waved goodbye, all sign of the earlier discord forgotten. "Come back and visit me. Don't wait too long."

The girls walked in silence, sometimes abreast but often single file, with Fumi taking the lead. It would take them a long time to reach home, especially as Fumi was moving more slowly than her usual brisk pace. Aya followed patiently behind. She wore the torn coat over her shoulders like a cape, the strips of cloth with her mother's writing stuffed safely in the pockets of her pants.

"You were right," Fumi said halfway through their trek home. "My sister doesn't want to come home anymore."

Aya didn't know how to undo the damage her careless words had done. "I didn't mean it when I said that. I don't know what I'm talking about."

"But it's probably true." Fumi sounded uncharacteristically resigned.

"You shouldn't listen to me. I don't know anything."

Fumi stopped walking and turned around so she was face-to-face with Aya. "No, I think you spoke the truth. I think you're the only person worth listening to."

43

Although Kondo had been the one to insist that they search in American Alley, once they arrived at the bustling market, Shimamura was clearly in charge. Kondo was surprised to see him move with such ease through the crowded passageways, clearly used to negotiating the twisting turns and crooked lanes filled with makeshift stalls. It was even more crowded than usual because of year-end shopping. People pushed with their elbows, shoulders, knees, even chins, anything to shove their way ahead of the person in front of them, anything to bring them closer to buying a tiny piece of *kazunoko* or *tai*, any kind of traditional treat that would help them mark the end of the year and welcome in good fortune for the new one. To Kondo the atmosphere didn't feel festive so much as frantic. He was glad he hadn't brought much money with him. The pickpockets would be out in full force on a day like this, he thought.

They walked past jumbled piles of canned peaches, stepped around baskets of onions, narrowly avoided tripping over buckets filled with live crabs. One man sat behind a dozen brown bottles lined up on a dirty bamboo mat. He was wearing a suit that had wide shoulders and broad lapels and looked too large for his bony frame. A woman was passed out under a tarp next to him. Shimamura was apparently undistracted by these scenes and looked neither left nor right. Kondo thought about how his students had come here on their own; he marveled at their boldness, and then he felt afraid. They were growing up fast and figuring things out for themselves.

Book learning, the kind that he was responsible for imparting, was only a small part of the knowledge they needed to live in the new era.

Coming here might have been a terrible mistake, though. There were too many people, too many places to hide or be hidden. And it was all Kondo could do just to keep up and not lose sight of Shimamura's stiff hunched back, not to fall behind and be swallowed whole into the churning mass of movement and noise and smell that surrounded them. He hadn't realized until now just how awful he felt. He was very short of breath, his chest hurt more than ever, and his legs felt as if stone weights were attached to his ankles. Every so often he was seized by a coughing jag and they had to pause until he could catch his breath again.

Shimamura abruptly stopped in front of a dark passageway with a piece of black cloth hanging halfway down the narrow entry. Kondo saw him stare at it for a few seconds, clenching and unclenching his fists. He entered, and Kondo followed. They had to turn sideways to squeeze through, and then the space opened up into a small room filled with stacks of boxes.

"Hello, Ozawa-san," Shimamura said. He didn't bow.

A man seated at a makeshift desk made out of old ammunition crates looked up and swiveled his toothpick to the side of his mouth. His shirt was unbuttoned halfway down his chest, and Kondo could make out the dense swirling pattern of an elaborate tattoo. "Well, look who's here. I must say this is a surprise." The man remained seated and resumed picking his teeth.

"I know it's been a while," Shimamura said.

Ozawa nodded slowly. The smile on his face was patently false. "So, to what do I owe the honor of this visit?"

"It's my daughter. She's run away, and I wondered if . . ." Shimamura finally bowed his head. "I don't know where to begin looking for her."

"Why come to me?"

"I don't know anyone else here except you."

"Yes, we used to know each other quite well, didn't we. At one point, we had a good business relationship."

Shimamura hung his head but Kondo saw how he clenched his jaw.

"As you can see, my business is flourishing." The man gestured to the neat stacks of boxes behind him. Except for a large open box full of syringes, the other boxes were sealed and labeled in English. Kondo's eye was caught by the medical names, most of which he wasn't familiar with. "But I am a generous man. If you're interested in resuming our relationship, I am willing to discuss it."

"You know I can't."

"Can't or won't?"

"You know."

"Oh, that's right, I forgot. You've got high standards, don't you."

"My daughter," Shimamura said. "I don't know who else to ask for help. She's missing and—"

"My help?" Ozawa's voice was cold. "You want my help?"

"I just wondered if you knew where I should look or what to—"

"I don't know anything about things like that. How dare you. What do you take me for? I'm a businessman, not a—" Ozawa's mouth curled in anger.

"I didn't mean that."

"Get out. We have nothing to say to each other." Ozawa spit his limp toothpick onto the dirt floor.

Kondo and Shimamura left the market and slowly made their way to the busy road leading to Ueno station. By this point Kondo was overcome with exhaustion. He could barely catch his breath, and every so often he found it necessary to put his hand on Shimamura's shoulder to steady himself.

"I didn't realize you were so sick," Shimamura said. "You should have said something earlier. You really need to go to bed. Do you want to stop somewhere for a bowl of hot soup?"

Kondo opened his mouth to say no thank you, but instead he started coughing again. Coughing and coughing and coughing until the stabbing pain in his chest made him double over and still he could not stop. He felt his legs buckle under him, and as he was sinking to the ground, a buzzing sound filled all the cavities of his sinuses and made his entire head vibrate. It felt like his head would explode. The buzzing was fierce and menacing. It sounded just like those bombers they'd all dreaded—the B-29s were coming again. They were coming back. Hurry, hurry! They needed to get to an air-raid shelter. Dive low! Hurry! Stacks of dried seaweed and canned meat and stockings and loose tea spun up into the air and whirled around and around like spinning tops.

Kondo was lying on his back, not sure if it was day or night. He had no clear recollection of going to bed. He could feel every bump in the tatami mat through the wafer-thin futon. Although he wanted to shift position, he had no strength and couldn't even lift his head. The last thing he recalled was the searching. Pushing through the crowds in the black market with Shimamura. Aya was lost. So was Fumi. Had they found them? Where had they gone? He felt someone tuck a blanket under his chin.

He was burning up and he was freezing cold and then he was burning up again. He couldn't find his arms, wasn't even sure if he still had arms. Or legs. All his limbs were plastered to the floor. He was like a starfish, flattened against the sand on the beach. Too far from the water. Flaccid and limp, all dried out, completely unable to move. His chest hurt. Every breath hurt. Every single breath was such hard work, like trying to suck air through a straw.

He tried to remember the last time he was this sick. It might have been when he was a child, when his mother had nursed him back to health, cradling his head in her arms and singing him lullabies. He wished he could rest in his mother's arms again, but she was long dead.

He felt as if he were adrift on a dark sea. People he knew floated by, appearing out of the darkness and just as suddenly receding back into the shadows. The woman from Love Letter Alley with the broken geta swam toward him, holding a baby between her teeth like a dog. His fellow translators Yamaguchi and Tabata were there, too, laughing and bobbing up and down in the waves.

He became aware of a funny rattling and wondered what it was. Then he realized it was him. The sound was coming from somewhere inside him, a sound like tissue paper being crumpled deep inside his lungs. The stabbing pains were sharper and more frequent. It felt like a giant snake was squeezing his chest, tighter and tighter, pushing out all the air.

He was no longer at sea. Instead he had reached a very high place. Not heaven but maybe partway up Mount Fuji. Yes, it was like that climb up Mount Fuji that he had made as a schoolboy. Their teacher had been a bit of a sadist and forced them to climb to the summit in one long march. There was no question of breaking the climb into two days, of resting overnight partway up the mountain. The teacher said it would toughen them up, turn them into real men, the kind of men Japan would need in the future. He remembered how hard it was to breathe, the air thinner and thinner the higher they climbed, and how his legs were so heavy it took all his strength and concentration to lift each foot.

"Keep on going, Kondo-kun. Don't give up!" his teacher had commanded. "*Ganbatte!* Don't give up. Just a little farther."

He was the last of his group to make it to the top, crawling the last few yards on his hands and knees like a beast. He collapsed on his stomach, not caring that his face was resting flat on the dirt. There was no air, but he strained to breathe.

From far away he heard more voices. Sweet, light voices. This time they sounded like the girls in his class.

Ganbatte, Kondo Sensei! Don't give up. *Ganbatte!* Kondo Sensei!

He sank into darkness.

44

Their search had ended abruptly when Kondo collapsed and Shimamura had to turn his attention to the problem of how to bring his daughter's teacher home. Asking Ozawa for help was obviously out of the question, and he couldn't very well carry Kondo onto the train by himself. Shimamura scanned the street for a taxi, one of the charcoal-fired cabs that had begun circulating in the city, but none was in sight. Finally he managed to hail a man with a cart attached to his bicycle and for an inflated price got him to agree to take them home. Together they lifted Kondo's limp body onto the bed of the wooden cart. The last load had been vegetables, and the surface of the cart was slick with bits of damp leaves and stems.

The cart owner refused to let Shimamura ride with Kondo. Two of them would be too heavy, he said. How could he pedal such a weight? So Shimamura had to half walk, half trot alongside the bicycle all the way home. Along the route he couldn't help thinking about Ozawa. He recalled the day he had made a delivery to the market and found Ozawa surrounded on one side by a pile of opened containers and vials and on the other by a neat stack of sealed boxes. When Shimamura came upon him, Ozawa was in the midst of re-taping a box shut.

"What are you doing?"

"Oh, Shimamura. Look at this. Good as new, don't you think? No one can tell. As long as the U.S. label is intact, that's all they care about."

"But what are you doing?"

"Conserving and recycling, Shimamura. Don't want to waste anything."

"But it's medicine."

"Oh, don't look so shocked. This is not a time to quibble about dosages and expiry dates. There's a shortage of everything. What's important is being able to supply enough to meet the demand. That's commerce."

Two days later Shimamura quit his job.

Not knowing where Kondo lived, Shimamura paid the cart owner extra to help carry him into his own apartment at the tenement house. By the time he unrolled the futon and put Kondo to bed, he was exhausted. Shimamura looked at the sleeping figure with a certain satisfaction that he had managed to bring him home, but he also felt a mounting sense of resentment.

Why hadn't Kondo Sensei said he was sick beforehand? He shouldn't have come to the market in his condition. If not for his collapse, Shimamura could still be there searching for Aya. Now he didn't know what he was supposed to do. Was he expected to stay here and tend to a sick man he barely knew when his own daughter was missing? It was growing dark, and every minute he spent with Kondo was time lost looking for Aya. He would go out and search for her on his own, he resolved, but the question was: Where on earth was she? How could she have run away? How could she have become so disobedient without his noticing? Faced with what seemed to be her assertion of independence, he was bewildered. Who had she become? The thought that she had not run away on her own, that rather she had been abducted or kidnapped, was too terrible to even contemplate.

He started to cry again, just as he had cried in front of Kondo in the school hallway. And this was the most confusing of all because he never cried. His generation had been raised to control their emotions, to hold their feelings in. To do otherwise was weak; it was womanly. He was a man, and a man did not cry. If ever he felt pain or hurt, he turned it inward. He let the sadness well up inside him, and then, through sheer force of will, he swallowed his sorrow. Nothing ever showed. Even when his wife had died, he did not show his emotion.

A man held things in. Hadn't he perfected this art?

On the tatami beside him, Kondo tossed restlessly on the futon. He groaned and began coughing again. Although he'd been semi-comatose during the ride in the cart, the coughing now returned in waves, so violent at times it sounded as if he could cough up his insides. When the last fit subsided, the quiet and stillness were worse. Shimamura could hear a rattling sound, faint but quite distinct. His gut instinct told him that wasn't good. Not good at all. When he touched Kondo's forehead, it was fiery hot.

Shimamura slipped out of the room and once on the street, he raced to find a neighborhood doctor.

"Everybody calls me when it's too late," the doctor grumbled, sitting back on his haunches. "Pneumonia."

"Pneumonia! What can you do for him?" Shimamura asked.

"Not much, I'm afraid. At this stage. Sometimes patients pull through . . . I really can't say. My advice is to make him as comfortable as you can."

"But there must be something . . ."

"Sulfa drugs might have helped much earlier. I don't know. Anyway there's a shortage of everything." The doctor's voice was hard and resigned. He began packing up his black bag.

"Wait, please. Don't go." Shimamura motioned for the doctor to stay seated where he was. He brought out his wife's old suitcase from the back of the storage cupboard.

"Maybe there's something you can use." He opened the lid and pushed the suitcase forward.

The doctor narrowed his eyes. "What's this?"

"Please."

"How did you get your hands on these?"

"Please. Take whatever you need." Shimamura felt his face flush but he had to press on. "There must be something in here that you can use."

The doctor picked up a small white box and examined it skeptically. The suitcase was full of boxes, all stamped PROPERTY OF THE U.S. ARMY.

"What are you doing with this? How can I be sure it's real? That it's not some watered-down serum you're trying to pass off?"

"It's genuine, I promise."

"I see. Well, I know all about the likes of you, hoarding this to keep your *panpan* women clean. Clearing up their VD so they can go back to servicing the GIs. You make a nice profit, don't you, while good honest people are dying."

"It's not like that. Please. If there is something you can use for him . . ."

The doctor's expression was thoughtful for a moment, then businesslike. He tore open the box labeled penicillin.

"This better be the real thing. I don't know how you managed to get hold of a supply like this when no doctor I know can, but this might save him."

He snapped the glass tip of the ampoule, filled his syringe, and gave Kondo his first shot, straight into his buttocks.

"He'll need more," the doctor said, standing up and checking his watch. "I'll be back in twelve hours to give him another injection."

Five minutes after the doctor left, Shimamura heard the sound of the door again and wondered if the doctor had forgotten something. But it was Aya. She looked cold and tired.

"Where were you!" he yelled, and then without thinking, he raised his arm. It was as if the strain of his earlier anxiety now sought some release through his body. Didn't she know how much she had frightened him? She should not have run away; she should not have scared him so. His arm hovered in the air and he saw that although he had never hit her before, she seemed to be expecting this punishment, for she did not flinch. Instead she lifted her jaw ever so slightly as if steadying herself for the inevitable blow.

"Where were you?" he repeated.

"I'm sorry. I know you're angry but I had to stay with my friend Fumi."

"Stay with your friend! Look at your teacher. He got sick when we went searching for you and your friend. See the trouble you two have caused?"

"I'm sorry." She hung her head and started to cry.

Shimamura suddenly felt all the strength drain from his muscles, as if some essence of himself were emptying out. He let his arm flop to his side. "Anything could have happened to you, don't you know that?"

"I know. I'm sorry."

"Anything at all. I keep trying to tell you the world is a dangerous place. It's a cold, mean, unfair place."

"I know."

"But you're safe now."

"I know." She was trying to hold in her sobs, almost choking with the effort of not making too much noise.

He put his hands on her shoulders and gripped them tightly, uncertain how to comfort her. You're safe, he thought to himself. You're safe.

"You came back. That's all that matters," he said softly. "Go wash your hands and face now. You have to help me take care of Kondo Sensei."

45

*M*att's headache lasted the entire week.

It had started the moment he sat down at his desk on Monday morning, the day after he and Nancy had gone to the Ginza, and no matter how many aspirins he took, the headache refused to go away.

The days leading up to Christmas were unbearable. Sab drove him crazy: either he was tapping his teeth with his pencil or drumming his fingers on his desk or whistling a medley of Christmas carols. He had to be the world's worst whistler. As if that weren't bad enough, even the ordinary noises of the office seemed amplified, especially the sounds from the typing pool where the keys clacked loudly in an uncoordinated rhythm, everyone typing at a different speed. Normally Nancy's typewriter would have contributed to the clacking, but she had not come in to work at all this week. Matt told himself he didn't care if she ever came back, but he kept glancing in the direction of the typing pool with a mixture of irritation and concern. Nancy had a perfect attendance record. She never took any time off.

"Getting into the spirit of things? Are you going to the Christmas Eve show at the Ernie Pyle Theater? Did you get all your presents from home? Have you opened them yet?"

To each of Sab's questions, Matt had simply grunted in reply.

Sab was undeterred. "I'm really looking forward to that big turkey dinner with all the trimmings, aren't you? They're putting up decorations in the mess hall later."

"I can't stand turkey," Matt muttered. He had then reached for an envelope and slit it open. When he pulled out the contents, he saw that he had sliced the letter in half. Setting the two parts side by side, he read.

Dear most honorable and courageous General MacArthur.

The handwriting was spindly, the style old-fashioned. Naturally it began with several convoluted sentences about the weather.

. . . the winter cold will soon pass. May you and all your troops look forward to an especially pleasing and beautiful spring. Japan is renowned for its exquisite cherry blossoms . . .

What the hell did the writer want? Just get to the point! They always wanted something. Ah, here it was.

. . . with misfortune . . . my fishing boat . . . extra costs incurred . . . could SCAP consider reimbursement . . . collision in which . . . thirty baskets of clams . . .

On the morning of the twenty-fourth, Sab dropped a crumpled square of coarse toilet paper on Matt's desk. "I don't know what's eating you, buddy, but let me give you a Christmas present. Take only one at a time. It'll help you stay awake. Might improve your mood, too."

There were four small white pills inside. Matt didn't hesitate or even bother to ask what they were. He put one in his mouth and swallowed it dry. Damn that little girl Fumi, he thought, rubbing his aching forehead. Damn her wayward sister. And most of all, damn that Nancy. How ludicrous he and Nancy must have looked traipsing around in the Ginza on that wild-goose chase. Even more idiotic than his outing with Eddie. Who had he been trying to kid, setting off on such a quest? A knight in shining armor? Ha! Did he really think he was the type of man who could rescue a damsel in distress? He wasn't the hero type. Not even close. Anyway, one hero in the family was enough.

On Christmas day Matt took the remaining three pills from Sab all at once. His headache miraculously disappeared. He spent the day in a bubble of serenity, and at Christmas dinner he felt like he was floating at least six feet above his plate of turkey and gravy. By evening, though, he had crashed back down. That night he dreamed about Henry.

He and Henry were in a black forest, crawling on their stomachs. They used their elbows to pull themselves forward through the cold wet sludge. It was so foggy all Matt could see of Henry were the soles of his boots, just inches in front of his nose. Wait for me, he wanted to shout, but he knew he had to be quiet. The enemy was behind the tree trunks. The enemy was in the fog. And then somehow he had caught up with Henry and they were lying side by side in the mud. Henry smiled and reached inside his chest. "Here, take this and give it to Mom," he said as he pushed something hot and beating into Matt's hand.

Matt woke up with a start, his whole body drenched in sweat.

Much of what they had learned about Henry's death came from the citation for bravery that accompanied the Purple Heart. As Matt's family was not free to travel, the army officers had to come to their camp to present the medal.

Henry Hiro Matsumoto made the ultimate sacrifice for his country, they intoned, reading from the official letter. He fought for democracy and freedom. America is proud of him.

Matt knew his mother had bowed her head to the ground because she didn't want to cry in front of the officers. The winds were blowing especially strong that day, and the desert grit was flying into everyone's eyes. The flag in front of one of the guard towers snapped back and forth like a whip.

We have to prove our loyalty. Show them which side we're on. That's what Henry always said.

Whose side were you on?

Were you a no-no boy or a yes-yes boy?

Were you loyal? Were you brave?

Whose side were you on, anyway?

What about the dead side.

His father was right, Matt thought. Forget the heart. Forget all the hearts.

46

Sumiko came back to the translator's stall every night. The other letter writers grew curious, and they teased and flirted with her and attempted to persuade her to hire one of them. But after it became apparent that she had serious business with Kondo, they turned protective. Someone named Yamaguchi took to giving her a hot roasted sweet potato as soon as she arrived, and from others she received bits of food they'd clearly saved for her—a rice cracker, a dried persimmon, a handful of chestnuts. Nobody had any idea where Kondo was or why he was absent. Some were even more worried about him than they were about her.

"It's so unlike him," Yamaguchi said. "I can't imagine what's happened."

She had gone to Love Letter Alley because she remembered what Yoko had told her, Yoko who went there often in the days of Jake and others before him. "The best letter writers aren't the ones with their stalls out front," she'd said. "There's a man who sits at the back all by himself. He wears thick glasses and he doesn't look very friendly, but I think he's the best." It wasn't far from the station, somewhere in an alley, somewhere up a slope. It was a well-known spot, someone would direct her.

When Sumiko met with the translator, though, she was certain she'd come across as a nervous fool. Now he had the newspaper in his possession. How could she have handed it over just like that? Was it wise to have trusted a total stranger? Yet she knew she'd had no choice. Every time she stared at those incomprehensible English words, she had felt increasingly overwrought. What did they say? What came after those words—Bar Lucky?

Night after night she returned, but he didn't show up.

On New Year's Eve, she arrived at Love Letter Alley as usual, but no one was there, neither the translators nor their customers. She was about to give up and return to the shelter she'd found in a nearby park when Yamaguchi arrived.

"I was worried you might be here. I thought I should check up on you. We're closing for the New Year's holiday, shutting down for five days."

She had never expected that a place like this would be affected by such a traditional holiday.

"Oh, of course. The holidays."

"Yes, we close down just like everyone else. Anyway there's hardly any business—everyone's gone home."

"I see."

"Funny, isn't it," he said.

"What is?"

"Funny we still use that phrase. Going home." He cast his gaze to the ground as if embarrassed at raising the topic. "When so many don't really have a home to go to. It's tradition, though. We have to close at New Year's."

"Yes, of course."

"Do you have a home? Any family?" he asked gently.

She nodded.

"Then you're very lucky, miss. That's where you should go. There's no point in waiting here." Yamaguchi reverted to his normal brisk tone. "We'll be open for business again on January fifth. We look forward to your patronage."

Go home? Just like that? Could it have been that easy all along?

Sumiko realized she was tired. Tired of hiding, tired of running away, tired of thinking, tired of worrying. Just plain tired.

By the time she arrived home, it would be the middle of the night.

Her parents had never locked the front door. She hoped that they still didn't.

47

When Fumi opened her eyes in the morning and saw a sleeping figure next to her in bed, she should have been shocked or at least slightly startled, but she wasn't at all. Because she knew in an instant. The figure had her back to her, but Fumi recognized those narrow sloping shoulders, the soft curving spine. She breathed in the rich scent of the coarse black hair that brushed lightly against her nose. It was her sister. Her sister had come home.

Fumi pressed the palm of her hand flat against the hollow part in the middle of Sumiko's back, wanting to wake her and not wanting to. She felt the heat of her sister's body, sensed the gentle rise and fall of her breathing. When Sumiko finally stirred and rolled over, it felt so natural, as if this were just another morning in the long series of mornings they'd always had.

Sumiko smiled. "I didn't wake you when I came in last night, did I?"

Fumi shook her head.

"That's good. Because it was very late. I tried to be really quiet."

"*Nechan*, you came back," Fumi whispered. She wasn't sure why she was whispering except some part of her thought she might be dreaming, and the only way to keep the dream going was to speak softly. She raised her hand toward Sumiko's face and touched her cheek. The skin was warm, the cheekbone solid.

"You came back," she repeated.

"Yes," Sumiko said, whispering just as softly as Fumi was.

After that they lay in silence with the blanket tucked up to their chins just looking at each other and smiling. It was cold in the unheated room, and Fumi could see her breath. She tried exhaling hard so the puff of her breath would brush against Sumiko's cheek.

Finally Sumiko said, "It's New Year's Day. *Akemashite omedeto gozaimasu.*"

"Happy New Year to you, too, *nechan.*"

"We should get up. I haven't seen Mother or Father yet. I hope they won't be too shocked to see me."

Fumi nodded but made no move to rise. If only she and Sumiko could stay just like this, Fumi thought, lying face-to-face, under the warm covers. She realized she didn't want to share her sister with anyone, not even her parents.

"*Nechan,* how long are you staying? Are you only here for the New Year's holiday?"

Sumiko closed her eyes and didn't answer right away. "No," she said, her eyes still shut. "I'm staying."

"For good? Forever?"

Sumiko opened her eyes then, and Fumi was aware that she was being stared at. It was almost as if Sumiko were seeing her for the first time.

"Yes," Sumiko finally murmured. "I hope so."

Fumi had imagined her sister's return for so long, but she had never gone beyond that point. Somehow she had always assumed that things would go back to exactly the way they had been before.

But it wasn't like that.

It was hard for Fumi to put her finger on it but Sumiko wasn't quite the same person. She was quieter, more distracted. She often said she was tired, but when Fumi peeked in on her, Sumiko would be sitting up with her eyes wide open just staring into space. Initially Fumi tried asking as many questions as she could. Who found you? Who ordered you to come home? What made you come back? Didn't you meet anyone famous? She sought to find out if in any way the letter had been responsible for her sister's return, but it did not appear to be so.

Sumiko got irritated with all the questioning. "I don't know what you're talking about, Fumi. Nobody ordered me to come home. I came home because I wanted to, that's all. Aren't you glad I'm back?"

"Of course, *nechan*!" And so Fumi gave up.

Still, Fumi took it upon herself to cheer her sister up. She couldn't think of anything funny except the things Akiko and Tomoko used to tell her at school. There was the story about Sanae, who was so worried about her bowed legs that she tied them together with string every night in an attempt to straighten them. And then there was Michiko's father, who wore a toupee and thought he looked very fine indeed except every so often the wind blew and twirled it around from back to front but he didn't even notice.

Sumiko laughed, and somehow that was more painful to hear because it didn't sound like a real laugh. It had a forced feel, a cloudy laugh tinged with darkness.

Fumi thought of another funny story to tell, about how Kondo Sensei had a small bald spot on the back of his head and how it was so smooth and shiny it looked just like an egg. Except she decided not to tell this story. She didn't think it was funny anymore, and besides, she liked Kondo Sensei and didn't want anyone to laugh at him. He was better now, but over the holidays he had been very sick. Everyone at school had heard about how he might have died had it not been for the penicillin from Aya's father.

"Mother told me what you did," Sumiko said. "I can't believe you stayed out all night in the Ginza. Don't you know how dangerous that was?"

"But I was looking for you."

"You scared Mother and Father to death. You should never have done that."

"But—"

"You could have gotten hurt. It was a very foolish thing to do. I don't blame Mother for being so angry."

When Fumi returned home after that night in the Ginza, she'd known her parents would be furious, but she had not anticipated the extent of the punishment she would receive. Even now, weeks after the incident, she still wasn't allowed to leave the house on her own except to go to school. As soon as class was over, she had to come straight home. Sumiko took their mother's side.

"But I didn't know where you were," Fumi protested. "I wanted to find you."

"I know, I know." A pained look crossed Sumiko's face. "Oh, Fumi, it was all my fault, wasn't it. Thank goodness you came back safely."

"And you came back safely, too."

"Yes." Sumiko nodded her head slowly. "Yes, I suppose that's right."

Gradually Fumi was allowed to take short walks in the neighborhood, but only if Sumiko accompanied her. She tried to persuade Sumiko to do this every day so that both of them could get out of the house. When they passed their neighbors in the narrow lane, however, Fumi quickly learned to merely nod hello and cut off any opportunity they might try to seize to start a conversation. Although the neighbors claimed to be concerned, Fumi knew they were merely curious and that their curiosity did not necessarily include compassion. They smiled but still they whispered. *Panpan desho*, they said, even though her sister looked nothing like she had before. Her hair was straight again, and she combed it the way she used to, parted in the middle and tucked neatly behind her ears. Her clothes, although Western in style, were modest and plain. She looked like all the other young women in the neighborhood, but still everyone whispered.

Every evening in the tiny bedroom on the second floor, Fumi and Sumiko laid out their bedding on the tatami floor, side by side,

futon pressed against futon, just as they always had. Fumi especially
liked the time between when they slipped under their covers and just
before one of them—usually it was Fumi—fell asleep. The nights
felt particularly still then, the only sound being the soft crunch of the
buckwheat-husk pillow whenever she moved her head. Those were
the times she really wanted to ask. Not about the letter—it seemed
clear that the letter had made no difference and Fumi didn't care
about that anymore. No, there were other questions on her mind.

Did you enjoy being with the *Amerikajin*? What was it like to
dance with them? Do you miss them? And then there were those
questions that she didn't even know how to put into words. Questions that, as much as she wanted to ask, she was afraid to. Were you
a *panpan*? What exactly does a *panpan* do?

"You've grown, haven't you," Sumiko said one night when they
were lying in bed. In the darkness her sister's voice was disembodied,
the words floating somewhere close to Fumi's ear. The pillow made
a crunching sound as Sumiko shifted the position of her head. "Has
Mother measured your height recently?"

"No."

"It's a sign of good health that you've grown so much. And
Mother looks healthier, too."

Fumi couldn't hold her thoughts in any longer. "Didn't you miss
us?"

"Of course I missed you."

"Then why didn't you come home?"

"I couldn't."

"Were you too busy?"

"Sort of."

"But you could have visited."

Sumiko was silent, but Fumi could hear a sharp intake of breath.
As soon as she spoke, she was sorry she had. She had not meant to
accuse, but it was hard not to. She had a storm of words inside her.

"I'm sorry." Sumiko's breath was like a feather tickling her ear. She had moved so her head was almost touching Fumi's. "I can't explain."

"Why not?"

"You're too young. You're only twelve."

"No, I'm not. I'll be thirteen in March."

"That's still too young to understand."

"To understand what?"

"Please go to sleep, Fumi."

"To understand what? I can understand. I know what's going on."

"You don't. You can't. Please go to sleep."

Sumiko abruptly turned and rolled onto her other side. Fumi could see only the outline of her back, and instead of the usual comfort it always brought, this time it struck her as such a rebuke. Their conversation wasn't over, she felt, it was just getting started.

"I know all about what you did," she said, declaiming this bold lie as calmly as she could into the darkness. "I'm old enough to understand everything."

Sumiko sat up and turned on the lamp that they kept on the tatami at the head of their futon. She twisted her body so that she was looking down on Fumi, and her face, lit from below, was cast in eerie shadows.

"What do you mean you know?" she asked sharply.

Fumi tried to turn away from this interrogation by rolling onto her side, but Sumiko grabbed her shoulder and forced her onto her back.

"What do you know?"

"I'm old enough," Fumi whimpered. "I know things. You can tell me."

"No, you tell me. Just what do you think you know about what I did?"

"You did special things. You did . . ." Fumi closed her eyes and hugged herself, wrapping her arms across her chest. Then she imitated the sound of kissing.

"Is that what you think?" Sumiko said.

Fumi opened her eyes. She nodded uncertainly.

"What else?"

"I—"

"What else?"

"I—I don't know."

"That's right. You don't know, do you. Someday you'll be older and then you'll know. And then you might wish you didn't." Sumiko turned away and clicked off the lamp. "No more questions, Fumi. Please go to sleep. It's late."

48

January 1948

Dear Capitalist MacArthur,

Happy New Year's greetings from the proletariat. Are you surprised to hear from us? You say you're bringing democracy and freedom to Japan, but isn't the truth that you're in bed with all the old industrialists and militarists. How long do you think you can suppress the people? When the Japanese workers rise up and shake off the chains of capitalist enslavement, then you'll see what real democracy is. Long live the revolution!

Yours,
Proud to be a Communist

It was one of the more unusual letters that had arrived in the office amid an avalanche of mail sent to MacArthur over the holiday season. Everyone's desk was overflowing with stacks of letters and cards waiting to be translated.

"If you think this is a lot, just wait and see," Sab scoffed. "The Old Man's birthday is coming up soon. We're gonna end up buried alive under the mailbags."

At the end of the day Matt took the work he had completed and placed the sheets of foolscap in the basket next to the typing pool. He paused briefly to look at Nancy. All he had was a view of her back, her head bowed over her typewriter, her shoulders hunched. She had returned to work in January but although two weeks had already gone by, they had not spoken at all. Whenever she had to pass his desk, she turned her head away.

During the period over Christmas and New Year's, Matt had had a lot of time to think. He realized that however bad he might have felt about failing Fumi and not finding Sumiko, whatever disillusionment he might have felt with himself, what bothered him most was what had happened between Nancy and him. During that failed search for a woman he didn't even know, he had ended up disappointing Nancy—no, hurting her—and now it seemed that nothing mattered more than restoring their relationship. He missed the way they had been with each other before, how comfortable he'd felt with her. He missed her sardonic wit, her no-nonsense directness, her friendship. Yes, friendship. He couldn't be more than friends, she would understand that, wouldn't she? He hoped it wasn't too late.

Sometimes Matt stayed behind after work to read at his desk. He was about three-quarters of the way through *Kokoro* and determined to finish. Although initially his only interest in the novel had been because Baker had given it to him, now his engagement with the book was personal. It was his own private embrace of the lives of Soseki's characters. One day he looked up from his reading and was surprised to see Nancy standing motionless at the window by herself. He wondered what she was looking at, how long she had been there.

He didn't want to startle her so he shuffled his feet as he approached.

"Oh, you're still here," she said turning toward him. "I guess I should have known. You're always working."

"No, I was reading." He showed her the book.

She took it from him and flipped through the pages. "Looks pretty serious."

"It's a novel."

She opened it to the title page and ran her finger under the author's name, then under the title, and finally under a name written in pencil in the top right-hand corner. *Kurisutofaa*, it said, in katakana. She tried pronouncing it aloud. "Christopher?"

"The book belongs to Lieutenant Baker," Matt explained.

She smiled and gave it back to him. "He's a nice man. He's a really special person, isn't he."

Matt nodded and felt his cheeks grow hot.

"I hope he comes back soon," she continued.

They didn't say anything for a few minutes, but the silence and stillness didn't feel unnatural.

"I wish those girls would come back, too," Nancy said. "I keep hoping that if I stand at this window long enough they'll magically appear the way they did that other time. I'd really like to see them again, especially Aya."

"Maybe they'll come back."

"Maybe. But not likely." She made a halfhearted effort to smile, but her mouth sagged in a lopsided grimace. "I'm sure they've given up on us. I hope they got someone else to help them find Fumi's sister. Not a couple of hopeless cases like us."

"You know, I made a mistake. I don't have the picture anymore."

"The picture?"

"Sumiko's photograph. I—it's gone."

"Oh, that's too bad. Well, you did your best to find her."

"*We* did our best," he said.

She gave him a full smile this time. "We did, didn't we. We tried darn hard."

"May I ask, have you heard any news about your status?"

She shook her head. "Not yet. Everything takes a long time. Patience was never my strong point, but I've sure had to learn it."

He nodded. Patience, yes. It was as important as hope.

Just as Sab had predicted, people began sending birthday greetings to MacArthur, who turned sixty-eight on January 26. Most were just short words of congratulations—*Happy Birthday! May you*

live a long life!—but occasionally a letter of substantial length would appear.

Haikei Makkaasaa Gensui-sama,
Dear General MacArthur,

> *Please allow this humble servant to extend sincere congratulations to Your Excellency on your sixty-eighth birthday and to wish you good health for many years to come. We, the Japanese people, are deeply grateful that you have chosen to spend the most vigorous years of your later life dedicated to bringing democracy to our country.*
>
> *I hope it is not too presumptuous of me to take this opportunity to seek your sagacious advice regarding a matter of personal concern.*
>
> *I myself am eighty-five years of age. They say that with advanced age one gains wisdom and understanding, but I have found the opposite to be true. With each passing year, I feel I know less than the one preceding.*
>
> *Perhaps I have simply lived too long? Everyone else in my family has gone before me—my wife and daughter-in-law of malnutrition and my son in a fire. I had two grandsons, both of whom served in the recent war. One perished at sea, but the other returned a strange, broken being. He suffered a terrible sickness of the heart, whether from actions taken or witnessed or some other cause, I do not know for he could not speak of it. Last year he died at his own hand.*
>
> *Ever since the beginning of our terrible war, I have been plagued daily by the same question: How should a man live? After all these years, even as I approach the time of my ultimate departure from this earth, I confess that I am still utterly unable to find a suitable answer. I feel that if I know the answer, I will know how to die in peace.*
>
> *How should a man live?*
>
> *If Your Eminence can offer any advice in this regard, I would be exceedingly grateful.*
>
> *With deepest respect,*
> *T. Inoue*

How could he translate this, Matt thought. *How should a man live?* What kind of question was that to pose to MacArthur? Or to anyone. Matt wished he could send an answer to the old man, but the question was too hard. How to live? It was a question for a philosopher.

He put the letter in his drawer. At the same time, he thought about the other letter he still had, the one from Fumi. That, too, had gone unanswered.

49

*X*ondo had been back at school for more than a month, yet each time he entered the classroom, he still felt the same rush of emotion that had hit him on the first day of his return after his illness. It was at that moment when he realized with unambiguous clarity that not only did he feel good standing in front of his class but that this was the one place where he really belonged. This was his true calling in life, to shepherd young people into the world. That first morning in mid-January, as soon as he entered the room, all the girls had stood up and clapped, and this unexpected enthusiasm and warmth had caused a salty lump to form in his throat. It was clear that everyone knew how sick he had been.

"That's enough," he said brusquely. "Sit down."

They didn't obey immediately. Instead they remained on their feet clapping even louder. He gazed at the sea of young faces, from Fumi and Aya in the front row all the way to the back where Tomoko and Akiko stood. They looked like the same students he had been teaching all year, the same but somehow different. He hadn't been away for very long, but something seemed to have changed. They were a little taller perhaps. Was that it? A little older. He supposed he must look different to them, too. He had lost a lot of weight during his illness.

On that first day of his return, Miss Ikeda had been standing at the back of the classroom and he'd felt a momentary puzzlement—why on earth was she here?—but recalled what the principal had explained: that she had volunteered to help out during his absence, somehow managing to run between his class and her own to supervise both sets of students. He'd nodded in her direction, in acknowledgment and in thanks, and in return she had bowed from the waist, a formal bow so low that her bobbed hair swung forward covering her face.

"Please sit down, everyone," he'd said again, louder and with authority. He was pleased to see that this time they did.

Long after he had recovered, Kondo continued to reflect upon what had happened to him. During a checkup, his doctor even alluded to how close he had been to not making it. "You were extremely lucky," the doctor said several times, although he stubbornly refused to go into further medical details. He would only say that he'd seen many cases where patients in Kondo's condition had died.

"You're getting a second life. Enjoy it."

Kondo hadn't needed the doctor's sermonizing. He knew how sick he'd been. He was grateful to the doctor but even more grateful to Aya's father.

He did not return to Love Letter Alley, for it was obvious that sitting outside for long periods would not be good for his health. Would he miss it, he wondered. Would he miss his customers? He had always prided himself on being a thorough professional. When he had started out, his goal was simply to be a conduit through which words in one language would pass and be transformed into words in another. A mirror reflecting meaning without distortion—pure and unbiased and impartial. But once he started working, he came to see that the words were not just letters or symbols on the page. Each word was bursting with emotion. There were the emotions felt by the writer and by the reader, but also by him, the translator caught in the middle, reading secrets between lovers or dark truths shared.

He hoped he had helped the women who had sought out his services. In the case of good news, that was easy to see. Everyone was happy to receive good news. But when there was bad news, an unwelcome truth? That was harder to determine. He still retained his conviction that it was better to know than not to know, that the truth, no matter how painful or ugly, held its own salve. Not knowing left such an empty gaping hole, a space one ceaselessly sought to fill. And yet how often was it the case that the truth was elusive.

Kondo decided that he needed to get some exercise to strengthen his resistance. Go slowly, his doctor had advised, so he began to take short walks every day after school. The late-winter air was bracing but the sun was strong by this time in the afternoon. Soon it would be spring. Sometimes he walked up and down the lane outside his boardinghouse, but most of the time he simply circled the school two, three, four, or as many times as he felt comfortable doing. He was a bit self-conscious of this exercise regimen, however, and always waited until all the pupils had gone home. On one of these perambulations around the yard, he was surprised to see Fumi and Aya near the entrance to the school. They were accompanied by a woman.

Fumi waved at him. "Sensei!" She pulled on the hand of the woman she was with, urging her forward. Aya followed, too. As the threesome walked closer, the woman's features came into focus, and then he realized who she was. When he saw the shocked look on her face, he knew she had recognized him in the exact moment that he had recognized her. And so there was no room for doubt. She was definitely the woman who had come to see him in Love Letter Alley, the day before he fell ill.

"Kondo Sensei, I want you to meet my sister, Sumiko."

He tried not to stare.

Sumiko lowered her head in an exaggerated bow and tugged on the ends of the large gray shawl around her shoulders, pulling it tighter. Her obvious discomfort further convinced him that there was no mistaking the connection they had.

"I'm pleased to meet you," he said, bowing in return. When he raised his head, she was still bent forward, clearly unwilling to look him in the eye.

He turned his attention to Aya. "How is your father? The last time I saw my doctor he told me he's putting the medicine he gave him to very good use. He said to pass on his regards."

After that there was nothing to say, so Kondo stood with his hands clasped in front of him and looked at the ground, wondering all the while if he could think of some way to make Fumi and Aya go away. He wanted to talk to the woman alone.

"I walk out here every day after class," he offered. "To strengthen my lungs. After an illness."

"Kondo Sensei had pneumonia. He nearly died!" Fumi said.

"I regret that my illness prevented me from fulfilling my obligations. It's important to follow through on one's duties, no matter how belatedly, don't you agree?"

Fumi and Aya exchanged puzzled looks, and after a moment of awkward silence, Fumi said goodbye and the three turned around to go home.

Kondo hoped that the woman might show up on her own, but she did not come back.

In his room at the boardinghouse, he dug through the pile of materials next to his desk. He realized with chagrin that he was not the thorough professional that he liked to think he was; a professional would have made an effort to return to Love Letter Alley after recovering from his illness and not simply assume that the woman had given up. Now to run into her like this—the coincidence was most unsettling. Who would have thought she would turn out to be the sister of one of his pupils.

He retrieved the draft of his translation and the crumpled newspaper from the bottom of the pile.

BAR LUCKY NOT LUCKY! OFF-LIMITS MEANS OFF-LIMITS!

All U.S. servicemen are sternly reminded once again not to enter any area designated as off-limits. Violations of these regulations will be considered as prejudicial to the goals of the Allied Occupation of Japan. For good reason SCAP has determined that certain districts must be out of bounds. Protect yourselves. Obey all regulations.

The recent increase in the incidence of alcohol poisoning in these quarters is of especially grave concern. All personnel should consider themselves fully warned about the dangers of not obeying military laws and regulations. Offenders will be considered to have engaged in disorderly conduct and will be tried appropriately in military tribunal.

He smoothed out the wrinkles in the newspaper as best he could and looked at it again. There was a long article about five servicemen who had gone to different bars in the same off-limits area and subsequently died of alcohol poisoning within a few days of each other. Their pictures appeared in a column beside the text. Almost the entire issue of *Stars and Stripes* was about the dangers of methyl alcohol, a clear indication of how concerned the authorities were. In recent months there had been a sudden surge in the number of such incidents throughout the city, and Kondo himself had heard stories of many Japanese dying like this. Such a sad way for a life to end, he thought. In their desperate search for a few hours of pleasure or forgetfulness or whatever it was that these powerful drinks promised, people didn't realize the risk they were taking. Or so Kondo assumed. Maybe he didn't understand, though. There were many things about the behavior of others that baffled him.

50

Aya's father showed her a bag he had hidden at the back of the cupboard. It was full of yen.

"It's not worth nearly as much as it looks, but it's a start. It will help us move to a better apartment," he said. "We can move anywhere in the city you want. You can go to a better school."

"Oh, no," she protested. She did not want to change schools.

"Well, we can take our time. We'll be okay for a while. These savings are from some work I did before, some work that I don't want to do anymore."

"Is that how you got the medicine, like the one that saved Kondo Sensei?"

He hung his head and nodded slowly, with obvious reluctance.

"I've been thinking. Maybe I can go to work," she said. "I'm old enough. I want to help out."

"No, you must stay in school." His tone was firm. "After you finish middle school, you must go to high school. After that, maybe you can do more. You have to study hard. It's what your mother would have wanted. She always wanted the best for you."

Aya felt her chest tighten. He so rarely mentioned her mother, hardly ever since they'd arrived in Japan.

"I have something to show you," she said, quickly standing up. She retrieved a knotted handkerchief from her drawer and sat back down across from her father. She undid the handkerchief and spread the strips of cloth it contained on the tatami in front of him. The stones were in the handkerchief, too.

"Mother did this. She wrote messages to me and hid them in the lining of my coat. I didn't know. I might never have known. It was an accident that I even found them."

Her father leaned forward. He picked up one of the stones, rolled it slowly between his fingers, and set it back down. Then he picked up one of the cloth pieces and smoothed the scrap of fabric in the palm of his hand. *Respect your elders*, it said. He patted the cloth absentmindedly with his other hand.

"She wanted to protect you. I suppose it was her way of staying near you, even after she was gone."

Aya started to cry. "But then why did she . . . ?"

He picked up two more strips of cloth. *Do your best. Be strong.*

"I don't know," he whispered hoarsely. "Sometimes people do things we don't understand. Things we can never understand."

They sat in silence. One by one her father picked up the cloth strips in front of him, examining each one slowly before laying it carefully on top of the others. The scraps of cloth were uneven in length and shape, but they all fit within the cup of his palm. He closed his fist around them. The last one said *Be kind.*

"She always said you were the strong one," he said. "No matter what, you would endure."

"Why would she say that? I'm not strong."

"You're stronger than you think. She always said you were so much stronger than she was."

"But I'm not," Aya protested, her voice catching.

"You are. You were. You have to be."

"But I don't feel strong."

Her father pushed the cloth strips into her hands, and closed her fingers around them by wrapping his own hands tightly around hers.

"Neither do I," he said, suddenly releasing her hands. "But maybe we can pretend."

51

*B*efore Matt knew it, the end of February was approaching. It was still cold, but he sensed that the days were getting longer, the sun a little stronger. For some reason, he felt that time was moving faster, too.

He finished reading *Kokoro* and immediately set off for the used-book district in Kanda, where he found a store that specialized in literature. He browsed the section on modern fiction, letting his fingers trail across the book spines until he came upon another novel by Natsume Soseki. *Sorekara,* it was called: *And Then*. An unusual title, he thought, not catchy at all but somehow very enigmatic. *And Then* ... the words felt incomplete. And then? What next? It was an open-ended question. He bought the book, and all the way home puzzled over the title.

If he saw Baker again, Matt would ask him what he thought. He'd return the copy of *Kokoro* and maybe he'd give him *Sorekara*, too.

"Every time I see you, you've got your nose buried in a book," his bunkmate, Eddie, complained when he came upon Matt one evening reading in bed. "You're gonna ruin your eyes. What the hell is it?"

"It's a novel." Matt no longer cared what anyone thought. "It's in Japanese," he added proudly.

"Oh, yeah? I don't care what language it's in, a book is too much work. Too many damn words, you know what I mean? Here, you should look at these." Eddie reached into the locker beside his bunk and pulled out a handful of magazines. He tossed them onto Matt's bed, and the glossy covers slid across the sheet. "Lots of photos, that's what I like. Believe me, a picture's worth a thousand words."

"Thanks."

"They're old—you can keep them," Eddie said as he left the room.

Matt picked up an issue of *Life* magazine and began flipping through it. There were pictures of housewives taking pot roasts out of ovens, long-legged young people marching in parades and twirling batons, men in cowboy hats, football players running on a field. How would pictures like this look to a Japanese person? he thought. This was America, the land of plenty.

Life. The name of the magazine said it all, didn't it. This was life, the good life. Carefree, glorious, unfettered life. The life they all wanted.

Matt gathered the magazines to put away in his locker when an issue with MacArthur's face on the cover caught his attention. Opening it, the first thing he saw was a full-page color photograph of MacArthur and his son posing for the camera on the steps of General Headquarters. The next few pictures were of the young boy getting out of the big black Cadillac, saluting the MPs at the entrance to GHQ, waving to the crowds of Japanese onlookers. Matt checked the date. The issue had been published last September and promised exclusive coverage of MacArthur's family life in Japan.

Matt rubbed his eyes, incredulous. That was the day, he was sure of it. The day when MacArthur's son had visited GHQ. The day when Matt met Fumi and Aya.

Turning the Japanese into the SCAPanese! one of the captions read. *General MacArthur shares Occupation tips!*

A formal family photograph showed Arthur flanked by his

mother and father, all three standing stiffly next to the American flag in the embassy reception hall. Most of the other pictures, however, were of a casual nature and had been shot in a variety of different locations: Arthur in his bedroom playing with his toy soldiers, Arthur holding a tennis racket, Arthur seated at the piano with his fingers poised over the keyboard.

The final picture in the series had been taken in the Ginza. Arthur and his mother were in front of the Tokyo PX surrounded by a crowd of GIs. The camera had caught the boy with his mouth wide open as he struggled to take a big bite out of his hamburger. The men standing behind him cheered. There was a long caption under the photograph:

> *Even living so long in the Far East, young Arthur is fast growing up to be a typical all-American boy. He especially enjoys going with his mother to the PX, where his favorite treat is the B-29 burger. They say you can't get anything better, not even in the States. There's nothing more American than a B-29 and a Coke!*

Matt used his connections at the Press and Public Information Section to obtain a highly detailed map of the city. As well as roads and streets, the surveyors had attempted to document the location of as many currently standing structures as they could. It was a long shot, Matt knew. He wasn't sure that such a small building of the type he sought would even have been included on the map. When, after hours of searching, he finally found what he was looking for, he still wasn't entirely confident that it was the correct place. The building seemed to be too far away. He thought about how long it would take to reach MacArthur's headquarters and how difficult walking would be: through all the dust-filled streets, through the maze of twisting paths, through the rubble. It wasn't impossible, of course, but it would have required real determination. Then he thought about Fumi, that blaze in her dark eyes and the fierce energy that radiated off such a small girl, and he knew he had located the right school.

He folded the map and put it in his pocket next to the letter. How fortunate that he hadn't destroyed Fumi's letter the way he had Sumiko's photograph. It was only when he'd looked at it again recently that he noticed something that had slipped his attention before, the name of the school: *Minami Nishiki Middle School, Chiyoda Ward*. Fumi had identified herself by her school.

Matt now knew exactly what he had to do. The first person he told was Nancy.

Eddie parked the jeep in front of the gate, next to the concrete pole carved with the school's original name in worn characters: MINAMI NISHIKI ELEMENTARY SCHOOL.

"You sure this is the right place?" Eddie asked. "It doesn't say it's a middle school."

Matt climbed out of the jeep. "This has to be it."

Sab and Nancy were in the back wedged among all the supplies: dozens of boxes filled with cookies, crackers, candy, chocolate, Spam, peanut butter, and anything else Matt had thought might be needed. Everyone followed Matt's lead and got out of the jeep. The four of them stood in front of the gate looking at the school.

The school yard was empty except for a small boy who was facing a big oak tree with his head lowered.

"Poor little guy. He's probably being disciplined," Nancy said.

The boy cocked his head in their direction. They could see he was trying to observe them surreptitiously but he couldn't help being very obvious. He glanced over his shoulder at the school building, stared at the tree trunk for a moment, and then, as if he couldn't stand it any longer, ran over to them.

"*Haro, haro.* Gimme!" he said, holding his hand out to Matt and flashing a hopeful grin. "*Chocoretto, puriizu!*"

Matt pulled out a chocolate bar and squatted down so he was at eye level with the boy. The name tag on his sweater said Masatomi

Hayashi. "Little boy, I wonder if you can help us. Is there a middle school nearby? We're looking for two pupils, Fumi Tanaka and Aya Shimamura."

The boy looked puzzled at first, then his eyes widened and his grin spread from ear to ear. He snatched the chocolate bar, turned on his heels, and began racing toward the school.

"*Oi! Amerikajin! Amerikajin ga kiteiru zo!*" he shouted at the top of his lungs. "The Americans are here! The Americans!"

Matt would come back to this moment in his mind for a long time afterward, replaying the event like a short film. The way all the children, including Fumi and Aya, had come running out of the school building. How their teachers, too, had followed, and instead of being angry at the disruption, had seemed quite elated to see them. Nancy had glowed. It occurred to Matt what a wonderful teacher she would make, she so clearly loved being with children. When it had ended and all the supplies had been distributed, down to the last chocolate bar and stick of gum, he realized that whatever self-consciousness he'd felt in this modest undertaking had completely dissipated. What they had done was such a small thing, but it was a good thing. Wasn't that all that mattered?

Amid all the gaiety, however, there had been one very hard moment when he'd had to force himself to approach Fumi. He brought out her letter and took a deep breath. Maybe if he spoke quickly, he could say what he needed to say.

"I'm really sorry your sister hasn't been found. I have a confession to make. I never gave your letter to General MacArthur. I thought I might be able to help you myself, but Nancy and I searched all over the Ginza and we couldn't find her. You have to understand, I never meant to . . . You see I really didn't . . . The truth is . . ." He foundered for words. Nothing seemed adequate.

"Here." He thrust the letter at her. "I'm sorry."

She accepted the letter from him and examined it briefly. He couldn't read the expression on her face at all. Slowly a smile began forming on her lips. The smile grew bigger and bigger until it looked as if she would burst out laughing at any moment. But she didn't laugh.

"Please don't feel bad," she said, patting his arm lightly as if he were the child and she the grown-up. "My sister came back. Everything is all right."

52

Sumiko followed Kondo Sensei into the empty teachers' room. He sat down at his desk and motioned for her to sit in the chair next to him.

"I've brought the material," Kondo said. "It won't take me long to explain what it says."

"I'm sorry to cause so much trouble."

"It's no trouble at all. I'm glad to be of service."

"I appreciate your kindness."

After this stilted exchange, there was nothing to do but wait for whatever Kondo would tell her. Everything would depend on what he said. Sumiko put her hands together in her lap and hoped he wouldn't notice she was trembling slightly. It had taken a long time to work up her courage to contact him, but now, although she was nervous, she was no longer afraid. She'd thought through what she might have to do, and she was prepared to go to the police and turn herself in if necessary. It had been an accident and she would explain exactly what had happened. But first she wanted to be certain that Wada would not be implicated and that he had not been mentioned in the article. Under no circumstances did she want to jeopardize his safety, his right to life as a free man.

Kondo laid the newspaper on the desk and opened it to the page she had originally shown him. She flinched momentarily, then forced herself to look. The GI's picture, small and grainy, appeared in a column under four other pictures, all of the same size.

"This is the article you were interested in, wasn't it?" Kondo said. "I can tell you what it says. It's actually quite straightforward. There was a big scare among the Occupation authorities about alcohol poisoning."

"Alcohol poisoning?"

Kondo ran his finger across the print. "It says, 'Why would a man choose to drink cheap hooch when the finest American whiskey is available for reasonable prices at any military-approved drinking establishment? Why would a man risk his life for a drink he can't trust?'"

"I don't understand," Sumiko said.

"The men whose pictures you see here died of methyl alcohol poisoning. They had all frequented bars in the same off-limits area near the Ginza. I guess the article was meant as a warning. They wanted to make an example of them. That's why the paper publicized the men's names and described the circumstances of their deaths."

"Circumstances?"

"One of the men came back to his barracks late at night and his bunkmates didn't bother to wake him the next morning because it was Sunday and they thought he was just sleeping off a night of heavy drinking. They didn't realize he was unconscious. By the time they tried to rouse him on Monday morning, it was too late."

Sumiko gasped. ·

"Methyl alcohol destroys the nerves in the brain," Kondo continued, "but it can take hours, even days. The problem is once you pass out, you might never wake up. A couple of the men were on weekend passes, and they died at their girlfriends' apartments."

"What about him?" she asked nervously, pointing to the last picture.

"He was found on the floor of the bar where he'd been drinking."

"Stabbed to death," she said quietly.

Kondo gave her a long, thoughtful look before returning his gaze to the newspaper. "No, it says he died of alcohol poisoning. The same thing that killed the other servicemen."

"It doesn't say he was stabbed?" She was suddenly confused.

"It's funny you should mention that. In fact, he had been in a fight of some kind in the bar. They speculate it might have been a warning by the yakuza."

"Oh, but wasn't he—"

"Actually this man's story is the most complicated of the lot. It seems he was a deserter with a gambling problem. Wanted by the army and in trouble with the yakuza, I suppose with a man like that, if it hadn't been bad liquor that got him, it was probably only a matter of time before something else would have."

What about the blood, she wanted to ask, but said nothing. She recalled how she had stared at the knife sticking out of the man's side, transfixed by the contrast between the smooth pale handle and the spreading stain on the man's shirt. Wada had pulled out the knife and dragged the man behind the counter. He tried to hide the body with a large dirty towel that he flung over the man's face and upper torso. Just before he and Sumiko fled, he threw the knife with all his might outside into the garbage-strewn darkness. She'd assumed Wada knew what he was doing. He'd been in the war; he'd seen plenty of dead men. It hadn't occurred to her that he might have been more afraid than she was.

She pictured the American lying in the deserted bar—how many hours or even days might have passed before he was discovered?

"I know this is a strange thing to ask, but about the man in the last picture—do you think he could have been saved? If he'd been treated right away, for instance."

"I'm not a doctor. I don't know," Kondo said. "Why do you ask?"

She shook her head. "Nothing. By the way, what happened to the bar owners? Did the newspaper mention their names?"

"No, there's no mention of any names. It seems like all the bars closed down and everyone vanished. That's understandable."

"I see." She was suddenly very, very tired. "I think there is something I should tell you. I don't know quite how to begin but I owe you an explanation."

"No, you don't have to explain anything."

"But you must wonder about me, why I would have asked you to read this."

He smiled gently. "Not in the least. You needed a translator, that's all." He went over to the corner of the teachers' room and picked up a small metal bucket. "I'm sure you don't need this paper anymore, do you?" Without waiting for a reply, he lit a match to the top of the newspaper and dropped it into the bucket. A tall blue flame shot up in the air, and the paper turned to ash in less than a minute.

Sumiko thought about the moment right before the man entered the bar. She and Wada had just clinked glasses. *Kanpai!* Her glass was almost to her lips. What would have happened to her and to Wada had it not been for the American stranger? Had he saved their lives when they had not saved his?

"There's one more thing," she said, bringing out the piece of paper she had tucked into her pocket at the last minute before leaving the house. She had been tidying up in the bedroom when she accidentally knocked over a pile of Fumi's schoolbooks, and the paper had fallen out.

"I wonder if you would mind taking a quick look at this."

He took the letter from her and read through it quickly, smiling when he got to the end. "Do you know what this says?"

"No, I'm not sure."

"Shall I translate it for you?"

She nodded.

Dear General MacArthur,

I am writing to ask for your great and kindly help. I have a serious problem. My sister is missing! Please help me find her.

Kondo read the entire letter aloud, in Japanese. When he finished, he said quietly, "Fumi must have been very worried about you."

My sister is missing! Please help me find her. Sumiko could almost hear Fumi's voice. Suddenly everything fell into place. She understood all those odd questions Fumi had peppered her with: Who found you? What made you come home? Didn't someone come and get you?

Kondo folded the letter and gave it back to Sumiko. "Well, I've always been impressed with Fumi. She's quite something, your little sister."

Sumiko looked at the piece of paper in her hand and then she fixed her gaze on Kondo. "You wrote this letter for her, didn't you."

"No, I didn't." He appeared genuinely taken aback.

"But you must have. Fumi could never have done this on her own."

"No, you're right. She couldn't have. But it wasn't me. I didn't know anything about this."

"Then who? Who helped her?"

Kondo thought for a moment. "I think I know who it was. In fact, I'm certain."

"Who was it?"

He smiled. "Aya."

Sumiko said goodbye to Kondo at the school gate, thanking him again for all he had done. She began walking home, slowly at first, then faster and faster, her steps trying to keep pace with her thoughts. There had been much to absorb tonight, much more than she had anticipated, and her mind was racing. The night in the bar, the American, Wada, her sister's letter. Before she knew it, she had broken into a trot and soon she was running. Racing headlong down the lane until she was right in front of their house.

She flung open the door, took off her shoes, and stepped up onto the landing. "*Tadaima*. I'm home," she shouted to her parents, the usual greeting she gave them whenever she returned. But she did not go into the living room to see them. Instead she scrambled up the ladder to the second floor. "Fumi!"

Fumi poked her head out of the bedroom.

"Fumi! Where are you?"

"*Nechan*, I'm here. What's the matter?" She'd been doing homework, and her notebooks were scattered across the tatami floor.

"There you are!" Sumiko said breathlessly.

"What's wrong?"

"Nothing."

"Are you all right? You look a bit strange."

"No, on the contrary, everything is . . ." Sumiko stretched her lips into as big a smile as she could manage so that she wouldn't be tempted to cry. Everything is wonderful, she wanted to say but she couldn't quite get the words out.

"Are you okay, *nechan*?" Fumi repeated.

Sumiko knelt on the tatami in front of Fumi, who was looking at her with a mixture of puzzlement and expectation. Without even thinking, she began stroking her sister's hair. It was so soft, like a much younger child's. "It's just . . ." she began. She stopped and took a deep breath, forcing herself to slow down so her next words would be clear and strong and without any ambiguity.

"I'm home," she said. "I just wanted to let you know that I'm home."

53

From his desk drawer Matt took out the letter from the old man and translated it. Once he set his mind to the task, it didn't take nearly as long as he thought it would. The letter had been written to MacArthur on the occasion of his birthday, so it was already long overdue. Matt put his handwritten translation in the typists' basket with a strong feeling of satisfaction.

It was early spring, and in a few days it would be a year since Matt first joined the section. The piles of mail addressed to MacArthur were as high as ever but somehow the work seemed more manageable now.

The others in the office had left not long ago. From the window Matt caught sight of his co-workers as they crossed the street and fanned out in different directions. He saw the typists, Yoshiko and Mariko, walking together, and then he spotted Sab running to catch up with them. Below, lining the route, was the usual crowd of Japanese onlookers waiting for MacArthur's car. They were so orderly and patient. Matt recalled the time Baker had brought them to his attention, how Baker had asked him if he would be willing to line up like that.

The people were so still. Too still, Matt thought. Too quiet.

Gazing beyond the line of immobile people, Matt was now aware of just how much activity there was elsewhere. Everywhere he looked, there was movement, rapid, darting, frenetic movement. There were many more people in motion than standing still. These people weren't in line; they weren't waiting around for anyone. They were running to catch a train, or hurrying to meet a friend, or rushing to go home. They could be going anywhere, he thought, anywhere at all, but one thing was very clear: They were all moving without hesitation toward whatever would happen next in their lives. Suddenly Matt made out Nancy's figure in the distance as she threaded her way through the crowds in that comical fast-walking way of hers. The loose sleeves of her blouse billowed out in the warm spring wind like small sails. She moved forward, only forward, never once looking back.

As Matt stood at the window watching the panorama of humanity before him, the sun began to set and the sky slowly changed color. Then there it was, what he had been hoping for, the rich crimson sky that sometimes appeared at sunset. The magic of those shifting shades of red always took his breath away. "It's just dust," Sab had once explained. "Beats me, but the more dust and dirt there is, the better the sunset." Was that really true? Matt only knew that in the desert some of the sunsets had been spectacular.

It had been like that on the evening before Henry shipped out for basic training. He and Matt had sat outside, just the two of them. They didn't talk much. Henry told Matt he should put on more weight, he was too skinny. He cuffed Matt playfully on the side of his head and said he'd never get a girlfriend unless he built up a few more muscles. Matt had laughed and punched his brother in the shoulder; then they'd wrestled briefly on the ground, Henry letting Matt win, as he always did. They lay on the ground, panting and covered in dust, when Matt looked up at the sky. It was covered with thick streaks of red and purple and orange, as if someone had run wild with buckets of paint and a giant brush.

That beautiful desert sky, with its unending vastness and freedom, how often it had seemed to mock him, Matt thought. But since coming to Tokyo, oddly, in this cramped dense patch of life, something had opened up. What it was he didn't understand, but something within him felt released.

Maybe life came down to this. In the end there was only the task of moving forward, one step after another, making your way through the dust and dirt of living. You lived your own share of life, and if you could, perhaps you lived someone else's share, too.

Ah, the old man's question. How should a man live?

Maybe there was no answer.

How to live? How to be?

Just day by day. Going forward.

And then?

Just live.

54

Fumi had suggested that Aya meet her in their special spot on the grounds of Shotoku Temple, adding that Sumiko would be joining them. It had been a long time since Aya had been to the temple. She recalled her first visit on that hot early-summer day last year. How her nostrils had recoiled at the sharp stink of urine and how dank it had been, how the furry moss grew everywhere like mold. The buzz of the mosquitoes, the feeling that in this dark part of the temple grounds the sun never penetrated.

But to see it now, at the beginning of April, was to see it completely anew. When Aya arrived, the first thing she heard was chanting. From inside the temple building came the low monotonous sound of voices repeating a Buddhist sutra, and through a wide gap in the not quite closed doors, she caught a glimpse of the worshippers seated on the tatami flooring. They sat with their feet tucked under them, and as their backs were to the door what struck her most were the soles of their feet, some stockinged, some bare. Those feet all seemed so vulnerable, exposed as they were. All along this had been a working temple, she realized, a place meant to offer comfort.

Aya went around the side of the temple to the grounds in the back. Again she was surprised at its transformation, for the area appeared to have been entirely cleaned up. Someone had recently swept the grounds, and the even marks of a bamboo rake were firmly etched onto the hard earth, giving the flat brown surface an appearance of order and tranquillity. There was no refuse, there were no bad odors. But the biggest difference was in the quality of the light. There was none of the darkness and gloom she remembered from before. The dramatic change startled her until she realized it was because of the time of year. Without the dense foliage of summer to block the sunlight from streaming in, the area was now bright and airy and, in an unexpected way, almost cheerful.

And to top everything off, one of the trees that stood in the spot where Aya and Fumi had always met was a cherry tree. It was at the peak of its bloom. Aya had never known what kind of tree it was until now, and she gazed with wonder at the frothy clouds of sakura blossoms that floated overhead. The petals were so light and so abundant that when she stood at the base of the tree and looked straight up, Aya saw nothing but pink, as if the entire sky were lit up with a luminous glow.

Tomorrow, she thought, would be a big day. Monday was the first day of the new school year. She and Fumi would enter second year, and although they knew they had been assigned to the same class, they did not know if they could sit together. They would have a new teacher, too.

While she waited for Fumi and her sister, Aya went to the far end of the grounds where the cemetery was. Whenever she had come here with Fumi in the past, they had never entered the section where the graves were. The worshippers in the temple Aya had seen earlier would probably come back here after the service to clean off the family graves and light incense. The headstones were close together and the calligraphy was too arcane for Aya to read, but she could tell from the worn surface of the stone markers that the graves were very old. The temple had been here for centuries, she'd been told. To her, an unimaginably long time. It was truly remarkable that both the temple and its cemetery still stood, that they had not been destroyed by fire or flood or earthquake. Or war. The cemetery was very small and cramped; it looked so crowded that Aya couldn't help wondering if there was room for any more dead, and if not, then where would they go?

In the summer she and her father would make a trip to a different cemetery, one she imagined was just as small and ancient as this one. It was in the tiny remote village on the northeast coast where he had been born, and they would take her mother's ashes and bury them in the family grave where his own parents already lay.

"The graveyard is on a hill overlooking the ocean," her father had said. "She can look out at the sea."

When Fumi arrived at the temple, she was alone.

"Where's your sister?" Aya asked.

"She can't come. It's really disappointing. She has to go to work."

Sumiko had promised to take Aya and Fumi cherry-blossom viewing in Ueno Park, but she had recently found a job at a small trading company that was just starting out, and it meant she had to help whenever they needed her, even on Sundays. Today she was called in at the last minute.

"She said we should go without her," Fumi continued. "I think she's feeling guilty because she gave me extra spending money. She said we can buy whatever we want."

"Oh, that's very nice of her," Aya said.

"Yes, it's really good." Fumi clutched Aya's upper arm and shook her. "So I have a much better idea. Why don't we go to Asakusa instead."

"Asakusa? But I thought we were going to Ueno. I want to see the cherry blossoms."

"Of course we can go there, too. Everything is in the same direction. You don't want to spend the entire afternoon looking at a bunch of flowers, do you? It's just row after row of *this*." Fumi pointed to the canopy of blossoms over her head. "That's all it is. I guess it's pretty, but Asakusa is more interesting."

The sakura cast a pink luster on Fumi's upturned face, and Aya thought she'd never seen her friend look happier or healthier.

"Okay. But what's so great about Asakusa anyway?"

Fumi beamed. "*Omiyage*. Souvenirs!"

As they browsed the colorful stalls in Asakusa, Fumi suddenly stopped, plucked an item from a shelf, and quickly paid for it.

"Here, this is a present for you," she said, handing it to Aya.

It was a man's head made of papier-mâché. The top, back, and sides of the head had been painted bright red to make him look like he was wearing a Buddhist monk's hood. His face was very strange—painted with thick exaggerated eyebrows, black whiskers for a beard, and a wide pink face, but where his eyes should have been were two blank white circles. There were many different sizes but Fumi had picked the smallest one because it was the cheapest. It was the size of a crab apple and as light as air. Aya shook it.

"What is it?"

"A Daruma. It's for good luck. You think about something you want, then you paint in one eye."

Aya looked at the blank circles on the Daruma's face. "Why only one eye?"

"Because when you get what you want, you can paint in the other eye."

"So it's like a toy? To make a wish on."

Fumi bristled. "It's not a toy. It's serious. You have to set a goal."

"What's the difference between a wish and a goal?"

Fumi thought for a moment. "A wish is something you hope will happen. A goal is like a wish, except you have to work hard to make it happen. It's like a promise to yourself. Does that make sense?"

"Sort of."

"Daruma was a famous Zen monk. He wants both his eyes, so he'll help you out. He's powerful, but he's also smart. He's not going to do everything for you. He wants you to work at making your wish come true. That's why you only paint one eye. Every time you look at him, he reminds you to work harder toward your goal."

They were standing in front of the souvenir stall and the owner was bemused by the conversation taking place between the two girls. He was also aware how a number of people had stopped to listen, including some curious GIs who were drawn by the crowd.

"Daruma for sale!" the stall owner began shouting. The opportunity was too good to let pass. "Asakusa Daruma, best prices! Good for your business, good for your study. Best prices, guaranteed good luck!"

He motioned for Aya to come closer, took the Daruma she was holding, and handed her a much bigger one, the size of a giant melon. "Please take this one instead. My compliments." He reached under the counter and pulled out a thick calligraphy brush and a pot of black ink. "And while you're here, I hope you don't mind giving everyone a demonstration."

He called out in his best English. "Oi, GI Joe. *Goodo subeniru!*"

Aya shot Fumi a look of panic. The crowd of onlookers pressed in closer.

"Get a load of this," she heard one of the GIs say.

"What is it?"

"I dunno. Some kind of kid's doll."

Fumi held the Daruma for her and the stall owner dipped the brush in ink. He wrapped Aya's fingers around the brush handle.

"Go on," he urged.

"Which eye am I supposed to paint?" Aya whispered to Fumi.

"The left, I think."

Aya raised her brush.

"Wait!" Fumi shouted. "Don't forget to think of something. Something you really want!"

Aya studied the Daruma's blank expressionless face. She should have been accustomed to Fumi's bossiness by now but there were still times when it came as a surprise. A year ago, she couldn't have thought of anything, but now? It might be like opening a bag that had been sealed shut for too long. What would come out? What did she want? What did she want so much that she would work harder than anything to make it happen?

She wasn't used to holding such a large brush, and the eye she drew was not a perfect circle. But it would have to do.

In fact, she decided, it would do just fine.

Acknowledgments

While there are many sources of inspiration for my novel, first and foremost was the inspiration I derived from Sodei Rinjirō's remarkable book, *Dear General MacArthur: Letters from the Japanese during the American Occupation* (translated by Shizue Matsuda). I was astonished by the sheer volume of letters sent to MacArthur and moved by the scope and nature of their content. I am also deeply indebted to John Dower's extraordinary study of Japan during this period, *Embracing Defeat: Japan in the Wake of World War II,* a work that transported me in time and space and from whose vivid pages I borrowed many rich details.

Many other books were of vital importance, including the following: *The Enemy That Never Was* by Ken Adachi; *American Caesar: Douglas MacArthur 1880–1964* by William Manchester; *The Least of These: Miki Sawada and Her Children* by Elizabeth Anne Hemphill; *Uprooted Again: Japanese Canadians Move to Japan After World War II* by Tatsuo Kage; *The Exiles: An Archival History of the World War II Japanese Road Camps in British Columbia and Ontario* by Yon Shimizu; *The Politics of Racism* by Ann Gomer Sunahara; *Unlikely Liberators: The Men of the 100th and 442nd* by Masayo Umezawa Duus; and *Dear Miye: Letters Home from Japan, 1939–1946* by Mary Kimoto Tomita.

I have been fortunate beyond all expectation in having the tremendous support of so many wonderful people. I begin by thanking my amazing agent, Hilary McMahon, for working so hard on my behalf and for making the impossible come true. My profound gratitude to Louise Dennys and Amanda Betts of Knopf Canada for being the first to have faith and to champion my novel; to Melissa Danaczko of Doubleday U.S. for embracing it with such spirited and unstinting enthusiasm; and to Susanna Wadeson and Lizzy Goudsmit of Transworld Publishers U.K. for joining with equal excitement and dedication. Thank you to all my editors, Amanda, Melissa and Lizzy, for countless insightful suggestions and for your willingness, individually and together, to push and to question. My book is better because of your commitment. Thank you to Suzanne Brandreth for kind support and to Margo Shickmanter for much appreciated assistance.

I owe a great debt of gratitude to Richard Bausch, who has a special place in the firmament of writing mentors and who gave me the courage and confidence to believe that these pages might someday become a book. My deepest appreciation to Elizabeth Ruth, whose generous act of uncommon kindness opened an important door to the publishing world. Thank you to Tim Bowling for important early advice and to Helen Humphreys and Dennis Bock for wise writerly lessons. To Kerri Sakamoto, thank you for words of encouragement along the long, winding way.

My heartfelt thanks to Momoye Sugiman, Ted Goossen, and Jennifer Hashimoto for reading earlier drafts and offering invaluable comments. Thank you to George Takashima for leading a tour of the Japanese Canadian internment camp sites in the B.C. interior and to Patricia Takayama for a memorable trip to Manzanar. Thank you to Ikuko Komuro-Lee for advice about Japanese phrasing. To Paul Kutsukake, thank you for your special help and support.

I wish to express my gratitude to the Ontario Arts Council for generous financial support received during the writing of my novel.

Finally, *kokoro kara no kansha* to Michael, for sharing the journey, and for making it all worthwhile.

About the Author

A third-generation Japanese Canadian, Lynne Kutsukake worked for many years as a librarian at the University of Toronto, specializing in Japanese materials. Her short fiction has appeared in *The Dalhousie Review, Grain,* the *Windsor Review, Ricepaper,* and *Prairie Fire.* This is her first novel.